D0378348

PRAISE FOR

"Author Jen Stephens has crafted a novel that is both tender and powerful, reaching out to engage readers' minds and woo their heartstrings. *The Heart's Lullaby* is just that—a story that sings to us of promises kept and dreams restored. This book will leave you encouraged about your own relationships and reaching out for more of God's plans and purpose for your life."

—Kathi Macias is the author of forty books, including *The Deliverer* and *Unexpected Christmas Hero*

"Filled with hope, *The Heart's Lullaby* is a story of redemption, second chances, and most of all, a tale of dreams that do come true."

—Alice J. Wisler, author of *Rain Song, How Sweet It Is, Hatteras Girl, A Wedding Invitation,* and *Still Life in Shadows*

"A beautifully told story of love and tragedy—and the intertwined lives of two women who needed each other more than they could have ever known, The Heart's Lullaby will draw you in and not let you go until you've turned the final page. And still its melody lingers."

—Kathy Harris, author of *The Road to Mercy*

"This book touched me deeply. Jen Stephens approaches some the most hurtful things life can throw our way with blunt honesty and earnest sincerity not often found in Christian fiction. The beauty of this story is that nothing is glossed over, and the contrast of God's love and redemption vs heartache and grief is on full display. You might need a box of tissues to get through the story because it will affect you, but it will leave you with feelings of comfort and hope. And it's a story you'll yearn to share."

—Shawna K. Williams, author of *No Other* and *In All Things*

"*The Heart's Lullaby* by Jen Stephens weaves a beautiful tale of hurt and hope, love and friendship, fear and trust. This story will be remembered long after the pages are turned. I loved it!"

—Carie Lawson, author of the Twisted Roots series

"The beauty of *The Heart's Lullaby* comes in one powerful, overriding message: Discover your roots, and embrace your wings. In this second installment of the Harvest Bay series, Jen Stephens crafts a moving journey of discovery, redemption, and faith-affirming love."

—Marianne Evans, author of *Hearts Communion*, 2012 Christian Small Publishers Romance Book of the Year

"Stephens crafts a heart-tugging story as she takes the reader into the life of a woman who is consumed with having a child. The hardships the character goes through are true to life, and will touch your heart."

—Beth Shriver, author of *Annie's Truth*

THE
Heart's Lullaby

JEN STEPHENS

Charlotte, Tennessee
37036 USA

The Heart's Lullaby
Copyright © 2012 by Jennifer Stephens.

Published by Sheaf House®. Requests for information should be addressed to:

Editorial Director
Sheaf House Publishers, LLC
1703 Atlantic Avenue
Elkhart, IN 46514
jmshoup@gmail.com
www.sheafhouse.com

All rights reserved. No part of this publication may be reproduced, stored in a retrieval system, or transmitted in any form or by any means—electronic, mechanical, photocopy, audio recording, or any other form whatsoever—except for brief quotations in printed reviews, without the prior written permission of the publisher.

Library of Congress Control Number: 2012948273

ISBN 978-0-9797485-5-4 (softcover)

Scripture quotations are from The Holy Bible, New King James Version, copyright © 1982 by Thomas Nelson, Inc.

Cover design and interior template by Marisa Jackson.

Map by Jim Brown of Jim Brown Illustrations.

12 13 14 15 16 17 18 19 20 21—10 9 8 7 6 5 4 3 2 1

Manufactured in the United States of America

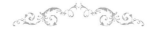

Acknowledgments

THE HEART'S LULLABY CHALLENGED ME, seriously pushed me to my limits, and I'm only half joking when I say I might not have survived without the support and encouragement of many, many people.

Gracious Father, how I've needed You! Thank You, Lord, for loving me with a love far greater than any human being has ever known. Thank You, my Savior, for picking me up and dusting me off every time I fall. Thank You, my King, for your endless grace and mercy. Thank You, sweet Jesus, for sacrificing everything so I may have the hope of a brighter tomorrow.

Chris, thank you for your love and support for thirteen years, especially during the long and trying process with this book. I also want to thank you for being the best daddy I could hope for to the girls and for your Christian leadership in our lives. It means more than you can know and we are all better because of it.

Alison, you have become a beautiful young lady right before my eyes, and it's so bittersweet. Your tender heart is the most precious thing I have ever seen and your creativity continually inspires me. Olivia, my beautiful baby, you're hardly a baby anymore. Your determination and confidence gives me strength, and the ever-present song in your soul makes me smile. My heart overflows with pride for both of you girls and I want you to know that nothing will ever compare to the joy of being your mother. I love you so much, Ali and Livi . . . all the way to heaven and back.

And speaking of heaven, Daddy, I miss you! I wish you were here to share this with me, but I take comfort in knowing that you are a big part of everything I am today. Thank you for teaching me about the joy found in storytelling. Thank you for teaching me about living and dying, laughing and crying, and loving every second in between. I'm so proud to be your kid.

To Joan Shoup and Sheaf House Publishers, thank you so much for believing in me yet again. You've given me the creative freedom I needed to bring this story to life, and you've placed my childhood dreams in my hands not once but twice. How can you thank someone for that? I don't know, but I hope I've made you proud.

It sounds cliche, but the truth of the matter is that you wouldn't be holding this book in your hands without two very special ladies: Bonnie Fellows, my sister and friend who talked me down off of a dozen ledges throughout this writing process, and Jodie Bailey, my friend and critique partner, who cleaned up my messes after I spewed words on a page. Bonnie helped me understand more about my character, Elizabeth, and Jodie helped me get to know my character, Amy. Thank you, ladies, for taking time out of your busy schedules to help me. At the drop of a hat (or text as the case may be) you were there, and I can't begin to tell you what that means.

Terri Petitt, once again you shot the perfect cover photo. You're not only an amazing photographer, you're also a great friend. Thank you! Kim Carver and Rachel Peacock, thank you for taking time out of your day to be my beautiful models and bringing my characters to life. Tina Hunter, thank you for letting us invade your home to shoot this cover. Your little girl's room made the perfect setting for this story. Marisa Jackson, not only did you do an amazing job in designing the cover, you made it pink! Again! Jim Brown of Jim Brown Illustrations, I just have to thank you again for bring Harvest Bay to life. The map is stunning, and I still find new little details that I love about it.

One of the themes of this book is the joys and heartaches of becoming a mom, and several times while writing this book I've wondered where I'd be without mine. Mom, thank you doesn't seem quite big enough for all you've done, but it's all I've got. Thank you for loving me when I was unlovable. Thank you for believing in me when I didn't believe in myself. Thank you for providing me with the best example of everything a mother should be. I pray one day my girls can look at me with all the admiration that I hold in my heart for you. I love you! Also, Shirley Dominick LaVoie, you became a mom in a different kind of way—by marrying my dad. I know it couldn't have been easy for you, but I thank you for the important role you played in my life and in making me exactly who I am today.

Julie Roeder, my "sneaky" sister and one of my most precious friends, I might not have survived writing this book without you. Thanks for keeping me sane. Karen Pantaleo, I can never thank you enough for sharing your experience with your first pregnancy, for helping me understand the loss and heartache. You're not only my sister, but also my hero.

The Heart's Lullaby touched on issues and situations that I have absolutely no experience in—infertility, miscarriages, adoption, foster families, military and legal matters, Post Traumatic Stress Disorder, and horses. Thanks to these individuals being willing to share their knowledge and personal trials and triumphs so I could better tell this story: Tammy Giles, Connie Roy, Carla Trawick, Chelsea Dowdy, Regan Jensen, Dr. Edgardo Padin, Tina Corte Thomas, Jen Stumpf, Jen Motz, Dr. Carolyn Thompson, Heather Martin, Shelley Surface, Jennifer Cruse, Michele Clark, and Michelle Marklin. Also, thank you Mark and Andi Soergel for allowing me to use your precious Haven William's name.

To my friends and fellow writers at MTCW, especially Kaye Dacus and Ramona Richards, who mentored me from the beginning, thank you for understanding every single step of this sometimes painful, yet incredibly rewarding process. I'm also so grateful to my talented author friends who took the time to read this book, and then write such lovely endorsements for it. Your words of encouragement were such an incredible blessing to me.

In life, everyone needs someone to encourage them to keep pushing, running toward the finish line, but, above all else, to just have fun with it. Thank you to the many cheerleaders I've been blessed with along the way, far too many to name, but you know who you are . . . and I do too.

Last, but certainly not least, I thank you, my reader, for picking up another Jen Stephens book. I pray this book sings to your soul long after you've turned the final page.

Congratulations to Lou Ann Gibson, who won the "What a Difference You've Made in My Life" contest. Lou Ann nominated her father, Bill Gibson, a gentleman who made a difference in many lives as you will soon see through his character in this book. Now it gives me great pleasure to introduce you to . . .

Bill Gibson

BORN ON NOVEMBER 30, 1934, Bill Gibson lived quite a life. Having to quit school in the tenth grade after the death of his father, Bill went to work to help pay the bills and put his younger brothers and sister through school. Despite his lack of education early on, he was a natural when it came to solving math problems. He always found the answer, even if by just using his common sense! Bill married the love of his life, Wilma, on June 19, 1959, while serving our great country as an MP in the Army. Following his service in the military, Bill provided for his wife and their two children—LouAnn and Billy—by working in the textile mills. Then, nearly twenty years after quitting school, Bill received his GED.

Bill had five hobbies—fishing, woodworking, gardening, animals, and cooking—but his greatest loves were his Lord and his family. His favorite scripture passages were Isaiah 40:31 and Psalms 23. Bill regularly spent time in the Word. If his family had a question regarding the Bible, they would go to him before even going to their preacher. Bill enjoyed a close—peaceful, trusting, loving, and caring—relationship with the Lord. He was active in his church even up until he passed away. He served as chairman of deacons, worked on several committees, taught Sunday school, sang in the choir, cleaned the churchyard, and even helped clean the church.

No job was too small or too large for Bill when it came to serving his Lord.

Next to his Lord, Bill's family was his top priority. He loved all his family greatly, but the love he shared with his wife was special, a once-in-a-lifetime kind of love. They were truly each other's best friend, and easily showed their affection. Bill's son and daughter were the lights of his life, but he loved all children and they were equally attracted to him. When a parent would scold a small child, you could always hear Bill saying, "A baby's gotta do what a baby's gotta do!" He was the ultimate grandpa!

In *The Heart's Lullaby*, Bill's character is a gentle, wise, dear friend of the family, lovingly referred to as Uncle Bill. He helps Elizabeth through her struggles with infertility and her marriage by guiding her to scripture and reminding her that "the God of the mountain is still the God of the valley." I pray that through this experience Bill's memory is honored in the utmost way: that everyone who reads *The Heart's Lullaby* will be inspired by Bill to "trust in the Lord with all your heart, and lean not on your own understanding."

Congratulations to Janet Haase who also won the "What a Difference You've Made in My Life" contest. Janet nominated her granddaughter, Stephanie McCorkle, who has overcome serious obstacles in life, while maintaining a positive attitude. A special thanks to Julie Kochan who provided me with additional information so that I could create Steph's character to the best of my ability. Now it gives me great pleasure to introduce you to . . .

Stephanie McCorkle

BORN ON FEBRUARY 20, 1981, Steph seemed to have a fiery spirit from the moment she entered this world. I'm told that as a child she would run from one thing to the next, and if you told her not to touch it, she'd snatch it, all the while looking at you with a try-and-stop-me look in her eyes. Steph was extremely curious about everything, always fearless, wanting to push things farther, always wanting to try new things. And if you're her friend or a part of her family, she loves you fiercely for life. These are all traits that have served her well later on in life.

Steph grew up in a Christian home, went to a Christian school, and attended church regularly. But that sheltered, safe lifestyle wouldn't prevent her from experiencing serious heartache and challenges. Shortly after she graduated from high school, her parents divorced and she was faced with the first of many obstacles in her life as she struggled with this new situation.

Several years later, Stephanie got married and had two beautiful children. However, more challenges were on the horizon. Her son, her firstborn, was discovered to be legally blind. The strength she exhibited in leaving her difficult marriage was surpassed only by her determination during her battle with breast cancer. She fought the cancer not once, but twice and WON! She is now cancer free!

Through all this she always looked at things, saying, "My life isn't as bad as someone else's. Things can always be worse." She has been an inspiration to many as she clung to the scripture passage, "Bear with each other and forgive whatever grievances you may have against one another. Forgive as the Lord forgave you."

In *The Heart's Lullaby*, we meet Steph's character at a single-parent support group meeting where she shares her testimony, seemingly speaking directly to Amy, a character who is coping with many issues. Steph befriends Amy and provides her with a source of strength and encouragement throughout the journey she is on. I pray that through this experience, everyone who reads *The Heart's Lullaby* will be inspired by Stephanie—by all she's overcome and by the positive attitude she's maintained through it all.

Dedication

THIS BOOK IS FOR PATTY, my best friend, who was one of my biggest fans and continues to be my biggest inspiration. Patty taught me about life as she faced her own mortality with such grace and dignity, with continued strength and determination. She taught me about real, hard-core faith as she praised God even through the fiercest moments of her storm.

Patty, you were everything I wish I could be, and your friendship meant more than I could ever put into words. My only hope is that I've made you proud with this story. I love you always, think of you every day, and will miss you until the day we meet again.

Patty (Spears) Smith
October 12, 1975–February 24, 2011

With my publisher's blessing and encouragement, I'm giving a portion of everything I make on everything I write to Ovarian Cancer National Alliance in Patty's honor. Whenever a book is bought, steps are being taken toward finding a cure for ovarian cancer to save our mothers, grandmothers, sisters, daughters, and friends.

To learn more, visit my website at *www.jenstephens.net*, and let's work together to find a cure once and for all!

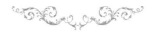

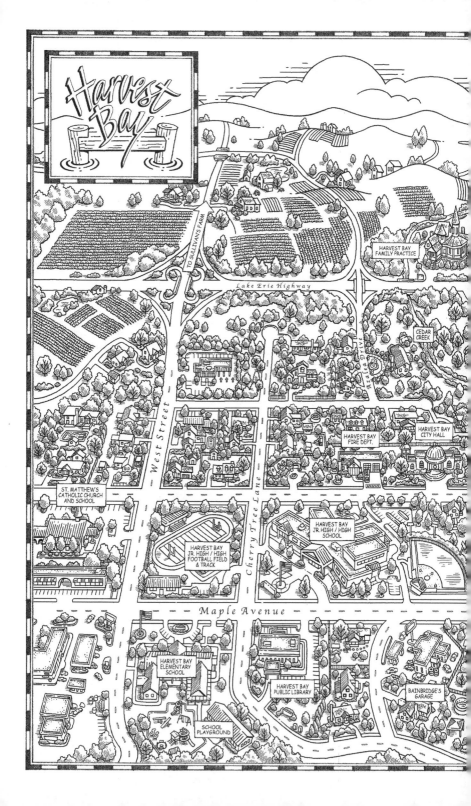

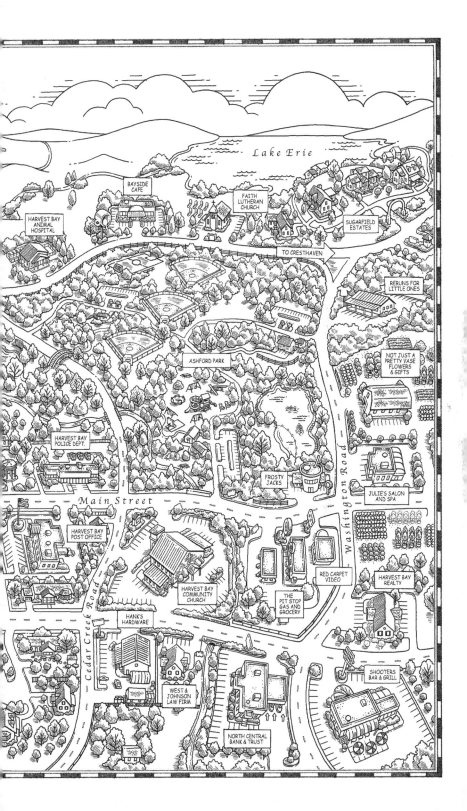

Also by Jen Stephens

THE HEART'S JOURNEY HOME
Book 1, The Harvest Bay Series

CHAPTER
One

Elizabeth Truman sat on the edge of the bathtub, her hands pressed together and wedged between her knees. The coolness of the beige marble penetrated through her soft cotton shorts to her thighs, but did little to soothe her fiery nerves.

The clock on the wall ticked off the seconds. Still the three-minute wait seemed unending.

This could be it. The wait may finally be over, and in just three minutes our lives could change forever.

She glanced down at her flat belly, imagining how she'd give Elijah the good news, smiling at the thought of how happy he'd be. Just the other day, when they were strolling through the mall together, a ball and glove caught his eye from the window of the toy store and he made a comment about playing catch with his son someday. He was ready to be a daddy.

And there was nothing she wanted more than to be a mother. Over the past several months the deep longing had intensified, preoccupying her thoughts during the day and her dreams at night. Her arms ached to hold their baby—a perfect combination of her and Elijah. Her soul yearned to nurture their child, to watch him or her grow day by day. She already loved this little miracle that she was sure the Lord would bless them with.

The second hand finally returned to twelve for the third time. Her heart thudded inside her chest. A hard knot formed in her stomach, and she pressed her hand against it in a feeble attempt to ease the discomfort. She stood and moved to the sink where the results waited on the end of a little plastic stick. Hand trembling, she reached for it and examined it closely.

One line.

In a matter of moments her heart went from almost banging out of her chest to barely beating. She looked closer, searching for a hint of that second line, but it wasn't there.

She glanced at her reflection in the mirror. "We did everything the doctor told us to do." Her bottom lip quivered. "I've recorded my temperature every day for three months and charted it on the Internet." Hot tears of disappointment blurred her vision. "I was so sure it would happen this month."

"What would happen, Aunt Liz?"

She blinked away the building moisture. She'd momentarily forgotten that her young nieces, Madeline and Chloe, had spent a couple nights with her while their parents, Kate and Adam Sullivan, were on their honeymoon.

She turned to Madeline and forced a smile. "That you and Chloe would come to stay with me for a few nights." Leaving the pregnancy test lying on the marble countertop, she swept out of the bathroom, snagging her niece as she went. They sat on her bed. "You're up early. Is Chloe still asleep?"

Madeline nodded.

Elizabeth grabbed a brush off her nightstand and ran it through the little girl's chestnut bob, wondering if it would ever be her own daughter in Madeline's place. Sorrow covered her heart like a heavy blanket. She'd have to endure another month of dreaming, hoping, wishing, and waiting.

She sighed. "So what do you want to do today before I take you and Chloe back to Grammy and Papa's?"

"Can we play Putt Putt?"

"That sounds like fun. How about lunch at McDonald's first?"

Madeline nodded, rubbing her belly and running her tongue back and forth across her lips.

Elizabeth laughed. Somehow this little ray of sunshine managed to burst through the gloom and brighten her day. "Why don't we scrounge up some breakfast, and then you can watch cartoons while I do some chores. After Chloe wakes up we'll get dressed and head out, okay?"

"Okay!" Madeline hopped off the bed and raced downstairs to the kitchen.

As Elizabeth trailed behind, she silently recited Philippians 4:11 until the pain in her heart subsided: *"For I have learned in whatever state I am, to be content."*

Running her fingers down the solid oak banister of the curved staircase, she reminded herself of her many blessings. Two months earlier, she'd celebrated seven years of marriage to her very own tall, dark, and handsome Prince Charming. Their two-story, elegantly decorated, stone home was a far cry from a fairytale castle, but it was her palace. Her career as a pediatric nurse fulfilled her, gave her a purpose. She had everything she'd dreamed of since she was a little girl . . . except a baby.

What if this isn't your problem? a nagging voice whispered in her brain as she poured Madeline a bowl of Fruit Loops. It wasn't the first time she'd thought it, and the idea came to her more often with each passing week.

Once Elizabeth had asked Elijah to go with her to a specialist, but he refused, arguing that if they were meant to have a baby it'd happen. Disappointed, she settled with tracking her cycle, but it still seemed like guesswork to her. Now, however, determination flowed into her spirit like the milk into the bowl of colorful rings. Somehow she'd make him understand the importance of making an appointment.

The rest of the morning, as she loaded the dishwasher and folded the laundry, Elizabeth prayed. "Please, dear God, give me the words to say, and let Elijah be receptive to whatever the next step may be."

Her heart sagged in her chest as she considered how quiet her house would be that evening after she took the girls back to her parents. "I know that you've created me to be a mother. I've known it since I was a child playing with my dolls. Please, God, make him want this as much as I do."

By half past eleven the girls were dressed and ready for a fun afternoon. Elizabeth slung her purse onto her shoulder and reached for her car keys. Just then the phone rang.

Stuffing the keys in her pocket, she swiped the handset from an end table and checked the caller ID. It came up Unknown and she didn't recognize the number, but with Madeline and Chloe staying with her, she was afraid not to answer it.

"You two go get in the car and buckle up. I'll be just a minute." She punched the talk button. "Hello?"

"Is Elijah there?" an unfamiliar female voice asked.

"No. He's at work. Can I take a message?"

The woman hesitated. "Um, yeah. Just tell him it's very important that I talk to him. He can reach me any time at this number."

"Okay. What is your name? It didn't come up on my caller ID." Another brief pause set off a warning bell in Elizabeth's spirit. "Hello? Are you still there?"

"Yeah. Just tell him it's Amy."

Amy Beauregard flipped her cell phone closed and set it on the counter of the busy café. Her world had been rocked hard over the past several months, and it was about to encounter another blow. She tried to brace herself.

The industrial-sized griddle sizzled and sputtered, reminding Amy of her fried spirit. Stopping to top off Amy's coffee cup, the waitress offered a warm smile. Politely forcing the corners of her mouth upwards, Amy ran a shaky hand through her short, spiky hair, wishing she was drinking something stronger. But she'd already made enough bad choices to last her a lifetime.

"Hey, Maggie!"

Amy started at the voice, sloshing a drop of the hot liquid on her hand. Biting her tongue to keep from cursing, she swiped up the moisture with a napkin and shifted her attention to the man who'd taken a seat at the counter a few stools down.

The waitress greeted him with a sweet smile. "*Hola*, Owen! Would you like a menu?"

"Nah. I'll take the usual with a chocolate milkshake."

"It will be *un momento*."

"*Gracias*."

Amy recognized the man's navy blue uniform as that of a firefighter. She also noticed how his strawberry blonde hair was just long enough that it curled at the ends. He met her gaze, and she jerked her attention back to her coffee.

She held her breath. *Please don't start a conversation. Please don't start a conversation . . .*

"Are you new in town? I don't think we've ever met."

Despite her shaky insides, she gave him her best pointed look. "And you know everyone in this town, I suppose."

He chuckled, revealing adorable dimples. "Just about. I still haven't decided if it's a curse or a blessing."

To her surprise the corners of her mouth turned up slightly, then she reminded herself that if he really knew her, he wouldn't be talking to her. She picked up her cup and took a cautious sip, refusing to be drawn in by his boyish charm.

"I'm here on business." Her tone rang with a note of finality.

"What do you do?"

"It's confidential."

He gave a nod as the waitress set a plate and a tall glass in front of him.

The mouth-watering aroma of the juicy burger and salty fries wafted to Amy's nose causing an immediate response in her empty stomach. She slid her hand over her belly as if covering the mouth of a boisterous child.

The firefighter picked up his burger. "Well, I'm Owen Sullivan. If you need anything while you're here, give me a shout and I'll see what I can do." Then he took a big bite and washed it down with a drink of his milkshake.

Amy stared at him, her guard up and on high alert. *A complete stranger is offering to help me.* Her initial instinct told her that if she didn't keep her mouth shut, she'd risk revealing her vulnerability. After all, predators fed on the weak and defenseless. Still, she needed some information in this God-forsaken town.

"Would you happen to know of a place to stay? The only motel I saw in town doesn't have any vacancies."

He swallowed and took a drink of his milkshake. "It's Friday and Cedar Point is in full swing. You'll be hard pressed to find a room anywhere in the area."

"Cedar Point?"

"An amusement park right on Lake Erie about half an hour from here."

Her shoulders fell. "Oh."

"But my mom and dad have a small apartment above their garage that my sister just moved out of. I'm sure they wouldn't mind if you stayed there for a few days." He pulled out his cell phone. "Let me just give her a heads up."

"That's okay," Amy said hastily. "I'll come up with something." She rubbed the crook in the back of her neck and prepared herself to spend another night in her car. After all, she had slept—or at least rested—in worse conditions.

"It's no problem. Really." He pushed a button and put the phone to his ear.

As he spoke with his mother, Amy's ten-year-old son came out of the bathroom carrying his overnight bag and plopped down on the stool next to her. She covered her face with her hands.

I can manage just fine, but my boy can't spend another night in the car. Still, who in their right mind would take in a strange single woman and her kid?

A minute later, Owen put his phone down. "It's all set. My mom's expecting us in a few minutes." He took another bite of his sandwich and flagged the waitress down. "Maggie, can you get me a to-go box and put the lady's check on mine, please?"

"Stop! We do not accept charity." *Or chivalry. This isn't a romance novel, and while he just may be a hero, I don't need saving.*

Acknowledging her son with a grin and a nod, he shrugged. "I didn't mean to offend you. It's just the way things are done in a small town."

She lowered her voice and dropped her gaze. "Not where I come from."

"I'm sorry to hear that." He packaged up what was left of his meal and handed the waitress some cash. "Use the extra for something little Justin needs."

The raven-haired woman lit up like the Christmas tree in Rockefeller Center. *"Muchas gracias!"*

Watching the exchange, a strange tingling occurred in Amy's heart.

He scribbled something on a napkin and handed it to Amy. "Here's the address. The offer stands. Mom's happy to have you both for as long as you're in town."

"Thanks."

He stood, picked up the Styrofoam box, and gave her a nod. "Well, if I don't see you again, enjoy your stay."

She put her hand up. "Bye."

Once he was safely out the door, she dropped her forehead into the crook of her elbow on the counter top. *I shouldn't have been so rude to him when he was only trying to help. And now it's too late to take it back.* She heaved a sigh from the depths of her troubled soul. *Will I ever believe that there are still good men left in this world?*

"Perdóname."

She glanced up to find the waitress staring at her curiously.

"More coffee?"

"Oh. No, but I need to place a to-go order." Right on cue, Amy's stomach growled again. "Can I see a menu, please?"

She ordered a late lunch for her and her son. When it was up, they headed to the park they'd noticed on their way into to town and claimed a spot under a huge shade tree. Everything was perfect about the mid-June afternoon, except for the reason they were there.

Dominick scarfed down his sandwich and fries, leaving nothing but a few crumbs, then motioned toward the playground.

She nodded and watched him scurry toward the equipment. He'd been through so much, including going months on end without seeing her. Yet he had such a tender heart. She tried her best to protect him, especially from the way she'd been hurt, but eventually she wouldn't be able to hide it anymore . . . from anyone.

All the decisions she'd made affected him—she could see it in his eyes—and this one would affect him most of all. She wished it didn't have to happen this way, but the time had come. She only hoped that this gamble would pay off, that coming to Harvest Bay would ease some of his loneliness and begin to fill the giant void.

They spent the rest of the afternoon at the park trying to make up for lost time, playing catch, swinging, racing each other on the obstacle course, and just relaxing. As the sun began its decent to the western horizon, she checked her phone again on the off chance that she'd missed a call. There were no messages.

Second thoughts set in. Maybe this was just a big mistake.

On their way back to the car, a beautiful little garden surrounding a huge flagpole caught Amy's eye and she strolled over to it. The bright, perky flowers sharply contrasted with her wounded spirit. She walked up a small brick path and sat on a bench at the base of the flagpole, while her son closely examined the manicured flowerbeds for anything that crawled or squirmed.

She inhaled the fragrant air. *I can't go back to the life I knew, not now after all that's happened. But I can't go forward, either. What am I going to do?*

She cast her gaze downward, and it fell on a bronze stone. Her heart nearly stopped as she breathed the words, "In memory of our brave soldier, Justin McGregor. We're forever proud of you."

In an instant she was transported back to that terrible day two and a half years earlier. As her second deployment drew to a close, screaming filled the foreign air that reeked of gunpowder, burning flesh, and the stench that seemed to permeate Iraq. She looked into the face of one of the casualties and recognized her friend, the young man who'd sat beside her on the long plane ride over. He'd been so kind and genuine. His eyes had shined as he told her of the girl he loved, the one he was going to marry when he returned home.

But at that awful moment his stare was blank.

It was her job to assess the wounded, save those she could and black tag the rest. She could easily see by the pool of blood surrounding him and the gurgling with each labored breath that she couldn't save him, but she couldn't leave him either. Oblivious to the sporadic gunshots echoing around her and the other medic yelling at her to move it, she very gently picked up Justin's head and set it in her lap. She stroked his hair, wet with sweat and blood, considering the price he'd paid for her. She thought about how this was somebody's son. Somebody's baby lay dying in her lap. She'd forced the thought out of her mind. She didn't have time to feel while she was on duty.

Grunting with the effort it took to reach out and place his dogtag in her hand, he gasped, "Harvest . . . Bay." And then he was gone.

Her insides shook and her stomach turned with the memory that had become her constant nightmare. Even the attack that came later didn't haunt her like that vision. Tears stung her eyes, but she quickly swallowed the sign of weakness. She meditated for a moment under the shadow of the American flag and gathered strength from it. She didn't have to reevaluate the situation after all. There was no mistake.

Filled with new resolve, she marched with her son to her old blue Taurus. After stopping by the Bayside Café to get directions for the address she had, she found the house and pulled into the driveway. She glanced at the clock on her dash. Half past six. Hopefully he was home from work by now because she didn't know if she had the nerve to go through this again. She put the automatic windows down, cut the engine, and turned to Dominick.

Putting her hand up, she said, "Stay here." He nodded.

Before more second thoughts set in, she got out and hurried to the front door. Closing her eyes in an attempt to calm her rattled nerves, she reached down deep for an extra dose of courage, and pushed the doorbell.

A moment later, a pretty woman with long, chestnut hair cracked the door. Moisture clung to her eyelashes, and her nose was pink. "Can I help you?"

It didn't take a genius to deduce that this woman had been crying. Rather than add to her grief, Amy seriously considered turning on her heel, sprinting back to the car, and never showing her face in town again. But then she thought about Justin, about his last words to her, and she knew she had to do this.

She cleared her throat. "Is Elijah home?"

As if on cue, the door opened further and he emerged. Tension creased his forehead and weariness filled his dark eyes. "Yes?"

Amy stood there, waiting for the dawning to occur. Nothing. She shifted her weight and crossed her arms.

"You don't remember me."

He stared at her hard. Finally, his eyes widened. "Daytona Beach?"

Amy glanced at the crying woman in that awkward moment and nodded.

Elijah stuffed his hands in his pockets. "It's been a long time."

"Eleven years."

"This is my wife, Elizabeth."

The women nodded something of a greeting.

Elijah rubbed the back of his neck. "Well, this is . . . this is quite a surprise. H-how are you?"

"I'm fine." She paused, shifting her gaze to her tennis shoes before looking him straight in the eyes. "And so is your son."

CHAPTER
Two

*S*eeking solitude in the shelter of her bedroom, Elizabeth lay on her bed and tried to read in between her tears. The usually soothing colors of pale mauve walls, sheer curtains, and soft sage quilt provided her with little comfort. As much as she tried to block them out, faint voices floated up the stairs as Elijah was introduced to his son.

His son.

Another wave of tears came. She gave up on reading and tossed the book aside.

"Why, dear God? Why? When You know that I want so desperately to have a baby, why did You give my husband a son with another woman? It seems like some kind of cruel joke. I trust You, God, but I just don't understand and my heart is breaking."

"I'm sorry. What can I do to make it better?"

Elizabeth looked up to see Elijah standing in the doorway. She rolled over with a humph. "It's a little too late for that, don't cha think?"

He strode to the side of the bed and knelt in front of her. "I know that you're upset and I'm sorry, but what else was I supposed to do? Slam the door in her face? Refuse to meet the kid after they came all this way?"

She turned her back to him.

"Please, don't turn away from me. I need you."

"No, apparently you don't."

"That's not fair, Elizabeth. This happened right after college before I even knew you . . . or the Lord. I asked the Lord to forgive me long ago. Can't you do the same?"

"Don't ask me that right now, Elijah. You know that having a baby is all I can think about. You know that. So some strange woman shows up claiming to have had your son, and you want to tell me I'm being unfair?"

"Look, you're not the only one upset here." He pushed to his feet, shoved his fingers through his hair, and began to pace back and forth. "Right now I don't know what to think or how to feel." He stopped and ran his hand over his mouth and down his chin. "It's like I've been thrown into the storyline of some bad drama. Something like this isn't supposed to happen to me, to us. Unbelievable!"

He started to walk the floor again. "Ten years! If this kid is really mine, I've missed out on ten years of his life." He stopped and looked pleadingly at Elizabeth. "How can that be okay? Why wouldn't she have told me sooner? I mean, why now when everything is so perfect?"

His words slapped her across the face leaving a sting so real she touched her fingertips to her cheek. "Perfect? You really think everything is perfect?"

He returned to the bed and sat beside her. "I meant our marriage and our careers." He touched her shoulder, but she wouldn't look at him. "You know that I want a baby as much as you do."

"Well, now you've got one."

A thick silence fell between them, heavy with all baggage they'd just been handed.

Finally, she turned back to face him. "So what are you going to do?"

He shook his head. "Nothing until we get a positive paternity test."

"Did she give you any idea why she showed up today?"

Elijah shrugged. "She said she has some issues to take care of and needed help with Dominick while she straightens things out."

"Issues to take care of? That sounds kind of shady. Are you sure you want to get involved?"

"If I am his father, how could I not?"

"Dominick? Is that his name?"

He nodded, his expression softening. "I don't know if he's mine, but when I looked in his eyes, it was like looking in a mirror. I saw the same need, fear, and hope that I had as a kid living with a couple relatives and a few different foster families, each time wanting to be able to call it home but always being let down. I know how bad he needs a father."

Elizabeth's voice was gentle but firm. "But if he's not yours, it's not your responsibility."

"I know."

Searching Elijah's chocolate eyes, she found the same turmoil that ate at her heart. "You want him to be yours, don't you?"

"I don't know. It would change everything, complicate our lives in ways we can't even imagine right now."

"But he would be your son."

Elijah met her gaze with an intensity that spoke the words he couldn't utter.

She took a deep breath. "So why don't you tell me about him?"

"He seems to be a great kid—really smart and athletic—but . . ."

"But what?"

"He's deaf."

"Really?"

In college, she'd enrolled in a sign language class, thinking it'd be a fun, easy elective, but the more she learned, the more beautiful the language became to her. She'd continued her education until she was fluent. It had come in handy several times during her shifts at the hospital, and she used it every week in her role as an interpreter during the Sunday morning church service.

"Does Amy sign then?"

"I'm not sure, but I don't think so. Dominick reads lips and carries around a notepad."

"That's hardly an effective way to communicate."

Taking her hand, he intertwined their fingers. "Look, I want to have a baby with you, and I promise nothing's going to keep us from trying to make that happen. But in the meantime, we have an opportunity to really help a boy who needs us, and we can choose to view it as a burden or as a gift. So what's it going to be?"

"Right now I just don't know."

"All right then." He sighed. "Let me know when you figure it out." Without another word, he strode out of the room.

Elizabeth heard the TV come on, most likely to ESPN. Her stomach growled. She thought about the supper they'd barely touched as she pleaded with him to see the doctor.

"He doesn't have to now. We both know he's not the problem." Tears blurred her vision and she closed her eyes. "I don't want this gift, God. I want my own baby."

She cried into her pillow until her emotional well ran dry and exhaustion set in. She closed her eyes and tried to sleep, but her mind continued to run wild.

Who was this woman and what exactly did she want? Elizabeth bristled as she considered the possibility that after all these years Amy might want a second chance with Elijah. Their marriage was strong, but Amy had given him the one thing she still couldn't.

Maybe Amy didn't want him as much as she needed the child support. That wasn't quite as scary as someone attempting to tear her home apart, but still a knot formed in her stomach at the thought of the financial responsibility.

Could Amy possibly be thinking of dropping her son off and disappearing? Elizabeth didn't know how a mother could do something like that, but it happened all the time, and the woman had told Elijah she had some issues to take care of. The knot in Elizabeth's stomach tightened as she wondered if she could be a full-time mother to someone else's special needs child.

She was born to be a mother, wanted nothing more, but she didn't want it this way. She wanted her own baby, one that she conceived, felt grow and move inside of her, and delivered the way God intended.

She flipped on her bedside lamp, reached into the drawer of her nightstand, and pulled out her Bible. "I need help, Father, or everything I know and love will be ruined. How do I deal with this? Please, God, give me some answers."

She opened her Bible to a page that had been marked by the thin scarlet ribbon and began to read 2 Corinthians 12. When she got to verse eight, her heart quickened and she read aloud.

"Concerning this thing I pleaded with the Lord three times that it might depart from me. And He said to me, 'My grace is sufficient for you, for My strength is made perfect in weakness.' Therefore most gladly I will rather boast in my infirmities, that the power of Christ may rest upon me. Therefore I take pleasure in infirmities, in reproaches, in needs, in persecutions, in distresses, for Christ's sake. For when I am weak, then I am strong."

It felt as though the Holy Spirit moved in her, stirring up tears from a deep reservoir. Determination filled her. If this boy was in fact Elijah's son, she'd find a way to make it work. She'd figure it out day by day with the Lord's help.

And in the meantime, she'd pray for *her* baby, as she had every day for the past two years.

Amy followed the directions Elijah had given her and, finding the number on the mailbox, turned onto the long gravel driveway. It was at least a half mile to the big brick farmhouse, long enough for her to figure out what to say, but when she put her car in park, her mind was still a blank slate.

She rested her forehead against the steering wheel as severe nausea set in. Every ounce of her being wanted to throw the gearshift in reverse and spin the tires as she flew out of there, out of Harvest Bay.

But when she glanced at Dominick her heartstrings tightened. If he was ever going to have a normal life, she had to see this through. And she had to have a place to stay for however long it took.

A long sigh dragged out of her throat. "Let's get this over with." She motioned for Dominick to follow her and trudged to the front door, hating that she felt like a charity case. She only hoped that the guy from the café—was his name Owen?—wouldn't be there. Seeing him while she asked for a place to stay would sting worse than Tabasco on a canker sore.

As the doorbell echoed through the house, she sucked in a deep breath and shoved her hands in the pockets of her jean shorts. She exhaled a moment later when a woman with wavy auburn hair and a friendly smile opened the door.

"Hi. I'm Amy. Owen gave me your address."

"Oh, yes! He said you might be by. I'm Anna Sullivan. It's nice to meet you."

"You, too."

Anna opened the door wider. "Would you like to come in?"

"We don't want to impose." Honestly, Amy just wanted a hot bath and a comfortable bed.

"Nonsense. I just brought in a pitcher of sun tea from the back porch, and I always keep a container of Nesquick on hand for the kids." She winked at Dominick. "Let's have a glass together, and then I'll walk you both up to the apartment."

Feeling as though she had no other choice, Amy motioned to Dominick and followed Anna into her country kitchen.

"So does your son make it a habit of bringing home strange women and children?" Amy asked in a sarcastic tone as she took a seat at the small, round breakfast table.

Anna chuckled as she crossed to the fridge and grabbed the pitcher of tea and a gallon of milk. "Ah, yes, my humanitarian. No, but he is always the first one to lend a helping hand." She brought a glass of tea to the table. "When did you arrive in town?"

Amy took a long, refreshing drink. "Late this morning."

"Enjoying your visit so far?"

"For the most part." *As long as you don't count how upset Elizabeth is that we're here or how Elijah asked for a paternity test.* "The city park is beautiful."

"How long are you going to be here?"

"I'm not sure yet."

"Well, you can stay here as long as you want."

Amy took another sip. "What is the rent?"

Anna stirred the chocolate powder into the glass of milk and carried it to Dominick. "There you go, sweetie." She leaned against the back of a chair and turned to Amy. "No charge. I'm sure you have plenty of other expenses."

Amy lifted her chin. "We don't accept charity."

"Well, I'm not going to take your money," Anna said planting her hands on her hips.

Unwilling to back down, Amy commenced a different strategy. "Then I can work off our room and board."

Anna tapped her finger against her chin. "What kind of work are you talking about?"

"Just name it. I grew up on a farm and spent almost ten years in the military. I know a thing or two about physical labor."

Anna gave a nod. "All right. It's a deal." She extended her hand and Amy shook it. "Spend the weekend getting settled in, and I'll meet you in the stables Monday morning."

Satisfaction curled the corners of Amy's lips. She could begin to get her life in order here, and she'd help this family in the process . . . at least until they figured out her secret.

Anna glanced at Dominick, who smiled at her after wiping away a hint of chocolate milk mustache with the back of his hand.

"Are you always this quiet?"

Amy felt her cheeks burn and she cleared her throat. "As a matter of fact, he is. Dominick's deaf."

Anna's shoulders fell. "Well, there I go putting my foot in my mouth." A sheepish grin crossed her face. "And a size nine is pretty hard to digest."

Amy chuckled. "It's okay."

"Nobody told me we were having a party." The chipper male voice cut through the tranquil kitchen, causing Amy to nearly jump out of her skin. "Who do you have here, Darlin'?"

"This is Amy, our new hired hand."

The silver-haired man sized Amy up and raised his eyebrows. "Really?"

Her blood simmered under his scrutiny. *If he only knew half the things I've been through . . .*

She stood and squared her shoulders. "I spent almost ten years serving as a medic in the Army. Before that I helped run the orange plantation that's been in my family for generations. I've done things many men wouldn't have the guts to try. I think I can pull my weight around here."

A warm smile crossed the man's face. "I think you might be right. Welcome aboard." He put his hand out and Amy tentatively shook it. "Jacob Sullivan."

Glancing at her ratty tennis shoes, disgust snaked its way into Amy's heart. Did she always have to be so defensive?

And did she really have to wear her oldest, most worn out pair of shoes today of all days?

"Thanks for letting us stay."

He nodded. "It'll be a good arrangement for all of us."

Anna gathered up the empty glasses and deposited them with a clatter in the sink. "What do you say I show you to the apartment now so you can get settled?"

"I can do that, Mom." Owen filled the doorway, stopping Amy's heart and draining the color from her face. He smiled at her. "Hello, again."

"Hi." Her face grew as warm as if she'd spent all day in the hot Florida sun, and she guessed it was just as rosy. She slipped a finger under the collar of her suddenly restrictive T-shirt desperately needing some fresh air. "Let me grab our bags and I'll meet you out front."

Owen stepped aside as Amy slipped by. "I'll help you."

She would've argued but was more concerned with getting out of that kitchen. Reaching her car, she turned on her heel expecting to find Owen right behind her.

"Listen, I appreciate . . ."

Amy intended to give him a piece of her mind once and for all, but he wasn't there. Instead, he and Dominick had stopped in the middle of the yard to play with a dog. She leaned against the car, watching them in the dim light. The dog dropped a ball at Owen's feet, which he picked up and handed to Dominick. The dog hopped around in a circle, tail wagging wildly.

Before Dominick could throw the ball, the dog jumped up on him, knocking him over and licking his face and neck in an attempt to get the toy. Owen quickly stepped in, swiped the ball, and catapulted it through the air. In a flash the dog bounded after the toy, and Owen helped Dominick to his feet.

"Are you okay?"

Dominick looked up at Owen with a smile as bright as the midday sun. Amy crossed her arms and turned her head. She wouldn't allow herself to get caught up in some warm and fuzzy moment between her son and some guy they'd just met. She couldn't take the chance of letting her guard down for someone who most likely felt sorry for them. Still, her gaze shifted just in time to see Owen tousle Dominick's hair, and her chest tightened.

A sad sigh escaped her lips as she returned to the task at hand. Yanking two black duffle bags from the trunk, she slung them over her shoulder surprised by how heavy they seemed.

Owen jogged up to her. "Hey, let me help you with that."

"I've got it." She reached up to close the trunk, struggling with the two bags.

He cautiously lifted the straps off her shoulder.

His persistence caused her to snap. "Who do you think you are?"

He slid the straps onto his shoulder. "I'm simply trying to be a gentleman. Please, just humor me. If Mom looks out the window and sees you carrying two bags, I'll never hear the end of it."

She worked hard to keep the smirk off her face as she slammed the trunk shut. "So really you need my help."

His light-hearted chuckle somehow lifted her heart as well. "I guess so."

"Well, in that case, have at it."

They walked together in silence toward the detached garage, her guard up and all of her senses on high alert.

Reaching the steps that led to the second story apartment, he turned to her. "Are you as hungry as I am?"

Right on cue, her stomach growled loudly.

He laughed. "How does pizza sound? I can call in an order and give you a quick tour of the farm while we wait for delivery."

Her mouth watered at the thought of a hot, cheesy pizza. If she was hungry, she knew her growing boy must be starved.

Across the yard, Dominick once again had the ball and was playing with the dog in the dewy grass. The stars and fireflies twinkled in the violet sky. She'd missed beautiful evenings like this on long patrols in Iraq.

She blew out an exasperated breath that ruffled her bangs. What was the point of crawling into a comfortable bed when she didn't sleep much anyway?

"Sounds good."

With a satisfied expression, Owen handed her the key, then pulled out his cell.

Amy lugged the bags up the steps, remembering well the weight of the equipment she had strapped to her when on duty in the desert heat. Try as she might, she just couldn't shake the heavy load she carried.

Just inside the door, she flipped on a light. The small apartment was surprisingly quaint for its location above a garage. The fully furnished living room was airy and decorated in neutral colors. The tiny kitchen waited to her right, and a little hallway that probably led to the bedroom and bathroom branched off to her left. Satisfied for the moment, she heaved the bags over to the side, switched the light back off and headed down to rejoin Owen at the bottom of the steps.

"Two large pizzas—a cheese and a meat lovers—will be on their way in twenty minutes. Let's head out to the stables while we wait."

She got Dominick's attention and waved him over. He and the dog followed closely behind as they headed across the yard toward a small red barn.

Owen shoved his hands in his pockets. "Can I ask you something?"

"I suppose."

"How long has Dominick been deaf?"

"Since birth. He came eight weeks early, and there were some complications during the delivery."

"Must be tough."

"Life's tough," she muttered.

In the twilight she could feel his eyes on her, studying her, trying to figure her out. Sweating under his inspection, Amy quickly put on a cool façade.

"He's a sport. And we have our own way of communicating so it works out okay." She shifted her gaze to those ratty shoes. "You just learn to deal with it."

His smile was so bright she felt its warmth. "When life handed you lemons, you made lemonade?"

"Something like that."

"Here we are." He pulled a door open and flipped on the lights. The horses nickered at the sudden movement. Amy stepped inside and inhaled the sweet, familiar scent of alfalfa. A comfort level she hadn't experienced in eighteen years set in and, for the first time in a long time, her smile came easily.

As Owen walked her and Dominick down the row of stalls, introducing them to the horses, it seemed as if she'd stepped back in time to a place before a one-night stand resulted in a special needs child, and the ravages of war stole whatever innocence she had left.

Back before God took the one person who meant everything to her—her one true hero.

In a stall set apart from the others, a beautiful palomino with bulging sides poked her head over the gate and whinnied.

Owen crossed the barn to the pregnant horse. "Don't worry, big mama. We didn't forget about you." He stroked her muscular neck. "Just planned on saving the best for last."

Safe with his back to her, Amy allowed her hand to find its way to her flat belly. There were many obvious differences between the two situations, but only she knew that while one was intentional, planned, and wanted, the other one wasn't.

She listened to Owen speak tenderly to the mare, knowing that she'd be ridiculed if her secret was ever revealed. Angry tears stung her eyes. She blinked them back and moved on to the last stall.

Amy immediately noticed the horse in this stall wasn't waiting at the gate for a bit of attention like the others. The bony paint watched her from the back wall, ears alert, nostrils flared.

When Owen finally joined her she inquired, "This one seems so different. What's her story?"

He rested his forearms on the top slat. "She's been on the farm for about a month. We call her Angel because she was in such bad shape when we rescued her that we figured somebody must've been watching out for her."

"She was abused?"

"Severely neglected, at the very least."

Amy's heart and fists clenched for the poor animal. "How could people do that to such a beautiful creature?"

"I wondered the very same thing." He gazed at Amy with an intensity that gripped her bruised and battered heart.

"Has it been twenty minutes? I think I just heard a car door." She turned and hurried back down the row of stalls.

While they sat around the small table in the apartment making quick work of the two pizzas, Owen filled Amy in on the history of the farm, but she was only listening with one ear. Her thoughts remained on that horse.

Who hurt you, Angel? She'd like to know, but it was a good thing she'd probably never find out for fear of what she'd do to the abuser. *You'll trust again, girl. So help me, God, you will. And maybe you'll even love again.*

lizabeth stared at the bright red numbers on the alarm clock, her eyes like sandpaper after a long, tearful night. 5:28 . . . 5:29 . . .

She reached over and turned off her 5:30 alarm. The blaring noise certainly wouldn't help her splitting headache. As her fingers kneaded her temples, she knew it would require pain relievers to make it through a twelve-hour shift.

Since they'd started trying to conceive, she made a point of avoiding medicines of any kind, including Tylenol. Still, as unpredictable as her PRN schedule tended to be, the day shifts she'd sign up for this weekend would be a welcome distraction.

She took an extra long shower, allowing the steamy water to melt away as much tension as possible. When the hot water began to fade, she turned the shower off and wrapped a towel around her. Examining herself in the mirror, she placed her hand on her tight, flat belly. Oh, to feel a little flutter, to see a tiny bulge.

"How much longer, God?"

My grace is sufficient for you, for My strength is made perfect in weakness.

Her bottom lip quivered. "I will trust You."

She twisted and clipped her towel-dried hair in a simple up-do, applied a little blush to her pale cheeks, and then added a touch of mascara. After brushing her teeth and covering her lips in a thin layer of gloss, she retreated to her closet and dressed in her Strawberry Shortcake scrubs. The young patients in the pediatric wing loved the characters on her uniforms, and Elizabeth loved the smiles it brought to their faces. She laced up her white tennis shoes, put in the diamond stud earrings that Elijah had bought her for their fifth anniversary two years ago, and then headed downstairs.

In the kitchen, her husband stood at the sink, staring out the window, a cup of coffee in his hand.

"Hey," she said softly, compassion flooding her heart.

He glanced over his shoulder. "Hey."

"Did you sleep at all last night?"

Elijah shrugged. "An hour. Maybe two. What about you?"

"I slept some."

He turned to face her. "I'm going to call Matt Johansen today."

Anxiety grasped her heart. "Isn't it a little soon to get our lawyer involved?"

"No. I have to know. If Dominick is my son . . ." He returned his gaze to their backyard. "I have ten years to make up for."

His son.

She bit her lip, wondering if those two words would ever become easier to chew, ever taste less bitter. Sighing, she grabbed her purse from the counter. "Well, I'll be home shortly after seven. If you need me, you know how to reach me."

He took her in his arms and gave her a weary smile. "Everything's going to be okay."

She wanted to believe him, but at that moment it felt like nothing would ever be okay again. Stretching up on her tip toes, she gave him a peck on the lips. "I love you."

"And I love you." He gave her a squeeze and let her go.

For a good part of the morning, Elizabeth managed to keep an upbeat attitude and focus all of her energy on the children assigned to her, but by one o'clock in the afternoon her restless night had caught up with her. After a quick check on her patients, she dragged herself to Cresthaven Medical Center's food court. Not having much of an appetite, she sat down at a table in a quiet corner and pulled an apple and her travel-sized Bible from her purse.

Closing her eyes, she silently prayed. *Be here with me, God. Give me strength to make it through this day.* Her thoughts drifted to Elijah, their new situation, and the baby she ached for. *And whatever is to come.*

"Having the Bread of Life for lunch?"

She glanced up at the friendly face of Dr. Nathan Sterling, one of Harvest Bay's two family physicians. "Just needing a little inspiration. Checking on a patient?"

"Why else would I be here on a Saturday?" He took a sip of steaming liquid from a Styrofoam cup. "Mind if I join you?"

"Not at all."

He sat across from her and examined her with a carefully trained eye. "So how are you?"

"I'm fine. Why do you ask?" Her answer was quick, even to her own ears.

He took another sip. "No reason."

Elizabeth fought uselessly against the moisture building in her eyes. She could've fibbed to anyone else, but Nathan was not only her primary care physician, he was the brother of her sister's deceased husband. Elizabeth knew she could confide in him. Maybe he could even help her.

"We found out last night that Elijah may have a ten-year-old son."

Nathan raised his eyebrows. "May?"

"Pending a paternity test."

"How does he feel about it?"

Spinning her apple on the table, Elizabeth worked to disguise the pain in her voice. "I think he's in shock."

"How do you feel about it?"

Elizabeth shrugged and gave him a wobbly smile. "I want my own baby."

"I understand that." Nathan had recently married his office manager, a woman with two teenage sons from a previous marriage, and Elizabeth took the opportunity to learn from his experience.

Leaning forward, she propped her elbows on the table and rested her chin in her hands. "So what's it like being a stepparent?"

"It has its challenges . . ."

She frowned.

". . . and plenty of rewards."

"Have you and Denise talked about having one of your own?"

"We can't without significant medical treatment. I knew the situation before we got married, and I'm okay with it. It's just not God's plan for me."

Elizabeth dropped her gaze as her heart sank low in her chest. "Do you think it's God's plan for me?"

Nathan reached out, took her hand in his, and gave it a squeeze. "I think it's still too soon to jump to any conclusions."

"I'm having a hard time being patient."

"Has your obstetrician informed you of your medical options?"

"We want to have a baby according to God's will." Tears tickled her nose and stung her eyes.

"Elizabeth, you're a nurse. You really think a prescription or procedure is above God?"

"Of course not!"

He drained his cup and tossed it into a nearby trashcan. "Look, any treatment—whether for fertility, cancer, or the common cold—is just a tool. Some work, some don't, and every individual is different. All you can ever do is try and leave the rest up to the Great Physician."

She nodded, letting his words soak in.

He stood. "I've got to run now, but talk to Elijah. Pray about it together. If you have any questions or want more information, I'll be happy to talk with you. Just call the office on Monday, and Denise will fit you in."

"Okay. Thanks." She watched him walk away, sure of two things. She definitely wouldn't be talking to Elijah about it. She couldn't. He had enough on his mind already. Yet, as wrong as it might be, as dishonest as it might seem, she'd make that appointment first thing Monday morning.

There was only so much settling in for Amy to do over the weekend. Early Saturday morning she'd unpacked the measly contents of their duffle bags into four dresser drawers.

When she was sure stores would be open, she headed out to pick up some essential items, including laundry soap, then returned to the apartment to wash, dry, and put away a small load of clothes. She spent the rest of the afternoon exploring the farm with Dominick, growing more comfortable in her surroundings with every passing minute. By sunset she actually felt somewhat at home.

Home. It had become a foreign word to her. It had lost all meaning when, as a vulnerable twelve-year-old, her home was torn apart, her whole world shattered. Eighteen years earlier her security had evaporated like a rain puddle on a hot summer day, and she'd run from anything that really mattered ever since.

"But my own son? What kind of mother runs from her child?" she whispered into the evening breeze, knowing the answer. "My mother. And I became just like her."

She sat on the bottom step of the stairway that led to the apartment and watched Dominick play with his new canine friend. He looked so carefree, and she wondered if he had been that happy in Florida. She honestly didn't know since she'd been in and out of his life, completely devoted to the military while her grandparents devoted themselves to raising him.

"Dominick deserves so much better." In the late afternoon heat, she shivered and hugged herself tightly. "I might put on a strong front, but I'm really just a big, fat chicken."

"There are worse things, I suppose."

Amy flew to her feet and spun around with her fists raised in a fighting position.

"Whoa." Owen put a hand up, palm out. "It's okay. It's just me."

Amy exhaled but couldn't relax completely. "Do you make a habit of sneaking up on people? Sheesh! Make some noise, why don't ya?"

"I was just checking to see if you survived your first day on the farm."

She sat back down, wondering how much he'd heard, and mumbled, "We managed."

He gestured at a basketball under his arm. "I thought maybe Dominick would like to shoot some hoops, but it looks like he's enjoying himself."

At that moment, Dominick noticed him and brightened as the dog leaped for the ball.

Owen laughed and waved Dominick over to them. Then he leaned over and asked Amy in a low voice, "How should I ask him if he wants to play?"

A sudden surge of warmth coursed through her. *This heat must be getting to me. Yeah. That has to be it.*

She uncrossed her arms to fan herself. "Just ask him. He reads lips and he carries a small notebook and pen with him so he can communicate with you."

Dominick threw the ball for the dog to fetch and trotted over with a questioning expression.

Owen held the basketball out. "Wanna play?"

Dominick nodded, a tuft of his hair whipping back and forth with the motion, and the two took off.

After a few steps, Owen turned and shouted, "Are you coming?"

Amy hopped up and took off after them. Basketball wasn't her game, but she wouldn't pass up the opportunity to spend a few fleeting moments with Dominick.

Besides, she knew nothing about Owen. He seemed genuinely kind hearted, and his family was very accepting. But appearances could be deceiving—she knew that all too well—and no matter what kind of mother she'd been over the past ten years, it was her duty now to protect her son.

For nearly an hour, they shot the ball into a hoop bolted into the side of a big, weathered barn. By the time the sky faded to a deep violet, Dominick had returned his attention to the playful pooch, and Amy collapsed on the soft grass, exhausted but more lighthearted than she'd been in a long time.

"That was fun." The words escaped on short puffs of breath as Owen stretched out a few feet from her.

"Thanks for joining us." He picked at the grass for a few minutes. "So . . . tomorrow's Sunday, and with you being new in town, well, I wanted to invite you and Dominick to come to church with me in the morning."

The way he asked—so gentle and thoughtful—tickled her heart, but the topic turned her stomach. "I think I'll pass."

"Maybe next week then."

She gritted her teeth. "No, I don't think so." The idea that people congregated to worship a God who allowed senseless tragedies to happen to good people repulsed her.

"Maybe . . ."

She pushed to her feet, her blood pressure rising with her. "Look, I'm here for one reason and one reason only, and it doesn't involve going to church or anything that has to do with God."

Owen stood, shuffling the basketball from one hand to the other. "Everything has to do with God."

"Butt out!" She turned on her heel to stomp off.

"When are you going to talk about being a chicken?" His voice held a hint of a challenge, but she refused to take the bait.

She spun around and marched right up to him, so close that the toes of their shoes touched. "With you? Never. It's none of your business, and you shouldn't have been eaves-dropping."

"Okay. Okay." He bounced the ball on the dirt court. "Just remember you're not the only one who's ever been scared."

She narrowed her eyes at him. "You have no idea what I've been through."

"I may understand more than you think." With that he turned and strode off into the darkness.

CHAPTER
Four

*A*my thought about Owen's words off and on the next day
and most of the night as she lay awake on the sleeper
sofa. *How could he possibly understand anything about me? He
doesn't even know me . . . and if he did, he wouldn't want to.*

Still, his voice had been so saturated with empathy that
somehow she believed him and tried to imagine what hardships he'd experienced that he could possibly understand
hers. After the way she'd snapped at him, she doubted she'd
ever find out. She wouldn't blame him one bit if he never
wanted to see her again.

Disgusted with herself, she got up and brewed a pot of coffee, wishing she'd packed a bottle of vodka and peach
schnapps since she hadn't seen a liquor store in town. A
strong fuzzy navel would be a good way to start this Monday.
After all, orange juice was loaded with Vitamin C, and the
alcohol would dull the sharp pain in her heart.

But it wouldn't be good for . . . Unable to finish the
thought, she leaned wearily against the counter. *What in the
world am I going to do about this mess I'm in?* She knew her
three options as any woman did, and she felt confident her
choice would be validated. Common sense told her it was a
no brainer, but she'd yet to make a final decision.

She stared at her reflection in the pitch black window. With daylight more than an hour away, everything was calm except for some crickets and a noisy owl.

That is peace. She found her eyes in the glass. *This is war.*

She longed for true inner peace, the kind she'd experienced long ago when her dad tucked her in at night and sang her to sleep, but her hope to know real peace had vanished long before the hell she endured in Iraq. It had boarded that plane with her father long ago and never returned.

Still, there had to be more to her life than continually battling the ghosts that haunted her days and the dreams that terrorized her nights. Her new mission and purpose for coming to Harvest Bay was to find a way to make life bearable again, whatever it took. Failing to complete this assignment was not an option.

While the coffeepot finished spitting and sputtering, she washed up and dressed in a pair of jeans and a T-shirt. She laced up her old shoes and filled her insulated travel mug with the steaming black liquid. Then, after scribbling Dominick a quick note, she slipped out of the apartment and headed for the stable.

Amy pulled open the heavy door and felt around for the light switch. The horses stirred and nickered when she found it. For a brief moment she stood there and let her guard down. The sweet, earthy scent of alfalfa filled her lungs and triggered countless memories of the best two years of her life. Suddenly she wished she trusted someone enough to share them. Of course, she could tell Dominick, but with the exception of only a few signs, she relied on his notepad for communication, and these memories were too special to be shared that way.

She sighed. *Too bad people aren't as trustworthy as animals.* With that, she got to work, mucking the stalls of Dixie and Dolly, two beautiful and very gentle palominos.

"Hey, girl," she said softly once in Dixie's pen. "I used to have a pretty baby just like you."

She carried a shovel full of manure and dumped it in the wheelbarrow that she'd positioned at the gate. The smell made her queasy, but she popped a stick of peppermint gum in her mouth and returned for another load.

"Her name was Mercy. Silly name, huh?" She scooped up another pile and dumped it. "Well, she was a gift from my dad, and he said that would be a good name because it would remind me that God gives us new mercies everyday." She shoveled up the soggy wood chips, dumped them, then moved to Dolly's pen. "Too bad there comes a point when that's just not enough."

"And when exactly would that be?"

Amy yelped and jumped. Although it didn't seem to faze Dolly, she still placed a reassuring hand on the animal's strong neck and the other over her own heart in an attempt to calm them both. She glanced in the direction of the voice, and found Anna standing in the open barn doorway.

"What is it with your family sneaking up on people?" She returned to cleaning the stall, making quick but thorough work of it, and walked the wheelbarrow to the dump pile out the door and around the corner. Back in the stable, she set the wheelbarrow down and eyed Anna warily, waiting for instructions but expecting a sermon.

"You did a good job with these stalls."

"Thanks." The simple praise released a few endorphins in her brain.

"Why don't you help me feed and groom these girls? Then we can put them out to pasture and you can level out the stalls with fresh wood shavings."

They worked together in silent efficiency. Amy stayed on edge, waiting for the questions that were sure to come and wondering how she would answer them. Before long, they led the horses to their individual fenced areas.

Anna fed and groomed Moses, their handsome thoroughbred stud, while Amy moved on to the very pregnant mare's stall on the other side of the barn. She dumped a shovel full of manure into the wheelbarrow as Anna approached with a bale of alfalfa and a bucket of water.

Amy leaned on the shovel handle. "When's she due?"

"In about a month and a half."

"Is this her first?"

Anna scratched the white patch between the palomino's eyes. "No. Bella's an old pro. Dixie and Dolly are both hers. We sold her last two, but we're keeping this one." She swiveled her attention to Amy. "Would you like to name it if you're still here?"

Amy almost dropped the shovel. Her heart tried to swell, but the walls surrounding it made it impossible. Shifting her gaze to the straw-covered floor of the stall, she kicked at a dirt clod until it broke apart and crumbled, perfectly illustrating her state of mind.

"I . . . I don't think so. That honor should be left up to your family." She returned to mucking the stall, the weight of her heavy heart slowing her pace. "Besides, I'm sure we'll be gone by then."

"Oh, well, that's too bad."

The look of disappointment on Anna's face tightened the ever-present knot in Amy's stomach. She didn't understand why this family had been so kind to her and Dominick since they arrived, but the last thing she wanted to do was to let them down now. Still, she couldn't promise them anything that she couldn't also promise herself.

After all the stalls were cleaned and most of the horses were happily grazing, Amy leaned against Angel's stall. She felt foolish for thinking about this animal so much over the past couple of days, but watching her now she felt a connection with the tortured spirit. Angel stood like a statue against the back wall. Her only movement was the flaring of her nostrils with each nervous breath, and an occasional swish of her tail.

"It's all right." Amy cooed, grabbing a handful of the sweet feed and holding it out as far as she could reach. "You can trust me."

Angel sniffed the air and fidgeted.

"I understand, girl, but I'm not like the others. I won't hurt you." She stretched a little further, her hand trembling. "C'mon."

Sniffing again, Angel pawed the ground.

At that moment, the trill of Amy's cell phone rebounded off of the stall.

Angel whinnied and reared back, her head raised high with panic in her big brown eyes.

"Damn it!" She rushed to answer the call before it spooked the horse anymore. "Hello." She didn't even try to mask the irritation in her voice.

"Uh, hi. It's Elijah." He paused. "Is this a bad time?"

She stared at the agitated horse. "No worse than any other." She forced a smile, hoping it'd brighten her tone a little. "What's up?"

"Oh, well, I wanted to talk to you about the paternity test."

"Okay."

"You understand that this is just a formality, right? I mean, it's not that I don't believe you."

She rolled her eyes at his need to clarify. "Of course."

He exhaled. "Good. Then you won't be offended when I tell you that I called the lab my attorney recommended, and they have an opening at three this afternoon. Does that work for you?"

"Sure. I just need directions." She found a pen in the tack room and tore off a corner of a feed bag to jot down the information. "Got it. We'll be there a little before three."

"See you then."

She slipped the phone into her pocket and stared at the directions. *And so it begins.*

"Everything okay?" Anna came into the stable carrying a bale of hay.

"It will be." She looked at Anna hoping to convey the necessity of her request without having to go into detail. "I've had something come up this afternoon, but I should be back in time for evening chores."

Dropping the bale, Anna stretched her back. "You were up before the crack of dawn, the stalls look great, and you were a big help in feeding and grooming. I'd say you earned your keep for today."

Her warm smile thawed the tip of Amy's frozen heart. She thought about the other appointment she'd been trying to forget. "I'm going to need Wednesday afternoon off too. Sorry."

"If you continue to work as hard as you did this morning, you can do whatever you want with your afternoons." Anna sat on the hay bale, studying her hands. "I know that we don't know each other very well, but if you need help with anything while you're in Harvest Bay, let me know, okay? I'll do whatever I can."

Amy turned back to Angel, a sense of hypocrisy nipping at her conscience. She closed her eyes and rubbed them with her thumb and first finger.

"Look, you and your family have been very kind to us and I really appreciate it. I do have some issues to take care of, but it's something I have to figure out on my own."

Anna eyed her for a moment then pushed to her feet and gave a nod. "Okay, then." She snipped the twine around the bale of hay and began distributing it between the stalls. "Just remember one thing. As long as you're staying on this property . . ." she turned and met Amy's gaze, ". . . you're never alone."

Elizabeth chewed on her thumbnail and flipped through a *People* magazine in the cozy waiting area of Harvest Bay Family Practice. The tan walls, each decorated with a Thomas Kincaid print, did little to ease the discomfort of sitting on pins and needles. She glanced at her watch, then at the doorway where the nurse would appear at any moment.

She set the magazine aside, closed her eyes, and tipped her face upwards. *God, what am I doing? It's not like me to be so impulsive, and I've never kept anything from my husband.* She took a deep breath, her determination and borderline desperation taking the place of rational thinking. *But if this results in us having a baby, the deception will be worth it.*

The bell above the door of the old renovated Victorian home tinkled, and her pulse quickened. In a small town word spread like the flu in a classroom of kindergarteners, and she certainly didn't need to run into anyone who might ask Elijah why his wife was at the doctor's on Monday afternoon.

Her jaw dropped when her sister, Kate Sullivan, came through the door like sunshine through a window, glowing with happiness from head to toe. Heaven knew with all Kate had been through she deserved to be happy. However, to witness it from the midst of such a fierce storm of emotion was almost more than Elizabeth could bear, and she wished her chair would swallow her.

Grabbing the magazine, she held it up to cover most of her face, and listened as Kate approached the office manager's window.

"Hi, Denise."

Denise squealed. "Kate! How are you?" A second later she rushed around the corner to embrace her friend. "So how was it? When did you get back? Tell me all about it."

Kate giggled. "One question at a time. Hawaii is a tropical paradise, and we had the honeymoon I always dreamed of. We got back late last night." A bright floral bag dangled from her fingertips. "We brought you and Nathan back a souvenir, and I couldn't wait to give it to you."

Elizabeth felt a twinge of guilt for eavesdropping, but she was curious as to what was in the bag.

Denise wasted no time digging into it. She pulled out a beautiful white pearl picture frame with gold accents.

"I thought you could use a special frame for your favorite wedding photo. Adam and I got one, too."

"Thank you. It's perfect!"

As they hugged again, Kate's gaze landed on Elizabeth over Denise's shoulder, and she gasped. "Elizabeth!" Kate squeezed Denise's hand and rushed to embrace her sister. "I would've brought your gift if I'd known I'd run into you. What are you doing here? Is everything okay?"

Elizabeth gave a little shrug. "It's no big deal. Just a checkup."

She looked toward the hallway for a way to escape just in time to see her nurse approach and call her name. Heaving an inward sigh of relief, she gave Kate a quick hug and gathered her belongings.

"I can't wait to hear all about your honeymoon. Bring your pictures to Mom and Dad's on Sunday, okay?"

Kate eyed her suspiciously. "Yeah. Sure."

Elizabeth turned and hurried down the hall before Kate had a chance to say anything else. While she sat on the hard table waiting for Nathan, guilt gnawed at her for being dishonest with her sister. It hurt just as bad as lying to Elijah, but Kate wouldn't understand. She'd listen with a compassionate ear like she always did, but she couldn't relate to Elizabeth's desperation.

Soon, though, this all will be a distant memory. Hope replaced the emptiness in her womb. Her heart swelled as she envisioned nursing her swaddled newborn. *It's just a matter of time.*

At that moment, Nathan knocked softly on the door and stepped in. "Hi, Elizabeth." He sat down on the rolling stool. "Elijah couldn't make it?"

"N-no," she stammered. "His schedule is pretty tight today."

"But you did talk to him about this, right?"

"Well . . ." She looked into the eyes of the one person she couldn't fool, and her shoulders drooped. "No."

"Elizabeth, I—"

"It wouldn't have done me any good to talk to him before today. Elijah is a facts and figures kind of guy. Please, Nathan, just give me the information, and I'll go home and talk to him. I promise."

Nathan stared at her for a moment, and then gave a nod. "All right, but I'm going to hold you to it."

Elizabeth smiled and held three fingers in the air. "Girl Scout's honor."

He explained some of the tests that a specialist might conduct to determine the cause of her inability to conceive, then handed her several brochures. "This is information on different drugs and procedures that might be options for you, depending on the test results. Insurance policies differ in coverage so you'll have to check on that, but I can tell you the farther you go in seeking treatments, the more expensive it is and the less likely that it'll be covered. Just to give you a head's up."

"Thanks, but I'm sure it won't come to that."

"I hope you're right." He jotted something down in his prescription pad, tore the sheet out, and handed it to her. "This is the name and number of a specialist in Cresthaven. I spoke with her today after Denise let me know that you were coming in. She's booked solid for two months."

"Two months!" Panic bells went off and hope shriveled.

"But she said she might be able to squeeze you in earlier."

Elizabeth exhaled but remained on edge.

"Go home and talk to Elijah. If he's on board, Denise will call and get you the earliest available appointment."

Elizabeth nodded. "Okay. Thanks."

He helped her down off the table. "Elizabeth, there are several issues to consider with fertility treatments, and it can put a lot of stress on a marriage. Communication with your spouse is the most important step in this process. Promise me you'll talk to Elijah."

She swatted his arm, dismissing his urgency. "Don't worry, okay? I'll talk to him. Everything will be fine."

He squeezed her shoulders. "I'll always worry. You and Kate are as close to sisters as I'll ever get." He paused. "Have you heard from her?"

"Yep. In fact you just missed her. She stopped in to bring you and Denise a souvenir."

"Well, give her a hug and thank her for me next time you see her."

"Why don't you do it yourself at my parents' annual Father's Day picnic next Sunday?"

He opened the door and walked her down the hall. "I'll check with Denise and we just might do that."

"All right. Hopefully we'll see you both then." She turned and hurried out to the lobby. Finding no sign of Kate, then glancing over her shoulder to make sure Nathan didn't follow her out, she stopped by the check-in window.

"Hey, Denise." She kept her voice low.

"Hi, there. Do you need to schedule another appointment?"

"Yes. With her." She handed Denise the name Nathan had just given her. She rationalized that it could be weeks before she got in to see the doctor. That would give her plenty of time to make good on her promise. "Is it too late to call today?"

Denise glanced at the digital clock on the counter. "Four forty-five. We're cutting it close, but let's find out."

She picked up the phone and dialed the number. A second later she perked up.

"Yes, this is Denise Sterling from Harvest Bay Family Practice. I need to schedule your first available appointment for one of our patients." After a brief pause, she put her hand over the mouth piece and whispered, "She can squeeze you in on Tuesday, July the fifth. That's just a little more than three weeks away."

"I'll take it." Elizabeth's heart suddenly grew wings and took flight, tickling her insides all over. The wait would soon be over, and when she could finally tell Elijah and the rest of her family that she was pregnant, nothing else would matter. Nothing.

CHAPTER

Five

With Dominick trailing behind, Amy marched up the sidewalk toward the Cresthaven Veterans Affairs outpatient clinic with a calm demeanor, though her insides could've registered 9.9 on the Richter scale. She dreaded this appointment, but her health and her ability to care for her son depended on it. The internal battle that ensued against the strong urge to hop back in her car and hightail it out of Ohio altogether could have compared to the Battle of Bunker Hill.

Owen's face drifted to her as Anna's words from a few days earlier echoed in her mind. *"As long as you're staying on this property, you're never alone."*

The inner turmoil eased. She'd been in Harvest Bay for five days, and she not only had a job, kind of, she and Dominick also had a decent place to stay, even if it was only temporary.

Something resembling hope flickered in her soul, and her lips curved upwards. Maybe . . .

"No." She shook her head, extinguishing the small flame before it had a chance to warm her heart. She wasn't foolish enough to trust a promise like that, no matter how genuine the source seemed to be. Knowing she'd already let her son down, she vowed not to let his heart get broken the way hers had over and over.

She stuck her chin out and picked up her step so that Dominick had to jog to keep up. She'd come to Harvest Bay for two reasons: so Dominick could meet his father, and so she could get her life straight. One down, and the sooner she got this appointment over with, the closer they'd all be to getting on with their lives.

They entered the building, surveyed the lobby, and finally found a sign pointing them down a long hallway. Amy glanced at her watch and picked up the pace again. She focused on her destination like a runner on the finish line and never saw the person come around the corner until it was too late.

They collided hard, setting her off balance. She closed her eyes, preparing to hit the floor, but a strong hand encircled her arm and helped steady her. Cracking one eye for a cautious peek, both flew open wide and a gasp escaped her lips.

"Elijah!" She shook out of his grasp. "What are you doing here?"

Surprise lit Dominick's face as he signed the word *father*.

A mixture of surprise and confusion swirled in Elijah's eyes. "I'm a physical therapist at the Cresthaven Medical Center, but on Wednesday afternoons I come over here to work with some of the vets." He planted his hands on his hips. "What are you doing here?"

"Take a guess. It's not that hard to figure out."

He crossed his arms and narrowed his eyes at her.

She sighed heavily. "I'm a veteran, okay? And I'm getting ready to be late for an appointment, so if you'll excuse me . . . "

She attempted to push past him but he held his hand up. "Wait a minute. I didn't know that you were in the service."

"You don't know anything about me. We shared one night." She paused and glanced at Dominick with a little smile. "And now a son."

She took a step forward, but he stopped her again. "What kind of appointment do you have? I mean, are you . . ." he swallowed, ". . . okay?"

Rolling her eyes, she jutted out a hip. "Please, Elijah. This isn't the movies. I didn't introduce you to your kid so I can go off to die in peace. I just . . ."

"Just what?"

Edginess set in. She didn't like being cornered. "Look, I need some help. He wanted to meet his dad. There you have it." She snatched Dominick's hand. "Come on."

"Hey, Amy!" he called after her.

Spinning around, she glared at him. "What do you want?"

He held his hands out. "I don't have anywhere to be. Why don't you let Dominick hang out with me while you're here? After all, I have ten years to make up for, ya know."

As the tension melted, she retracted her claws and turned to Dominick. "Do you want to stay with your . . ." she made one of the few signs she knew, ". . . father?"

Dominick stared at Elijah for a moment, a smile creeping across his youthful face. He nodded, gave her a hug, and hurried to Elijah's side. He got out his notepad from his back pocket, scribbled something on it, and held it out.

Elijah laughed and ruffled his hair. "You bet. Let's go." Elijah walked backwards a few steps. "We'll be in the courtyard, out the door and to the right."

"I'll find you."

Elijah's hand rested on Dominick's shoulder as they walked away from her with the same gait, looking every bit like a father and son should, and satisfaction filled Amy. She'd done the right thing by coming to Harvest Bay. She felt a little guilty that she hadn't done it sooner, but they'd have forever now.

She closed the short distance to the office labeled with the sign "Dr. Olivia Kimball, Psychiatrist", opened the door, and stepped inside.

A young blonde receptionist looked up and pushed her fashionable glasses higher on the bridge of her thin nose. "Can I help you?"

"I'm Amy Beauregard. I have an appointment to see Dr. Kimball at four o'clock."

The receptionist scrolled and clicked on her computer. "Ah, yes. There you are." She printed up a couple sheets of paper, attached them to a clipboard and grabbed a pen. "Look over these forms and correct any information that might have changed. Obviously your residence will need to be updated. Also, make sure we have an emergency contact." She handed the paperwork to Amy. "Dr. Kimball will be with you shortly."

The hard, plastic chair made Amy feel like a schoolgirl in the principal's office as she breezed through the forms, filling in what she could remember of her new address and jotting down her grandmother's name and number as her emergency contact. The walls of the small waiting area were the color of sand, and the knot in her stomach pulled tight again. She'd seen enough sand to last her a lifetime. She used to love the Florida beaches, spending all day surfing and soaking up the sun. After returning from her second tour in Iraq, however, she sold her surfboard and avoided the sugary sand she used to love to sink her toes in.

Anger curled its strong fingers around her heart. *It's not fair the way war changes people.*

"Amy?"

She jumped and turned toward the gentle voice. "Yes, that's me." She got to her feet and met the doctor halfway across the small room.

"I'm Dr. Olivia Kimball. It's nice to meet you."

They shook hands. "Thanks for seeing me today."

"That's what I'm here for." Dr. Kimball gestured toward the open door. "Let's step into my office, shall we?"

Once inside, Dr. Kimball shut the door and motioned for Amy to have a seat on the brown leather sofa.

"Would you like something to drink?" She picked up a coffee cup and brought it over to the small glass end table.

"No, thanks." Amy's gaze swept over the small office. Distinguished degrees and licenses hung in heavy frames on the wall. Smaller frames holding pictures of children decorated her organized desk. A couple potted plants in the corner added a peaceful touch as did the meditation music playing in the background. Dr. Kimball was a perfect fit to the scene, with her dark hair pinned up in a neat bun, a few stray curls framing her face, and wearing a navy suit that was just a few shades darker than her gentle eyes. She sat in a chair perpendicular to the sofa.

"Okay, Amy. Why don't you start by telling me a little about yourself and how you came here?"

Amy took a deep breath. "Well, I spent the last ten years as a medic in the Army and have been deployed three times. I started having trouble sleeping after my first tour, but when I came back from my second deployment two and a half years ago it got really bad."

"Do you have nightmares?"

"They're worse than nightmares. It's like I'm reliving the whole thing."

"Is that why you're here?"

Amy shook her head. "I could deal with that, but the anxiety has gotten worse too. I get startled at the tiniest noise or movement." Amy was silent for a moment, staring at her hands in her lap. "One night a few weeks after I got back from my second tour, my son, who is deaf, had a bad dream and came into my room. I'd actually fallen into a sound sleep that night, and when he tried to wake me . . ." Tears stung her eyes and she bit her lip.

"What happened, Amy?"

"I attacked him." Almost choking on the guilt, she swallowed hard and continued, "I didn't mean it. I just reacted when he tapped my arm. I screamed and lunged at him, and by the time I realized what I was doing, I'd laid my own son out on my bedroom floor."

She sniffed. "Thankfully, he wasn't hurt physically, but that's when I really understood that I had a problem. I made an appointment with a counselor, but before long I was deployed again. After my third tour, I got out for good. I'd already realized that a ten-year-old boy needs his father, and since Dominick's father lives in Harvest Bay, I had the counselor on base schedule the earliest available appointment here. And the rest is history." Not realizing she'd been holding her breath. she dragged every ounce of air from her lungs and refilled them with a measure of relief.

"First, let me tell you that the fact that you heeded the warning signs to get help is a huge step in the right direction, okay? I also want you to know that these symptoms, the nightmares and anxiety, are typical for someone who has gone through a traumatic experience."

Amy ran her fingers through her stylishly unkempt hair. "That's great, but how long will it take for me to get better?"

"That all depends on you. Typically I'll see a patient with post traumatic stress disorder for twelve to sixteen weeks, but it really varies based on their ability to open up, process the trauma, and determine how it changed them physically, mentally, emotionally, and spiritually."

Amy nodded. Three to four months. Not exactly the answer she'd hoped to hear.

"I can promise you one thing, though." Dr. Kimball leaned forward. "I will see you through this. You will not go through this alone."

Amy thought of Anna's words again, and that tiny flicker of hope returned. This time, though, she didn't extinguish it.

Dr. Kimball sat back and took a sip from her mug. "Can you tell me a little about your time overseas?"

Amy stared at a tiny black spider scurrying up the wall toward the ceiling. Compared to the spiders in Iraq, it was nothing more than a speck, but she decided not to share that with Dr. Kimball.

"During training, I learned how to handle every possible scenario, but nothing could prepare me for the environment, the constant stench and dirt." Her stomach turned at the memory. "Where I was stationed was like being on another planet. As a combat medic, I provided emergency medical treatment to soldiers in the field and sometimes assisted in the hospital. Being in the hospital wasn't too bad, but trying to treat my guys with sand and filth caked in their wounds was pretty tough." She dropped her gaze to her hands in her lap. "But none of it was as hard as having a friend die in my lap."

Dr. Kimball's words were drenched in compassion. "Oh, Amy, I'm so sorry. No one should have to experience something like that."

"Soldiers do. All the time."

"Do you want to talk a little about your friend?"

"He was from Harvest Bay. His name was Justin McGregor."

"I think I remember the name."

"He was just a genuine guy, honest and good-hearted. He was engaged to be married and planned to continue his career with the fire department as a paramedic when his enlistment was up. He had his whole future laid out in front of him and in the blink of an eye . . ." A thick lump formed in her throat, blocking the last few terrible words.

"When this happened, were you injured?"

Amy swallowed. "No, not that day."

"Does that mean you got hurt on another occasion?"

She hesitated, holding her breath again, not ready to regurgitate that memory. "Yes."

"Can you tell me about it?"

Amy remained silent. Her gut warned her against opening up so much to a stranger, but her head rationalized that Dr. Kimball wasn't an ordinary stranger. She might be the only one who could help her.

Amy wanted to tell someone what they did to her. She longed to be reassured that it wasn't her fault, and to seek advice about the resulting situation she now faced, but she'd been strong for so long that the thought being vulnerable even just for an hour-long counseling session made her nauseated. Tears of frustration blurred her vision and she shook her head.

"It's okay. We're going at your pace. If at anytime you feel overwhelmed, we'll stop. You did really well opening up about your friend, but let's move on to something else for now. Why don't you tell me more about your son?"

The subject change lifted her mood. "Dominick is an amazing kid. He was born early and there were some complications that resulted in his deafness. He's really smart though and he loves any game with a ball."

Dr. Kimball chuckled. "Typical boy then, huh? Did he stay with his father during your deployments?"

"No. My grandparents raised him in Florida."

"How did you feel being away from him for so long?"

"Honestly, I didn't think about it. I couldn't. While I was in the military, I had a job to do. I couldn't dwell on the fact that I missed my son's first steps, first words, and first day of kindergarten. He's been playing baseball since he was five, and I've never been there for any of his games." She swallowed a wad of emotion back down to her knotted stomach. "I hate that my grandma learned to communicate with him in sign language, but I never did because I was gone more than I was there. For most of his life I was a robot, an unfeeling machine."

"That must've been hard."

"No. Not feeling is easy. *This* is hard."

Dr. Kimball nodded. "You mentioned your grandparents. Did you have a happy childhood?"

Amy's heart began to race. "My mother deserted us when I was a baby, but my dad did his best to make up for her absence until I was twelve."

"What happened when you were twelve?"

A long moment passed. Memories of the day her world stopped spinning came in waves, nearly knocking her over. Feeling like she was drowning, she shook her head. "I'm sorry. I can't . . ."

"It's okay, but we'll have to address those issues at some point. Do you understand that?"

Amy nodded.

"Now, in order to help you, I have to know if you've used any drugs to help you cope."

Amy hung her head. "Sometimes I drink when I'm having a bad night, but that's it and I haven't since . . ." She caught herself. "I haven't for several weeks. I don't want anything else around Dominick."

Dr. Kimball leaned forward again. "This question might be difficult to answer, but I need you to tell me if you've had any suicidal or harmful thoughts."

A tiny tear slipped out of the corner of her eye, and she angrily swiped it away. She hadn't shed a tear in eighteen years and she wasn't going to start now.

"Yes. Once."

"Can you tell me about it?"

"It happened right after the episode with Dominick, when I realized that there was really something wrong with me, something that I didn't know how to fix. I dropped Dominick off at school and drove out to one of my favorite beaches. I remember the sand alone brought on an anxiety attack, but I thought if I was going to die, that's where it should be. So I walked out onto the pier, got all the way to the end, and my cell phone rang. It was the school. Dominick had thrown up, and they needed me to come and get him. I never thought about it again." She gave a little shrug. "That was my wake-up call. I made up my mind right then to finish my enlistment, and then do whatever it took to get my head on straight so I could be the kind of mother my son deserves. I can't desert him the way my mom left me."

"I'm glad you shared this with me, Amy. You have a healthy way of looking at this issue, but if ever you find yourself in that frame of mind again, please call the emergency number right away. Sometimes an antidepressant is needed just to get you over that hump."

Amy pressed her hand to her belly. "I don't want a prescription."

"I understand, and you may never need one. I'm really impressed with how well you're opening up. Just know that it's an option." Dr. Kimball paused to take a sip of her coffee. "Now tell me a little about your beliefs. How has your spirituality changed as a result of the trauma?"

Amy's voice was flat. "It hasn't."

"Meaning?"

The edginess returned. "I didn't believe in God before, and I don't believe in Him now."

They talked for another half hour, just skimming various topics but steering clear of her childhood and Christianity. Finally, Dr. Kimball looked at her fancy gold watch and cleared her throat. "I think that's good enough for today. Let's plan on meeting once a week. Is this day and time good for you?"

"Sure." *One session down.*

Dr. Kimball rose. "All right. I'll have Tabitha put you down for Wednesdays at four o'clock. Now for your home-work—"

"Homework?" She groaned inwardly. *As if this hasn't been torture enough.*

"Don't worry. It's not as bad as it sounds." She went to her desk and picked up a black and white composition book. "But it could be very helpful in your recovery." She handed the book to Amy. "Between now and next Wednesday, I want you to write at least one journal entry a day. It doesn't have to be any certain length. Just write down your thoughts and feelings from the day."

Amy flipped through the empty pages. "That's it?"

"It may seem silly and pointless at first, but after a while it'll get easier, and as you get better it'll be rewarding to look back on your progress."

Amy stood, wedging the book under her arm, and grabbed her purse. "Thoughts and feelings. Got it." She took a step toward the door.

"There's one more thing."

She stopped and turned, dread weighing heavy in her gut.

"I want to encourage you to get involved with a support group, one that will help you deal with everyday life issues. There are a few that meet here at the clinic. I can have Tabitha get you that information, or you could check with some of the local churches. Regardless of where you go, the support and encouragement of people who have had similar experiences will be very important the further you get in this process."

Amy's stomach wrenched at the thought of sitting amongst a group of strangers with "everyday life issues." And in a church no less.

She worked to put a lid on her negative attitude. "Write in the journal. Find a support group. Anything else?"

"That's a good start."

Heading toward the clinic doors as if marching into battle, she prepared herself for recovery, certain it'd be every bit as painful.

Elizabeth sat at the table, folding and refolding her napkin. She'd set out her grandma's china, poured two glasses of sparkling cider, and lit a few candles. The lasagna and garlic bread rested on the stovetop filling the kitchen and adjoining dining room with the rich aroma of tomatoes, garlic, and herbs, which mingled nicely with the romantic melodies of Jim Brickman filtering in from the stereo speakers. She'd even put on the little black cocktail dress she knew was Elijah's favorite.

Tonight she'd make good on her promise to Nathan . . . and she'd make it impossible for Elijah to disagree.

She glanced at her watch. *A quarter after five. He's usually finished by three-thirty on Wednesdays. Where could he be?*

Fifteen minutes later, just as she was about to blow out the candles, the front door opened.

"Lucy, I'm home," Elijah called in a chipper voice. His bad imitation of Ricky Ricardo made her smile.

"In here!"

Her excitement built. He'd agree to fertility treatments and they'd have a baby by spring. She just knew it.

"Oooo. Something smells goo . . ." He came around the corner and stopped short when he saw her sitting at the beautifully set table. His big, happy grin fell and he scratched his head. "What's all this? Did I miss something?" He rubbed his chin. "Our anniversary was two months ago . . ."

Elizabeth laughed. "Can't I just do something nice for the man of my dreams?" She went to him, wrapped her arms around his neck, and gave him a lingering kiss. "Have a seat. I'll dish you up some lasagna before it gets cold."

He tightened his arms around her waist. "Or we could skip right to dessert."

"There'll be plenty of time for that later."

She wiggled her way out of his arms and headed to the kitchen, grabbing the Pyrex casserole dish in one hand and the basket of garlic bread in the other. When she returned, he'd already filled both of their bowls with tossed salad. She served up healthy portions of the lasagna, relieved that it was still warm, and joined him at the table. Elijah said the blessing, and then they both hungrily dug in.

After a couple bites, Elizabeth took a drink and wiped her mouth on her napkin. "Actually, there's something I want to talk to you about."

"There's something I need to tell you too."

"It sounds important."

"It is." He took a bite, chewed, and swallowed. "To me, at least."

Her nerves kicked in and her courage stalled out. "Okay then. You go first."

He put down his fork and folded his hands. "I ran into Amy and Dominick today at the VA clinic."

Suddenly, her appetite dissipated with the steam rising off the food. "Oh? What were they doing there?"

"It turns out that Amy's a veteran and had a doctor appointment."

She stabbed at a noodle on her plate. "Hmm. That's interesting."

"I got to hang out with Dominick while she took care of her business."

Elizabeth stared at him, recognizing the gleam in his eyes. "Do you think that was a good idea? I mean, you don't even know if he's yours yet."

"I don't need the results of a paternity test to spend time with him."

"What if it comes back negative? You're already attached."

"But what if it comes back positive?" He reached across the table and grabbed her hand. "Please try to understand."

She sighed heavily. Ready to get to the reason behind this meal that he was late for, she prompted, "Is that all you had to tell me?"

"Well, I guess you should know that Amy and I made a temporary arrangement that I'll get him every Wednesday after work while she takes care of her business."

"You what?" Elizabeth retracted her hand, dropped her fork, and pushed away her half-eaten plate of food. There was no way she could eat now when her insides had come to a rapid boil.

"And I asked her if he can spend Sunday with us."

It took a minute for the dawning to occur. "You're bringing him to my parents' Father's Day picnic? Elijah, what were you thinking?" She rarely raised her voice at him, but at that moment she couldn't help it.

He shoved his fingers through his dark hair. "I don't know, all right? I don't know what I was thinking. I got caught up in spending time with Dominick, and the invitation was out before I could take it back." He held his hands out. "I'm sorry."

"You're sorry? That's all you have to say?" She stood and carried her plate and silverware to the kitchen.

Elijah followed her. "What else do you want me to say?"

She scraped her plate into the trash and loaded it in the dishwasher. "For starters, what am I supposed to tell my family?"

He placed a hand on the counter, the other on his hip. "The truth. Exactly how long were you planning on keeping this a secret?"

Elizabeth didn't have an answer for that. Honestly, she didn't want to tell her family at all.

"What's next, Elijah? Are we going to give him a room upstairs? Wallpaper and paint it and buy him a sports-themed comforter to match?"

He only stared at her.

She pointed a finger at him. "You've gotten in over your head now. If that test comes back negative, his heart will be broken." She turned away from him. "And so will yours." She started to walk away, but his words stopped her in her tracks.

"And if it comes back positive yours will be broken."

She couldn't look at him. "It already is."

CHAPTER
Six

*S*unday morning, after chores were done, Amy sat cross-legged under a sprawling shade tree, the composition book on the ground next to her.

How do I feel today?

Dominick played in the yard with Harley, laughing loudly every time the dog licked him. Dixie and Dolly grazed in the pasture, while several different birds took turns serenading her and a gentle country breeze fingered her hair. She tipped her head back and closed her eyes in an attempt to experience true peace for just a moment, but the ghosts returned almost immediately, bringing the pain of the day with them. Her eyes dampened as she opened her journal to where her pen marked her page.

Day 5 – Father's Day, the eighteenth one without my dad. I can't help but wonder what we'd be doing if he was still here. I'm sure we'd go to church, and for that reason alone I was tempted to go with the Sullivans this morning, but figured it wouldn't have made a difference. At the end of the service there'd still be that same ol' emptiness, and I can feel disconnected sitting right here, so what's the point?

Maybe I'd still have Mercy, and maybe we'd take her out for a ride along the beach like we did the day before he left.

Of course, I'd introduce Dad to his grandson. Dominick would've adored him. He's so much like Dad. I see it more and more every day in his positive attitude, cute sense of humor, and genuine charm with everyone he meets. Dad would be proud of him . . . and of me. Despite my mistakes, I'm sure he'd be proud of me.

So, how do I feel today? Gypped. Abandoned. And just really . . . hopeless.

The pop of gravel under tires turned her attention to the driveway. Sighing, she closed the book, hooked the cap of the pen on the front cover, and got to her feet.

Elijah parked, got out, and strolled over to her holding a piece of paper. He handed it to her.

"I guess I don't have to show you this, huh?"

She unfolded it and read the words " . . . confirms paternity . . . "

"It came yesterday by certified mail."

She forced the best smile she could manage past her deflated spirit. "Happy Father's Day."

"Thanks." He gave her the goofy grin of a brand-new father, but it soon faded, and he shoved his hands in his pockets. "Amy, I want to have legal parental rights."

She crossed her arms, her only means of protection against the fight that she was in for. "Meaning?"

"I want to know that I'll be a part of his life. If you go back to Florida—"

"Are you talking about court?"

"If we're both in agreement of joint custody and have a workable arrangement prepared for the judge, my lawyer said it could possibly be settled in one session."

She nodded, anxiety already clenching her heart. "I understand."

"Well, we can talk about that later." He took his hands out of his pockets and rubbed them together. "So, is there anything I should know? Any allergies or other issues?"

"No food allergies, and he's a good eater so make sure your pantry and fridge are stocked. He's allergic to amoxicillin, though." She paused, reluctant to give up the control she'd only recently regained. "You'll call me if there's an emergency, won't you?"

He held up his cell phone. "I've got you on speed dial." He caught Dominick's attention and waved him over. "Hey, Bud! Are you ready to go?"

Dominick glanced worriedly at Amy, who gave him a smile and a nod. He hugged her tightly, then turned to his father and signed, "Let's go!"

Elijah took a few steps backward. "I'll have him back by nine."

Amy waved. "Have fun."

As she watched the car head back down the long gravel driveway and turn onto the country highway, she couldn't help feeling a little bitter. Dominick deserved to be with his dad . . . but so did she. When she could no longer see the dust from their tires, loneliness rolled in like fog so thick she could almost touch it. Not having anywhere else to go or anyone else to be with, she trudged toward the stable, Harley following close at her heels.

"You're lonely now, too, aren't you?" She felt silly for talking to a dog, but it soothed her. "Well, we have twelve hours without him, Harley. What are we going to do with ourselves?"

He barked, and she scratched his head. Stepping inside the barn, Amy checked on Bella. The pregnant mare had plenty of water, but Amy got her some fresh water and repositioned a fan to give her more air. Then she moved down the row of empty stalls until she came to the last one.

Angel greeted Amy with a nervous snort and pawed at the ground.

Amy sighed. "How can I help you trust again?"

At first glance, it seemed the white and bay paint hadn't moved even an inch since early that morning, but Amy noticed some of her pellets and water were gone. She refilled the bucket with cold water and grabbed a scoop of sweet feed from the tack room.

"Hey, girl," Amy cooed. "You should be getting used to me after a whole week of this." She took a handful of the corn and grain mixture and held it out. "You're a stubborn girl, but so am I and I've got all day today."

Angel lowered her head and flared her nostrils, sniffing the air.

Amy stretched a little farther. "It's all right. I'm not going to hurt you."

Angel swished her tail and snorted, then took a step back. After several minutes, the mare still hadn't budged. Realizing this could take a while, Amy laid her head down on her already aching arm.

"I'm not going anywhere, Angel, so you're going to have to give in." She closed her eyes. "And the sooner the better."

"Patience truly is a virtue."

Sweet feed dotted the air as Amy's yelp echoed off the barn walls.

Angel backed up as far as she could into the corner.

Annoyed, Amy spun around, her eyes landing on a brawnier version of Owen with shorter, sunny blond hair. Next to him was a beautiful young woman who resembled Anna in the face but had long strawberry blond corkscrews.

"You must be the new hired hand. I'm Adam and this is my sister, Kennedy." He stuck his hand out. "Sorry to startle you."

"Don't worry. I'm getting used to it with your family." She shook his hand, and then Kennedy's. "I'm Amy."

Kennedy stepped forward and leaned against the stall. "I don't know how Mom and Daddy found you, but I'm glad they did. Usually Adam and I are more available to help out during the summer, but I've been tied up with volleyball camp, and Adam just got married."

Amy offered Adam her sincere congratulations despite her opposition to relationships in general, and turned her attention to Kennedy. "Actually, I bumped into Owen at the Bayside Cafe my first day in town. I needed a place to stay, and he told me about the apartment. Your parents were nice enough to offer it in return for help with chores. It's that simple."

Adam hooked his thumbs in his belt loops. "Well, as far as we're concerned, you're a godsend."

A slight wave of warmth tingled Amy's heart, but she reminded herself that if they knew her—and she'd make sure they never would—they wouldn't have described her that way. She shifted her gaze to the grains of sweet feed scattered on the stall floor. "It's really the other way around."

"Well, regardless, we're glad you're here."

"That's right," Kennedy chimed in. "Hey, we're taking Dixie and Moses for a trail ride, but Dolly could really use the exercise too. Do you want to join us?"

Amy perked up with a shot of excitement, but fear quickly tamped it out. What if riding Dolly brought back more memories? "Uh, no, thanks. I've spent all week trying to wear Angel down, and I think I might be getting somewhere. Can't stop now. Besides, it's been far too long since I've been on a horse. I probably wouldn't remember how."

Kennedy swatted the air. "Nah. It's like riding a bicycle, and Dolly's the most laidback horse we have."

Adam gestured toward the skittish rescue horse. "As for Angel, how long you stand there is not nearly as important as how many times you come back."

She understood the wisdom in Adam's words better than most. Suddenly she wanted nothing more than to experience the freedom she once felt in Mercy's saddle. She only wished it could be with Angel.

Someday, girl. Someday. She turned to Adam and Kennedy, grains of sweet feed crunching beneath her boots. "Okay. Why not?"

They gathered up the saddles, saddle pads, bridles and reins from the tack room and went out to where the horses waited in their designated pastures. Amy surprised herself by how much she remembered, but she was still glad she had Kennedy's guidance in saddling Dolly. Within just a few minutes she timidly mounted Dolly, the leather saddle squeaking beneath her.

Kennedy sat naturally in Dixie's saddle. "Are you ready?"

Amy swallowed her nerves and nodded.

"All right then. Let's go." Kennedy clicked her tongue and eased Dixie out of the fenced-in area.

Amy followed suit. Adam joined them at the gate of Moses' separate pasture, and the threesome headed off down a dirt path through a hayfield toward a grove of trees. Memories floated back to Amy on the warm breeze, but they lacked the sharp pain she expected. The gentle sway of Dolly's gait comforted her like a mother rocking her baby.

Like the way Dad used to push me on the tire swing in the back yard. Her stomach fluttered at the memory of flying toward the sky until the rope brought her back to her dad's waiting arms.

Or the way he played his guitar and sang to me before bed. The sweet melody of the special lullaby he wrote for her filled her mind.

Or the way he sat with his arm around me during the Sunday morning church service. She inhaled humid country air and thought she caught a hint of his familiar cologne.

They emerged on the other side of the small woods into a grassy meadow and stopped. Several yards ahead, the meadow transformed into a pebbly beach that led right into the waters of Lake Erie, where gentle waves lapped lazily.

Kennedy dismounted and led Dixie to the water for a drink. "We thought since you're staying here and working with our family, you might like to see the whole farm and not just the horse barn." She winked at Amy.

"You're from Florida, right? I'm sure Lake Erie is no comparison to the ocean." Adam shrugged. "But we like it."

"It's different, that's for sure. The ocean is never this calm." She glanced down at the rocks and shells that led to the water, muttering, "And I've seen enough sand to last two lifetimes." She nodded. "This is really nice."

After the horses drank their fill, Adam, Kennedy, and Amy climbed back in their saddles and took off again, this time at an easy canter.

Adrenaline coursed through Amy's veins and invigorated her soul. The breeze tousled her hair and swept away every thought from her cluttered mind. For that moment the absence of her dad, the horrors overseas, and the challenges of being a single mother to a deaf child drifted away. She wasn't trying to escape her problems this time, but just the same the heavy burdens fell from her shoulders one at a time, and she happily left them in Dolly's dust.

They made a big loop around the vast hay field, and by the time they returned to the pasture, Amy's spirits were higher than they'd been in a long time. As she brought Dolly to a halt, the faint buzz of a motor landed on her ear like an annoying bumble bee. She turned in the saddle and watched a four-wheeler approach. The corners of her mouth lifted when she recognized Owen, but fell flat as it became obvious he wasn't alone.

The pretty raven-haired waitress from the Bayside Café sat behind him, her arms wrapped around his waist.

Suddenly, the troubles she had left in Dolly's dust returned with hurricane force. When she dismounted her legs nearly collapsed under the pressure. Having already put Moses back to pasture, Adam walked over to talk to Owen while Kennedy and Amy led the horses through their pasture gate.

Kennedy lifted the saddle off Dixie's back. "Have you met Maggie?"

Amy unfastened the saddle and pulled it and the saddle pad off Dolly's back. "She's the waitress at the café, right?"

"Only on the weekends. Monday through Thursday she's a receptionist at the Harvest Bay Family Practice. Oh, and on Tuesday evenings she leads a single-parent support group at our church."

Support group? Amy's stomach lurched as she recalled the dreaded homework assignment. "Really? Tuesday evenings at what time?"

"Seven, I think. Why?"

Amy shrugged as she unhooked the bridle and slipped it off. "Just wondering. She and Owen seem pretty close."

Kennedy nodded. "Her fiancé was his best friend before he died a couple years ago. Since then, Owen has really stepped up to the plate and helped out with her baby."

Amy watched them, remembering her first day in Harvest Bay—how Maggie knew what he wanted to order the minute he sat down and the way she lit up when he paid his bill. "Sounds like she's been through a lot. She's lucky to have someone to help her through it." A stab of jealousy caused a pain in her heart so sharp she sucked in a breath. She quickly scooped up the equipment and started for the gate. "Well, thanks for the ride. It was fun."

"Nice meeting you," Kennedy returned sweetly.

As Amy stalked off toward the stable, curiosity about Maggie nagged her. She dumped the equipment in the tack room and returned to Angel's stall with an uneasy heart. Unfortunately, she knew there was only one way to get the answers.

Elizabeth sat on a thick quilt under one of the two huge maple trees she used to climb as a kid. Sunlight streamed through leaves dappling her crossed legs. Those trees had transported her to far-off places and transformed her into anything she wanted to be, from Rapunzel trapped in a castle tower to a fearless explorer in an Amazon rainforest. She wished for a moment she could climb into those strong limbs and be whisked away from this life that had suddenly veered so far away from what she expected, from what she'd dreamed of since she was a little girl in that tree.

Several yards away, the man she loved with all her heart and his son played a game of backyard baseball with her family, who'd welcomed the young boy with open arms. She wished she could be happy for Elijah, but the irony of the whole situation just made her sick.

She was the one who wanted a baby so badly her empty womb ached endlessly. *She* was the one who cried for hours on Mother's Day, yet Elijah was the one celebrating Father's Day with his son.

"Looks like Dominick fits right in." Elizabeth's sister, Kate, took a seat beside her on the blanket and handed Elizabeth a plastic cup of lemonade.

"Guess so." Elizabeth took a drink to keep from saying anything she'd regret. Truthfully, she was a little annoyed by how well her family accepted him. His language barrier didn't hinder Madeline and Chloe's ability to communicate with him. In fact, they seemed to have developed a language all their own. And her father was over the moon that he now had a grandson.

Nathan hit the ball toward Dominick, who fielded it and threw it to Adam on first base for an easy out. Nathan returned to home, patting Elijah's back on the way, and a knot formed in Elizabeth's stomach.

God, please don't let Nathan say anything about my appointment. I'll tell Elijah . . . eventually.

Kate draped an arm over her sister's shoulders. "Do you want to talk about it?"

Overwhelmed by the complexity of the situation, Elizabeth simply shook her head and leaned into Kate feeling heavier than ever.

Kate rocked her gently. "I can only imagine how hard this is for you."

"It's just not fair, Kate." Elizabeth swiped at a tear rolling down her cheek. "I keep thinking each day will get easier, I'll get a little more used to the fact that Elijah has a son, but instead it gets more complicated and I feel more upset and betrayed and . . . empty." She paused to swallow a sob. "And lately I just can't help but wonder where God is in all this."

Kate smoothed Elizabeth's hair. "Did I ever tell you that I had a similar conversation with Gramps right after I moved back to Harvest Bay?"

Elizabeth sniffed. "No."

"I asked him how he made it through Grandma's death with such unwavering faith. He said there were times when he was tempted to question the Lord, but the Bible says, 'Trust in the Lord with all your heart and lean not on your own understanding.' No, it doesn't make sense, but you're going to have to trust the Lord on this too."

"I really miss Gramps."

"I know. I do too." Kate squeezed Elizabeth, and then let her go. "But if he was here, he'd want us out there joining in the fun and putting the guys in their place. What do you say?"

Elizabeth had no desire to play baseball with the others, but she never wanted to let her sister or her Grandpa Clayton down. "Let's make him proud."

They each homered by the time their father announced that supper was on and everyone rushed toward the smorgasbord of picnic food. Elizabeth's stomach growled as she loaded her plate with grilled chicken and her mom's homemade potato salad. She claimed an empty spot at the picnic table with the kids and Bill Gibson, a dear family friend.

"Hey, Uncle Bill! How's your garden this year?" She greeted the older man as she shoveled in a bite of tangy potato salad.

The thin, lanky man with snow-white hair nodded. "Good, good. I brought two paper sacks over. Tomatoes, cucumbers, onions, squash. Oh, and a dozen eggs from our chickens too. Take some home with you."

Her chuckle was the first genuine one of the day. "Thank you. I think I will." She glanced at Dominick and shifted her attention to young Madeline. "Did you introduce Dominick to Uncle Bill?"

She gave a sheepish grin, her cheeks full of hotdog. "Oops."

Elizabeth ruffled the little girl's hair, turned to Dominick, and signed as she spoke aloud. "This is Bill Gibson. He was a good friend of my Grandpa Clayton's."

Dominick gave Bill a little wave, then signed, "Where is your grandpa?"

"He died a year and a half ago."

"My grandpa died too. I never met him."

He went back to his plate of food while Elizabeth examined him through new eyes. For the first time she tried putting herself in his shoes. This boy faced a challenge every day of his life. He'd spent ten years without knowing his father, months at a time away from his mother, and was now thousands of miles away from his home. Yet he maintained a healthy attitude and a sunny disposition. Shame broke her spirit, while compassion softened her heart.

"So did ya bring us anything today, Uncle Bill?" Madeline wiped watermelon juice from her chin.

Elizabeth patted her niece's leg. "Maddie! Where are your manners?"

"Now, now, Elizabeth. A baby's gotta do what a baby's gotta do." He turned to Madeline. "As a matter of fact . . ." He reached into the breast pocket of his shirt and pulled out three small wooden crosses each hanging from a thin rope. "I made these necklaces in my shop last week."

"Wow! Cool!" Chloe took one and studied the intricate details.

Madeline slipped hers over her head. "Thanks, Uncle Bill! I love it!"

He held the third one out to Dominick. "The last one's yours if you want it."

Dominick brightened, accepted the gift, and signed, "Thank you."

Elizabeth shook her head in amazement. "Bill, how did you know to have three?"

He shrugged. "I didn't, but there were three crosses on Calvary. No other number felt quite right."

"Hey, look right there." Chloe held her cross up for Elizabeth to see. "It says, 'Psalm 23:6'."

Bill's eyes shined behind his glasses. "That's my prayer for you."

Madeline laid her head against his arm and looked up at him with big chocolate eyes. "What does it say?"

Dominick perked up and began to sign, while Elizabeth translated. "'Surely goodness and mercy shall follow me all the

days of my life and I will dwell in the house of the Lord forever.'"

Bill nodded. "That's right. Good for you."

Elizabeth winked at Dominick, hiding her astonishment,
and signed, "Good job."

So Elijah had been right after all. Dominick was a good
kid, full of surprises, and somehow he'd managed to find a
comfortable spot on the fringes of her heart. But it didn't
change the fact that he wasn't her son.

Two weeks. Just two more weeks.

She would trust in the Lord, just like Kate said, and in His
holy Word. Surely goodness and mercy would follow her to her
appointment with the specialist and maybe, just maybe, next
Mother's Day she'd really have something to celebrate.

CHAPTER
Seven

*A*my pulled into the parking lot of Harvest Bay Community Church, found an empty spot, and turned off the engine. For a long moment, she stared at the building remembering the last time she was inside a place of worship.

"At Dad's funeral." Her whisper seemed loud in the silent car. From that terrible day on, she refused to go to church with her grandparents. Not quite thirteen years old, she was still too young to make her own decisions regarding church attendance, but her tired and weary grandmother eventually quit fighting her.

"Amy Grace Beauregard, your father would be very disappointed in you."

She'd crossed her arms in a preteen huff. "Oh yeah? Well, I'm disappointed in him!"

Her heart sagged to her nauseated stomach at the memory. She'd long since forgiven her grandmother for the words spoken out of overwhelming grief, but she'd yet to get over shooting the wrong target.

She took a deep breath and hurried toward the church entrance before any more regrets tormented her. Pulling open the heavy wooden door, she stepped inside and looked around. With a set of doors straight ahead, hallways branching

off on both sides and nothing to point her in the right direction, her pulse started to race. Being alone and unarmed in a
strange place of any kind set her on edge, but being both
physically and spiritually lost inside a church pushed her over
the top.

"That's it. I'm outta here." She turned on her heel and
grabbed the handle of the door just as a man emerged from
the hallway on the left. He stopped whistling "Amazing
Grace" when he noticed her and his puckered lips spread into
a warm, friendly smile.

"Well, hello there. Can I help you?"

"Uh . . . I—I'm looking for the single-parent support
group."

"I just happen to be headed in that direction. I'll walk you
there."

They started around a corner and down a pale blue hallway with framed illustrations of Bible stories decorating both
sides. "If you don't mind my saying, I don't recall seeing you
around town. Are you new to this area?"

"Yes. My son and I arrived a week and a half ago."

"Well then, welcome to Harvest Bay. I'm Pastor Ben
Andrews."

"Amy Beauregard. Nice to meet you."

He rounded another corner and stopped at the second
doorway they came to. "Here we are. I think these folks will
make you feel right at home, but if there's anything else I can
help you with, just let me know." He pulled a business card
from the breast pocket of his button-down shirt, handed it to
her, then moved on down the hallway.

Recognizing the kindness in the gesture but certain that
she'd never need it, Amy slipped the card into her pocket.

She took a step out of her comfort zone and inched across a tightrope, taking in her surroundings as she went. The average-sized room buzzed with positive energy as men and women of different ages mingled at a little snack table in the corner or chatted from the seats they'd claimed in the circular arrangement. She spotted Maggie across the room, talking to a captivating woman with a beautiful heart-shaped face and very short hair.

"Are you here for the single-parent support group?"

Maintaining a casual front, though every nerve in her body jumped and the knot in her stomach pulled tighter at the sudden interaction, Amy turned to face the woman who had spoken. "Yes."

"Great! My name's Letisha Jackson, but everyone calls me Tish. Come on in, Sugar. Do you need child care today?"

"No. My son's with his father."

"Well, it's available, just so you know. Here's a nametag you can fill out while I grab some information for you."

Needing space in a hurry, Amy scrawled her name on the small white rectangle with a shaky hand, peeled off the back, and stuck it to her T-shirt.

"Perfect! Feel free to visit with the others or find a seat and get comfy. The meeting will start in just a few minutes. In the meantime, you can look over these." Letisha handed her two stapled packets. "The first is a new member application. It just gives us your basic information, and then discusses the policy on confidentiality. The second handout covers today's topic."

"Thanks."

"Sure thing, Honey." Letisha moved on to help someone else.

Amy eyed the circle of chairs, suddenly wishing someone would just blindfold her and set her in front of a firing squad. She'd be equally exposed, and a dozen bullets penetrating her flesh would certainly be less painful than this. A small bubble of panic floated up from her toes and expanded in her chest until she could barely breathe, and she fought hard against the urge to make a quick exit. Forcing her feet to move to the closest seat, she busied herself with filling out the form although she didn't intend on being a member any longer than it took for her to get well.

"*Hola,* everyone! It's time to get started," Maggie announced in her thick Spanish accent. She waited for everyone to find their seats, and then continued. "If you're new tonight, welcome. My name is Maggie Martinez. I became involved with this group almost two years ago, right after I had my *niño.* I've been leading it, with Tish's help, for about one year now. You can find mine and Tish's numbers in your new member packet. Please call if you have questions or need anything at all."

Amy tried to keep an open mind but found herself listening with a cynical ear. What could Maggie possibly do for her?

"And please take *un momento* afterward to visit. Usually I would ask you to introduce yourselves, but we have a busy schedule tonight . . . "

Amy breathed a sigh of relief. She'd dodged one bullet.

" . . . so let's open with prayer and get started. Tish, will you lead us tonight?"

Amy groaned. Prayer was pointless. While everyone folded their hands and bowed their heads, Amy sat with her arms crossed.

"Lord Jesus, hear our prayer. You know that our hearts, our needs, our wounds . . . You know each one of us far better than we know ourselves. And you know that we're hurtin' here tonight. We got so many needs in this room, and we got nowhere else to turn but you, Lord. We need you, Lord Jesus. We need your sweet embrace. Wrap your arms around each one of us, Lord, and help us feel your presence. We get so tired and lonely. We get all worn down, 'n feelin' like we can't make it one more minute, but we gotta be strong for our babies. And that's so hard when we doin' it all by ourselves. Oh, sweet Jesus, only you can help us. Fill us up with your Holy Spirit and give us the strength to make it one more minute, one more hour, one more day . . . Thank you, Jesus. Thank you. From the bottom of our hearts, we thank you."

"Amen," the circle murmured together.

Amy stared at her lap, wanting to stay cold and bitter. God had proved to her on several occasions that He didn't answer prayer. But Letisha prayed with such fervor and passion it seemed as if she had an intimate one-on-one conversation with the Big Man Himself. Amy almost felt guilty for eavesdropping except that Letisha seemed to be talking about her. Confusion filled Amy and she reacted the only way she knew how—she fought it.

"*Gracias*, Tish."

Letisha's bright red lips spread into a big grin. "Sure thing, Sugar."

"Now, onto tonight's topic: Forgiveness."

Amy's stomach turned. Thankfully she'd had a light supper.

"I know that this is a hard subject for many of you, but it's the key to true peace and freedom. No one knows that better than Stephanie McCorkle." Maggie shifted her attention to the woman she'd been talking to before the meeting. "Steph joined our group a few months ago, and as I've gotten to know her *un poco* over the past several weeks, I realized that she needed to present this topic, not me, so I asked her to give her testimony and share her thoughts with us tonight."

"Thanks for thinking of me, Maggie." Steph smiled looking remarkably like a porcelain doll with her exotic eyes and ivory skin. "But, truthfully, my story's not much different than the rest of yours. Tish hit the nail on the head when she prayed that we're all hurting, tired, and lonely. And I know that sometimes we all wonder how our life ended up this way."

Intrigued, Amy tuned in to what Steph was saying.

"I grew up in a Christian home, attended a Christian school, and went to church every Sunday and Wednesday. I guess I just figured my life would always be practically perfect . . . until I was fourteen."

Amy narrowed her eyes at Steph, whose story sounded all too familiar.

"Something happened that caused my life, and everything I believed in, to fall apart. What happened isn't nearly as important as the effect it had on me. I turned my back on my faith as others I had trusted seemed to turn their back on my family and me. That was just the beginning of the landslide."

Amy felt her heart connecting with this woman.

"I never imagined being a single mother of my two amazing kids." She paused. "Or that my oldest would be legally blind. Still, with his disability, he's taught me to see things in a whole new light, and I've come to realize that there are blessings even in challenging situations."

Blessings? Amy thought of Dominick and how many times she'd cursed God because of her son's disability.

"It wasn't as easy to find the blessing three years ago when I was diagnosed with breast cancer. I went through the treatments, was declared cancer free, and then a year ago it showed up in my liver."

Amy could've heard a pin drop in the stunned silence. She met Stephanie's gaze from across the circle and recognized the carefully concealed pain. Amy had seen it many times before and every day when she looked in her mirror. The battles might have been different, but war was war, and cancer was as ruthless an enemy as they come.

When Amy looked closer, though, she found something else swimming in the depths of Stephanie's crystal blue eyes. It wasn't dull like the pain. It kind of danced like . . . hope.

"When I got sick, most of the people I thought were my friends disappeared. I tried to stay positive for my kids, but I'd hit a pretty low place. Although sometimes I felt lonely, I didn't go through it alone. I had my family, and gradually I developed a new perspective. No, my life didn't turn out the way I planned it, but it was still my life and I could choose to waste it being angry, bitter, and cold or I could learn to forgive and make the best of it. When I looked at my son and daughter, who looked at me as an example, the answer was clear."

Amy shrank down in her chair and tried to become invisible.

"There's a passage in the Bible I often turn to when I'm tempted to be angry, and I want to share it with you." Her well-worn Bible fell open in her lap and she turned a few more pages. "Colossians 3:13 says, 'bearing with one another, and forgiving one another, if anyone has a complaint against another; even as Christ forgave you, so you also must do.' Heaven knows it's not easy, and it certainly doesn't happen overnight, but here's the thing I've found: Forgiveness is a gift. You'd think it's for the person who wronged you, but it's not. It's for you. When you finally reach a point of acceptance and complete forgiveness, your chains will be gone, and you'll be free."

Amy longed for freedom, for the true peace that Steph experienced despite all she'd been through, but Amy's eighteen-year-old grudge had grown and solidified with every additional hardship. Now it would be like wiping out the Empire State Building, nearly impossible and not worth the time or energy.

"Thank you for being so open and honest, Steph. You've given us all something to think about," Maggie said. "May I ask how your health is now?"

"I still get a mild chemo treatment every three weeks just for maintenance, but all of my tests indicate that I'm cancer free."

A cheer erupted from the circle, startling Amy and reminding her that, although she shared some similarities with Steph, there were differences too. For starters, she'd been programmed to never surrender, never admit defeat, and it'd take more than one remarkable testimony to change that.

It might just take a miracle.

Eight

The morning of July 4th, after chores were done, Amy stood at Angel's stall, rested her arms on the top slat, and contemplated Stephanie's words from almost two weeks earlier.

"When you finally reach a point of acceptance and complete forgiveness, your chains will be gone, and you'll be free."

"You understand, don't you, girl? It's just not that easy." Sighing heavily, she grabbed a handful of the sweet feed from the scoop beside her and stretched her arm out as far as it would go. Now, on day twenty of this ritual, her patience was growing thin. "But I'm not the one who hurt you, Angel. What else can I do to make you trust me?"

"I was wondering the very same thing."

Amy jumped, sending the sweet feed flying, along with her temper. "What the . . . !" She turned as Owen stepped up beside her, close enough that a hint of his cologne drifted to her and set all of her senses on high alert. She wasted no time in reinforcing the barrier around her heart.

"Okay. Is it just me or do you sneak up on everyone?"

"Nope. Just you." He gave her a wink that melted her anger like a summer ice cream cone and turned his gaze back to Angel. "Trust issues are hard. Sometimes there's nothing you can do but wait." He moved around to her other side, unlatched the gate and, keeping a close eye on Angel, slipped into the stall.

Obviously annoyed, Angel pinned her ears back and pawed at the ground.

Amy managed to keep her voice calm. "What are you doing?"

"And then sometimes you have to do something a little crazy to show her you really do care. . . " he glanced over his shoulder at Amy, " . . . that you would never think of hurting her. Ever."

Amy's blazing cheeks set a distress signal off in her brain. If her erratically beating heart was any indicator, the enemy had infiltrated the barrier. She had to find the weak spot and secure the breach.

Keeping a cautious eye on Angel, he gestured toward the gate. "Well? You aren't going to let me go through this alone, are you?"

Every nerve in her body twitched as she joined Owen inside the stall and closed the gate, leaving it unlocked, just in case. "Now what?"

"You still have to wait." The soft hay crinkled as he sat down with his back against the wooden planks and patted the ground next to him. After she got settled, he leaned toward her. "She'll come to you when she's ready."

"It's hard to be patient," she whispered.

"It'll be worth it."

A lull fell between them as they watched Angel fidget and sniff the air. Finally, Owen turned to her.

"I haven't seen Dominick around this weekend."

"He's with his dad. He actually spent the night with them last night."

"That day in the café you said you were here on business. Was that the business?"

Bouncing her gaze from Angel to Owen and back again, she considered her response. It might have been safe to reveal information about Dominick, but he'd never know the extent of her business. He couldn't.

"Part of it."

"So you've been here for three weeks—"

"Twenty-three days," she corrected. In some ways, it felt like a lifetime.

"How do you like it?"

"I'm glad that Dominick is getting to know his dad. I don't think I've ever seen him so happy, although I don't think his new stepmom is too crazy about the whole situation." She shrugged. "It's been an adjustment for everyone."

"Maggie told me you were at the last two single-parent support group meetings."

Her ears burned. "I thought there was a confidentiality rule."

Owen was quick to clarify. "She didn't tell me anything that was discussed, just that you were there. I think she was happily surprised."

If she wasn't sitting in a stall with a skittish horse, she would've bolted up and stormed out of the stable altogether. "I didn't go to make her happy. In fact, I didn't even go to make me happy. I hated every minute of it."

"Well, then, why did you go?"

"Because I had to, okay?" When he didn't respond, she noticed his eyes fixed on something just past her.

She followed his gaze and gasped. Angel cautiously stood just a few feet from her.

"Keep talking," Owen commanded, his voice low and steady. "As long as we ignore her, she won't feel threatened."

"Okay." She picked at a piece of hay, trying not to look at Angel and wracking her brain for something to say. "Did I ever tell you I had a horse?"

He shook his head, shifting in slow motion to a squat position, in case he needed to jump into action.

"She was a gift from my dad on my tenth birthday. Her name was Mercy. She was supposed to be the first of many that would start our therapeutic program for special needs kids, but I only had her until a few months before I turned thirteen."

"What happened?" He glanced at her with curiosity in his eyes, then returned his cautious gaze to Angel.

"My dad died, and without the extra help on the farm we had to downsize." She wrapped the piece of hay around her finger so tight the tip turned beet red. "Besides, riding her made me miss him even more." It surprised her how easily she admitted that.

"I'm sorry." Owen picked at a piece of hay. "So your dad was a farmer?"

"No. He was a paramedic, but on his off days he helped out on my grandparents' orange farm."

Owen nodded. "I understand that. Did he pass away while responding to a call?"

Amy considered the various definitions of *call*. "Not exactly." She quickly searched for a change of subject. "I guess that explains why I like it here. In a lot of ways it reminds me of that place in time."

"Do you like it here well enough to stay a while?"

Amy tore the piece of hay in half. "I don't have any other choice right now. I've got to deal with something here for at least the next three months. Plus, Dominick's dad wants legal parental rights, and our court date isn't until the middle of September. School will have started by then, I'm sure." She sighed in defeat. After ten years in the military, her life was once again not her own. "It's looking like we'll enroll Dominick here and stick around until Christmas vacation."

Owen twirled a piece of hay between his fingers. "Christmas, huh?"

Suddenly shy, she hugged her knees to her chest. "Unless something happens to change my mind." At that moment, something rustled her hair and she sucked in a sharp breath. She glanced at Owen as warm puffs caressed her scalp.

He smiled, his eyes wide in astonishment. "You don't, by chance, use a fruit-scented shampoo, do you?"

"Is she . . . ?"

Amy turned very slowly to find Angel's velvety muzzle mere inches from her face. Amy's heart brimmed with a joy she hadn't felt in years. Moving in slow motion, she lifted her hand. Angel sniffed it and licked at the residual dust from the sweet feed. Amy's eyes grew misty.

"Look at her. Isn't she beautiful?"

"More than she knows."

She shifted her gaze to find Owen watching her intently. Her heart, already lighter than a butterfly on the breeze, took a flying leap off of the wall she'd built around it. He'd risked his safety to help her reach this step with Angel. If she wasn't so afraid of spooking Angel—or of a crash 'n burn landing—she might have leapt into his arms.

"This is amazing, Owen. How can I ever thank you?"

At that moment, Angel nipped her finger.

Yelping, Amy yanked her hand back and held her throbbing finger close to her chest. The sudden noise and movement caused Angel to skitter to the protection of her corner.

"You thanked me too soon. Are you okay?" Owen reached over and took her hand in his to examine the injury.

Becoming heady from his gentle touch, she pulled out of his grasp. "Are you kidding? I'm more than okay. That was awesome."

He stood and held out a hand to help her up, which she ignored. "Well then, let's discuss payment, shall we?"

"Excuse me?"

After they crept out of the stall, Owen fastened the lock and turned to Amy. "You wanted to know how you could thank me."

She narrowed her eyes in suspicion and planted her hands on her hip. "Go on."

"A bunch of us are taking the four-wheelers down by the beach tonight for a little Fourth of July get-together." He shifted his weight from one foot to the other. "I'd really like for you to come with me."

"Why don't you take Maggie?"

He scratched his head and scrunched up his brow. "Why should I?"

"I saw you two together on Father's Day. I just figured . . ."

"That we're friends?"

The urge to scoff nearly overcame her. "Does she know that? I've seen the way she looks at you."

"Look, I just sat in a wild horse's stall for you. Now will you go to the party with me or not?"

Her resolve evaporated like dew on a late July morning, leaving behind only a drop of an argument. "I'm leaving in a little bit to pick up Dominick, and I don't have a sitter."

"My mom will watch all the kids here. She's already stocked up on sparklers and popsicles."

She had to admit it sounded fun, and she knew Dominick would want to join the kids even if she didn't go to the party. She faced Owen.

"All right. You win."

"Great!" He smiled, his blue-gray eyes twinkling. "Meet me here at seven."

Amy forced herself not to watch Owen walk out of the barn, but as she inhaled the trace of cologne he left behind, she knew she was fighting a losing battle. No matter what strategy she put in place at this point, there was a good chance that Owen would succeed in capturing her heart, and for the first time in her life losing didn't sound all that bad.

By a quarter after six that evening, Amy regretted agreeing to go to the party with Owen. After all, history did have a tendency to repeat itself, which guaranteed it would be a disaster.

She rummaged through the two large boxes of clothes her grandmother had shipped. However, since Amy had requested clothes for work, there wasn't much to choose from besides jeans and T-shirts. After transforming the bedroom into a ransacked Old Navy store, she found a pair of white Capris and a navy sleeveless scoop-neck sweater at the bottom of the second box.

"I guess this will have to do." She dressed and slipped into matching sandals. After spending extra time on her hair and makeup, she stood in front of the full length mirror, satisfied with what she saw, but her confidence ended there. Her hands slid to her flat stomach. There was so much she still hid. If Owen ever found out, he'd regret this date as much as she already did.

Anxiety clenched her heart so hard in its iron fist that she had to sit on the edge of the bed and catch her breath. She had her hand on the phone ready to call the whole thing off when Dominick came into the room.

His eyebrows arched, and he spelled out the word *wow* with his fingers, followed by the sign for *pretty.*

Amy smiled and signed, "Thank you."

Her fate was sealed. She wouldn't be a coward in front of her son. She took a deep breath and spoke slowly so he could read her lips.

"Are you ready to go to the farmhouse to hang out with Mrs. Sullivan and the kids for a while?"

He grinned and nodded.

She grabbed her keys and her cell phone, and they headed out the door. Across the lawn, several kids already played in sprinklers, laughing and squealing through Popsicle-stained lips. Dominick gave her a quick hug and ran off to join the fun while Amy headed to the back porch where Anna watched over them like a mother hen.

"Thanks for letting Dominick join you. I hope he's no trouble."

"He is such a good boy, no trouble at all. Go have a good time and don't worry one bit about us."

Amy hesitated, shifting her attention toward the stable. Owen had just pulled up on the four-wheeler, looking every bit the part of a handsome cowboy who'd just lassoed her heart. Too bad she didn't fit the part of a damsel in distress.

"Amy, you look like a million bucks. Go have fun," Anna urged.

Amy's insides tingled. She stepped off the porch and turned.

"Thanks again. I mean, for everything."

"My pleasure." She waved Amy off. "Now shoo."

Amy took a few steps backward. "I have my cell on me if you need anything."

Anna planted her fists on her hips.

Amy put her hands up. "All right. I'm going." With every step toward the stable, her heart raced faster, and she wondered if Owen felt even half as nervous.

When he finally noticed her approaching from halfway across the yard, he did a double take, not bothering to mask his approval of her appearance. She grinned and relaxed. She'd always held the position that it was degrading for a woman to use her looks to her advantage, but at that moment she relished the feeling of empowerment.

"Hey, sorry I'm late."

"You look great. Uh . . ." He shook his head. "I mean, you're not late."

"The time on my cell phone says I am." She pulled it out of her back pocket, looked at it, and replaced it, avoiding his captivating gaze. "By two minutes."

"That's not late. That's fashionable."

He winked at her and disappeared into the horse barn to turn off the light. By the time the door clicked shut and he turned, Amy was perched on the four-wheeler in the driver's position, a mischievous expression on her face.

"Do you know how to operate one of those?" Owen crossed his arms, amusement dancing in his eyes.

"Are you kidding? I've been riding them for years."

He walked over and climbed on behind her. "All right, then. Let's go."

"You're going to trust me just like that?" While it was true she'd driven an ATV, she wasn't prepared for the way his closeness would turn her brain to mush.

"Is there a reason I shouldn't?"

"No. No reason."

She inhaled deeply. *Focus*. Turning the key, she reviewed the steps in her head, and took off.

The breeze they created did little to cool this fever that spiked every time Owen leaned in to shout directions above the buzz of the motor. The perfect way his body fit behind hers gave her a high that no drug could induce, and she wondered how she could be driving the four-wheeler while floating on air. Just then, she hit a rut. They bounced hard, and Owen's arms flew to her waist like a seatbelt, holding her securely to him.

He leaned closer. "You okay?"

His breath on her neck sparked an electric current that ran down her spine, setting the core of her being on fire. "Never better."

A minute later, they emerged from the woods to the meadow by the lake, where a dozen or so people visited, chatting and laughing, around a blazing bonfire. Amy parked the four-wheeler with the others along the tree line. Owen hopped off and extended his hand to her.

She studied it for a moment, impressed by the strength and determination she found in the calluses. Knowing very

well she was headed for dangerous territory with such a dilapidated barrier around her heart, she slipped her hand into his
and they headed off to join the others.

As he introduced her to the two brothers she hadn't met,
all three of his sisters-in-law, and some family friends, she
appreciated how easily they accepted her. The lapping of gentle waves mixed with the crackle of the bonfire to create a
soundtrack similar to beach parties she had attended in
Florida and aided her comfort level.

Owen swiped two Cokes from a nearby Igloo, cracked one
open, and handed it to her. She sighed inwardly, unable to
remember the last time she had experienced a night so . . .
perfect.

"Hey, guys! Sorry we're late!"

The familiar voice severed her blissful thoughts and she
spun around.

"Amy?" Elijah stopped in his tracks.

In an instant, the cloud she'd been sitting on vanished,
and she crash landed into reality. "I don't believe it."

"Did I miss something?" Owen asked.

Amy shoved her fingers through her hair before stuffing
them in her back pocket. "Hi, Elijah."

Elizabeth crowded close to him, her violet eyes dark with
the pain of the circumstance.

"What are you doing here? And where is Dominick?"
Elijah asked.

The stares of the group bored a hole in the middle of
Amy's back, leaving her feeling exposed and vulnerable, but
it didn't hurt half as bad as the questioning expression on
Owen's handsome face. "You mean besides the fact that I live
here? I was invited. And Dominick is having a blast with

Anna and the other kids." She crossed her arms. "Now it's your turn."

Apparently past the initial shock of seeing her, his demeanor softened. "Elizabeth and Kate are sisters. Adam invited us."

She should've been prepared to run into them like this. Such is life in a small town, but this was the one place she'd assumed she was safe. It reinforced the fact that safe didn't happen in real life.

Owen pulled her aside. "I need you to help me understand what's going on here. Is Elijah . . . ?"

She nodded. Expecting the questions she found swimming in the depths of his eyes after all he'd done for her, she offered slightly more information. "It was one night eleven years ago. He didn't even know that he had a kid until I came to town."

The creases in his brow smoothed and he nodded. "Makes sense now. Look, we don't have to stay. Do you want to do something else?"

She took a deep breath and smiled. "No. It'll be okay. I just didn't plan on dealing with this tonight."

He reached for her hand again and led her to the opposite side of the bonfire. "Well, you can relax now. Everything's out in the open, and I'm not going anywhere."

As the deep fuchsia sky faded to dark violet, she almost forgot that Elizabeth and Elijah were just across the blazing pit. Gazing at Owen in the glow of the firelight, she almost forgot she was all wrong for him. Almost.

A near-sonic BOOM! shattered the serenity. Amy yelped and jumped as an explosion of color filled the sky.

"You okay?" Owen asked, his eyes clouding over with concern.

"Where did that come from?" Amy frantically searched for the explosion's source.

"Cedar Point is right across the water. Their fireworks show is the best in the area."

"Oh no," she groaned, then shrank at the sound of two loud POPs.

The large blue and red circles that bloomed in the sky blurred behind threatening tears. In an instant, Amy returned to Iraq and her constant nightmare—the stench, the filth, the brutality, the blood. All the blood. She stared down at her hands, sure she'd find her fingers wet and red. Another BOOM drove a shudder through her, and she instinctively backed away from the group.

"Amy, what's wrong?"

A rocket whistled into the air. Amy covered her ears. "I'm sorry. I have to go." She jumped as another rocket exploded. "Right now." She turned and raced for the four-wheeler. Three quick POPs made her jump, stumble, and fall.

Owen was there in a heartbeat. He scooped her up and carried her the last few feet to the four-wheeler. Climbing on in front of her, he turned the key and took off, kicking up clods of dirt and grass.

As he sped toward the safety of non-hostile territory, Amy held onto him with her left arm. She pressed her left ear tightly against his back and covered her other with her right hand.

The explosions and gunfire threatened her life but weren't as terrifying as the labored breathing of her dying friend. She could feel the weight of his head in her lap, feel his blood soak through her clothes, warm and wet against her skin. The metallic smell of the blood laced with the stench of that godforsaken place filled her brain and she had to swallow hard to keep from gagging. She touched the dog tag that hung to the middle of her chest as tears oozed down her cheeks like the Euphrates and repulsed her just as much as that nasty river.

In record time, Owen reached the horse barn and decelerated. Before he brought the four-wheeler to a stop, Amy jumped off and scrambled into the barn. Inside the dark haven, she practiced the deep breathing techniques Dr. Kimball had taught her. The soft nickering of the horses and earthy smell of the barn calmed her rattled nerves and soothed her soul, but when she glanced up to see Owen standing in the open doorway, moonlight surrounding him, she nearly fell to pieces again. Her only form of defense kicked into high gear.

She threw her arms out. "Why didn't you tell me there would be fireworks?"

He crossed his arms. "It's the Fourth of July." He approached her with a soft demeanor. "Do you mind telling me what just happened?"

Turning away, she shook her head. "I can't."

He reached out and touched her arm, but she shrugged it off. "Okay then. Let me guess."

"Go ahead and try."

"You were in the war, weren't you?"

Her breath caught in her throat.

"You saw things no one should have to see."

In slow motion, she turned to face him. *How . . . ?*

"Maybe someone even hurt you."

Her pulse pounded hard against her skin. "You have no idea what I've been through."

"You're right. I don't, but I know what the aftereffects of war look like." Owen went over to Bella's stall and stroked her bulging side as he continued. "This guy and I came onboard with the fire department at the same time. We got real close. I thought of him as a little brother." His voice wavered. "Just a few months later, September 11th happened. He felt it was his duty to go fight." Sighing heavily, Owen rested his head against the slats of the stall. "He asked me to go with him, but I didn't." He met her gaze. "I guess you could say I was a big, fat chicken."

Her cheeks burned as she remembered their spat from a few weeks earlier right after they'd had so much fun playing basketball with Dominick.

"He served a tour in Iraq, and when he came home he was . . . different. Edgy, jumpy, paranoid . . . "

She nodded. "That's Post Traumatic Stress Disorder."

"He asked Maggie to marry him before he deployed again. His enlistment was almost up, but he never made it home."

Legs trembling, Amy sat down on a nearby hay bale, her expression like stone. "My closest friend died in my lap. I was a medic and I couldn't save him. I couldn't do anything to help him."

Owen leaned against the stall. "I don't know how many times the thought crossed my mind that, if I would've enlisted with him, I would've been able to do something, anything, and Justin McGregor would still be with us today."

All the air in Amy's lungs escaped, leaving her to gasp for breath. "What did you say?"

"I know that it sounds ridiculous. I just wish I could've been there for him." Owen shook his head. "He never even knew about his son."

Amy's chest rose and fell, but no air reached her lungs. Tiny black spots floated through her vision. She had to get out of there before she suffocated.

She dashed to the stable door, turned to meet his gaze. "I'm sorry," she choked. "For everything."

With that, she half sprinted, half stumbled, toward the farmhouse. She grabbed Dominick, a sparkler still in his hand, and dragged him back to their apartment. He only fought her for a moment before she made it perfectly clear he wouldn't win this struggle.

"Get ready for bed. I'll be there in a minute."

After he stomped off, she stepped into the kitchen. Leaving the lights off, she peeked through the blinds at the stable. Her heart a cold, heavy stone in her chest, she watched Owen climb onto the four wheeler and drive away.

Her head began to pound. She pressed her trembling fingers to her temple and cursed aloud, wishing for a strong drink, anything to numb this pain.

"I was there and I couldn't do a damn thing. Owen wouldn't understand that. He'd never forgive me." She snorted and sagged against the window casing. "I can't forgive myself. Why would he?"

When you finally reach a point of acceptance and complete forgiveness, your chains will be gone, and you will be free.

"It won't work this time. Acceptance? Maggie would hate me and it'd drive her right into Owen's arms." She shook her throbbing head and backed away from the window. "They can never find out the truth. Never."

lizabeth woke up with a troubled spirit on, of all days, the very one she'd been holding her breath waiting for. She blamed Amy.

"She just had to be at the party last night looking so . . . beautiful and . . . happy," Elizabeth grumbled, kicking off her covers and plodding to the bathroom. "What does Owen see in her anyway? I mean the girl is a walking tornado. As if turning my life upside down isn't bad enough, the scene she caused when she stormed out of there last night was embarrassing." Elizabeth undressed and got in the shower. "She has obvious attention issues."

Elizabeth hung onto that excuse all morning, not willing to admit even as she sat alone on an overstuffed floral print sofa in the waiting room at the specialist's office that part of her unrest could be due to this appointment. Her emotions were like a giant pendulum. While hope bloomed in her heart, guilt wrung her stomach.

She'd never in her life broken a promise. But as the days went by, the fear of Elijah's response and her ever-increasing desperation overpowered her honorable nature. Elijah would never understand her need to have her own baby now that he had a son. She was sure of it. So what other choice did she have?

Still, she was embarking on an incredible journey, and she didn't want to travel this road alone. She wished Elijah was sitting there, holding her hand and dreaming with her about what their baby would look like or trying out different name combinations.

Elizabeth hugged her purse to her abdomen and dropped her gaze to a photo album on the glass and iron coffee table in front of her. Curious, she set her purse aside, put the album in her lap and opened it. Page after page was filled with pictures of babies born with this specialist's help. Her eyes brimmed with liquid joy as she looked at a photo of a mother cradling a newborn swaddled in a pink blanket, and she smiled. "Macy Elizabeth." On the next page a daddy showed his ruddy-cheeked bundle in blue to the camera and a tear escaped. "Anthony Elijah."

These babies were living proof that miracles truly did occur. They might've been conceived with medical help, but they were miracles just the same. Maybe even more so.

A nurse stepped into the waiting room. "Elizabeth?"

Elizabeth took a deep breath. *This is it.* She returned the album to the table, rose on shaky knees, and followed the pink-scrub-clad nurse to an examination room.

Pink. I wonder if that's a sign. She almost giggled at the thought.

The nurse asked her some questions regarding her medical history and made notes on her chart. Then she moved to the door and slipped the file folder in its designated slot.

"Dr. Monroe will be in to see you shortly," she said and stepped out, leaving Elizabeth with her rattled nerves and hopeful heart.

In the stillness of the pale green examination room, it felt right to bow her head, but her cluttered mind couldn't form a prayer. Prayer had always come as naturally to her as breathing, but now, when she needed it most, she struggled to get past, "Dear God . . . " Next to tears and feeling very alone, she wondered if this was the sign. Just as she clutched her purse, ready to up and leave, a voice whispered in her soul.

"My grace is sufficient for you, for My strength is made perfect in weakness."

She froze, listening for it again. When it came louder and clearer than before, Elizabeth exhaled.

"Thank You, God, that Your grace is sufficient for me, that Your strength is made perfect in my weakness."

A soft knock on the door grabbed her attention, and her nerves shifted into high gear as Dr. Alison Monroe came into the room.

"Mrs. Truman? I'm Dr. Monroe. It's nice to meet you."

Elizabeth shook her hand. "You, too."

"Let's just talk for a few minutes. I understand that you're on pins and needles. I've been in your shoes, so I want to go over what we'll cover at this appointment and lay out a plan that you'll be comfortable with. Is Mr. Truman here with you today?"

Elizabeth hung her head. "No. He's not the problem. He already has a son."

Compassion flooded Dr. Monroe's eyes. "It's very possible that you aren't the sole problem either."

Elizabeth's forehead creased. "I'm confused. It has to be one of us, doesn't it?"

Dr. Monroe sat on a stool. "How old is his son?"

"Ten years old."

"A lot can happen to a person's ability to conceive in ten years. It could also be the combination of both of you, but I'll need to see him to determine that."

Elizabeth didn't know whether to laugh or cry.

"In the meantime, let's get some tests started on you. I see you've tracked your cycle for three months. That's good. Today I'm going to ask you several questions regarding your family history, and we'll run blood work to test thyroid hormones along with estrogen and progesterone levels. But first, do you have any questions or concerns?"

Elizabeth took a deep breath. "Not at the moment."

"All right. Let's get started then." She opened Elizabeth's chart to make notes. "Is there a history of infertility on your mother's side?"

Forty-five minutes, many questions, and a couple vials of blood later, Dr. Monroe flipped through the paperwork in the file folder as she wrapped up the appointment. "The charts of your cycle show no indication that you ovulated two of the three months and the last one is iffy. We'll get your blood work back in a day or two, and if there's nothing that concerns me, I'll call in a prescription for Clomid. You'll start it on day five of your cycle, take it for five days, and begin trying after that. Keep tracking your temperature for an idea of when you're ovulating. If the Clomid doesn't work, it will be imperative that your husband come in for testing."

Elizabeth was afraid to ask but she had to know. "D-do you think it will work, Dr. Monroe?"

The doctor placed a reassuring hand on her shoulder. "Elizabeth, you are young. The odds are in your favor, but we'll know a lot more when your test results come back." Dr. Monroe moved to the door. "We'll be in touch then."

"Thank you."

Dr. Monroe nodded and slipped out, allowing Elizabeth time to gather her things and her thoughts.

She made her way out of the room and down the hall, a smile working its way to her face as she did some quick figuring. If her blood work came back okay, she'd start the medicine later that week, and there was a chance, albeit slim, that she could be pregnant in two weeks! She stifled a squeal as she threw open the office door and practically skipped into hallway . . . just as Nathan came around the corner. She turned to duck back into the cover of Dr. Monroe's office but it was too late.

"Elizabeth?"

The color drained from her face. Her palms dampened and she swiped them on her shorts.

"Nathan!" She forced a smile. "What a surprise running into you like this!" She looked up, but couldn't meet his gaze.

"I'm on my way to a consultation with one of my patient's cardiologist. What are you . . ." He glanced at the name on the door and brightened. "You saw Dr. Monroe? How did it go?"

She fidgeted. "Good."

He narrowed his eyes. "Where's Elijah?"

She didn't respond. She couldn't.

"Elizabeth, please tell me you talked to him."

Tears of shame stung her eyes. "I can't because I didn't."

"You promised."

"I'm sorry."

"I'm not the one you should be apologizing to."

"I had every intention of talking with him, but something always came up." She cast her gaze to the floor. "Besides, if he didn't want to try fertility treatments before, he certainly wouldn't now that he has Dominick."

"And how do you know that?"

She gave a little shrug. "Because I know my husband. You mean you've never predicted what Denise thought or how she felt?"

"This isn't about Denise and me, but just for the sake of argument, even though I may know her opinion on certain topics, I respect my wife enough to talk to her about something that could potentially affect our family."

Hot tears slid down Elizabeth's cheeks. "I've got to go." She attempted to side step around him but he blocked her.

"You're making a big mistake, Elizabeth. He deserves to know how you feel."

She pushed past him and hurried down the hallway, but Nathan's words stayed with her long after she returned home.

"Everything okay?" Elijah asked that evening when they sat down to dinner. "You've been awfully quiet."

He might deserve to know how I feel, but I deserve to have a baby.

She wondered if she should run the risk of his rejecting the idea of treatments now that she'd had her initial appointment. If she didn't get pregnant this month, she'd have no other choice. Maybe if she approached it from a different angle . . .

"I've just been thinking about how great it'd be if Dominick had a little brother or sister to play with when he comes to visit." She reached across the table for his hand. "With just a little help we could possibly give him one by spring."

Elijah shoved a forkful of pot roast into his mouth and chewed. "Help?"

"Yeah, you know, nothing major. Just maybe a prescription or a minor procedure."

He stared at her, chewing in silence. Finally, he swallowed.

"Dominick's used to being an only child and he seems to be adjusting pretty well. Why take a chance at complicating things?"

Elizabeth nearly choked on her water. "Complicating things? Tell me, how could things get any more complicated than they are right now?"

"You don't think a baby is an adjustment?"

"You don't think a ten-year-old deaf boy is an adjustment?"

"Look, I'm not saying no. Let's just give it a few months."

"A few months?! I've already waited two years!"

He put his fork down and pushed his plate away. "I see what's going on. This isn't about Dominick at all. It's about you. It's always been about you."

Tears blurred her vision as his words pierced her heart. "How can you say that? I thought this was about us. I thought you wanted a baby too." She stood with such force that her chair clattered backwards, almost tipping over. "Oh. Right. *You* have a kid now so why bother?"

He slammed his hand on the table so hard it made her jump. "That's not fair, and you know it."

The dam she been trying to maintain burst and tears poured down her cheeks. "No. What's not fair is you have never wanted a baby like I do. Yet *you* are the one with the kid. But even that doesn't hurt as bad as the fact that you don't even acknowledge how important it is to me."

"That's ridiculous! How could I not acknowledge it? It's consumed our lives. Do you know what I want? I really want to go through just one day without being reminded that I'm not enough for you anymore." He shook his head. "Nothing I can say or do will make you happy, Elizabeth. You won't be completely happy unless we have a baby."

Elizabeth covered her face with her hands and sobbed.

He stood, his demeanor softening. "Look, I'm sorry. I don't want to fight with you about this anymore. You know that nothing would make me happier than for us to have a baby, but I also want to know that we'll be okay regardless of what happens."

The tears slowed and she sniffled. "Of course we'll be okay. How could you think such a thing?"

He stared at her for a long moment. "I believe I've already answered that."

They stood together in silence, close enough to touch, yet miles apart. Then, shaking his head, he stalked out to the garage.

Elizabeth lowered herself to the chair feeling nothing short of completely miserable. The guilt she harbored for being dishonest paled next to the shame she felt for her selfishness.

At that moment, the sound of the doorbell resonated through the house, startling her. She was in no state of mind to entertain visitors, but she realized that in a small town like Harvest Bay not answering the door when both vehicles were sitting in the driveway could raise a few eyebrows. The doorbell sounded again as she wiped her eyes with a napkin. Hoping her makeup wasn't smeared all over her face, she went to the door, pasted her best smile over her true emotions, and swung it open. She almost cried with relief when her gaze landed on Uncle Bill holding a brown paper sack.

"Uncle Bill! I'm so sorry it took me a second to get to the door. I . . . " She stopped. She couldn't tell him the truth, but she was done lying. She shrugged. "Well, I'm sorry."

"Oh, no problem, kiddo. I won't keep you." He held out the bag. "I just wanted to bring you some tomatoes and onions from my garden."

"Thanks." The paper sack crinkled as she accepted it, and she relaxed in his unassuming presence. "Have you had supper yet?"

He nodded. "Wilma made a roast."

Elizabeth chuckled. "That's what we had." *Though we didn't eat much of it.*

She glanced up into Bill's thin face. His eyes were bright behind his glasses, and she prayed he didn't sense the storm of emotions battering her soul the way Grandpa Clayton could. Gramps had the ability to forecast depressions, cold fronts, and every other kind of disturbance with pinpoint accuracy, but he could also ease those spiritual storms with gentle words of truth and wisdom.

"Well how about dessert then?" She held up the bag. "Think of it as a trade."

He gave a nod and stepped into the foyer. "That sounds fair."

They walked into the dining room. Bill took a seat at the table, while Elizabeth moved into the open kitchen, set the bag on the counter, and pulled a serving bowl out of the fridge.

"What are we having?"

"Homemade banana pudding." She dished up two bowls and carried them to the table.

Bill dove right in. "Mmmm. Delicious. How'd you know that this is my favorite dessert?"

"I didn't. I just had some ripe bananas that I needed to use up. I'm glad you like it."

He took another bite and closed his eyes as he savored it. After he swallowed, he pointed his spoon at her.

"You know, your grandma had a knack for banana pudding. She made some of the best I've ever had."

Elizabeth nodded. "This is her recipe." She fell silent, taking a few bites of pudding in between making designs in it with her spoon.

He tipped his head to the side studying her. "Does Elijah know what he's missing out on?"

She snorted. "Yeah. He made it perfectly clear." She caught her sarcasm and her tone softened. "I'm sorry. He's in the garage putting a basketball hoop together for Dominick."

Catching a glimpse of her practically untouched dinner plate, he put his spoon down and folded his hands on the table. "I don't mean to pry, but is everything okay?"

"I don't know, Uncle Bill." She shook her head and pushed her bowl away. "I've wanted something for a long time now. It's always been my heart's greatest desire, but recently it's consumed my whole life. I've really hurt Elijah, and I feel just rotten about it, but . . . " she blinked back threatening tears, " . . . I still don't want to give it up."

"Has Elijah asked you to?"

"Well, no. Not in so many words."

"Has the Lord asked you to?"

She shrugged, her bottom lip quivering. "I don't know."

"The Bible says in Philippians, 'For I have learned in whatever state I am, to be content.'" He reached across the table and patted her hand. "That doesn't mean give up on your dream, Elizabeth. Just be happy with what you already have while you're waiting."

She smiled as a tear slipped out of the corner of her eye. "Thanks, Uncle Bill."

He scraped the last bite of pudding out of his bowl. "No. Thank *you*. This was a nice surprise." He stood and carried his bowl to the sink. "But I'd better be getting home before Wilma starts to worry."

Elizabeth walked him to the door and gave him a warm embrace. "Stop by again soon, with or without veggies."

"Will do. Tell Elijah hello for me," he called over his shoulder as he descended the front porch steps and started down the sidewalk.

Elizabeth watched his car back out of her driveway onto the quiet country road and she waved as he beeped the horn twice before heading off out of sight. Then she closed and locked the door, tidied up the kitchen, and headed upstairs to relax in a warm bubble bath.

While the tub filled with jasmine scented water, she grabbed her Bible from her bedside table, sat on the edge of the bed and flipped right to the passage in Philippians. She knew the verse by heart, but tonight she needed to see it in black and white.

" . . . in whatever state I am . . . "

Her heart sank as she lifted her tearful eyes to the ceiling. "But how, God? How can I be content? This state I'm in hurts. Nothing about it is fair." She returned her gaze to her Bible as a tear rolled down her cheek and plopped onto the page. "I've served You as faithfully as I know how, and I always will, but I can't be content loving another woman's son. I just don't have it in me."

Overwhelmed with hopelessness, she snapped her Bible shut, went to turn off the water, then fell back on the bed. Closing her eyes, she lay perfectly still, praying the vicious emotion that'd been eating her alive would think she was dead and leave her once and for all.

In that quiet moment, a voice whispered in her soul. *"Therefore I take pleasure in infirmities, in reproaches, in needs, in persecutions, in distresses, for Christ's sake. For when I am weak, then I am strong."*

The words wrapped around her heart and squeezed. New understanding filled her and with it came the pain of dying to herself.

"But not my will but Yours be done." Then she rolled over to her side and wept hard.

CHAPTER
Ten

"So after I freaked out like some kind of raving lunatic, Owen drove me back to the stables where he told me about a friend of his who served in Iraq." Unable to sit still with three days worth of bottled-up tension, Amy walked the floor of Dr. Kimball's office.

"Did you tell him about your experience?"

She shook her head. "His friend was Justin. You know, the guy who died in my lap." She stopped and ran a hand through her hair. "*His* friend . . . Maggie's fiancé . . . died in *my* lap. There's no way I could tell him that."

"Why not?"

Amy plodded to the couch and sat down, chewing on a thumbnail. "It's the reason they're so close . . . and why they'd hate me."

"Aren't you exaggerating a little? They may be surprised, but what reason would they have to hate you?"

"I couldn't save him, all right?"

"But it wasn't your fault either."

Amy remained silent staring at the trace of blood behind her nail and wondering if she had the guts to finally face the ugly truth.

"So what did you do?"

She snorted. "What I do best, of course. I ran." She got up and strode to Dr. Kimball's bookshelf, faking a sudden interest in the dozens of psychology books on display. "I knew I shouldn't have gone to the party in the first place. I just knew it would be a disaster, and I was right. First, Dominick's father and step-mom show up at the party, and I had to explain that whole humiliating situation to Owen. Then I have a full blown panic attack at the sound of some dumb firecrackers. Finally, he poured his heart out to me and like a jerk I left him sitting there. I went back to my apartment and watched him leave from my kitchen window, wishing that I could either live a normal life or somehow get a grip on this one."

"Wait a minute. It's only been four weeks. I told you it'd take twelve weeks at the very earliest, but most likely closer to sixteen. Maybe even a little longer than that." Dr. Kimball closed the gap between them and put a hand on Amy's shoulder. "You might be taking baby steps, but you're moving. The fact that you went to a party is progress. Focus on that, okay?"

Amy nodded just to satisfy her psychiatrist, knowing very well that concentrating on one positive point in the midst of so much negative would be like trying to see the glow from a candle at the end of a long, dark tunnel. Nearly impossible.

Dr. Kimball gave her an encouraging smile and crossed the room to where a coffee pot had finished spitting and sputtering. "Would you like a cup?"

Amy shook her head. She needed something stronger than coffee. It'd been months since she had a drink, but at that moment her nerves screamed for a Bloody Mary. Feeling a little woozy, she staggered to the sofa and sank down into it.

Dr. Kimball poured the steaming black liquid into a mug. "Owen sounds like a pretty special friend."

Amy shrugged but couldn't stop her lips from curling upwards at the thought of him.

Dr. Kimball's eyes sparkled as she stirred in some cream. "That's what I thought." She carried her cup to her chair, sat down, and took a cautious sip. "You're opening your heart to someone. That's a very good sign."

"Well, I mean, he sat in a horse's stall for me."

Dr. Kimball knit her brow together in confusion.

"There's a rescue horse on the farm that I've been working with, but I wasn't making any progress with her until Owen convinced me to sit in her stall with him. Now she's eating out of my hand."

"Animals have proven to be very helpful in recovery from PTSD. That's another step in the right direction." She took a swallow of coffee, her long slender fingers encircling the blue ceramic mug. "But tell me more about Owen."

"There's nothing to tell, really. He's taken an interest in Dominick. They spend time playing ball together and with the farm dog, Harley." She shrugged again. "As crazy as it sounds, it seems like he knew me before we even met."

"But there's nothing to tell?"

"No. I'm sure of it. Not after the Fourth of July disaster." She did her best to mask the disappointment in her voice.

"Don't be so quick to draw conclusions based on your own assumptions."

Amy put her hands out. "Okay. If he could see past the scene I made and the way I deserted him after he opened up to me, I know that he'd never want to see me again when he found out about Justin." Her shoulders fell with her gaze, which rested on her abdomen. "And that's just the tip of the iceberg. I'm not what he needs. Plain and simple."

Dr. Kimball put a hand up. "Hold on. One issue at a time. Why do you think Owen would hold Justin's death against you?"

The knot in her stomach pulled so tight she doubled over. "Do I have to spell it out for you? It. Was. Because. Of. Me."

"What do you mean?"

Tasting bile in the back of her throat, Amy took a couple of deep breaths in through her nose and released them through her mouth. She eyed Dr. Olivia Kimball, so beautiful with her dark curls pinned up on her head and her piercing blue eyes examining her. There was no way she'd understand. Maybe she'd even judge her.

"I'm sorry. I can't."

Dr. Kimball leaned forward. "Amy, you're very close to a breakthrough. Please try."

Amy's hands grew clammy, and she rubbed them vigorously on her jeans. Her heart raced as if to escape the memories about to ambush her. She ached to move about the office again but didn't think her knees would hold her. She inhaled and held it. A moment later, as she exhaled, the words came tumbling out.

"My platoon was just outside a village that intel said was overrun with Taliban. We took on heavy fire. I went out to check on my guys—assess their wounds, provide temporary treatment if I could, call for a medical evacuation if needed—that kind of thing. Justin came with me for extra cover. As we reached the first casualty, I saw something fly at us." She glanced up at the ceiling and began to shake.

"Stay here with me, Amy." Dr. Kimball reached out and touched her knee, but it was too late. She'd already been transported back in time.

"I saw a kid standing on a rooftop nearby so I thought it was just a rock. I remember thinking that his mother needed to turn that boy over her knee, but before I could finish the thought, the object rose up and started spinning. Justin yelled, 'Grenade!' and gave me a really hard push. I went flying. He turned to run when the grenade went off." She rocked back and forth holding her stomach.

Dr. Kimball shook her arm. "Come back to me."

"His body jolted like he'd been struck by lightning or something. He looked right at me and I saw it in his eyes. He knew he wasn't going to make it home." She choked on a sob rising in her throat. "I got to him the second he fell, but there was already so much blood. There was just so much blood."

She placed a hand on her tightening chest as she recalled the gurgling in each of his labored breaths. "He didn't suffer long. He only had enough time to hand me these." Tears streamed down her face as she pulled his dogtag out of her shirt.

She turned to Dr. Kimball. "His last words were, 'Harvest Bay'. I thought it was because I'd told him Dominick's father was there, but now I know that he was thinking of his home. He was thinking of Maggie and Owen." She squeezed the oval piece of metal and met Dr. Kimball's gaze. "So you see? If it weren't for me, he'd be here with them. If it weren't for me, his son would have a father."

She crumpled. Her head dropped to her knees, her body wracked hard with months of dammed up sobs. "It was my fault. It was all my fault."

Dr. Kimball scooted over to the sofa and rubbed Amy's back. Her voice cracked when she finally spoke. "I think we're done for the day."

Amy slid behind the steering wheel of her old Taurus and rested her forehead against it. An hour of purging toxic emotions and memories had left her so drained she had to find the strength to breathe.

"And Dr. Kimball called it a breakthrough," she muttered, then snorted. "More like a breakdown." She shook her head. "How could I just fall apart like that and spill my guts about Justin?"

Speaking his name ignited a fiery determination. Setting her jaw, she jammed the keys in the ignition and turned. "It doesn't matter. It won't happen again."

She put the car in gear and peeled out of the parking lot. As she sped down the country highway that would lead her into the heart of Harvest Bay, voices and images took over her mind.

It should've been me.

Justin's blank, lifeless stare filled her windshield. She glanced at her sweaty palms to make sure there was no blood. Just as her heart was about to hammer out of her chest, the picture morphed to Owen's handsome face, regret and sadness reflecting in his eyes. She lifted her hand from the steering wheel to touch the image before his voice echoed in her brain.

"If I would've enlisted with him, I would've been able to do something, anything, and Justin McGregor would still be with us today."

"I'm sorry, Owen," she whispered as a fresh wave of tears streamed down her face. "It's all my fault and I'm so sorry."

As the tears dried and her eyes cleared, she spotted a plastic bag up ahead on the side of the road. A bubble of panic started at her toes. She eased her foot off the gas, wondering if it had been a mistake to disregard Dr. Kimball's suggestion to call a cab.

"It's just trash. No big deal."

She tried the deep breathing technique Dr. Kimball had taught her, but her chest was so tight she couldn't fill her lungs.

"Keep driving. It's just trash. Everything's fine."

Sweat beading her brow, she pressed the accelerator in an attempt to outrun the deafening blasts . . . the screams . . . the looks of terror . . . the putrid smell of gun powder.

As she drove up on her biggest fear, the sharp trill of her cell phone split the silence. She jumped, jerked the steering wheel, and lost control. She heard tires squealing, glass shattering, then screams rent the air and a huge blow slammed against her face.

In the stillness that followed, she envisioned Dominick with his sweet ten-year-old boy smile. She reached for him, desperate to protect him. He signed the word *father* and she dropped her hand.

"He'll be okay," she breathed.

And everything faded to black.

CHAPTER
Eleven

*E*lizabeth glanced at her watch, then scanned the lobby of Harvest Bay Community Church. Still no sign of Elijah, and the Wednesday evening service would be starting in fifteen minutes. She checked her cell phone, but there were no missed calls or text messages. She sighed, tossing the phone into her purse, and turned to Dominick.

"He'll be here," she signed, forcing a smile while battling serious disappointment. Swallowing her pride, she'd taken a huge step in Elijah's direction. She'd called Amy that morning and asked her to allow Dominick to spend the night. She'd planned several activities in an honest attempt to bond with her stepson. After a brief interrogation Amy agreed, but Elijah didn't seem to acknowledge any of it.

Okay, God. I'm trying really hard to be content in this state, but my efforts seem kind of lopsided. Please, show me where to go from here.

At that moment the muffled ring tone of her cell phone filtered from her purse. She fished it out and checked the caller ID. Her heart fell when she saw it wasn't Elijah but instantly gathered speed when she recognized the number. Hands trembling, she accepted the call and put the phone to her ear.

"Hello?"

"This is Dr. Monroe. Is this a good time to discuss the results of your blood work?"

Elizabeth moved to a less populated corner of the lobby where she could still keep an eye on Dominick who was pre-occupied with his Nintendo DS. "Yes. Is everything okay?"

"Nothing turned up overly abnormal. Your progesterone levels were a little low so I'm calling in a prescription for oral progesterone to be taken with the Clomid. It's one pill once a day. Continue taking it after you've finished the cycle of Clomid and you begin trying to conceive. Do you have any questions?"

Elizabeth had dozens of questions, but the cork had popped off her bottle of hope and effervescence filled her brain. "Not right now."

"Okay, then. Your file says you use Judy's Medicine Shoppe in Harvest Bay?"

"That's right."

"Excellent. I'm calling these prescriptions in now, and they'll be ready for you later this evening."

"Great. Thank you."

She hung up just as the prelude music began. Tears filled Elizabeth's eyes as she recognized the beautiful melody of "How Great Thou Art".

Everything's going to be okay now. I just know it.

Just before she silenced her phone and put it away, it chimed, indicating she had received a text. With her spirits floating near the peaked beams of the ceiling, she had to concentrate to flip it open and read the message.

Won't b @ church 2nite. Needed @ hospital. Take Dominick home w/ u. I'll c-ya there.

The happy little bubbles in her brain burst as she reread, *Needed @ hospital*. Elijah was a physical therapist and she highly doubted any patient in the small town hospital needed therapy at seven p.m.

What goes around comes around. Remember, you lied first. She shoved the voice of reason to the back of her mind. Nothing could get her down now.

As Elizabeth took her place at the front, satisfaction filled her. She'd serve her faithful Lord by interpreting this service, and then she'd find out what Elijah was hiding . . . right after making a stop at the pharmacy.

Amy stood on shaky legs at the small sink in room number thirteen, filling a Styrofoam cup with water. Taking a mouth-ful, she swished it around and spit, hoping the metallic taste went down the drain with it.

Catching her reflection in the mirror above the sink, she recalled the last time she looked and felt like this. She'd been able to repress the memory of that night a few months ago until now, when her bruised and swollen face stared back at her with the same hollow expression. Merely a shell of a being, she was lost and alone, her heartbeat dull inside her chest, lacking any luster for life.

But this shell contained an unexpected and unwanted pearl.

She touched her stomach as tears slid down her cheeks, adding to the anger that burned inside her. She'd had her pride and dignity stripped from her that night, her strength and confidence beaten out of her. Every ounce of goodness and innocence she'd managed to salvage from life's circumstances had been stolen from her. In return, she was left with a baby as a constant reminder.

She shook her head, wincing at the pain the sudden movement caused. "It's my body and my life. I don't have to accept a destiny I didn't choose."

Moving at a snail's pace, she returned to the bed, the stark white sheets crumpling under her weight of her aching body. "It would have been better if this baby didn't survive the accident." She paused, unwilling to voice her next thought. *Maybe it would have been better if I hadn't survived.*

Shame struck her so hard that tears blurred her vision, and she had to rub her eyes to make out the figure that appeared in the doorway. Her stomach sank to the white tile floor as Elijah came into view.

"What are you doing here?"

"Owen called me."

Her heart lurched. "What?"

"He said he'd been meaning to call you since the party and finally got the nerve today."

"It was him?" Amy groaned.

Elijah nodded. "The phone must've picked up the call on impact. He heard the whole thing, and a few minutes later the accident report came over the scanner at the fire department. The description of the car matched yours, and they reported a female with minor injuries being transported to the hospital, but there was no mention of a boy. He was frantic, Amy. He wanted to get to you so bad and to make sure Dominick was safe, but there was no one to cover his shift, and he knew I could get here quicker."

Amy's heart swelled . . . and burst when she remembered how wrong she was for him.

Elijah moved farther into the room. "So what happened?"

Amy blew out an exasperated breath. "I had an episode at my doctor's appointment . . . "

"An episode?"

"A flashback. I thought I'd worked through it and I was safe to leave, but halfway out of town I saw a bag of trash on the side of the road and panicked. I swerved to miss it, then overcorrected, and wrapped the car around a utility pole."

"A bag of trash?" His eyebrows arched with skepticism. "Really?"

Her cheeks burned as she closed her eyes and counted to ten. Steam must've been rolling out of her ears. She'd come to despise the fact that most people had no idea of the dangers soldiers faced on a daily basis while fighting for the liberty and security Americans enjoyed.

"Are you questioning me? In Iraq, the bad guys like to plant improvised explosive devices in potholes or junk alongside the road. I saw a guy lose an arm and an eye to a loaded baby doll. You learn to avoid the stuff if you want to live."

"Oh." Elijah examined her, concern creasing his face. "Well, are you okay?"

"I'm fine." She managed a weak smile. "The airbag did a number on my face, but it saved my brain."

"And what if Dominick had been with you?"

Her shoulders fell. Somehow she knew this would be an issue.

"It was an accident, Elijah. It could've happened to anyone."

Elijah's voice was gentle but stern. "Not everyone would swerve to miss a bag of trash."

"Look, when I was a soldier, my duty was to take care of my guys, but I'm home now, and Dominick is my first priority. Yes, I have some things to work through, but I'd never let anything happen to him. You have to believe me."

Elijah ran his fingers through his dark hair. "Okay, but try to see my point of view now. I missed out on ten years of his life. Ten years. I can't miss out on any more. I'm just getting to know him."

She hung her head. "I know. I'm sorry."

The sounds of the busy ER filled the space between them. When Amy finally spoke, remorse filled her voice.

"So then, you wouldn't mind keeping him for a few days? I don't want him seeing me like this. Just tell him I'm not feeling well."

Elijah's demeanor softened. "I don't think that'll be a problem."

"Good." She cocked her head toward the door. "Now that you've checked on me and you see I'm okay, go be with your wife and kid. I'll take a cab home. I need some time alone to figure out what to tell the Sullivans."

"How about the truth?"

She carefully shifted, trying to lose the storm cloud hanging above her. "I can't risk losing my job."

"In case you haven't noticed, they're good people. They wouldn't let you go because you were in an accident."

"There's more to consider than just the accident."

He straightened. "Like what?"

At that moment, a young nurse breezed into the partitioned room, the squeak of her tennis shoes on the floor announcing her arrival. She glanced at Elijah, and then turned to Amy.

"Do you mind if your discharge orders are discussed in front of your visitor?"

Amy leaned back heavily against the pillows. "I don't care. I just want to get out of here."

"All right, then. Here's your paperwork, and you're free to go. I just want to go over a few things. If you experience dizziness, vomiting, confusion, severe headache, cramping in the lower back or vaginal bleeding within the next forty-eight to seventy-two hours, come back immediately. Rest is the most important thing you can do for your body right now. Use heat for muscle pain and ice for bruising, but you can only have Tylenol for discomfort. Any other pain reliever may put your baby at risk."

At Elijah's gasp, Amy's eyes flew open. The nurse paused, looking back and forth between them.

Amy squeezed her eyes shut in dread. "Please continue."

The nurse hesitated before moving on. "If Tylenol doesn't take care of the pain, come back in. Also, be sure to make an appointment with your obstetrician as soon as possible. The ultrasound showed no signs of trauma to the baby, but you can never be too careful when you're pregnant."

Amy held her breath until the nurse left. She glanced at Elijah and exhaled slowly. His shocked expression blurred behind her unshed tears.

"You're pregnant?"

She sensed his judgment, could almost hear him thinking, *Another child out of wedlock?* She didn't need a reformed playboy reminding her that she was damaged goods to be discarded at the first opportunity. Tears slid down her cheeks.

"It wasn't my fault."

He ran his hand down his chin and shook his head. "Well then whose fault was it, Amy? It typically takes two, as we both know."

At that moment she wished with every fiber of her being that Dominick hadn't cared about knowing his father, that she alone could've been enough for him. But she wasn't and if she didn't recover from all her physical and emotional wounds, she knew she'd be lacking as a mother too.

"It's none of your business." Her teeth were clenched, her blood simmering.

"If it's going to affect my son, it is my business."

She rolled her eyes. "Oh, give it a rest. If you're so concerned about your son, why are you here? Go home to your perfect life, Elijah, and leave me the hell alone."

He crossed his arms and set his jaw. "What are you hiding?"

Her stomach knotted under the pressure. She lifted her chin and tried to turn this heavy table.

"I could ask you the same thing."

"Does Dominick know that you're pregnant?"

Her heart seized with panic. "No, and he's not going to. I'm going to take care of it before anyone else finds out, so if you breathe a word, I swear I'll—"

"What do you mean take care of it?" His eyes grew dark with disgust and disrespect. "How could you?"

Suddenly, the time bomb in her soul exploded and the ugly truth spewed out of her. "Because I was raped! Okay? Are you happy now?"

Elijah's hard expression melted like a candle under the heat of her shame. "What?"

She turned her head so she wouldn't have to watch the pity overtake his face of stone. "It happened while I was still in Iraq this last time. There were three guys. It was so dark I couldn't make out their faces, but they didn't speak much English so I'm pretty sure they were part of the Iraqi military that were on our base. They beat me up pretty good, and then . . . "

Her voice cracked, but she quickly built up the reinforcement. She refused to shed a single tear over those good-for-nothing, sorry excuses for men, and certainly not in front of Elijah.

"They each had their turn with me."

When Elijah finally spoke, his voice was barely more than a whisper. "I'm so sorry, Amy. I had no idea."

Amy sat up and glared at him. "No you didn't. Next time get your facts straight before you jump to conclusions."

Elijah stared at floor. "But do you think abortion is still the right answer?" He rubbed the back of his neck. "I mean, lots of women would give anything to have a baby and can't. It doesn't seem right to just . . . get rid of it."

"Did you hear anything I said? I. Was. Raped." She got off the bed and gathered her belongings, grimacing with each wrong turn or sudden movement. "This *thing* is a product of abuse, a result of a crime. It served its purpose. Because of my condition, I received an early discharge." She snorted in contempt. "Yeah, the process went remarkably smoothly, but now I'm done with it." She moved toward the door and turned to face Elijah. "Look, I promise I will never ask you for anything else, but please don't breathe a word of this to anyone, not even Elizabeth. Just let me handle it the way I see fit."

Elijah held his position a minute longer before conceding, "All right, on one condition. At least let me take you home."

She agreed and they headed toward the only set of open doors in the hospital at that hour. Stepping into the fading sunlight, she inhaled the warm, humid air as she waited for Elijah to lead her to his car.

Instead, he froze, all the color draining from his face. She followed his gaze and shivered as her blood ran cold.

Elizabeth stood fifteen feet away, pain glistening in her icy stare. Questions hung in the air between them, just waiting for a voice.

In that moment, it dawned on Amy that maybe Elijah's life wasn't so perfect after all. And maybe, just maybe, she wasn't the only one with something to hide.

CHAPTER

Twelve

Amy chewed her thumbnail all the way up the long driveway. One of the few body parts not achy from the accident contained a trace of blood by the time they parked.

To her relief, she saw no sign of Owen's truck. Before she could relax, however, Anna stepped out on the porch.

"I suppose Owen told her too," she moaned.

Elijah shrugged. "Is it a crime that people care about you?"

"These people don't know me. You don't know me. How can people care about someone they don't know?"

"Caring is a heart thing, not a head thing."

She grabbed the door handle and it popped open. "Thanks for the ride, but you need to go make things right with Elizabeth now."

He tipped his head back against the seat, and remorse saturated his voice. "Yeah."

Giving careful thought to each movement, she maneuvered out of the car, gravel crunching under her feet. Turning in slow motion, she peered back in.

"Give Dominick a hug for me and tell him I'll see him soon."

"Will do."

She shut the door and watched his tail lights fade along with her pride. The slight breeze carried Anna's fragrance, and Amy protectively wrapped her arms around her aching body.

"I'm sorry I missed evening chores."

"I don't care about the chores. I've been so worried. Why didn't you call?"

She fingered a piece of hair that was matted with dried blood. "You're right. I should've called, but I'm fine. I just need to take some Tylenol and go to bed."

She took a few steps toward her apartment, her traumatized muscles beginning to throb. She wondered if she'd be able to move in the morning and if there was such a thing as a full body-sized heating pad.

"Amy?"

She reluctantly faced Anna, bracing herself for the pity she so despised, but instead was met by genuine concern.

"Stay in the farmhouse with us. I have the bed in Kennedy's old room already made up for you."

Amy hesitated, her independence screaming at her to stay strong and keep moving.

"How long have you been taking care of yourself?" Anna placed a gentle hand on Amy's arm. "For once let somebody take care of you."

The tender words struck a chord, nearly causing Amy to buckle. "Okay. You win, but can I at least get a change of clothes and my toothbrush?"

"I made a quick trip to the store and picked up everything you'd need." Anna slipped her arm around Amy. "Come on."

Amy allowed herself to be led to the farmhouse without any further arguments. Kennedy's old room was at the top of the staircase, and after climbing it, Amy was thankful she didn't have to tackle the steep steps to her apartment.

"Well, here we are." Anna opened the door, the hinges creaking softly. "I guess it's a little out of date."

Amy entered the room, wondering if she'd somehow stepped through a portal into the past. Everything from the pale pink walls to the sheer curtains to the flowered bedspread reminded her of the bedroom where she'd colored pictures for her father and had tea parties with her dolls. Where her father would tuck her in at night after she'd said her prayers and sing the lullaby he wrote for her. Where she felt safe and happy and loved.

She shrugged the sentimental thoughts away. "It's nice."

Anna made a beeline to the bed and turned it down to reveal crisp, pink sheets that seemed to call Amy's name. "I keep telling myself to remodel in here, put up some fresh paint and new window treatments." She ran her fingers across a pillow encased by a pretty sham. "But sometimes it's hard to let go."

The feeling of intrusion smothered Amy and she took a step back. "Maybe this was a bad idea."

Anna chuckled. "Don't be silly. It'll be nice having someone in here again." She returned to the door. "Can I get you anything? Are you hungry?"

Amy's stomach growled as she realized that she hadn't eaten anything since lunch. "A little."

"Be right back with some vegetable soup and a roast beef sandwich. How does that sound?"

"Perfect, thanks."

Anna nodded and disappeared into the hallway.

As Amy inched further into the room, the strange sensation that she'd glimpsed her alternate life prickled her skin. She ran her fingers along the delicate vine of blue and purple flowers painted across the top of the oak headboard, imagining how different her life would be if her father hadn't gotten on that plane.

"Everything would be perfect, even without mom. Just like this."

She imagined sitting at the simple desk near the window, working on homework . . . or maybe college applications. After all she'd been through in the past ten years, college sounded refreshing. Maybe she would've planned out the fine details of their therapeutic equine program at that desk.

Amy's gaze shifted to Kennedy's senior picture, centered on the wall, surrounded by several framed awards and various team photos.

"That could've been me," Amy whispered. "But I never had senior pictures made, and after losing Dad, Mercy, and our dream I didn't care about sports or my grades. What did it matter?"

At that thought, she stumbled to the beautiful antique dresser, set her bag down, and leaned heavily against it. "If only I'd known it did matter. Just a few bad choices changed everything."

"But a few positive decisions can turn your life around." Anna stood at the doorway carrying a tray. "And it's never too late."

Not having the energy for a rebuttal, Amy gestured toward the frames on the wall. "You must be very proud."

"That I am." Anna set the tray on one of the bedside tables and pulled up the desk chair.

Amy crossed the small room, sitting gingerly on the edge of the bed facing Anna. She picked up the bowl of soup and, inhaling the rich aroma, managed to refrain from scarfing it down like a wild beast. She savored three bites, taking advantage of the brief lull to survey the security around the dilapidated wall of her fragile heart. She'd have to be very careful not to let her emotions overtake her, but the envy she battled proved to be a strong opponent.

She recalled how genuine Kennedy had been on Father's Day when they went riding. Of course, the whole family had been wonderful to her and Dominick, but something about Kennedy pinched her spirit.

Having made a large dent in the soup, Amy set down the bowl, picked up the sandwich, and swallowed her negative attitude. "So tell me about her."

"You want me to tell you about Kennedy?"

Amy nodded as she chewed.

"Well, here's a little known fact: Her first name is really Grace."

Anna stood, crossed the room to a chest of drawers, and reached for a frame sitting on top. Staring at it whimsically, she brushed the thin layer of dust off as she carried it back to the bedside and handed it to Amy.

"She was named after my mother, Emily Grace Kennedy."

In the aged photo, a beautiful young woman posed in her simple but elegant wedding gown and veil. "Wow. Kennedy looks just like her."

"She has Mom's strong will too. From the moment she was born I had fantasies of dressing her up in frills and lace with bows in her hair, but she wouldn't have any of it." She chuckled. "Of course, it didn't help that Adam gave her a ball and glove for her first birthday. You could probably guess what Owen gave her."

"A fire truck?"

Anna nodded and they both laughed. "Jake and Isaiah put her on a horse when she turned three, and she never got down. On her first day of kindergarten, she insisted on wearing a shirt and pants instead of the dress I had picked out, and when the teacher took roll, she said her name was Kennedy—Ken for short—and it stuck."

"Are you disappointed?"

"No. Never. It's who she is, and, after all the Lord has brought me through, I'm just thankful He gave me a second chance."

"I don't believe in second chances." Amy also didn't believe that the Lord had anything to do with the outcome of a situation, but she decided against voicing that opinion.

"I'm sorry to hear that." Anna carried the picture back to the dresser, set it in its spot, and stared at it mournfully. "The summer before I turned fifteen, Mom was diagnosed with cancer. What I remember most about those scary and uncertain months is how much time we spent together."

Anna smiled and returned to her chair. "We must've played a thousand games of Scrabble, and she beat me every time. We painted each other's nails and she'd brush my hair. I'd make us tea, and we'd both put on one of her fancy hats and have a tea party in her bed. She'd get sleepy easily, so a lot of the time I curled up next to her and read. She would always say, 'Anna, I pray that one day you have a daughter. Then you'll know how very much I love you.'"

Amy placed a hand on her chest in an attempt to ease the stabs of the beautiful mother/daughter image. She hated her mom, where ever she was, for all she'd missed out on.

Pushing to her feet, Anna stepped to the window and peered out through the delicate, sheer curtains. "Mom fought hard—like I said, she had a strong will—but the cancer stole a little more of her every day until one day, just a few weeks before I turned seventeen, I came home from school and she was gone."

Heavy grief that Amy had boxed up long ago and stashed away in a dark, unreachable corner of her heart resurfaced and pooled beneath her lashes. "I'm so sorry."

"I managed to finish my senior year, though it didn't seem to matter much." Anna glanced at Amy with knowing eyes. "And right after graduation I ran away with my boyfriend. We got married in Las Vegas, and a few months later I found out I was pregnant."

Amy finished her last bite of sandwich and edged forward a little. "What happened?"

"Well, we were living in a hotel room and had no money. We couldn't afford to feed ourselves let alone a baby, so he insisted that I have an abortion. 'It's your problem,' he said. 'Take care of it.' I went to a clinic the next day, but I couldn't go through with it."

Amy swallowed hard. "Wh . . . Why not?"

"Because after watching Mom fight for her life, I valued it more than the average eighteen year old. And even though I'd fallen away from my faith, I was raised to believe that the Lord has a plan and purpose for all of His creation from the very second we are conceived."

"Even if it's the result of a crime?" The words tumbled out before she could stop them, and Amy began to sweat under Anna's watchful eye. "I—I mean, hypothetically speaking, of course."

"Hmm." Anna moved to the bed and fluffed up the pillows.

"That's a tough one. God certainly doesn't condone assaults against women."

Hope filled Amy's heart, lifting it like a hot air balloon. Maybe, just maybe, she could open up just a bit and wouldn't have to make the difficult decision alone after all.

"But He also doesn't condone assaults against children. Oh, I know that opinions differ regarding when a baby's considered a baby, but I believe that at the moment of conception she's a living soul."

Amy slumped against the pillows, deflated. Square one never felt so much like a prison.

Anna perched on the edge of the chair. "The truth that's hard to see during any difficult time is that God can use even the worst situations for good."

Filled with skepticism, Amy challenged Anna. "So what happened in your situation?"

"Well, eventually he found out that I didn't have the abortion. He got mad, dragged me out our front door, and threw me down the stairs of our second-floor hotel room."

Amy gasped. "Were you okay?"

"I had a list of injuries—several broken bones, deep tissue bruises, excessive bleeding—but nothing hurt as bad as the doctors telling me my baby didn't survive. I delivered a tiny, lifeless baby girl." Anna sniffed, her eyes becoming misty. "I named her Emily."

"After your mother." Amy groaned. "I'm so sorry, Anna. I had no idea you've been through so much."

"You couldn't have known. Not too many people do, but that's why Kennedy is such a special blessing. She's my second chance at Mom's prayer. And I pray the same thing for her."

"So why did you share it with me?" Amy slipped under the covers, the cool fresh sheets feeling like a sigh to her aching body, and her eyelids growing heavy in response. "And how can you possibly think God used that terrible situation for good?"

Anna stood and gathered the dishes. "Amy, when I told you that day in the stable that you weren't alone, I really meant it. Everyone has their own baggage. I don't know what you're carrying around, but I know that your heart's been broken. I recognize the pain in your eyes."

Amy squeezed her eyes shut, but a small tear squeaked out at the corner.

"The good that came from that dark place in my life is I made the decision to let someone help me put the pieces back together and turn my life around. But that's a story for another time." Anna walked to the doorway and faced Amy. "I want to do that for you. I can help you put your pieces back together, but you have to want it too."

Amy didn't respond. Her eyes remained closed, her breaths coming in a relaxed rhythm.

"Just reach out to me," Anna whispered, stepped into the hallway, and pulled the door shut.

In the stillness, with sleep beckoning her, Amy lifted a heavy arm and reached out.

In the kitchen, Elizabeth's tea kettle whistled. She stood and hurried to pour a cup of chamomile tea, hoping it would soothe her frayed nerves. She sipped the hot liquid and filled her lungs with the sweet fragrance, but when her gaze fell on her purse, which contained the prescriptions, she tensed up again.

"As long as I'm dishonest with Elijah, our marriage will never be restored. But what more can I do? I've tried talking to him and he doesn't hear me out."

She sighed. "God, please, just let the medicine work and all these issues will fade away. A baby will solve everything."

At that moment, she heard the front door open, and a second later Elijah appeared in the dining room adjacent to the kitchen. Tossing his keys on the table, he glanced at her with weary eyes. She held her breath, hoping for an apology, waiting for an explanation.

He shoved his hands in his pockets. "Where's Dominick?"

The fragile bubble of hope burst and escaped with all the air in her lungs. "Upstairs."

Without another word, Elijah turned and strode toward the staircase.

Elizabeth hesitated for just a moment before she set her cup in the sink with a clatter and hurried after him. Slowing as she approached Dominick's room, she peeked around the doorway, straining to listen.

"Hey, Champ."

Dominick tossed his video game aside. He reached for his note pad, scribbled for a moment, and then thrust it at Elijah.

"I know I missed church and I'm sorry." Elijah sat on the edge of the bed. "Forgive me?"

Dominick shrugged and went back to his video game.

"Hey." Elijah rested his hand on Dominick's shoulder and gently shook it when Dominick didn't look up. "I know that I let you down, and you have every right to be mad at me, but I had something very important to take care of."

Dominick threw his game down, picked up his notebook, and scribbled away.

Elijah read it aloud. "What's more important than me and Elizabeth?"

Elizabeth's heart swelled and tears gathered under her lashes at the realization that Dominick was sticking up for her. *Take advantage of this situation. They both need you now.*

She sucked in a breath and stepped into the room wearing a compassionate expression. She sat down next to Elijah and began to sign. "Nothing is more important to your daddy than you and me, but someone needed his help. Isn't being a Christian about putting your faith in action and not just going to church?"

Dominick nodded and softened. He began moving his hands and fingers while Elizabeth voiced, "He still should have called."

Elijah nodded, looking at Dominick. "You're right." Then he shifted his gaze to Elizabeth. "And I'm sorry."

Satisfied, Dominick returned to his video game, while Elizabeth mused over how three little words could provide such instant healing for a hurting heart.

Elijah took the electronic toy from Dominick's grasp.

"Hey," the boy signed, reaching for it.

"Dominick, I need to tell you something. Your mom is sick." He shot his gaze at his son and clarified. "Just with a cold or flu or something like that. She'll be just fine, but she has to rest so you'll be staying with us for a few days, okay?"

Dominick's shoulders fell.

Elizabeth's heart broke for this boy who had been through so much. "Hey," she signed as she spoke so Elijah could hear her idea. "Would you like to make her a get well card? Maybe we can get her some flowers or balloons. How does that sound?"

Dominick shrugged and picked up a book from his night stand.

On that note, Elizabeth pushed to her feet and slipped out of the room. Just down the hall, in the privacy of her own room, she knelt beside her bed and fought off the insecurities that plagued her.

"God, I'm not his mother, and I know that it'll never be the same, but I care for him. I'm pretty sure he likes me too. Strengthen that relationship. Help me build some sort of a relationship with his mother." She paused. "And please restore my relationship with Elijah to what is was before she turned our world upside down."

"Hey."

The voice startled her. She jumped to her feet and turned to find Elijah in the doorway with his hands in his pockets.

"Hey."

He trudged to the bed and sat on the corner rubbing his hands together. "Thanks for your help in there."

She nodded and sat next to him, close but not touching. "What happened tonight?"

"Amy was in a car accident. Owen heard it over the scanner and called me. I went for Dominick's sake."

"I understand, but why didn't you tell me?"

"I didn't know what I'd find when I got there. I didn't have any details besides that there'd been an accident and she was transported to the hospital. And . . ."

"And what?"

"Well, to be completely honest with you, Elizabeth, I didn't know how you'd react."

Elizabeth opened her mouth to argue, and then closed it. "I know. I'm sorry I made you feel like you had to sneak around. I have these insecurities that I'm trying to work through, but regardless, I should've trusted you more."

He shifted his gaze to meet hers. "Do you mean that?"

"Yes, I do." She paused turning her wedding band on her finger. "Is she going to be okay?"

Elijah rubbed the back of his neck. "She's pretty banged up, but I think she'll be fine."

She glanced at him with misty eyes. "Are we going to be okay?"

His lips curved upward. "Yeah, we'll be fine too." He reached out and pulled her into a warm embrace.

And Elizabeth trusted him. As long as he didn't uncover her secret, she believed that they'd be just fine.

CHAPTER
Thirteen

*A*s the days passed, Amy's bruises faded, and her sore muscles healed. By a week after the accident, she'd returned to what had become her normal routine.

She settled back in her apartment and convinced Anna she needed to be in the stables. The sweet, earthy smell of alfalfa and the peaceful presence of the gentle horses provided more comfort than a whole day's worth of Tylenol. Working with Angel again and receiving her timid, but positive response acted like a band-aid covering the deep wounds of her heart.

Her pregnancy, however, remained a heavy burden, heavier now that Elijah knew about it. She'd procrastinated, but at almost 15 weeks, she knew she'd soon be feeling the baby move and wouldn't be able to avoid a decision any longer. Her window of opportunity slid shut a little more everyday. Some people might say she'd already waited too long, and her sense of urgency heightened.

With her heart hammering in her chest, she hurried through morning chores, dashed back to her apartment, pulled out her yellow pages and searched for a health clinic. If they couldn't do the procedure, she reasoned that they could direct her to a clinic that could. Three phone calls later, she'd made an appointment for the following Monday. Now all she had to do was wait . . . and remind herself that it was the right choice.

It's the only choice, she wrote in her journal later that evening as she sat under a shade tree, watching Dominick play fetch with Harley. It wasn't until Elijah had dropped him off after church that she'd realized that she'd missed him more in one week than in all of her deployments combined.

I won't miss this . . . She couldn't even bring herself to write the word baby. *I could never love it. In fact, I hate it. And I hate that I feel guilty for admitting that. This is not my fault. I am the victim here.* She sighed, the journal pages blurring behind unshed tears as she remembered Anna's words.

"But He also doesn't condone assaults against children."

She blinked hard and returned to her journal. *Would it be better for me to have this baby, and then just give it away to a stranger like it's nothing? I know very well how it feels to be abandoned by a mother. Growing up, I remember times I wished I'd never been born. The way I see it, I'd be doing this kid a favor.*

"Amy!"

She snapped her gaze up and her journal shut as Owen emerged from the stable. Her pulse quickened as he jogged a few steps toward her waving his arm.

"Come here! Hurry!"

The urgency in his voice magnified the initial jolt of seeing him, and Amy popped to her feet. Her heart skittering, she rushed to his side.

"Is it Angel? Please tell me she's okay."

"Angel's fine." Excitement, not panic, danced in his eyes, and her concern morphed into curiosity.

"Well then what—"

"Just come on." He grabbed her hand, causing a surge of emotion so powerful it shook the rickety walls around her heart. He pulled her along on wobbly legs to the stable door, where Anna met them.

She patted her son on the shoulder and met Amy's gaze. "I'll take Dominick to the house and fix him a snack. You two take your time."

Confusion replaced the curiosity and stole Amy's patience. She yanked her hand away from Owen. "Will someone tell me—"

"Shh." He crept inside the stable and motioned for her to follow.

Shifting into high alert, she stepped into the dimly lit barn and paused for her eyes to adjust. Heavy breathing punctuated by a few low grunts drifted to her ears, and her eyes widened. She moved to stand next to Owen at Bella's stall door and found the horse lying on her side.

When their shoulders brushed, Owen glanced at Amy, and then turned back to Bella. "Ever see a foal be born before?"

"No. Is it time?"

Owen nodded.

"Do we need to do anything to help her?"

"Not yet. Just watch."

Bella grunted and rocked her big body. Her nostrils flared with each hard breath.

As Amy stood there mesmerized, taking in this beautiful yet excruciating scene, not a sound could be heard from the other stalls. It was as though every living creature in the stable understood the sacredness of the moment.

A few minutes later, Owen leaned so close she could feel his breath on her skin, heightening intimate experience. "Look," he whispered sending tingles down her spine. "It's coming."

Amy gasped as two little, bony legs emerged from Bella covered by a thin white sac. Bella's sides heaved with the powerful contractions.

Owen slipped on a pair of latex gloves. "We should see the head next."

Her stomach in knots, Amy stepped just inside the roomy stall and knelt on the straw. "You're doing good, girl. Keep pushing," she said, her voice low. From out of nowhere her eyes grew damp. "Your baby will be here soon."

Amy held her breath as Bella worked. Anna had called the mare an old pro, but that didn't mean it was any less difficult. Finally the foal's muzzle appeared and several pushes later they saw the head.

"Amazing," Amy breathed.

Owen stepped inside the stall and crouched next to Amy. "She might rest a second now. The shoulders are the hardest part."

Bella didn't rest long. Her nostrils flared with heavy breaths, and her sides seemed to heave more ferociously than before. The anxiety building with each passing minute, Amy winced as the sweet mare rocked and grunted.

"Is she okay? Is it supposed to take this long?"

"She's doing great."

Several moments later, Bella passed her foal's shoulders and delivered the slimy, squirmy seventy-five pound bundle. Amy smiled, certain she could see pure relief in the proud mama's large brown eyes.

Owen moved in and, without interrupting the mare and foal's bonding time, helped remove the placental sac from the newborn.

"We've got a boy," he announced.

Amy's bond with the mare strengthened. "That's good. A son holds a special place in his mother's heart."

"And vice versa." Owen discarded the gloves and retreated to the corner with Amy, allowing Bella plenty of room to finish cleaning her baby.

Sitting cross-legged in the hay, they laughed together as the colt tried out his new long, skinny legs, teetering back and forth, falling down and rolling over. The harmonious sound of her laughter mixing with Owen's acted like a strong medicine, healing Amy from the inside out. The electric spark that zapped her core every time their knees brushed made the experience almost perfect.

Almost.

Bella nudged her baby and licked his head as if encouraging him to get back up and try again. The tender interaction that contrasted with her own grim reality caused Amy's soaring spirits to take a nose dive.

"I wish I could be a mother like that." Too late, she realized that she'd vocalized her private thought. "I—I mean, look at what she just did."

"There's nothing more beautiful than the miracle of life."

His unassuming words stabbed her in the gut, piercing her biggest secret. She blamed herself. She'd let her guard down, but as unintentional as it might've been, it was still an attack and she planned to retaliate.

"Why did you call me in here?"

Not wanting to disturb Bella and her baby, she rose and stormed off toward Angel's stall. Owen stepped out of the stall but moved no farther.

"What do you mean? You've been helping take care of Bella. I didn't think you'd want to miss this."

"I haven't talked to you since the party. For a week and a half you've avoided me, but now you act like nothing ever happened?" She spun around to shoot her words like arrows to his soul. "What makes you think I want to have anything to do with you?"

"This was never about me. It's about the horse." He moved toward her. "But since you asked, you're here aren't you?"

She took a step back and jabbed a finger at him. "You didn't leave me much choice. Bottom line, you deserted me when I needed a friend the most."

"Correction: *You* left *me* standing right over there." He cocked his head in the direction of Bella's stall. "Since then, I've just been trying to give you the space I figured you needed."

Sweat beads formed on Amy's brow. "You have no idea what I need. You don't know anything about me."

"You're right." He propped his forearms on the top slat of Angel's stall and slid his gaze to Amy. "So why don't you tell me something about you?"

"Okay." She stuck her chin out. "I can't stand nosey men."

Owen chuckled. "I deserved that."

He turned his attention to Angel and held his hand out to her. Keeping her head low, she moved toward him with cautious steps.

"It won't be long before we can start working with her using a lead rope."

Amy perked up. "Really? How do you know?"

"It's just a guess, but it's a good sign that she came when I held my hand out, even though she was a little unsure."

Maintaining a safe distance from Owen, she stepped up to the stall and reached out to Angel who placed her velvety muzzle in Amy's hand. The tension in Amy's soul slipped away as she stroked the horse's neck with her free hand.

"I was worried I'd lose ground with her this past week."

"Nah, I wouldn't let that happen."

Amy shifted her attention to Owen. "What exactly does that mean?"

"I spent some time working with her since you couldn't, that's all." He shrugged. "It's no big deal."

"Oh." Her heart melted like a candle under a flame. "Well, thanks."

He nodded. "I was thinking maybe Monday we can try to walk her to the arena, and in the meantime we can work on getting her used to the lead."

Amy's heart froze. "Monday?" She crossed her arms over her abdomen and turned away. "I—I can't on Monday."

"I've got to be at the fire station Tuesday and Wednesday so Thursday then? She should be good and ready to work with the lead by then."

Amy spun around to face him and planted her hands on her hips. "You just won't give up will you?"

"Not when something's worth fighting for."

The warmth from his gaze lit a fire in the core of her being. The heat radiated up her neck and settled in her cheeks.

"Thursday works."

"Good." Owen grinned. "Should we go check on Bella and her baby?"

Amy nodded, and they headed down the row of stalls. Bella had already gotten up and appeared to be coaching her still unsteady colt with nudges and licks on his little chestnut head.

Amy smiled at the entertaining pair. "When will he start nursing?"

"As soon as he figures out how to use his legs. Probably within the hour."

"I could sit out here and watch him all night. He's so cute."

Anna appeared in the stable doorway then. "The offer still stands if you want to name him."

Dominick sped over to the stall and squeezed in between Amy and Owen. His face shined with excitement, and wonder danced in his eyes. His hands flew with everything he wanted to say, but Amy could only pick out a word or two. Her heart squeezed as she pondered whether she'd ever be able to make up for her failures as a mother.

She wrapped her arms around him, rested her chin on the top of his head, and glanced at Anna. "Could Dominick name him instead?"

Anna nodded. "I think that will be perfect."

Amy turned Dominick to face her and spoke slowly. "He needs a name. Got any ideas?"

Dominick thought a second and reached for his notepad. He scribbled and handed it to Amy.

Amy read it and chuckled. "I know that you're a fan of *The Chronicals of Narnia*, but I don't think Aslan fits this colt." She held up her index finger. "Try one more time."

Dominick leaned against the gate and watched the colt for a long moment. Then he brightened, snatched his pad from his mom, scribbled on it, and handed it back to her.

This time a lump grew in her throat so large she couldn't manage to fit the name around it. Helpless, she looked into Dominick's questioning eyes, eyes so much like her father's. He'd be proud of his grandson's choice. She, on the other hand, was not.

Owen reached over and gently slipped the notepad from her hand. "Beauregard," he read aloud. "Beau for short."

Anna clapped her hands together. "Bella and Beau. That's precious."

Owen rustled Dominick's hair, further rustling Amy's heart. "That's a great name. Good job, Bud."

"It's settled then," Anna announced with finality. "The colt will be named Beauregard, Beau for short."

Dominick watched the wobbly colt with obvious satisfaction while Amy made a desperate attempt to sort out the whirlwind of emotions stirring up her soul.

Now that Dominick had given the colt their last name, Amy realized, a part of her would always be on this farm even after she'd returned to Florida. In many ways, that comforted her. She'd never felt such a sense of belonging.

If circumstances were different, maybe she'd consider staying permanently. But if the Sullivans ever discovered her secrets, they'd wish they never heard the name Beauregard much less own a horse by that name.

Amy awoke with a start before dawn Monday morning, the ever-present knot in her stomach pulled so tight she felt as though someone had kicked her in the gut. Mopping her damp forehead with the edge of her sheet, she took several deep breaths and relaxed enough to sit up.

Since her breakthrough with Dr. Kimball, her nightmares had eased up a bit, but this one wasn't about Justin. In this dream she saw a baby. With her face. Another causality of war, but instead of helping the infant, she sat and watched the brutality happen. She heard the baby's desperate cries but didn't lift a finger to save it.

She stood on shaky knees and stumbled to the bathroom, thankful that Elijah had asked if Dominick could spend the night with them again. Knowing sleep wouldn return anytime soon, she figured she might as well get dressed for chores. She'd already decided to do more than the required amount just in case she couldn't work that afternoon. Hopefully, if she started early enough she could get in and out before running into anyone, especially Owen. She didn't need her emotions going haywire today, and Owen Sullivan had a way of making that happen every time. Just the thought of the two of them working together with Angel later that week set off butterflies in her abdomen.

Amy froze. *Wait a minute.* She pressed her hand to the ever-so-slight curve of her belly and felt her skin twitch under her finger tips. *Those weren't butterflies.*

She groaned. "This wasn't supposed to happen. I'd planned to take care of it before I felt anything." She sank to the edge of the tub and dropped her head to her hands. "But I kept putting it off, avoiding the situation altogether." She choked on a sob. "This is ridiculous. With all I've been through, with everything I've seen, this should be a piece of cake."

She washed her face with a cool rag, finished dressing, and headed out the door. In the stable, she focused all her energy on the tasks at hand, completely detaching herself from the harsh reality of her situation. That exact mindset had been a requirement during her military career, and for the most part it came as second nature to her. But she'd never been at war with her own body, and with each passing hour, her anxiety heightened. At half past nine, she stared out the window of the cab at the gloomy afternoon and battled painful memories of her attack.

I am the victim here. She balled up her fists. *I don't deserve a constant reminder of what they did to me. I don't care if God doesn't condone assaults against children. It's time for me to take control of my future and experience real happiness again. After this procedure is over, I'll be able to do just that.*

In keeping with her story of having a doctor's appointment, she instructed the driver to drop her off at Cresthaven Medical Center, paid him, and, after he was out of sight, hurried the three blocks to the rundown brick building with the sign Cresthaven Women's Clinic above the door. The door banged shut behind her, causing her to yelp and a heavy-set woman behind the counter to look up with an annoyed expression.

"Can I help you?"

Amy took a deep breath, but the stale air didn't do a thing to calm her rattled nerves. "I-I'm Amy Beauregard. I have a ten o'clock appointment."

The woman turned to her computer, tapped the keyboard a few times, and then reached for a clipboard. "Here. Fill out these forms. It'll be a few minutes before we can get you back for an ultrasound."

"Wait. Why do I need an ultrasound?"

The woman stared at Amy for a long moment before answering slowly and deliberately, "Because in order to determine what method will be used, we have to know how far along you are. Certain procedures shouldn't be performed past a certain number of weeks of gestation."

"I can provide you with that information." The thought of having an ultrasound, of actually seeing it on a screen, made her insides twist.

"I'm sure you can, but it's very important that we get an accurate measurement." She dismissed Amy with a wave of her hand. "It's all right there in your paperwork."

Feeling small and insignificant, Amy retreated to a corner of the dismal waiting room, perched on the edge of a hard plastic chair, and started on the forms. They only asked for basic information so she flew through them without much thought until she got to the last page. At first glance, it appeared to be a disclaimer with lines for her signature and the date so she slowed down and read it carefully.

As with any medical procedure, there are certain risks involved, some of which may include: very heavy bleeding, infection, injury to the cervix or other organs and, in extreme cases, death. The risks tend to increase the longer you are pregnant . . . I understand these risks and do not hold Cresthaven Women's Clinic responsible for any injury that may occur . . .

Amy's eyes flicked back to the words *in extreme cases, death,* and suddenly she couldn't hold the pen in her shaking hand. Of course, she knew the risks involved, but seeing it on the paper made the slim possibility very real. A picture of Dominick's face formed in her mind and her heart sank to the knot in her stomach. She'd come close to taking her own life once, but she couldn't go through with it because her son needed a mother.

The words on the disclaimer blurred behind unshed tears as she imagined how disappointed Justin would be to know the risk she was taking after he sacrificed everything for her. She remembered how adamantly her father supported pro-life issues.

What would he think of his daughter now? A tear plopped onto the papers in her lap, and she swiped at the few sliding down her cheeks. *But what else can I do?* Filled with deep despair and hopelessness, she fought hard against the urge to break down and cried out in silent desperation, *Dear God, help me!*

A song softly filtered through the heavy fog of her grief. For over eighteen years, she'd only heard the melody in her mind, but she remembered every note. When her father sang her special lullaby, everything was right with her little world.

. . . Soothe your weary mind, paint a radiant scene. Won't be long until you drift to dream . . .

Her mind had definitely become weary, but so had her body and spirit. All her life had been a steady uphill climb, and now, sitting in this musty-smelling waiting room, she'd come to a fork in the road. There were so many uncertainties with both choices that neither path seemed right, but with that song in her heart she believed that everything would be okay. Somehow. Some way.

"Amy, they're ready to do your ultrasound." The receptionist leaned over the counter. "I'll take your paperwork."

Amy's heart stopped. Her stomach lurched. Sweat beads formed on her brow. She stood on wobbly knees and walked to the counter, trembling as she handed the clipboard to the woman.

The woman flipped through the paperwork. "Oh, I need you to sign and date this one." She shoved the clipboard at Amy.

Putting her hand up to block the pass, Amy shook her head. "I can't."

The annoyed expression hardened on the receptionist's face. "Ms. Beauregard, we can't help you until you sign and date this form."

Thinking of Anna and the brave choice she'd made years ago, Amy squared her shoulders and lifted her chin. "You're right. You can't help me, but there are people who can."

"Look, I understand that you're nervous. Most women are, but if you walk out that door right now, you'll be taking the easy way out. Can you live with that?"

"Excuse me?" Amy's blood became molten lava coursing through her veins, and she suspected if she looked in a mirror she'd see steam billowing from her ears. "I have a ten-year-old son, and I can tell you that having a child is most certainly not the easy way out." She stormed to the door and grabbed the handle. "I've made lots of mistakes that I'm learning to live with, but I don't know if I could ever forgive myself if I have an abortion today." She shrugged. "And I really don't want to find out."

She pushed through the door, relief washing over her as she stepped into a cool, gentle rain. However, she soon felt as though she was drowning.

"What am I going to do now?" She dropped to a sidewalk bench, thankful for the rain that hid her tears well as she tried to imagine being a single parent to a special needs child and a biracial result of a crime. She slid her hand over her belly and right on cue her skin twitched beneath her fingers.

"Maybe I could learn to love you."

Even as she said it she knew every child deserved more than that. At that moment, the dam she'd been reinforcing all day burst and powerful sobs wracked her body. Anxiety wrapped itself around her like a mammoth python, suffocating her.

"Oh, God! I can't love this kid. I don't have it in me. Somebody help me, please! I don't know what to do."

"Hey!"

Startled, Amy lifted her gaze through the heavy drizzle to find a car pulled over at the curb. Seeing that the passenger window was rolled down, she shifted her guard to high alert.

"Hey, are you okay?"

Amy peered through the open window and recognized the driver as the short-haired woman who had given the talk on forgiveness at the first single-parent support group meeting. She searched her memory for the woman's name and found it just in the nick of time.

"You're Stephanie, right? Stephanie . . . McCorkle, is it?"

Steph leaned across the passenger seat for a closer look and, as the dawning occurred, her crystalline blue eyes widened from behind stylish square glasses. "You're from the support group." She scrambled out of the car, put up an umbrella, and hurried to Amy's side. "Yes, I'm Stephanie, but everyone calls me Steph. I'm sorry I don't know your name. You left before I had a chance to talk to you."

Amy sniffed and wiped the rain and tears off her face with her wet hand. "I'm Amy and I'm fine." She shivered, but not from the temperature.

Glancing at the door of the clinic, Steph turned back to Amy with concern creasing her forehead. "Well, you really need to get out of this rain. Can I give you a ride home?"

Amy realized that she hadn't even called a cab yet. Hard telling how much longer she'd sit there waiting for one, but she'd waited in worse conditions.

She lifted her arms. "I'm soaked. I'll ruin your seat."

Steph chuckled. "I've got two kids. If they haven't ruined it by now, you certainly won't. Come on."

At that point, Amy didn't have any fight left in her. She allowed Steph to help her into the front seat of her Altima and closed her eyes as they started down the road.

"Are you like some sort of superhero or something?" Amy's words dripped with sarcasm. "Does a signal light up the sky whenever a woman is sitting in front of the clinic in the pouring rain, lost and alone?"

Steph burst out laughing. "Do I look like a superhero to you? No, I had a chemo treatment at the hospital this morning and decided to go home this way today. It's as simple as that. No bat signal here."

"Oh. I'm sorry. I didn't mean . . . "

"Don't worry about it. These treatments are a breeze compared to when I was first diagnosed." She transferred her gaze back and forth between Amy and the road. "So, are you really okay?"

"I told you. I'm fine."

The country station on the radio fittingly played a song about how everyone bleeds red. Steph, too, had seen her share of hardships. Maybe, just maybe, she'd be the one person to understand Amy's.

She sucked in a deep breath and took the plunge. "And so is the baby."

Steph snapped her attention to Amy. "What?"

"I didn't have the abortion." Amy stared out the window. "And now I'm more confused and scared and lost than before."

"Do you want to talk about—"

"No!" She swiveled her gaze to Steph. "Please don't ask me anything about this pregnancy and don't tell anybody. The only other person that knows thinks I had the abortion." She propped her elbow against the door and rested her head in her hand. "I should have gone through with it. I can't have this baby. I can't." Dread sat in her chest like a lead weight, making it hard for her to breathe.

They drove for a while in silence. When they coasted into downtown Harvest Bay, Steph turned into the parking lot of Ashford Park. "Sometimes I come here when I need to think." She glanced at Amy. "Or pray."

Amy shifted in her soggy seat. "I don't like to do either of those."

"You don't have to. I said I come here when I need to think or pray." Steph turned the radio down and bowed her head. "Dear God, thank You for all Your gifts. I thank You for the gift of friendship and companionship. The way You brought Amy and me together today was no accident, but intentional and according to Your plan. Whatever Your reason might be, Lord, I thank you for that too. Thank You that we are never alone, even in our darkest hour, for Your Word says that You will never leave us or forsake us. I thank You, God, that You were with Amy today at the clinic, and I pray that she would feel Your presence more and more every day of this trial she's going through now.

"Most of all, I thank you for every life because in every life there is purpose. Every baby is a perfect gift, even if he's not meant for the woman carrying him. Just as Mary carried Jesus though He was meant for the world, I thank you for women who choose to carry a baby meant for someone else. I pray that you comfort and protect these women and their babies in Jesus' name. Amen."

Silent tears slid down Amy's cheeks. "No one ever prayed like that for me before."

"I'm glad I could be here for you now, and I'll continue to pray for you."

Amy stared at her hands in her lap. "Thanks."

"You know, Amy, you really aren't alone."

Amy thought of Anna's words her first day of work, and then again in Kennedy's room. Dr. Kimball had reiterated the same thing.

"Yeah, I know, but sometimes I feel alone even when I'm in a crowd."

"You must've had a rough life."

"I guess you could say that, but from the sounds of it, you have too."

Steph nodded. "And I've learned the one good thing about hitting rock bottom is there's only one way to go." She pointed her index finger up.

"It's going to be a long, hard climb, though."

"As long as you're climbing, that's all that matters. In the meantime, come back to the single-parent support group. We'll carry you through your weak moments."

That sounded like heaven to Amy, and her heart softened. "Maybe I will, but no one else can know about this baby. At least not until I figure out what I'm going to do."

"You have my word." Steph put the car in gear and made a left onto Lake Erie Highway.

With the rain tapping out a soothing rhythm on the windshield, Amy mused at the turn of events that had taken place. She had awakened planning to have an abortion, but got a new, real friend instead. Between Owen, Anna, and now Steph, Harvest Bay was feeling more and more like home every day.

By the time they reached West Street, the rain had slowed to a steady sprinkle, and the thick clouds parted just enough for a sliver of sun to peek through. Up ahead Amy easily picked out the Sullivans' farm, and they both stared in wonder at the beautiful rainbow that arched from one side of it to the other. Everyone knew it was a symbol of God's promises, but Amy wondered what it meant for her. At that moment, as she felt a flutter near her bellybutton, she was afraid to find out.

Fourteen

"But I couldn't sign the disclaimer that released the clinic from liability so I walked out, and now I have no idea what I'm going to do." Amy sat in her usual spot on the couch in Dr. Kimball's office. After telling Elijah and Steph certain details about her situation, she was ready to report the whole sordid story to her therapist, hoping, if nothing else, that Dr. Kimball could help her figure out what to do next.

Dr. Kimball leaned against her desk. "First, you need to know that the rape wasn't your fault. Do you understand that?"

"It's hard to tell someone who experienced what I did that there was nothing she could've done to prevent it from happening."

"What could you have done differently?"

Amy thought hard. The night it happened she'd been on her way to the latrine. She wasn't out of line, but simply in the wrong place at the wrong time. If it wasn't her, it might've been another poor woman. And although she could have put up a good fight against one, she didn't stand a chance with three men.

Finally, she shook her head. "Nothing."

"Did you report it?"

"Yes, but it was dark and I couldn't make out any faces. There wasn't much that could be done short of testing the DNA of the entire Iraqi military. When my higher-ups found out it resulted in a pregnancy, they were quick to push paperwork through to get me out." She snorted. "Nice of them, huh?"

"I can imagine the battle you've been fighting within yourself—moral issues versus painful reality."

Amy bit her quivering lip and nodded.

"You were very brave to follow your gut and leave the clinic."

Amy popped to her feet and began to walk the floor. "That's fine, but what do I do now? Tell me how I can look into this child's eyes every day and not hate him or her."

"You'll start by directing your anger at the men who hurt you. You have every right to hate them, but the baby didn't commit any crimes against you. He is as innocent as you are."

Guilt stabbed Amy in the gut. "Probably more so."

"Also, understand that if you feel incapable of raising this child, you don't have to. There are many couples just waiting for a baby to love."

"You mean adoption?" She recalled how Steph's prayer hinted at that option, but she found it hard to swallow the bad taste it left in her mouth. "There is no pain in this whole world worse than being rejected by your own mother. If I give this kid away, I won't be any better than my mother, and I promised myself a long time ago that I'd never let that happen. Never."

"Stop right there. You are not your mother. You're you." Dr. Kimball spoke with a gentle firmness. "But for just a moment, you have to quit dwelling on what you're afraid you'll become, shake off the ghosts of your past, and swallow your pride long enough to consider what will be best for this baby. You made the choice not to abort. Now you have to decide if this child will experience a more abundant life with you or someone else."

Amy sank to the soft leather sofa, leaned forward, and rested her forearms on her knees. "I don't feel anything for it." She sniffed. "When I was pregnant with Dominick I found every little movement fascinating. Even though I spent a lot of time away, I always wanted him." She shook her head as her eyes grew damp. "I don't want this one."

Dr. Kimball's heels clicked as she crossed the floor to her chair, sat, and reached out to touch Amy's knee. "You've been given the opportunity to be a hero, not only to this baby, but also to some woman out there who will get the chance to be a mother only through your sacrifice."

A tear slipped out of the corner of Amy's eye. "I don't feel like a hero."

"Real heroes never do." Wisdom coated Dr. Kimball's words, and Amy couldn't help wondering if her comment was based on professional or personal experience. "Think about it. If you want to talk to someone more knowledgeable about the process, I can give you the number of a social worker I know. For now, though, you need to see an obstetrician. We don't have one here at the VA clinic, but I'll have Tabitha get a list from the medical center and set you up with an appointment." She stood and used the phone at her desk to page her receptionist with the task.

Amy chewed on her thumbnail in silent reflection. "Tell me something," she said when Dr. Kimball had hung up. "In the two weeks since my accident, two different women told me that everyone has a purpose. Even babies. Do you believe that?"

"You tell me what the alternative would be? Just existing?" She returned to her chair. "Yes, I believe that we all have a purpose, and it's when we discover that purpose that we find true happiness."

True happiness? Amy salivated at the thought. "I don't know what my purpose is." She dropped her head into her hands. "I don't feel like I have one."

"That's okay." Dr. Kimball smiled. "It just means your journey of self-discovery will be that much more satisfying."

"Journey of self-discovery?" Amy turned her nose up. "That sounds . . . painful."

"At times it very well may be."

Amy left Dr. Kimball's office with a loose plan. She had a doctor's appointment, the social worker's business card, and a lot to think about. But as she finished her afternoon chores later that day, the only thing on her mind was how much longer she could hide her situation from the Sullivans. And how would they judge her after they found out? They'd accepted her so easily that she didn't know if she could take their rejection. That left only one option.

"We'll leave after I go to court with Elijah at the end of September, and they'll never have to know." She looked into Angel's big brown eyes and stroked the side of her face. "I'll miss you, girl, but I don't have any other choice." Her shoulders sagged, heavy with regret. "I just wish I could have a chance to ride you."

"Then I guess we'd better get started."

Amy jerked around as Owen walked up beside her and rested his forearms on the top slat of Angel's stall. "Geez! What are you doing here? You said we'd work with Angel tomorrow afternoon."

"Well, that was when I thought we had until Christmas."

The blazing furnace in her cheeks scorched any argument before it had a chance to form. She swallowed twice in an attempt to get moisture to her bone-dry throat.

Owen pushed off the stall and disappeared into the tack room. He emerged a minute later, his strong arms full with a halter, lead, and a rod with a rope wrapped around it. The latch clanked as he opened the gate, stepped inside, and glanced back at her.

"Well? What are you waiting for?"

She gathered herself together and joined him in the stall. "How'd you know?"

"Know what?" He handed her the rod. "Here. Hold this training stick for me."

"What you always know. Just when to show up. It's like you're psychic or something."

He held the harness out for Angel to smell and even grab at with her lips.

"What are you doing?"

"Building her trust." After several minutes, when she seemed a little more comfortable with the new object, Owen draped it over his hand and began to stroke her nose.

Amy watched in awe as he gradually moved up Angel's head, scratching between her eyes, and then slipping the harness in place. Angel reared up, as did Amy's nerves, and they both pressed themselves as far as they could into their separate corners. Owen quickly gained control over Angel by keeping a firm grip on the lead rope and speaking in low tones, soothing Amy's anxious spirit in the process. He moved Angel around the small pen to get her used to the feel of being led with a rope.

"As for your comment, no, I'm not psychic. If I was I'd know why you need to leave in two months."

Hearing unmistakable disappointment in his voice, Amy dropped her gaze to the training stick. After all he'd done for her, she didn't want to hurt him, but she had to protect herself.

He looped Angel around the tight quarters again. "I'd also know how she'll react when I take her out of this stall, and I don't have a clue about either."

Amy grew uneasy. "We don't have to. I mean, if she's not ready maybe we shouldn't push her."

"It's all about trust. When the horse feels safe, she'll be ready." He turned his intense gaze to Amy. "The real question is: How much does she trust me?" He shifted his attention back to Angel. She bobbed her head as he stroked her neck. "Time to find out."

Amy scurried out of the way.

No sooner did Owen lead Angel out of the gate than she reared up again, but he calmed both Amy and the horse with his gentle voice. He grabbed the rope close to Angel's halter and unknowingly tugged on Amy's heartstrings. As she watched from the safety of a corner of Angel's stall, she reminded herself that he'd taken this time out of his day and once again put himself in very real danger because of her love for this horse. It stirred up new emotions she'd never felt before.

"You know, maybe this was a bad idea," she said as Angel tried raising her head and backing up. "She's obviously spooked."

Owen gave a firm tug on the rope and tightened his grip. Angel fidgeted and pawed the ground while Owen waited for several minutes until she settled down. His patience with the skittish animal caused Amy's heart to swell.

"All right. We're ready." He shot Amy a glance over his shoulder. "Are you?"

"Uh . . . yeah. Sure." She took cautious steps toward him. "What do you want me to do?"

"Give me the training stick and grab the rope right here."

She followed his orders, trying to ignore her skyrocketing pulse as their hands brushed. He slipped his hand farther down the rope, wrapped it around his hand twice, and leaned in to Amy.

"Don't let her sense your nerves. It'll make her feel insecure."

His breath tickled her ear and raised her blood pressure. "Good to know." She filled her lungs to capacity and slowly exhaled.

"Now give her a little tug and lead her to the door."

Amy hesitated, doubting herself and her ability to control this nine hundred plus pound animal.

"Don't worry. I'm right here."

His strength gave her an extra measure of courage and she pulled on the lead rope. "C'mon, girl. You know that I won't hurt you."

One careful step at a time, Angel emerged from the stable. As Amy encouraged and instructed the horse, Owen encouraged and instructed her. She knew they were bonding, all three of them. She could feel it forming between them, and knew it'd make it that much more difficult to leave, but she told herself this moment would be well worth the heartache.

As they neared the circular arena, Owen moved ahead to open the gate and close it after Amy led Angel through. The clank of the metal gate in this new environment spooked Angel. She stepped backward, swishing her tail, her head raised, ears pinned back, eyes wide.

Amy held her breath waiting for the horse to rear up, waiting for her to lose control, but Owen was by her side in a heartbeat. He reached up, placed his hand over hers, and pulled down on the rope.

"Talk to her," he instructed. "Make her feel secure."

"Whoa, girl. You're okay."

"Rub her neck."

Amy continued to speak in a soothing voice as she stroked Angel's neck until they both relaxed.

"Good job." Owen squeezed Amy's shoulder, turning her knees to Jell-O. "Now let's get to work."

He held up the end of the rope, which resembled a thin leather tassel, and tapped Angel across the nose with it. The horse jerked her head up, almost yanking the rope out of Amy's hands. Just as before, she calmed Angel and rewarded her with verbal praise. Then she turned to Owen.

"A little warning would've been nice."

His eyebrow quirked in amusement. "What do you think let's get to work means?" He handed her the end of the rope. "This is called desensitizing the horse, and it has to be done before you can even think of riding her. When she doesn't spook with you tapping her face, give it a little more length and swing the rope over her neck. Then we'll work with the training stick."

Amy nodded, took a deep breath, and began the routine.

Angel progressed more quickly than Amy imagined, which boosted her confidence in handling the horse. It took all evening, but as the sun set in the western sky Amy succeeded in using the training stick to touch either side of Angel's body without her flinching. The feat was nothing less than exhilarating, but not quite as satisfying as the approving grin on Owen's face.

"If she keeps doing this well, we'll be able to start using a saddle pad to work with her soon." He patted Angel's neck. "Let's call it a day."

Amy agreed, fighting disappointment over the end of their time together. They led Angel back to her stall, removed her harness, and gave her a scoop of sweet feed as a treat. Then they leaned against the stall watching Angel munch away.

Amy's soul sighed in contentment. "That was amazing, and once again I'm wondering how I can ever repay you." She turned to him with smile and pointed a playful finger at his face. "But if you invite me to a party the answer will have to be no."

"Stay." His tender gaze melted her firm stature and her hand sank to chest level. He reached out then and captured her hand. "Don't leave in September or at Christmas."

She shook her head and tried to widen the gap between them, but he pulled her so close a breath could barely pass through.

"If you don't like it here on the farm, find a place in town. Harvest Bay is a better place with you and Dominick in it."

He glanced away for a moment and returned his gaze, intensified with emotion so strong it left Amy breathless. "And I'm a better person."

"Owen, you don't even know me."

"But I know how I feel when I'm around you." He bent his head close to hers. "Please. Give me a chance to get to know you."

Warning bells sounded in Amy's brain. She yanked her hand out of his grasp and pushed him away.

"Look, it's complicated—*I'm* complicated—and I can't tell you why, but I can't stay."

She swallowed rising tears. Fighting the urge to touch his handsome face, she shoved her hands into her pockets.

"It'd never work anyway. We're from different worlds, and you deserve so much more than I can give you."

She made the mistake of looking into his pleading eyes and, in doing so, pulled the pin in her heart. It'd soon explode and she'd fall to pieces. And he'd witness the whole ugly thing if she didn't run for shelter.

"I'm sorry. I just can't."

She side-stepped around him and dashed out of the stable. Stumbling up the steps to her apartment, she burst through the door and crumpled to the floor. She clutched her chest, rocking back and forth and weeping hard.

Dr. Kimball had been right. Self discovery hurt. In many ways it seemed like cruel and unusual punishment. What good did it do her to know that she had fallen in love with Owen Sullivan when their relationship didn't stand a chance of surviving?

"But Dr. Kimball was wrong too."

She pulled herself together and wiped her face. Her heart returned to a cold, hard rock, heavy in her chest.

"There's no such thing as true happiness."

Elizabeth was sitting at her kitchen table, cradling a cup of tea in her hands, when she heard Elijah's car pull in the driveway. She worked to suppress her smile as he came through the front door a minute later.

"Hey." He came to kiss her forehead.

"Is Dominick back home safe and sound?"

"Yep." Concern creased his forehead. "I'm sorry you got sick at church this evening. You know, Amy didn't look very well either. I wonder if she has the same bug you have."

She took a sip of her tea. "I'm pretty sure she doesn't."

He went to the sink and poured himself a glass of water. "Do you think it was something that you ate?"

"No. Not exactly."

"Well, are you going to be okay?"

"Yep." A big grin spread across her face. "In about nine months." As Elijah started to choke on a gulp of water , Elizabeth hopped up and patted him on the back, giggling.

"Are you going to be okay?"

He took her by the shoulders and looked at her with gleaming eyes. "Are you saying what I think you're saying?"

She nodded, her eyes filling with liquid joy. "I'm pregnant."

Laughing, Elijah picked Elizabeth up and twirled her in a circle. Then he held her in a warm, tender embrace.

Elizabeth's spirit sighed. *I just knew if I got pregnant everything would be okay, and it is. It really, really is.*

He pulled back, kissed her lips and her forehead, and held her close to him again. "I can't believe that it's finally happening. After trying for so long, we're going to have a baby."

She shrugged the niggling sense of guilt off her shoulders. "God's timing is perfect."

"That it is." He swept her up into his arms. "What do you say we go upstairs and celebrate?"

"I'd say that's the best idea you've had yet." With that, she allowed herself to be carried far away from the real truth and any lingering regrets.

CHAPTER
Fifteen

E lizabeth agreed with Elijah that they should keep their good news a secret at least until she'd seen her doctor. She promised to wait that long to go shopping for the tiny booties and soft blankets she'd dreamed about. However, as she strolled down a booth-lined street with Kate, Madeline, Chloe, and Dominick two and a half weeks later, taking in the sights, sounds, and smells of the annual Harvest Festival she thought she just might burst.

She stopped at a craft booth that displayed knitted baby sweaters with matching hats. "Hey, Kate, look at this." She held up a beautiful sage green set.

"That's just like one Maddie wore." Kate wrapped an arm around her sister's shoulders and squeezed. "Don't worry, sis. It'll happen for you and Elijah."

Elizabeth tenderly fingered the cute embroidered giraffe with teardrop eyes. "You're right. It will." A wide, joyous smile spread across her glowing face. "In about nine months."

Kate gasped. "You mean you're . . . "

Elizabeth nodded and both women squealed, embracing in the middle of the sidewalk.

The gray-haired woman behind the booth stepped up. "Does that mean you'll be taking the sweater set?"

"Yes." Kate grabbed her purse. "I'm getting a head start on spoiling my niece or nephew."

The woman put the sweater set in a bag and handed it to Elizabeth.

"Thanks, Kate. I couldn't wait to tell you."

"I'm so happy for you." Kate hugged Elizabeth again, and the sisters started down the street arm in arm. "Isn't it amazing to think that two years ago at this time Maddie and I had just moved back to town? And I was so sure I'd never love anyone again after Ryan. Now I not only have an amazing husband, but another beautiful daughter."

On cue, Madeline skipped around the women, picking off bites of her cotton candy, while Chloe and Dominick trailed behind, nibbling theirs and communicating in their own language.

"In one year's time you'll have a sweet stepson and a baby. See? The Lord knows just what we need and exactly when we need it."

Elizabeth nodded. "And right now we need to get to our husbands' baseball tournament or we'll never hear the end of it."

Floating through the rest of the afternoon, Elizabeth didn't even notice the hard, metal bleachers as she cheered with Dominick, Kate, and many of their friends. To add to the lightness of her mood, it turned into a special time of bonding with her stepson, surely an answer to her prayers. While her baby grew little by little in her womb, he grew by leaps and bounds in her heart.

In between games, Elizabeth and Kate walked all over town with the kids, stopping at every carnival ride and food stand. Thanks to the cloud she was on, her feet never ached. The corndog, fried pickles, and funnel cake she splurged on tasted like heaven. The happy chatter that filled the steamy early August air made a wonderful soundtrack to her perfect day.

Later, when they all ran home so Elijah could clean up before the Sullivans' annual barn dance, Elizabeth decided to catch a short nap. Just as she laid her head on the pillow she heard a soft knock on her door.

Dominick stood there timidly.

She sat up and patted the bed beside her. "What's on your mind?"

His fingers started flying. "I was wondering what you and Aunt Kate were so excited about earlier."

"Well . . ." Quickly evaluating the situation, sensitive to the needs and feelings of this ten-year-old boy who'd just found his father, she realized that Dominick might not consider a baby great news and tried to brace herself. "Why don't you take a guess?"

"Maddie said you're having a baby."

Elizabeth sighed. She should've tried harder to hide it from her perceptive little niece, who must've put two and two together, reporting her findings to Dominick and most likely the rest of the family by now. "I'm sorry you had to hear it from her instead of your dad and me, but she's right."

Dominick cast his gaze to his lap and her heart dropped with it.

She patted his knee to get his attention. "You're going to be a big brother. That's exciting!"

He meditated on those words for a moment. "You mean you'll still want me after you have your own baby?"

"Want you?" She dammed up threatening tears. "I'll need you!"

Dominick smiled and signed, "Really?"

"Absolutely! Who else will teach the baby to play ball?" She gave him a teasing grin. "And there'll be plenty of dirty diapers to change."

He scrunched up his nose and stuck out his tongue, and they both laughed.

Growing serious, she started moving her hands, hoping the emotion in her eyes spoke louder than the signs. "Don't ever think I don't want you."

It might have been true when he showed up on their doorstep two months ago and maybe even a few weeks ago, but the Lord had worked a miracle in her heart. Now she not only wanted him, she truly loved this boy.

"You're a part of our family and nothing, nothing at all, will ever change that, okay?"

He gave a nod and lunged forward, the bed squeaking with the forceful movement as he encircled her neck with his arms. Elizabeth smiled. Having the wind knocked out of her never felt so good.

By the time they arrived at the barn dance, only a thumbnail of the sun remained visible on the violet horizon, but the barn glowed with party lanterns and white Christmas lights. An upbeat country song greeted her and coaxed her into tapping her toe. Half the town crowded into the huge red barn, mingling with smiles and laughter.

Dominick hung back, taking in the ordeal. Elizabeth tried to imagine the event without hearing the music or the people, and she guessed it seemed like utter chaos. Her heart sagged a little for him until Madeline and Chloe found him.

"Hey, Dominick! Come play with us! We're doing the Hokey Pokey," Madeline announced and dashed off, while Chloe waited, motioning for him to join them.

He brightened and looked up questioningly at his dad.

Elijah nodded toward the girls. "Go have fun."

Elizabeth leaned into Elijah, watching her stepson join in the fun, more content than she'd been in years. In all her bliss, she'd been able to overlook the pesky sliver in her spirit until she scanned the large area and found Amy at a picnic table in the corner by herself. Then it began to fester. Remembering her prayer for some kind of a relationship to form between them, she felt the Holy Spirit nudge her.

A relationship will never happen if someone doesn't extend an olive branch. Now that she carried Elijah's baby, her insecurity faded enough that she could take that first step.

"Honey, could you please get me a Sprite? I'll find us a table."

"Sure." Elijah kissed her forehead and started toward the coolers.

Elizabeth sucked in a long, slow breath, second guessed herself for half a minute, and then headed toward Amy uttering a silent prayer.

God, please let her be receptive to my gesture. For Dominick's sake, if nothing else. I don't know if I can do this again.

Amy glanced up and bristled.

Pasting a smile over her uncertainty, Elizabeth forced herself to bridge the gap. "Hi, Amy."

"Hey." Amy avoided making eye contact.

Elizabeth wrung her hands. "Dominick had a lot of fun at the festival today. He won you a stuffed animal at one of the games."

Amy swiveled her gaze to Elizabeth and locked it on her. "What do you want?"

Elizabeth's casual front crumbled as she sank to the bench across from Amy. "Look, I'm sorry we got off on the wrong foot.

It was a bit of a shock to find out Elijah had a son, and I didn't handle it too well, but now I'm really glad we get to be a part of his life. So . . . I just wanted to say thank you."

Amy narrowed her eyes. "Again, what do you want?"

Elizabeth stood and shook her head. "Nothing. Nothing at all."

Just as she turned to leave, Dominick ran up to the table and began speaking animatedly with his hands.

Amy put a hand up. "Whoa. I don't know what you're saying. Where's your notepad?"

Elizabeth stepped up and placed her hand on his shoulder. "He told you that he's going to be a big brother."

"What?" The color drained from Amy's tanned face. "How did he find out?"

"I told him." Elizabeth tucked her hair behind her ear. "It's a little soon—I'm only a few weeks along—but it's hard to keep something like that a secret."

"You mean you're . . . "

Elizabeth nodded.

"Oh." Amy exhaled. "Well, then, congratulations." She stood abruptly. "I've got to go. Send Dominick to the apartment after this thing is over."

Dominick put his hands up to stop her, and then used them to speak. "Can I go to church with Dad and Elizabeth in the morning? Please?"

Elizabeth translated, shrinking a little at the incredulous expression on Amy's face. She gave a little shrug. "I'm fluent in sign language."

"I see that." Amy lifted her chin and shifted her attention to Dominick. "I guess you can go."

He hugged her, then signed while Elizabeth interpreted. "Will you come too?"

"I don't think so." Her gaze pierced Elizabeth straight through to her soul. "Have him home by lunch." With that Amy stormed out of the barn.

Dominick's eyes clouded over with disappointment, stirring up a storm in Elizabeth's heart. "We'll pray for her, okay?"

He nodded.

"Good." She smoothed his hair. "Now go find the girls and enjoy the party." She watched him disappear into the crowd, and then turned to stare at the empty barn door. Had she misunderstood the Holy Spirit? Wouldn't the Lord want her and Amy to have some sort of a relationship? She didn't expect to be friends, but she'd hoped to be friendly.

Dominick's unique laughter floated to Elizabeth above the joyful racket. She slid her hand over her flat, firm belly. She'd done the right thing, and the Lord would once again reward her for her obedience. Somehow, someway.

He hugged her, then signed while Elizabeth interpreted. "Will you come too?"

"I don't think so." Her gaze pierced Elizabeth straight through to her soul. "Have him home by lunch." With that Amy stormed out of the barn.

Dominick's eyes clouded over with disappointment, stirring up a storm in Elizabeth's heart. "We'll pray for her, okay?"

He nodded.

"Good." She smoothed his hair. "Now go find the girls and enjoy the party." She watched him disappear into the crowd, and then turned to stare at the empty barn door. Had she misunderstood the Holy Spirit? Wouldn't the Lord want her and Amy to have some sort of a relationship? She didn't expect to be friends, but she'd hoped to be friendly.

Dominick's unique laughter floated to Elizabeth above the joyful racket. She slid her hand over her flat, firm belly. She'd done the right thing, and the Lord would once again reward her for her obedience. Somehow, someway.

Amy made a bee line for the stable. She needed to see Angel. She tried to convince herself she didn't need to see Owen, but when he hadn't showed up at the barn dance, she couldn't deny the flicker of hope that he'd opted to hang out with the horses instead.

She shoved the door open and flipped on the lights. Some of the horses nickered at the sudden movement. Little Beau skittered in the stall he still shared with Bella.

There was no sign of Owen.

She slumped against Angel's stall. "It's just as well. There's nothing left to say." Since the first evening they'd worked with Angel two and a half weeks earlier, he'd continued to help train her, but he'd become distant. She recognized the wall he built between them, and she didn't blame him—it was what she intended. However, she didn't expect it to hurt so badly.

"And it doesn't feel too great that Elizabeth is getting along so well with my son. Not only can she sign, she's giving Dominick the brother or sister he always wanted." She glanced down at the slight curve of her belly and shook her head. "I can't do that either. Even after seeing this baby in the ultrasound last week, I can't make myself love him."

Inadequacy beat down her soul, stealing whatever self-worth she'd managed to regain. Next to tears, she spun around and stomped to the tack room, pieces of hay and alfalfa crackling beneath her boots. She grabbed a saddle, saddle pad, bridle, and reins and carried them back to Angel's stall.

"You ready for this, girl?"

Angel bobbed her head and stomped the ground. After two and a half weeks of training, it seemed she not only understood, but looked forward to the next step.

Amy rewarded this major progress with a good scratch between the horse's eyes. She strapped on the saddle, fastened the bridle, and led Angel out of the stable. The training arena, lit up by a powerful floodlight, reminded her of Dominick's bright, happy face as he tried to tell her about being a big brother.

"He'd hate me if he ever found out that I gave this one away. The only way I know for sure to keep it a secret is to go back to Florida alone until this kid is born, but then he'll hate me for leaving him again." She snorted. "Classic case of damned if I do and damned if I don't." Her shoulders sagged. "Oh, who am I kidding? Elizabeth can take care of him better than I can anyway."

Amy's breaths came in shallow puffs as she cautiously moved to Angel's side and slid her foot into the stirrup. She shifted some of her weight onto it, gauging Angel's reaction.

Angel lifted her head and whinnied.

The knot in Amy's stomach yanked taut, and she pulled her foot out of the stirrup before Angel had a chance to rear back. She rested her forehead against Angel, wearier than she'd been since arriving in Harvest Bay.

"I can't do this. I can't do any of it."

"Why do you always try to do everything on your own?"

Amy snapped her head in the direction of the familiar voice, her heart galloping away as her gaze landed on Owen. The glow of the flood lights gave him an ethereal appearance, and she wondered if she was hallucinating, if he was just a mere figment of her imagination.

Owen pushed through the metal gate, locking it behind him, and joined Amy in the arena. "Let somebody help you."

Amy concentrated on keeping her voice low and even so Angel wouldn't sense her building emotions. "I didn't see you at the barn dance."

"I didn't know if I was going to come." He reached up and stroked Angel's neck. "This girl's come a long way since we started working with her. It seems she's a different horse."

"She just needed to know that someone wouldn't give up on her."

"She needed you." Owen slipped his fingers under the leather straps of the bridle and tightened his fist around it. "Why don't you try getting on?"

Amy's pulse picked up speed, and every nerve in her body stood at attention. "What if she's not ready?" She dropped her head against the saddle. "What if I'm not ready?"

"You will be leaving soon, right?"

She nodded her head against the smooth leather.

"How disappointed will you be if you don't take this chance?"

Amy didn't respond.

"We rarely regret the chances we take." Owen placed his hand on her shoulder. "Even if it doesn't turn out quite like we hoped."

The electricity in his touch jolted her. "I'm afraid of falling." She couldn't believe that she'd actually admitted weakness, but an unexpected wave of relief washed over her.

"No, you're afraid of getting hurt. You've experienced so much pain in your life that it's what you expect in every situation. I've fallen off a horse many times, and I promise you it doesn't hurt quite as bad if there's someone there to pick you up and dust you off." He reached over and lifted her chin to meet his gaze. "I'm right here and I won't let you fall."

During her two months in Harvest Bay, Amy had learned that among his many admirable attributes, Owen was dedicated, persistent, reliable, but above all else, he was honest, more honest than anyone she'd ever known. And that was enough to give her the strength to try.

Trusting him with all her heart, she shoved her foot into the stirrup, swallowed the last of her fear, and hoisted herself into the saddle. Her heart thundered in her chest like a timpani as she sat there, bracing herself for Angel's reaction.

The paint fidgeted a little, swishing her tail and stomping the ground.

Amy held her breath while Owen gripped the bridle and calmed Angel with his low, gentle voice.

"Okay, Amy. Loosen up on the reins and give her a nudge with your heels."

Amy's nerves were like hot wires as she followed Owen's instructions. Her heart lurched forward as Angel started to move.

Owen continued to hold onto the bridle, helping to guide the horse. "Very good. Now pull back on the reins and say, 'Whoa.'"

Amy did as she was told and, after Angel tried unsuccessfully to side step and lift her head, she stopped in her tracks. The corners of Amy's mouth turned up with satisfaction.

"I'm riding her," she whispered. "I'm actually riding her." She might as well have been sitting in a saddle on top of the world.

That is, until Owen's smile put her over the moon. Gazing down at him, not bothering to mask her deep affection, liquid gratitude filled her eyes. *And it's all because of you.*

"All right. Let's get her moving again, and we'll work on turning her to the right and left."

Amy could have spent all night training Angel with Owen's help, but after introducing right and left turns, he suggested giving Angel a rest.

"You can work with her more tomorrow. Let's reward her for her good work and let her process what she's learned tonight."

Amy fought her disappointment and dismounted. Reins in hand, she rubbed Angel's side and neck as she worked her way to the horse's head. Looking into Angel's trusting eyes and feeling the warmth of Owen's presence only intensified the sting of the sand slipping through the hourglass. She had to cut the ties or leaving Harvest Bay would be nearly impossible, but now she risked slicing herself in the process.

"So . . . " She scratched Angel between the eyes. "Um, do you think you'll be around tomorrow?"

Owen released his grip on the bridle and stepped back, slipping his hands in his pockets. "I could be persuaded."

Amy gave the reins a gentle tug and led Angel toward the gate. "I just wondered. I'm not twisting your arm."

Owen walked ahead of her, unfastened the latch, and opened the gate for them. "No, but you could ask for help."

She shook her head. "It isn't easy for me. When you take care of everything on your own for as long as I have, you grow accustomed to figuring out a way to do it all."

"Believe it or not, I understand that."

Curiosity made her brain tingle. "But you live five miles from your parents. You have three brothers and a sister, sisters-in-law, nieces and nephews, and a whole town that loves you. I can't imagine you not having help when you need it."

"Reaching out is a choice. It doesn't matter if you have a hundred people near you or just one. You have to make a conscious effort to receive help in any circumstance."

As they reached the stable and led Angel into her stall, Amy considered Owen's words. She unfastened the buckles and lifted the saddle off Angel's back.

"Sometimes it's best not to get anyone else involved. That way no one else will get hurt."

Owen removed the bridle. "If they really love you, they're hurting anyway."

Amy lugged the saddle to the tack room, set it in its place, and scooped up some sweet feed. She dumped Angel's reward in the feed trough, turned, and planted her hand on her hip.

"I don't disagree, but every situation is different and everyone copes in their own way. Your family and friends helped you through your problems. That's great, but there's something called privacy." She shrugged, a tiny movement under the heavy weight of her secrets. "I just prefer to take care of my own business, okay?"

Her strong independence had always been a source of inner pride. Now it seemed more like a stumbling block. She bit her lip to keep it from quivering, but knew it wouldn't last long.

"I've got to go."

"Amy, wait." As she brushed past him, he reached out, caught her by the arm, and spun her around. "Have you ever been in love?"

Staring at him, she knew she'd never in her life been so in love as she was at that moment, and it scared the living daylights out of her. She shook free from his grasp and backpedaled, almost tripping over herself in a frantic attempt to put space between them. She crossed her arms and lifted her chin defiantly.

"Yeah. What's it to you?"

"Me, too." He walked over and sat on a hay bale. "Her name was Julia."

Amy inched closer, strangely jealous of, and yet curious about, this woman who once held the key to Owen's heart.

"We were first-year teachers together at the high school."

"Wait a minute. You were a teacher?"

"Yep." Owen dragged a long breath out of his throat. "I taught the upper level math classes and coached junior varsity basketball. Julia taught honors English and coached softball."

"Sounds like a match made in heaven." She kicked at a dirt clod gloomily. *While you and I would be a match made in hell.*

"It sure seemed that way." He shook his head. "I can't believe that I'm telling you about her. I don't typically talk to my family and friends about her, let alone someone I've only known for a couple months."

The honor Amy felt didn't compare to the fear that shar-ing his weakness would bring them closer, making her leaving that much harder. "You don't have to. Really."

"No, it's okay." He leaned forward, resting his forearms on his knees and rubbing his palms together. "About two years after our first date we got married and just a couple months later were expecting our first baby."

Amy had trouble finding her voice. "Y-you were married?"

"Yes, for almost a year."

Feeling her heart about to explode, she sank to a hay bale next to him. "What happened?"

"I was in Columbus at a seminar on effective teaching strategies one Friday evening in January when my dad called my cell. I knew right away something was wrong."

Amy held her breath.

"He told me there'd been a fire and I needed to come home right away. My only thought was Julia. I didn't care about the house or any of our stuff. I had to get to her, but . . ."

Amy was on the edge of the hay bale. "But what?"

"I was too late." He sucked in a sharp breath. "It was an electrical fire that started in our utility room. As far as we can tell it started sometime after she went to bed, and it must've spread quickly because the fire chief said by the time the call came in the house was fully engaged."

Stunned, Amy wasn't sure how to respond. She ached to wrap her arms around him and comfort him, but it didn't seem appropriate. So she waited in silence.

Finally, he continued. "It's my fault. The small, old house had no working smoke detectors when we bought it. For months I'd meant to install a new one in every room, but I always found something else to do." His shoulders fell. "The death of Julia and my unborn son was the price I paid."

The bomb in Amy's heart went off and she clutched her chest. "It's not your fault. You couldn't have known what would happen." Realizing how close to home her words hit, she winced and clamped her lips shut.

"True, but it was preventable."

Being with him like this made her want to stay even though she knew she couldn't. Still, the tug of war going on inside her heart began to hurt, and she needed this conversation to be over.

"Why are you telling me this, Owen?"

He turned to her, his storm blue eyes glistening with unshed tears. "Do you remember what I told you your second day in Harvest bay? You aren't the only one who's ever been scared or lost or heartbroken. Whatever you've been through, Amy, you aren't the only one who's had to figure out how to start over, and you don't have to figure it out alone. Let people help you, people who've been there. People like me."

Her eyes flickered to his lips and suddenly she wanted, maybe even needed, more than just his help. "So how did you move on?"

"One day at a time. Sometimes moment by moment." He stared at his folded his hands. "I quit teaching. I couldn't drag myself out of bed knowing I wouldn't see her in the halls, and I was certainly in no shape to inspire of a bunch of teenagers to learn."

"Is that when you became a firefighter?"

"Eventually, but first I just grieved. Pastor Ben counseled me weekly for several months, and Mom helped me a lot.

Sometimes there was nothing to say, but it helped having someone there who understood that."

Amy nodded, her heart swelling. She didn't intend to be drawn in by him, but their connection strengthened every time they were together. And as she learned more about him, she found she learned more about herself. Now, as he opened his heart and bared his soul to her, Owen Sullivan managed to touch a cold, unreachable part of her soul. The warmth radiated through her, incinerating the already dilapidated wall around her heart, but she had a hunch that he'd protect her as well, if not better than, any of her own defenses.

"When the time felt right, I went through the training and joined the fire department. In the ten years since then, I've created a fire safety program that I take to the area schools, of course, stressing the importance of working smoke detectors." He rubbed his hands together. "And that helps. It gives me peace and the strength to move on, knowing that I'm making something good come from my loss."

Peace. The thought made her salivate, no matter how futile it was. "I don't think I can make anything good come out of my situation."

"I'm only suggesting that you open your heart to the possibility."

Amy gently rested her head against Owen's shoulder. She closed her eyes imagining for a moment that he was hers and they could be like this forever, but a little flutter in her belly yanked her back to reality. She could only squeak a whisper past the large bundle of emotions in her throat. "I don't know how to do that."

He took her hand, intertwined their fingers, and leaned his head against hers. "This is a good start."

CHAPTER
Sixteen

*L*ong shadows stretched out from the boys' cleats by the time Elizabeth set up her lawn chair and waved to Elijah on the field. She didn't plan on sitting through all of Dominick's practices, but his disability threw Elijah a curve ball, and she promised him she'd be there. She strolled over to meet him at the chain-link opening of the dugout.

Shifting his weight from one foot to the other, Elijah adjusted his hat. "Thanks for being here."

"No problem. It's a beautiful evening." She reached up on her tiptoes to give him a quick peck on the lips. "Do you remember the signs I taught you?"

Elijah signaled "go" and "stop".

She clapped. "Very good. You'll be fluent in no time."

"Doubt that. Thank goodness Dominick can read lips." Rubbing the back of his neck, he added, "This is my first stab at coaching my kid. I don't want to screw it up, you know?"

"You'll be great." The corners of her lips turned up. She couldn't help thinking he was adorable with his high hopes and nervous jitters.

He scanned the park and glanced at his watch. "We're almost ready to start. Where is he?"

"Don't worry. Amy said she'd have him here and she will."

Elizabeth patted her husband's back. "Now go have fun." As she turned to head back to her chair, Dominick barreled up to them, putting the brakes on just in time. "There you are. We were wondering," Elizabeth both spoke and signed.

Dominick's eyes sparkled as he moved his hands and Elizabeth interpreted. "I'm ready, coach. Put me in."

Laughing, Elijah patted his shoulder. "Come on, son. Let's go play some ball."

As Elijah led Dominick into the dugout, Elizabeth marveled at how the very term she'd seethed at just two months earlier now caused her heart to radiate with joy.

Son. She ran a hand over her belly, wondering if the sesame seed-sized baby would be another son or a daughter. Either way, she loved this life growing inside her with every ounce of her being. She'd never imagined how immense love could be. Of course, she loved Elijah as much as any wife could love a husband, and she'd grown to love Dominick like her own, but this baby was a part of her, the answer to years of fervent prayers, and the fulfillment of her life-long dream.

"I hear congratulations are in order."

Elizabeth immediately recognized the voice of their family friend and the office manager of Harvest Bay Family Practice. She brightened and swiveled her gaze to meet Denise's smiling eyes.

"Word travels fa . . ." Then her gaze landed on Nathan, and she couldn't finish her thought under his critical stare.

Denise didn't seem to notice. "Such is life in a small town." She leaned over and embraced Elizabeth. "A new baby! Isn't it wonderful, Nathan?"

"It's amazing after all you've been through." He gave her a stiff hug, adding in a low voice, "I'll bet Elijah is thrilled."

Elizabeth lifted her chin, refusing to let him burst her bubble. "He is. We both are."

"Well, I wish we could sit and chat, but Greyson's practicing on the next field." She pointed. "And first practices are packed with information for the parents."

Elizabeth nodded. She had helped Elijah put together packets containing the game and snack schedules, contact numbers and email addresses of the players, and a few other important tidbits.

"Let's have lunch one day this week. That is, if your boss will let you off." She gave Nathan a teasing grin.

"If it's okay with Doc Brewster, I don't think that'd be a problem." Nathan slipped his arm across Denise's shoulders and gave Elizabeth a pointed look. "She's never given me a reason not to trust her."

Elizabeth's blood ran cold. Nathan was the only one who knew the whole truth. He held the mallet that could drive a wedge between her and Elijah. She doubted he'd act on it, but the only way to be sure was for her to come clean with Elijah.

After Denise and Nathan moved on, she shifted her attention back to the field and her smile easily returned. Elijah was a natural coach and a wonderful father.

Maybe he won't be mad that I was dishonest. Maybe he'll understand the importance of medical help. Maybe he'll feel partly to blame for shutting me down when I brought it up. Maybe . . .

"Hey."

Elizabeth jerked her gaze in the direction of the voice that interrupted her thoughts and met Amy's jade stare. Remembering her cold attitude at the barn dance, Elizabeth straightened at the uncomfortable prick of pins and needles.

"Hi."

Amy squatted down beside Elizabeth's chair. "Sorry Dominick was a little late."

"It's fine. Practice hadn't started yet."

"And . . . " Amy picked at a few long blades of grass. "I'm sorry for the way I treated you Saturday. You're right. It's been an adjustment for us all."

Elizabeth worked to keep her shock hidden in her heart. "Thank you for that."

Dominick appeared at the fence in front of them and began speaking with his hands.

Remembering Amy's hateful expression after she had interpreted for Dominick at the barn dance, Elizabeth shifted in her chair and swallowed hard. "He asked if you saw him hit a double a minute ago."

"Sure did." Amy gave him a thumbs up. "You're doing great."

Dominick smiled and returned to the field, while Amy returned her attention to the tuft of grass. "He signs when you're around because he knows that you can translate for me."

"I never thought about it that way. I'm sorry."

Amy's voice wavered. "It must be comforting for him to know that you understand him."

"I suppose." Elizabeth picked at the pearl pink polish on her thumbnails, imagining how badly it must hurt to realize that someone else could communicate better with her son.

"Think you can teach me?"

Elizabeth met and held Amy's misty gaze. A lump she couldn't explain formed in her throat. She had no idea what had happened in just three short days, but there was no mistaking the change in Amy. Still, while her heart leapt for joy, Elizabeth remained calm and made no sudden movements, as if she'd encountered a wounded and frightened wild animal.

"I'd be happy to."

"Thanks." Amy stood. "I've got to run or I'm going to be late for a meeting." She got Dominick's attention and waved. "Take good care of him for me tonight."

"We will. See you tomorrow."

Amy put a hand up in a parting gesture and hurried toward the parking lot, leaving Elizabeth scratching her head. She replayed the conversation in her head and concluded that there were three possible explanations for her exchange with Amy. Either she was dreaming, Amy was scheming, or God was working a miracle.

Amy pulled her car into the parking lot of Harvest Bay Community Church twenty minutes early. As she killed the engine of the used Honda Civic she'd recently purchased with her insurance settlement, her nerves kicked into overdrive. Taking a shaky breath, she opened her door.

"I have a feeling I'm going to regret promising Owen I'd start letting people help me," she muttered as she stepped out.

"Amy?"

Amy jerked toward the voice, exhaling when her gaze landed on Stephanie's friendly face. "Hi, Steph. It's good to see you."

"I thought that was you." Steph hurried to join Amy. "I pulled in right behind you."

"I'm surprised you recognized me since I'm not a sopping wet basket case."

Steph dismissed her comment with a wave. "We all have our moments. I've been thinking about you though. How are you?"

"Still clueless but in a much better place. Thank you."

"Well, I'm glad you're here."

Amy's jitters settled as they started toward the church together. After a few silent steps, Amy cleared her throat.

"Can I ask you something?"

"Sure thing."

"That day when you prayed in the park, something you said stuck with me. I believe that it was something to the effect of every baby is a perfect gift, even if he's not meant for the woman carrying him."

Steph nodded.

"What did you mean by that?"

"Well, God doesn't make mistakes. Some women can't have babies. You'd think that was a mistake or maybe a curse. But I believe that those women are specifically chosen for unwanted babies." Steph studied her. "Are you considering giving this baby up?"

Amy shrugged. "I don't know. I've been taught that you play the hand you're dealt."

"I understand that, but you have to remember, this isn't just about you. You have a child to think about. In my opinion, if a woman can't love or take care of her baby, giving it to someone who can is the most selfless, honorable choice they can make."

She pulled open the big, creaky, wooden door and faced Amy before walking through. "If you can't love this baby, maybe, just maybe, God created him or her for someone else to love."

Amy considered what Steph had said as they jig-jogged through the hallways of the large church. *Could I be carrying someone else's baby? Could God have actually planned this?*

She scoffed at the ridiculous thought. She didn't know if she believed in God, but if He truly planned for her to be raped, and then get pregnant so another woman could have a baby, she didn't want to believe in Him. She shook her head as they neared the beehive of activity in the meeting room . It was all too much for her to process and now entering a room of strange people, she began to feel nauseated.

Amy leaned closer to Steph. "You know, I'm not feeling very well. I think I'm going to go."

"Wait. Give it a few minutes. Why don't you find a seat? I'll grab you a 7-Up and some crackers and maybe that'll settle your stomach."

Amy did as Steph had suggested. The crackers worked on her belly but did little to soothe the churning in her heart.

But Anna said God didn't condone assaults against women. What if He's just making good come of something bad like she and Owen both said? It doesn't seem fair, but if any good could come from Owen losing his wife and unborn son, He could certainly do the same for my situation. Her shoulders drooped. *But I'd have to let Him. I promised Owen I'd start letting people help me. I didn't say anything about God. I don't want Him messing with my life, not after what He did with Dad's.*

Amy checked her watch. If she was going to stay, she wanted to this meeting to get started and over with.

After several long minutes, Maggie finally made her way to the circle of chairs. "*Hola.* It's time to get started. If everyone could find a seat, *por favor.*" She paused while the milling members wandered to their seats.

Practicing her breathing techniques helped Amy tolerate the circular arrangement of the chairs with a manageable anxiety level for the time being.

"Would someone like to lead us in a word of prayer?"

"I will." Steph raised her hand, and then folded them in her lap. "Dear Father in Heaven, I ask You to be present here with us tonight. We all come bearing our own burdens, some heavier than others."

Amy held her breath, wishing she could become invisible. *She's talking about me. I just know it.* She studied the exit, calculating a fast and silent escape.

"Those burdens weigh on our hearts and minds, shifting our focus away from You as we try to take care of them on our own. Please help us to lay them at Your feet day by day and trust You as our help in times of trouble, not just as our Father, but also as our best friend. You are everything we need and You have every answer we're seeking even when we don't know what questions to ask. Dear God, if there's someone here who doesn't know You, I pray that You'll reveal Yourself to them. As days go by, I pray their desire for You will multiply and their relationship with You will become more important than any other."

Amy sank down in her seat. *Relationship? Desire? No, thank you.*

She barely listened as Steph concluded by thanking the Lord for Maggie and Tish's leadershipa and asking for God to bless the group's members and their children.

"*Gracias,* Steph," Maggie said when Steph finished. "Most of you know me, but in case we have any new members tonight, my name is Maggie Martinez. I have *un nino*, Justin, who just turned two and keeps me *muy* busy. I've been leading this group for a year now with the help of my co-leader, Letisha Jackson." She gestured toward the eccentric woman who had welcomed Amy on her first visit, and Tish waved like a beauty pageant contestant. "Are there any first-time visitors who would like to introduce themselves?"

Having managed to dodge one bullet, Amy heaved an inward sigh of relief. Technically, she was a second-time visitor, but, regardless, she would not like to introduce herself.

After a few takers shared their name and important details, Maggie welcomed them and moved the meeting along. "As I mentioned, Justin has reached his, how do you say, terrible twos?"

The circle unanimously responded with a light-hearted groan. Even Amy found an amused smile playing on her lips.

"And I've learned that I have a lot to learn about being *la madre*."

Murmurs and chuckles floated up from the circle.

"Between Harvest Bay Family Practice and the Bayside Cafe, I work six days a week and I'm thankful to provide for *mi nino*, but I'm tired and most days very, what's the word, overwhelmed."

Nodding heads indicated that many could relate.

"That led me to today's topic: *Donde esta*—" She stopped and shook her head. "Where is God?"

Amy leaned forward. *That's a good question. And where was He when Dad died?*

"I've asked myself that question. I've asked others. I've even asked God Himself, 'Where were You when *mi novio* died fighting for our country?'"

Amy's heart stopped. *Mi novio?* A cold chill ran through her causing the hair on her arms to stand at attention. *God wasn't there, Maggie, but I was.*

"Where was God when I had to tell our parents, just days after Justin's funeral, that I was pregnant? Oh, the shame I felt at having given in to temptation, but even more the grief that came with the fact that Justin would never know about his *nino*. As Steph just prayed, it was too much for me to bear on my own, but I couldn't find God to lay anything at His feet. I was abandoned, left all alone to be *un madre y padre* to *mi nino. Si?*"

The guilt twisted Amy's gut until she doubled over, resting her forearms on her knees. *It's my fault. It's all my fault.*

"No. I want to read to you what God Himself said to His servant Joshua, right after Moses died." She opened up the Bible that lay in her lap. "I imagine Joshua felt overwhelmed too. Not only did he have big shoes to fill and a big job to finish, I'm sure he was missing his leader. But God said to him in Joshua 1:5, 'as I was with Moses, so I will be with you. I will not leave you nor forsake you.' He goes on to encourage Joshua in verse nine, 'Be strong and of good courage; do not be afraid, nor be dismayed, for the Lord your God is with you wherever you go.'"

Tears stung Amy's eyes and tickled her nose. Although she hadn't thought about that verse in years, she could've recited Joshua 1:9 by heart. It was the same verse her dad had used whenever they prayed for her mother.

And for her tenth birthday, in addition to giving her Mercy, he gave her a gold medallion with a cross etched on one side and those words engraved on the back. She remembered squeezing it, feeling its weight when she prayed for her mother. Two and a half years later, she clung to it, reciting the verse when her dad boarded that plane that took him halfway around the world. Now she longed to hold that quarter-sized pendant in her hand and soak up all the strength it emitted, but she'd lost it when she lost her dad.

"That is one of many times God promises that He will not leave His servants. I believe that promise as true for you and me as it was for Joshua. *Si*, times and circumstances have changed, but God will never change for all of eternity. We may still get lost along the way. We may feel like God has left us, *pero* it's because we leave God."

Amy winced. The truth in those words stung like a mad hornet. She knew she'd turned away from God, but she believed that He left her first, just like her mother.

How could Dad have died the way he did if God was with him? A loving God wouldn't have let it happen, not to Dad. And what about Justin? He was so young and good. What about Anna's baby and Owen's wife and son? How can such tragedy happen if God never leaves us?

"Bad things happen. That's just life, but I believe that God is with me through it all. Even when I can't feel Him, I know that He's there. And if I'm faithful to lay my burdens at His feet, as Steph prayed, He is faithful to hand me back blessings. Now instead of being angry that I'm raising *mi nino* alone, I understand that it's a gift and I'm *muy* thankful."

Amy's blood began to boil. *Thankful? That is the most heartless . . .*

Maggie's eyes glistened with unshed tears. "Because I have *mi nino*, I'll always have a part of Justin."

Amy melted against the heat of her shame and pressed a hand against her chest, feeling Justin's cool, metal dogtag on her skin. Grief gripped her heart as the dawning occurred. Justin had given them to her to bring to Maggie, not for her to keep as a crippling memory of his sacrifice for her. Needing to stand and bolt, her legs tingled.

"Does anyone want to share about a time when you felt God's presence? Or when He turned your burdens into blessings?"

Someone on the opposite side of the circle piped up, and Amy accepted the distraction as an opportunity to sneak out. Stepping out into a warm summer rain she welcomed the natural camouflage for her tears. She dashed to her car and in its seclusion slipped Justin's dogtag over her head. The chain rattled as she squeezed it so tightly in her fist she could make out the imprint of his name on her palm.

You gave me your dogtag because you knew that since you weren't married it was the only way to get them to Maggie.

She rested her head against the steering wheel and heaved a ferocious sob, realizing that she'd have to give up the only part of her dearest friend she still held, that she'd have to let him go, that he was never hers to begin with. But saying good-bye never hurt so much. She still hadn't completely recovered from telling her father good-bye, and she knew she'd soon have to let Owen go. She clutched her chest in an attempt to soothe her aching heart. The flood waters of her anger rose, and like a tree limb in the current, she snapped.

"It's not fair!" She slammed her palm on the dashboard with a loud thwack. "Why do I have to say good-bye to everyone I love? Why?"

The answer came as a whisper in her soul. *'Be strong and of good courage; do not be afraid, nor be dismayed, for the Lord your God is with you wherever you go.'* . . . *And so am I.*

The gentle tapping of the rain on the windshield kept a steady beat as the melody of her lullaby floated back to her. She loosened her grip on the dogtag and ran her thumb over the engraved letters of Justin's name. Although it was lighter and more oblong than her medallion, she gathered the same amount of strength and comfort from it. She'd miss wearing the flat metal oval, holding close its significance, but she found some peace in knowing the biggest part of it would never leave her.

After what you did for me, Justin, I'll do this for you. I promise.

CHAPTER
Seventeen

The rest of August passed in a blur. In addition to morning and evening chores, Amy worked with Angel every
day, went to support group meetings, counseling sessions, and
another prenatal appointment, and shared the duties of getting Dominick to his baseball practices and scouts.

Above all else, though, registering Dominick for school
took top priority. During the entire painstaking process of setting up his initial Individualized Education Program meeting,
requesting and receiving all the required documentation, and
then sitting through the meeting, Amy battled guilt over the
fact that her grandma and grandpa had taken care of this
every year before.

*I should've been there for my son. I should've been more
involved in his education, learned sign language, taken him to
baseball practices, and cheered at his games. I'm his mother, yet all
this time I've been nothing more than a paycheck. I took care of
him that way, but does a ten-year-old boy care about that? Will he
hold it against me someday that I wasn't there? It's true I spent a
good amount of time out of the game, but I've stepped up to the
plate now. That should count for something.*

Early Labor Day morning, the negative thoughts continued to float through her mind like passing storm clouds. After

Amy finished chores, she carried an insulated cup of coffee to the pasture and climbed up to sit on the fence. As she watched the sun rise over a distant soybean field, the dew on the crop sparkling like hundreds of tiny diamonds, thoughts of Justin warmed her heart.

Because of his sacrifice, she had the opportunity to make up for lost time with her son, and she would make him proud. She'd keep her promise to him and, regardless of the outcome, she'd be a better person. Today, for the first time in ages, she viewed the dawning of a new day as a gift, instead of a curse.

"Maybe that means I'm finally healing."

Filling her lungs with the fresh, sweet country air, she swung her leg over the fence and hopped down, yelping when she almost landed on Dominick. *Okay. So I still have a ways to go.*

"I'm sorry," he signed.

She searched her brain for the hand motions Elizabeth had been teaching her, but since she'd only had a few short lessons, she settled on a combination of speaking and signing the words she could remember. "Why are you up so early on the last day of summer vacation?"

Using his fingers he spelled, "N-e-r-v-o-u-s."

Having learned the alphabet on her first lesson, she understood. "Why are you nervous?"

Pulling out his pad, he scribbled on it and handed it to her.

"New school. What if no one likes me? What if I get made fun of 'cause I can't hear?"

Agony gripped Amy's heart. She turned away from him so he wouldn't misread the apprehension on her face. Crossing her arms, she chewed on the inside of her cheek, silently cursing herself.

Of course it's going to be harder for him to adjust than for a regular education student. How could I have not considered that?

She motioned for him to follow her to her favorite shade tree where she sat and patted the ground beside her. He sat in front of her, studying her face and picking at the damp grass between them.

"Did I ever tell you that I had to change schools once?"

He thought a minute and shook his head.

"I'd gone all the way through seventh grade at a private school . . . "

He perked up and began to spell "C-h-r-i-s-t-i-a-n?"

"Yes, it was a Christian school, but when my dad died, Grandma and Grandpa couldn't afford to send me there anymore. So I started my eighth-grade year at the public middle school. I was really scared, but I viewed it as a mission. Every day was a new adventure. Some days my mission would be to uncover the truth behind the mystery meat in the cafeteria."

Dominick burst out in a loud laugh.

"Some days it would be to make a new friend, which was not easy for me." She shrugged. "I found ways to make a hard time in my life bearable. Understand?"

He nodded.

She tipped her head to the side and patted his knee. "Tell you what, let's give it till Christmas, then decide whether we stay or move back to Florida. I know that you'll miss Grandma, Grandpa, and your friends, but you'll have Maddie, Chloe, and most of the boys on your baseball team in your new school. And you'll be in your Aunt Kate's class. How cool is that?"

He scrawled in his notepad and handed it to her.

"An adventure," she read and smiled at him, her heart beaming with pride not just for him, but also for her. Maybe, just maybe, she's gotten this one right. "That's my boy."

He leaned over to write on the notepad in her lap. "I'll try to be brave like you."

She couldn't force any sound past the lump of emotion in her throat so she wrote back under his words, "You're the brave one, son."

He shook his head and used his fingers to spell out, "H-e-r-o."

Tenderness pooled behind her lashes. "What did I ever do to deserve you, huh?"

"You love me." Dominick's three simple signs spoke louder than if someone shouted it from the rooftop.

"Yes, I do very much." She sniffed and wiped her eyes with the sleeve of her light-weight flannel shirt. "Now what do you say we play some catch before I take you to your dad's?"

Scrambling to his feet, Dominick dashed off to get his ball and glove.

Amy's smile followed him, and although the last of her doubts as a mother evaporated with the dew, new ones rose with the bright morning light.

It took about ten minutes to drive from Elijah and Elizabeth's house to the fire station, and Owen's shift ended in five. Amy couldn't miss him or she'd chicken out. After backing carefully out of the driveway, she put the hammer down and thought she actually felt the car lift off the old country road for a split second. By the time she neared her destination, her heart rate matched her speedometer and only accelerated after she parked next to his truck.

"The sooner I get it done and over with the better." Summoning all her courage, Amy climbed out of her Honda just as Owen stepped out of the building and met her gaze.

"Amy?" He jogged over to her. "This is a surprise. What are you doing here?"

Amy's knees turned to Jell-O and she leaned against her car for support. "You know how you said I should let people help me?"

"Yes."

"Well . . ." Her voice wavered. "I need your help."

"You've got it. What's up?"

Amy expelled all the air in her lungs. "I need to see Maggie."

"Okay. Hop in the truck."

The peaceful streets of Harvest Bay contrasted sharply with Amy's tumultuous insides. She was doing the right thing, but that didn't make it any less scary.

She wiped her damp palms on her jeans and silently rehearsed what she would say. She prepared herself for Maggie's reaction knowing she deserved it, but she doubted she could withstand Owen's rejection. Just imagining the disappointment on his face caused her heart to start to crumble. By this evening she was sure it'd be nothing more than a pile of dust on her diaphragm.

They pulled up in front of a quaint duplex near the park and Owen cut off the engine. "This is it, and it looks like she's home. Do you want me to wait here?"

Amy shook her head. "I can only do this once so you'll have to come with me." Her hand trembled as she reached for the door handle.

Genuine concern clouded Owen's eyes. "Are you all right?"

She slid out of the truck and steadied herself on her wobbly knees. "Ask me in a half hour."

Her fist was heavy as she lifted it to knock, but before it made contact the door opened revealing Maggie's smiling face.

"Owen! Amy! I thought I heard a car out front, *pero* didn't expect such a *bueno* surprise." Maggie stepped aside, opening the door wider. "Come in, *por favor*."

Amy entered first, her eyes sweeping the adjoining living and dining rooms. "You have a pretty home."

"*Gracias*. It is small, but it is all we need."

Amy moved farther into the living room, perched on the edge of the sofa, and motioned toward a few trucks, a ball, and some blocks scattered on the floor. "Where's the little guy?"

"Napping. He'll be up soon, though. Can I get you both something to drink?"

"No, thank you," Amy answered while Owen, leaning against the archway to the kitchen, put a hand up and shook his head.

Maggie's cheerful expression faded as tension flooded the room. She shifted her gaze back and forth between Owen and Amy. "What's going on?"

Amy cleared her throat. "I think you need to sit down."

Maggie crossed the room, sat rigidly in an antique-looking rocker, and folded her hands in her lap. "What is this all about?"

"There's something you ought to know."

All at once, Amy's throat closely resembled the Arabian Desert, and she swallowed wishing she'd taken Maggie up on her offer for something to drink. Her heart hammered in her chest and echoed in her ears. Her hands shook. Her stomach lurched.

She should've expected a full blown anxiety attack, but she'd hoped maybe she'd moved past that stage. Now she wondered if she would ever be fully healed from them. She closed her eyes, meditating for a brief moment as Dr. Kimball had taught her.

After one last deep breath, she opened her eyes and met Maggie's gaze. "I knew Justin McGregor."

Maggie's lips parted as her jaw dropped. "*¿Qué?*"

"He was my closest friend. More like a brother, really." Amy's bottom lip quivered as she glanced over her shoulder at Owen, who was rubbing his chin. "I made the connection that he was your fiancé and Owen's friend on the Fourth of July."

"*¡Dios mío!*" Maggie's hands flew to her mouth as tears sprang to her eyes.

"I'm sorry. I know that I should've told you both sooner, but I was afraid that you'd hate me. Honestly, I'm still scared."

Owen stepped further into the room. "Why?"

There it was, the moment of truth. Amy's heart plunged to rest heavily on the knot in her stomach as the floodgates opened and tears flowed down her cheeks. "Because it's my fault that he's not here with you. It's my fault that he doesn't know his son. It's all my fault."

Maggie wiped a rivulet of tears away as her brow creased in confusion. "His *padres* said he died in an explosion."

Amy nodded. "He did. It was a grenade. He pushed me out of the way, but it went off before he could run."

A sob bubbled up in her throat. She tried to swallow it, but it burst with the release of this secret and there was no stopping it. She hid her face in her hands as she wept.

"I'm so sorry, Maggie. I can't tell you how long I've carried the guilt around that he gave up his life for mine, but getting to know you and Owen and finding out about his son has made it that much harder to bear."

She lifted her wet eyes to meet Maggie's and found not anger or resentment amidst the tears but compassion. She didn't have the courage to see if Owen's mirrored Maggie's.

"Oh, Maggie, he loved you so much. He talked about you all the time, but he never mentioned your name. He always called you *Alma*—' "

"*Gemela.*" Maggie lips curled in a sad smile. "It means soulmate."

Amy sniffed. "In his final moments, he thought of you. I was there with him. I held his head in my lap. He said, 'Harvest Bay' and he gave me this." She slipped the dogtag over her head, squeezed it one last time, and handed it to Maggie. "It took me a while to figure out what he meant, but I know that he wanted me to bring it to you."

Maggie cradled the oval piece of metal in her hands as if it was a priceless, delicate cameo from her great grand-mother's jewelry box. Her tears dropped steadily unto it. Running her fingertip over the engraved letters, she whispered his name and moaned as a powerful wave of emotion engulfed her.

"Oh, how I miss you!"

Amy wept with Maggie, but hers were tears of sweet relief. The tag was where it belonged. Letting go of Justin hurt, but the closure felt good.

"Mama?"

They all looked in the direction of a tiny voice and found little Justin in the doorway sucking his thumb, a blanket in the crook of his arm, as he twirled a lock of his honey blonde hair with his other hand. His eyes were still heavy with sleep. This was Justin's son, a real living, breathing part of him. The realization warmed Amy's heart. The resemblance took her breath away.

"Mama, who's dat?" He toddled over to climb up in Maggie's lap.

"This is Amy. She was a friend of your *papi*."

"*Papi?*" He slid off her lap and raced out of the room. A second later, he tore back into the room with a picture frame in his hand, which he carried to Amy. "*Papi.*"

Amy took it and found herself gazing at a picture of Justin in his Class A uniform. "Your daddy was a real hero."

Little Justin tipped his head to the side. "Heeero?"

"Yep. Someone who works really hard to help keep others safe."

The little guy scrunched his face up as he processed the information. Then he turned and pointed. "Uncie Owen is heeero!"

Amy glanced up at Owen. The amused expression on his handsome face started her heart jitterbugging. "Yes, he is."

"Uncie Owen is a fireman." Little Justin raced to his pile of trucks, plucked the fire truck out of the bunch, and rolled it in a circle on the carpet. "I a fireman too! Vroom, vroom! Woo woo woo woo!"

He alternated making the sound of the engine and the siren, while Amy and Owen chuckled.

Maggie wiped her face and leaned forward. "Justin, do you want to go to the park?"

"Yea!" In a heartbeat, he dropped his truck and ran to Amy. He caught her hand and gave it a tug. "I go to park. You come too?"

"I came with your Uncle Owen. You'll have to ask him."

He ran to Owen, who'd already squatted down. "You come to park wiff me?"

"Sure, buddy. We'll come for a little while."

Little Justin leapt into his arms, while Amy's heart leapt in her chest.

"*Pero* we can't go to the park until you go find your shoes, *mi hijo*." After he raced out of the room, Maggie scooted from the rocker to the sofa. "Amy, I do not hate you. I am so grateful to you. You were a good friend to Justin. You were there when he needed someone the most."

Amy stood and began to pace, shaking her hands as she made a last ditch effort to drive home the facts. "Maggie, you don't get it. It's my fault that's he's not here with you, with his son, with his friends." Making the mistake of glancing at Owen, she felt her stomach lurch at his intense stare and hurried back to the sofa before her knees gave way. "Justin was there for me, not the other way around, and it cost him everything. How can I begin to repay that?"

"You just did." Maggie slipped the dogtag around her neck, closed her eyes, and squeezed the flat oval metal as if giving it a hug. "Did you know that someone gave His life for me too? I didn't deserve it. Sometimes I didn't even act like His friend." Maggie's voice wavered. "But He followed His orders anyway. No, He didn't want to die, but He loved me so much He was willing to do whatever had to be done to save me. I know about shame. I spent a long time carrying it around until I realized that the only way I could bring Him honor and justify His sacrifice is to tell others about Him and His amazing, redeeming love."

Amy heaved a sigh. "I know that you're talking about Jesus, and it's a clever parallel, but you have to understand that it's not the same. I mean, I watched Justin die with my own eyes all because of me."

"*Sí, pero* Jesus said, 'Blessed are those who have not seen and yet have believed.' " Maggie lifted a different chain off her neck, placed it in Amy's hand, and closed her fingers around it. "Try seeing with your heart instead of your eyes." She removed her hand as little Justin ran up to her with his shoes on the wrong feet.

Amy opened her fingers and a small gasp escaped her lips. Her eyes grew as round as the quarter-sized gold medallion that lay in her palm.

"It can't be," she breathed.

She examined it through blurred vision. She ran her thumb over the exquisite cross etched on one side. Every detail was exactly as she remembered.

It can't be the same one. Surely there were dozens of these necklaces sold. The answer lies on the other side and there's only one way to find out for sure.

Part of her didn't want to turn the pendant over. She wanted to see with her heart as Maggie had just suggested, to hope and believe that somehow, some way, she'd gotten back the necklace her dad had bought her.

However, the urge to know the truth was too strong. Holding her breath, she flipped the medallion over in her hand and blinked.

"Be strong and of good courage . . . for the Lord your God is with you wherever you go."

She blinked again and reread the engraving. Unbelieving, she glanced up at Maggie. "Where did you get this?"

"Umm . . . at a flea market, I think, about a year ago. *¿Por qué?*"

Amy shook her head. "Just wondering." For the first time in ages, her smile reached her damp eyes. "Thank you for this. It means more than you know."

"Well then, we're even." The warmth in Maggie's smile wrapped around Amy's heart like a soft, fuzzy blanket. "Now who wants to go to the park?"

Little Justin jumped up and down. "Oooo, me! I go, I go!"

Amy spent over an hour at the park with Maggie and Owen, pushing little Justin on the swings, catching him at the bottom of the slide, and playing chase. After the spunky toddler had played his little heart out, they strolled over to the memorial garden. Maggie sat on the bench and gestured for Amy to sit next to her.

Little Justin pointed to the plaque. "Dat's *papi*." He hopped back and forth over the engraving singing, "*Papi, papi, papi, papi* . . . " to the tune of "Twinkle, Twinkle Little Star".

In that sacred moment, the hairs rose on Amy's arms. She felt Justin's spirit with them so strongly that she finally understood that he'd never really left the ones who loved him most.

And neither did Dad.

During the short drive back to her car, she kept reaching up and touching her medallion, making sure it was real and not one of her crazy dreams.

It's a miracle.

She worked on wrapping her brain around the idea. There was simply no other way to describe it. She found it hard to believe that instead of hating her, Maggie and Owen embraced her, empathized with her, and shared her loss.

But when she handed me a piece from my own past that I'd chucked into the ocean a week after Dad's funeral . . . She shook her head. *It's nothing less than a bona fide miracle.*

Later, after Amy finished evening chores, she stood with her arms propped on the fence of the pasture, watching Angel graze while she continued to finger the medallion.

"Amazing," she mused.

"Are you talking about Angel or what happened today?" Owen walked up behind her and placed his hands on her shoulders.

"Both, I guess."

"Now I understand why you took off on the Fourth of July when I told you about Justin." He stepped closer and lowered his voice. "But you have to know that I'd never hate you."

Thankful he didn't have a direct view of her burning cheeks, she tried to lighten the moment with a teasing tone. "Never say never."

"Never." He ran his hands up and down her arms. "So are you going to tell me about the necklace, or am I going to have to find out about that the hard way too?"

"You won't believe it."

"Try me."

"It's mine. It was a gift from my dad, but after he died I was so angry—at Dad, at God, at myself, at the whole world—that I stood at the end of a pier and threw it into the ocean. How it ended up at a flea market in Ohio is beyond me."

"And how, out of all the stuff there, Maggie just happened to find it, and then give it to you a year later. That really is amazing."

"Yeah. So I was thinking . . . "

"About?"

"If it was all right with you, maybe I'd go to church with you on Sunday."

"It's all right with me." He slid his hands down her arm, encircling her waist, and dropped his chin to her ear. "You know, Angel's not the only one who's come a long way since you got here."

Swooning from feeling his breath against her cheek, she leaned into him and closed her eyes, losing herself in his closeness, longing to be closer . . . until she felt a twitch just under her bellybutton.

Trying hard not to panic, she unhooked his hands and side-stepped out of his embrace. "Speaking of Angel, I need to bring her in, and then I'm going to retire for the night." She stretched and faked a yawn. "It's been a long day."

In the blink of an eye, Owen snatched her hand out of the air and reeled her in to him. "No more running, Amy." He ran his fingertips down the side of her face. "I told you to open your heart to the possibility of something good." He lowered his face so their lips were just inches apart, their breath mingling in the skinny space between them. "That includes love."

He leaned in and brushed his lips over hers like butterfly

wings on a delicate flower petal. Amy had read in a few books about a moment as beautiful as this, by far the sweetest moment of her entire life. Fireworks exploded in her soul. The core of her being burned with love for this man until flashbacks of her attack smothered the flame, morphing his gentle touch into hard blows and his delicious kiss into a disgusting act male dominance.

Her anxiety building, she pushed hard against him and worked to catch her breath. She pressed her fingertips against her forehead in a feeble attempt to get the images to stop. At the familiar sting of tears, she squeezed her eyes shut.

If I ever get past the trauma of the attack, I'll still have the end result. Once Owen finds out about this baby, he'll hate me for sure.

He examined her with tender eyes. "Are you okay?"

In all of her time in Iraq, she'd never been so petrified—to love him and to lose him. "I'm sorry, but this is moving really fast, and there are some things I still have to work out. I promise I won't run this time if you think you can just be patient."

His smile caused a small earthquake inside her and her legs nearly collapsed. Thankfully, he held his arms out to her just in the nick of time.

"Come here."

She fell into him soaking up the scent of his cologne, recording the rhythm of his breathing, memorizing the shape of the muscles in his shoulders and arms because she didn't know when or even if she'd ever be this close to him again.

His baritone voice near her ear sent shivers down her spine. "Take as long as you need. I'm not going anywhere."

That's what I was afraid of.

CHAPTER

Eighteen

On the last Sunday in September, a front moved through bringing dark skies, storms, and cooler temperatures. As Amy sat in an uncomfortable wooden pew, she thought it reflected her mood perfectly.

A big part of her gloomy attitude may have been due to the court date scheduled for the following day. She, Elijah, and Elizabeth had worked together through mediation to come up with a near perfect parenting plan that appeased everyone involved. Still the idea that she was going to legally give partial custody of her son to someone else when she was just beginning to feel like a parent struck a nerve.

But also her stormy spirit could've been directly related to Owen's absence. It was his weekend to work, and she could've dealt with that if she would've felt something, anything, during her last two visits. Instead, she'd sat there feeling detached and out of place. She'd expected something big to happen, something equivalent to Maggie handing her the long lost medallion and couldn't help being disappointed.

The pianist played a few introductory measures of "Great is Thy Faithfulness", a song Amy remembered well from her youth, and the entire congregation lifted their voices in song until the refrain reached the high, peaked beams above them. Amy closed her eyes and listened, remembering, longing.

Dad and I had a good life, even without mom. We had a dream. Our therapeutic equine program for disabled kids could have happened, but instead Dad didn't even get to see me graduate from high school. And that was just the beginning of a trip to hell and back that I never bought a ticket for. Her gaze fell to her lap. *In the process, I wandered so far away from the faith I once knew that I don't think I'll ever find my way back.*

With her spirit sagging under the weight of her shame, Amy grabbed her purse and waited for the right moment to make a break for it, but just as she was about to dart out of the pew, Maggie slipped in, blocking her exit. The hymn concluded and Pastor Ben made his way to the pulpit, while Amy tried to settle in for what was sure to be a long hour.

"Grace and peace to you from God our Father." He set his Bible on the wooden podium and pulled out a coffee cup from a shelf inside. "This week I had the pleasure of accompanying the seniors' group on an outing to East Liverpool in southern Ohio, which was at one time known as the Pottery Capital of the World. The folks at the Museum of Ceramics held a workshop where we all got to create a piece of pottery. My piece . . . ." he beamed with pride at the white mug with the Ohio State emblem painted in red, and then swiveled his gaze to the full sanctuary, " . . . didn't make it back with us. Apparently my talents don't involve pottery so I cheated and bought this in the gift shop." The congregation chuckled. "But as I sat there working with that ball of clay, I couldn't help thinking of all it could become—a mug, a vase, a bowl, anything. It reminded me of how God is actively shaping us into His perfect creation."

Pastor Ben set the cup on the podium, picked up his Bible, and flipped to a marked page. "Let me read to you Isaiah 64:8. It says, 'But now, oh Lord, You are our Father; We are the clay, and You our potter; And all we are the work of Your hand.' "

He closed his Bible and slipped it under his arm. "There are two truths that go along with this verse that I realized after having clay in my hands. First, to mold a piece of clay into something useful took some friction and pressure. I couldn't just barely set a finger on it and expect it to become something." He stepped off the altar and into the congregation. "Ladies and gentlemen, I know that many of you are hurting. I've heard your stories of lost loved ones, sudden unemployment, failed marriages, and struggling with addictions. I know that your heart may be feeling some friction or pressure right now."

Becoming increasingly uncomfortable, Amy fidgeted and dropped her gaze to her hands in her lap. It felt as though the pastor saw right through her, and she was determined to avoid making eye contact at all costs.

"Even though the times of trial hurt, don't lose hope. It's often what shapes your character and faith so God can use you for His purpose."

So God could use me? She crossed her arms and set her jaw. *No, thank you. I saw what happened when He used my dad.* Her shoulders fell. *Besides, why would He want me? I'm* . . . moisture gathered behind her lashes, . . . *nothing.*

"And if that isn't encouraging enough, understand that while the Potter is molding and shaping His clay, He never takes His hands off of it."

Very nice sentiment, but do these people really believe it? Amy swept her gaze in a big arc around the sanctuary and found

many congregants nodding. Others murmured amens and hal-
lelujahs, leaving her feeling like an outsider, like the only one
in a crowd who didn't get the punch line of a joke.

What am I missing here? Owen's suggestion from the barn
dance several weeks earlier came to mind. *Okay, let me try this
again.* Leaning forward, she opened her heart a crack and
tried to concentrate harder.

"Second, clay is clay. Dirty, messy, filthy, and sloppy. I
couldn't change that, but when I thought about everything it
could become, I really didn't care about the mess. In fact, the
bigger the mess, the more I looked forward to the result, and I
can't help but wonder if God views His creation in the same
way."

Creases of perplexity formed in Amy's brow. *Try seeing
with your heart instead of your eyes.* Remembering Maggie's
advice, she tuned Pastor Ben in more clearly.

"You see, John tells us a story about a woman who'd had
five husbands and was currently living with another to whom
she wasn't married. Sounds pretty messy, doesn't it? I imagine
she experienced pressure and friction in her heart. I'm guess-
ing that she felt a great deal of loss, shame, maybe rejection
and betrayal."

Heat rose up Amy's neck and settled in her cheeks. *He
might as well be talking about me.*

"Knowing all of this, Jesus came to her anyway. When she
was quite possibly at her lowest, He met her and took the time
to visit with her. He asked her for a drink of water, but according to the scriptures, He never got one. His purpose for stopping in the first place wasn't His thirst, but hers. Unlike
anyone else, He didn't care that she was a Samaritan or that
her past was questionable. Those were things she couldn't

change anyway. But Jesus cared deeply about her future. He believed in all that she could become. Folks, after experiencing Jesus, that woman not only gave her life to Him, but also led many from her city to be saved."

Just like that? She resisted the urge to stand up and argue with him. *But it's not that easy. It's certainly not practical, and it takes time when you have a special needs kid, not to mention one on the way that you don't know what to do with.*

"Human beings are sinful, messy people. God knows that. Most of us have a past. I'll be the first to admit I'm not too proud of some of the things I've done and said, and I'll be the first to tell you I'm so thankful He already made provisions for my mess. Listen, we all know John 3:16. The very next verse says, 'For God did not send His Son into the world to condemn the world, but that the world through Him might be saved.' Through His grace alone we receive what we messy humans don't deserve, and through His mercy, new every morning, we don't have to face all we do deserve."

Amy sat captivated, not expecting such a thorough ministering to her spirit.

"Hear me when I tell you it doesn't matter how big of a mess our lives have become because God sees past all that to everything we can become through Him."

Wanting to believe that somehow, someway, she could have a fresh start, Amy's demeanor softened. Still, she couldn't help being skeptical. *If it's so easy why doesn't everyone turn their life around?*

"There's just one thing we have to do. Unlike the ball of clay placed in my hands, we have to make the choice to accept Christ. If you already have, you know the peace that accompanies that decision. If you haven't yet, don't wait. Rest yourself in the Potter's hands and let Him work through your mess to mold and make you into more than you could imagine and everything He already sees." Pastor Ben spread his arms out and while the pianist softly began playing "What a Friend We Have in Jesus", he concluded, "The altar is open and all are welcome."

As several individuals and a few couples walked forward, Amy shrank lower in the pew, unable to make herself follow suit. She sneaked a glance at Maggie, who had her head bowed and hands folded.

Across the aisle, Steph watched misty-eyed as new believers and those recommitting their lives knelt together praying. Amy had to admit it was a beautiful scene, but it couldn't be that easy.

Or could it?

Desperate to find out, Amy slipped past Maggie, darted out the door at the back of the sanctuary, and continued through the heavy wooden church door. Once in the safety of the parking lot, she pulled out her cell phone and hit a number on her speed dial. After three rings the line picked up.

"Hi, Grandma. It's Amy. Can you please do me a favor?" Amy reached her car, unlocked it, and slid in.

"Sure, Honey. What do you need?"

"One of your Bibles. And I need it as soon as possible."

"I can ship it FedEx first thing tomorrow. Is everything okay, dear?"

Amy put the car in gear and pulled out onto the quiet street. "Yes. I just have some questions, and I need to find the answers. Thanks, Grandma. Our court date is tomorrow. I'll call you afterwards and let you know how it went."

"I'll be praying for you."

"I know you will. Give Grandpa a hug for me."

"I will. We love you."

"Same here." Amy hung up and sped off toward the farm. Only Angel could soothe her troubled mind now.

"Wait up, Elizabeth and Elijah."

Mingling with other church members on their way out after the service, Elizabeth and Elijah stopped and smiled at Sarah Ellsworth.

"Good morning." Elizabeth greeted her friend with a warm embrace. "Where's Tom?"

"He's rounding up the kids."

Elijah slid his arm across Elizabeth's shoulders. "That shouldn't be too hard. Your girls are angels."

Sarah chuckled. "I don't know about that, but he's not only gathering the twins. That's why I stopped you. I wanted to introduce you to our new foster child, Zander." A light skinned African American boy approached them, walking slowly as he played a handheld video game, Dominick by his side looking over his shoulder, and Tom a few steps behind with their seven-year-old identical blonde girls. "He'll be joining your Sunday school class next week."

Elizabeth smiled. "I see he's already made a friend, but then with Dominick that doesn't surprise me. It's nice to meet you, Zander."

The boy lifted his piercing topaz eyes and met hers for a fleeting moment. " 'Sup."

Dominick moved his hands, while Elizabeth put a voice to his words. "Zander is my new friend at school I was telling you about. He's in my class."

Sarah squeezed Dominick's shoulder. "Thanks for making him feel welcome. He was nervous about switching schools again."

A crease formed in Elizabeth's brow. "Again? Zander, how many times have you changed schools?"

He didn't bother to look up this time. "Eight."

"And you're in fourth grade?"

"Yep."

Unbelieving, Elizabeth glanced first at Sarah, and then Elijah who wore a knowing expression.

"Well, we're glad you're here now." Elizabeth's warm enthusiasm fizzled as it met Zander's cool stare.

Elizabeth thought about Zander off and on for most of the day. As planned, they took Dominick to an indoor water park in Cresthaven, and she wondered how often Zander experienced such a fun afternoon. Did he ever have a dad who played catch with him like Elijah often would? Did he have any real friends if he'd moved schools eight times in four years?

Later that evening, as she pored over a parenting magazine while eating a small bowl of Butter Pecan ice cream, she wondered how a woman could give her child up to foster care. Elizabeth already loved her baby with all her heart, and she'd grown to love Dominick just as much.

"I'm home." Elijah came in from dropping Dominick back off to Amy. He tossed his keys on the coffee table, leaned over, and kissed Elizabeth on the top of the head. "What are you thinking about?"

"Zander."

Elijah nodded. "I've been thinking of him too." He sat next to her on the sofa and she cozied into the crook of his arm.

"How does a kid adjust to being shuffled around like that?"

Elijah shrugged. "Some kids are lucky. They're placed in a good, stable home and don't have to be moved until their parents are able to care for them again."

She hesitated, unsure of how to proceed and finally deciding to tiptoe. "You know, you've never told me much about your experience in foster care."

"Because that's a dark time in my life, Elizabeth. I don't revisit it if I don't have to."

She prodded gently. "Were you a lucky one?"

He exhaled a heavy breath. "My folks liked to party. Once when I was about four or five years old, I remember having hunger pains so bad I couldn't sleep, and there wasn't a crumb in the cupboards. From my secret hiding place behind the couch, I watched my mom and dad drink and smoke pot while my stomach growled. When I was six years old, I got caught shoplifting a bag of chips and a carton chocolate milk, and that's when the Department of Human Services stepped in. By that time we'd been living on the streets for a few months. Before I knew it, I was being sent off to live with my grandma."

Elizabeth's eyes filled with tears. "I'm sorry." She squeezed his hand, wanting to somehow make up for his miserable childhood.

"When Grandma died a few years later, I went into the system, and by then I was mad as a hornet. It took a handful of families to find one that wouldn't give up on me."

"Mr. and Mrs. George?"

"Yes, and their son, Jeremy. He was several years older than me and every bit as much a mentor as his parents.

Though it took some time to take root, they were the ones who planted the seed of Christianity." Elijah wrapped his arms around her. "So to answer your question, no, but I'm blessed now and that's all that matters."

The Holy Spirit urged her on. "Have you ever thought of being a mentor like they were?"

He rubbed her flat belly. "Now that we have Dominick and a baby on the way, it'd be too much."

"True." Silence thick with thoughts and ideas filled the room for a long moment. "But what if it wouldn't be too much?"

Elijah leaned forward to search her face. "What is this all about?"

Elizabeth's bottom lip quivered. "I don't know. Maybe it's just my hormones, but maybe it's something more. When Sarah talked about having a foster child on top of her twins, she didn't make it sound like a burden, but a privilege, and it makes me sick to think there are kids out there not being taken care of." She clutched his hands. "Elijah, our home is plenty big enough, but more important, I know that my heart is big enough for another child."

"Elizabeth, are you sure? If we have a child placed with us and you decide it's too much, we'd be doing more harm than good. Do you understand that?"

She wasn't sure of anything except the fact that the Holy Spirit had laid this on her heart, and truthfully she wasn't a hundred percent sure about that. She believed that giving a child a chance was the right thing to do, but it was a huge decision, one in which they should maybe even include Dominick.

"I think I'll give Sarah a call and see if she's free one afternoon this week. I'd like to talk to her about her experience."

Elijah sank back into the sofa, exhaling deeply. "That's a good idea, but first thing's first. Let's focus on getting legal parental rights for Dominick. We can talk more about this after court in the morning."

Elizabeth nodded, but that night lying in bed, she couldn't think about Dominick or the baby she carried when she knew a child could be out there, possibly sleeping on the streets like Elijah had, desperate and hungry. Needing someone. Needing her.

CHAPTER
Nineteen

As Elizabeth sat on Sarah's front porch swing that sunny Wednesday afternoon, her heart danced with hope. The late September breeze carried a bit of a chill and caused her to smile.

Soon the leaves won't be the only thing changing in Harvest Bay. Excitement bubbled in her spirit like the effervescence from her glass of Sprite.

"Here we go." Sarah pushed open the screen door with her hip and joined Elizabeth on the porch, carrying a tall glass of iced tea in one hand and a large silver tray in the other. "I hope finger sandwiches and fruit salad are okay for lunch." She sat in a white wicker rocker adjacent to the swing and set the tray on a matching wicker table between them.

"Mmm. Sounds great." Elizabeth's stomach growled loudly as she helped herself to a small bowl of fruit.

Sarah washed down her small triangular sandwich with a drink of her tea. "So tell me how court went."

"It went as well as court could go, I suppose. Honestly, the whole ordeal was nerve wracking. Just stepping inside that building is intimidating. The paperwork was overwhelming, but it helped that Amy, Elijah, and I agreed on all terms. We met with the arbitrator and signed a Stipulated Joint Custody and Parenting Agreement, and that was that." Elizabeth grinned. "As soon as the judge signs the documents—hopefully by the end of the week—we'll legally be a part of Dominick's life."

"Aw, that's good. Dominick's a great kid."

Elizabeth laid her hand over her chest. "He's touched a place in my heart I never even knew existed."

Sarah nodded. "That's how I feel about the kids who come into my home. Each one teaches me something new about life and the human spirit."

"How many foster children have you had?"

"Zander is our sixth."

Elizabeth suddenly wished she'd thought to bring a pad of paper to take notes on. "Sarah, if you don't mind my asking, what made you and Tom want to become foster parents?"

"I don't mind at all." She set her glass on the tray next to the sandwiches and folded her hands in her lap. "I had a difficult pregnancy with the twins, and when they were born there were complications that made our chances of having more slim to none. We tried for a while, but it never happened.

"Now don't get me wrong, we felt blessed to have our girls, but despite all we'd been through with them, Tom and I both felt that we were meant to have more children. So we prayed together and handed it over to the Lord. Not long after that, we were tossing around the idea of adopting when a friend approached us about becoming foster parents. We contacted a caseworker for more information, and that got the ball rolling. Five years ago next month, we received our first foster child, a fourteen-year-old girl who was 2 months pregnant."

Elizabeth's hand flew to her mouth to cover the gasp that escaped her throat.

"Oh, Elizabeth, the stories are just heart breaking. The baggage these kids carry is unbelievable. Many have been abused in some way."

Zander's face filled Elizabeth's mind and moisture gathered behind her lashes at the thought of someone hurting him.

"I can't even begin to tell you how many tears I've cried over the kids we've cared for. I've hit my knees and pleaded the blood of Jesus over their lives and the lives of their families more times than I can count."

Serious second thoughts washed over Elizabeth like a tidal wave. "Then why in the world do you continue to do it?"

"To give them hope. To provide them with some stability and help them understand that the choices their parents made don't have to determine their future. Every kid deserves that chance." Sarah brought her folded hands up to her chin. "After we met our first foster child, it stopped being about me, my wants and needs. The focus shifted to these kids and what I can do to help them."

Elizabeth dropped her gaze to the last lonely grape in her bowl For years her whole life had revolved around her obsession with having a baby, while there were kids needing homes, needing to be loved.

"But more than anything else, to me being a foster parent is about showing kids real love—earthly and heavenly," Sarah continued. "These kids have such a warped idea of what love is. To them it's a one-sided, empty emotion because they've given it to parents who were unable to fully love them back."

Elizabeth shook her head. "I don't understand how a mother could not love her own child."

Sarah held up a finger. "Don't be so quick to judge. True, some of these parents have made bad decisions, but you never know what they've been through in their lives. History does tend to repeat itself, and not always, but often, these parents are products of the same lifestyle." Sarah reached for another sandwich. "It's really sad when you think about it."

As regret rained down on her and deep pity replaced her criticism of these parents, Elizabeth became more determined than ever to help them as well as their children. "So . . . how would one go about becoming a foster parent?"

"Well, first you'd contact an agency. You have to go through an interview process and fill out paperwork, then go through several hours of training, and have a home inspection. If you choose to, you can list preferences. For example, Tom and I will take children with severe disabilities, and for a short time we had a sweet boy with Mitochondrial Disease. You can choose not to accept kids with special needs, but, truthfully, every child comes with his or her own issues."

Sarah leaned forward. "Listen, Elizabeth, give it careful consideration. Talk with Elijah and Dominick about it. The whole family has to be onboard or you'll sink fast. Becoming a foster family is a big decision. It will try your patience. It may even try your faith at times."

"Has it tried yours?"

"I've had my moments."

"Do you regret it?"

"No. It's rewarding to plant seeds of faith, hope, and love in these children. I nurture them while I have them, and when they leave I trust the Lord to finish what I started, in His perfect timing. But also everything I've gone through with our foster kids has made me a better mom. It's made the girls appreciate things most kids take for granted, like full cupboards and closets. Since we became foster parents, Tom and I are a team. We have to work together or our home would fall apart. And my relationship with the Lord is stronger now than I've ever experienced in my adult life because I've had to rely on Him, meditate on His Word, and trust His promises like never before. Being a foster family definitely has its challenges, but it's been worth every minute of it."

Elizabeth smiled warmly at her friend. "Thanks for sharing, Sarah. You've given me a lot to think about."

Time grew wings and took flight as the two women visited. Before she knew it, Elizabeth had fifteen minutes to get home before the school bus dropped Dominick off. Fortunately Sarah only lived five minutes away.

She embraced Sarah and hurried to her car. As she backed out of the driveway, she was already praying for Elijah's receptivity to their becoming foster parents, for Dominick's adjustment, for the baby growing inside her. And for the safety of the foster child the Lord was going to bring to them.

Amy stared at the package on her kitchen counter. The FedEx courier had delivered it the day before, but Tuesday was one of her days with Dominick. The last thing she wanted was for him to see the Bible her grandmother sent and start asking questions that Amy couldn't answer. It'd kill her to let her son down again.

Now, with Dominick safely at his dad's for the next two days, she had no excuse. Sucking in a deep breath, she ripped the cardboard tab across the end of the box, tipped it up, and caught the Bible as it slid out. A piece of paper fluttered out and landed on top of the worn leather cover. Her eyes became misty as she recognized her grandmother's perfect penmanship.

My dear Amy,

Here you go. I hope you find what you're looking for.

Love you forever and always,
Grandma

"I hope I do, too." Amy hugged the Bible, a poor substitute for her grandmother, but as the strong scent of oranges laced with a hint of Sunday morning's White Diamonds wafted from the gold-rimmed pages, somehow she sensed the presence of the woman who had selflessly cared for her and her son. "The problem is that I don't know where to start looking."

For the sake of her sanity, she decided to view uncovering the truth about Christianity as a new mission and not the overwhelming, daunting task it seemed to be. Grabbing a small backpack from the coat hanger by the door, she loaded it with the Bible, her journal, a few snacks and a bottle of water, and headed out to the field.

Angel looked up from the patch of grass she was munching on as Amy slipped inside the pasture gate.

"It's okay, girl. It's just me."

Content, Angel returned to grazing while Amy set up camp near the fence and worked on coming up with a strategy.

"First things first. What facts do I already know?" Amy's shoulders fell. "None. There are no facts, just stories I've been told through the years."

The story of Jacob surfaced in her mind. Amy had always respected that Jacob figured out a way to get what he wanted, even if by dishonorable means. Now, however, she didn't know what to think about that attribute.

"He wrestled with God for his blessing, and though he ended up crippled, he still won." Amy exhaled an exasperated breath that ruffled her bangs. "But that's what doesn't make sense. Jacob was a liar and a cheat. He didn't deserve God's blessing."

Pastor Ben's words from the past Sunday echoed in her brain. *"Through His grace alone we receive what we messy humans don't deserve, and through His mercy, new every morning, we don't have to face all we do deserve . . . it doesn't matter how big of a mess our lives have become because God sees past all that to everything we can become through Him."*

Running her hand over the Bible, she shook her head. It seemed like the more she tried to figure it out, the more confused she became. But, like Jacob, she wouldn't give up that easily.

Taking a deep breath, she opened the leather cover to find not the table of contents as she expected, but a family tree. Thin and scrawny, it didn't have the impressive sprawling branches of some family trees, but it was hers and it filled her with pride. Her great grandparents, none of whom she knew, were listed at the top. Written under those names were her grandma and grandpa's names, each of their dates of birth and their anniversary.

"David Beauregard," she whispered.

Battling tears, she ran a finger over her dad's name wishing somehow she could feel him and hear his voice again. She seethed at her mom's name and swooned at her son's name. Staring at her own name, however, caused a complex mix of emotions to swirl in her heart.

"Amy Grace Beauregard, who are you and what is your purpose?" As expected, she received no answer from the pages of her grandmother's Bible. She sighed and moved to turn the page, but something caught her eye.

Set apart from the rest of the tree with a line attaching them to her grandmother were the words: *Baby Girl Whitlowe, born December 25, 1955.*

"Huh?" Creases of bewilderment formed on her brow as she reread the words. "This baby had Grandma's maiden name but no first name." Her heart sank at the thought that this baby was stillborn. "No, that's not right. There's no date of death like there is with my great grandparents." She stared harder. "Wait a minute. Grandma and Grandpa weren't even married until 1960."

Her eyes grew wide at the dawning. "Grandma must have had a daughter that she gave up. I wonder why no one told me. Did Dad know he had a sister? Does Grandpa even know?"

She glanced at the subtle roundness of her belly, her shoulders tense with her anxious spirit. "What was her situation? And, more important, did she ever regret it?"

She picked up her cell phone, determined to find out the truth, when the clank of the metal gate caused her to jump and fumble the phone. She cursed under her breath. After twelve weeks of therapy she'd hoped she wouldn't react like that to sudden noises anymore and she began to doubt if she'd ever be completely healed.

She stuffed the Bible back into the bag and glanced over her shoulder, brightening as her gaze landed on Owen. "Hey, this is a . . . " Then she noticed Kennedy and her smile wavered. " . . . surprise. I thought we were working with Angel later this evening." She transferred her gaze back and forth between Owen and Kennedy, her nerves on high alert. "What's up?"

Owen hooked his thumbs in his pockets. "It's time to transition Ken in as Angel's trainer."

"What? No."

Amy scrambled to her feet, a hard task after having the wind knocked out of her. She glanced at Kennedy.

"Look, no offense," then returned her hard stare to Owen, "but I've spent almost everyday for three and a half months working with this horse. You know that. You even said yourself that Angel needed me. How could you—"

"You're leaving any day now, right? Someone's got to continue what you've started and Ken trained both Dolly and Dixie." He nodded. "Don't worry. Angel will be in good hands."

Amy jabbed her finger at him and opened her mouth, but she snapped it shut when she realized that she didn't have an argument to stand on. She turned on her heel, crossing her arms in a huff, and watched Angel through blurred vision. Couldn't he see that to her Angel was more than a horse to be trained? Angel was determination and resilience and . . . hope.

Pulling herself together, she lifted her chin and narrowed her eyes. The bell sounded in her soul and the wrestling match began. Like Jacob, she might end up crippled, but she would win.

"That won't be necessary."

Owen stepped toward her. "What are you saying?"

Amy spun around to face him, finding a satisfied expression on his face that both infuriated and excited her. "I'm saying that I'm not going anywhere, and I'll be the one to continue her training." She reached down and snatched her backpack. "Now if you'll excuse me, I have to get ready for an appointment."

She brushed past them, slipped out of the gate, and rushed to her car. Halfway to the VA clinic she realized what she'd done. She'd doomed herself. Now that she was staying in Harvest Bay, the Sullivans' would find out her secret. The only questions that remained were: When and how?

Elizabeth repeated the same prayer throughout the rest of the afternoon and as she curled up in her bed that night. Hearing Elijah shut their bedroom door, she opened her eyes and uttered a silent amen.

"I'm sorry. I didn't mean to disturb you."

"It's okay." She set her Bible on the bedside table and propped herself up on her elbow. "Is Dominick settled in for the night?"

Elijah nodded and sat heavily on the edge of the bed his expression reflecting worry. "Have you ever felt like you were living someone else's life?"

Concern creased Elizabeth's brow. "What do you mean?"

"While we were at church this evening it all finally hit me. Less than four months ago I didn't even know that I had a son. Now we're a signature away from being Dominick's parents and seven months away from having a brand new baby."

"It's been a big adjustment, that's for sure, but our house feels more like a home with Dominick here." Sliding her hand across her belly she smiled. "Our baby and any other children we're blessed with will just add to it."

He shook his head. "Elizabeth, please. I can't think of any more kids. Between baseball, and boy scouts, diapers and formula, I don't know if I can handle two, let alone any more." He shoved his fingers through his hair. "Before we went to court . . . " He dragged a long breath out of his throat.

"What, Elijah?"

"I had an out, okay? Now I'm legally and financially responsible for that boy. And there's another one on the way. Everything's changing so fast. I don't know if I'm ready."

Her smile faded. "Elijah, I don't think anyone's really ready to become a parent. I guess you just have to do the best you can and trust the Lord for the rest."

"That's easy for you to say." Elijah pushed to his feet, crossed his arms, and walked the floor.

Elizabeth sat up in slow motion, raw fear gripping her heart. "Elijah, what's wrong? What's this all about?"

"Your parents are great. You've had the perfect examples to learn from. It's no wonder why you've always wanted to be a mother." He turned to her, holding his hands out. "I didn't have the greatest role models. What if . . . "

"No, Elijah. Don't even think it."

"I can't help it, Elizabeth. What if I turn out just like them?" He sank to the corner of the bed, his shoulders falling further. "What if I'm a failure in the one area that matters most?"

Crawling up behind her husband, Elizabeth wrapped her arms around his neck. "You won't be."

"How do you know?"

"Because I've seen you with Dominick." She leaned around him and directed his gaze to meet hers. "You're one of the kindest, most thoughtful and loving people I know, and above all else, you're a dedicated Christian. That's how I know you won't fail."

He jerked his chin out of her grasp, mumbling so low she could barely hear him. "Being a Christian doesn't automatically make someone a good parent." Shrugging out of her loose embrace, he stood. "I'm going to take a shower." He strode into their bathroom.

Her gaze followed him until he shut the door, leaving her spirit throbbing. A minute later, she heard the water running and slunk back to her place on the bed.

What just happened here? Did I bring on Elijah's uncertainties when I asked him about his experience as a foster kid? He told me it was a dark time in his life and he didn't like to revisit it, but I pushed him.

Heavy with disappointment, she slumped against her pillows. *If he's overwhelmed by Dominick and our baby, he'll never consider having a foster child. Maybe I didn't sense the Holy Spirit after all.*

She imagined the child she'd been praying for and tears streamed down her face as deep despair filled her heart. *But then why does it hurt so badly to let go of a child I've never met?*

CHAPTER

Twenty

By late Saturday afternoon, the deep concern that continued to gnaw at Elizabeth's spirit caused her to ache all
over.

*It's just not like Elijah to come all undone. He's usually the
one holding me together, but he made it sound like he doesn't even
want this baby.*

Her abdomen knotted at the thought, and tightened even
more when she considered that he still hadn't snapped out of
his mood. While Dominick played his handheld video game
and ate a snack at the table, she leaned against the kitchen
counter, chewing on her lip and wracking her brain for an
explanation of this change in her husband.

Dominick interrupted her thoughts by dropping his dishes
in the sink with a loud clatter. Elizabeth started and snapped
her attention to him.

"Sorry," he signed.

She used her fingers to spell, "OK," just as the doorbell
reverberated through the house. Signing, "They're here," she
started toward the door, but Dominick beat her there, threw
it open, and greeted their visitors with gusto.

Elizabeth came up behind him, forcing a smile at Sarah
and her three kids. Wednesday afternoon when they visited

together, Elizabeth had thought watching the kids so Sarah and Tom could have a date night was a good idea. Now, however, she wasn't so sure.

"Hey, guys. Come on in."

With a wave good-bye, the kids tore off to Dominick's room while Sarah remained in the foyer, eyeing Elizabeth. "Are you okay? You really don't have to do this."

"I'm fine, just a little achy today." Elizabeth rubbed the back of her neck. "I want to keep the kids for you. You and Tom deserve a night out, especially now that's it football season, and I happen to know that my brother-in-law works his assistant coaches almost as hard as his players."

Sarah stepped out onto the porch. "Thank you, Elizabeth. We'll be back to get them between nine and ten o'clock."

"Don't mention it." Elizabeth shooed her down the steps. "Now go have fun."

After Sarah drove out of sight, Elizabeth shut the door and headed upstairs, her lower back aching more with every step she climbed. "This stress can't be good for me. I have to just let go of it." But as she stood in the doorway of Dominick's room and watched Zander laugh and play like any other child, the longing for her own foster child returned.

She'd learned from her deep desire to have a baby that obsessing over it would only make the situation worse. Instead, she vowed to try to be patient. If the Holy Spirit moved her, He could move Elijah, too. It might take a miracle—she'd never seen Elijah so distraught—but the Lord worked miracles every day. And in the meantime, she'd pray like never before.

She moved into the room and sat on a corner of Dominick's bed. "Don't get too comfortable in here. We're going to the park to have a picnic. Maddie and Chloe are going to join us there."

Later, as Elizabeth loaded all four children, a full picnic basket, and a king-sized quilt into her Mountaineer, a familiar black truck pulled up beside her. She brightened as Uncle Bill approached carrying a large Tupperware container, and greeted him with a hug.

He handed her the container. "I see you're heading out. I won't keep you. Just wanted to bring you some melon from the garden, already sliced."

"Nonsense. You're just in time. This melon will be perfect for our picnic, but it won't be the same without you. What do you say? Join us?"

Bill glanced inside the SUV at the four young faces staring back at him with hopeful expressions.

Elizabeth grinned with satisfaction as she watched him melt before her eyes. His soft spot for kids was one of the many things she loved about him.

"Well, Wilma's out with her prayer group so I'm on my own for dinner tonight. A picnic sounds like fun." He gave a nod. "All right. You talked me into it."

They climbed into their separate vehicles and motored to Ashford Park. Kate, Adam, Chloe, and Madeline had already arrived, staking claim to a spot near the small Ashford Lake with a clear view of the playground.

Dominick and Zander dashed to an open area to play some catch, while the twins rushed to visit with Madeline and Chloe. Elizabeth strolled along with Uncle Bill, partly because she enjoyed his company and his peaceful spirit, but also because her body was too sore to hurry.

"Hey, Uncle Bill," Kate greeted as they neared. "This is a nice surprise."

Uncle Bill chuckled. "For me, too. Your sister over here is a good arm twister."

Winking at Elizabeth, Kate embraced Uncle Bill. "True, but she comes by it naturally."

Elizabeth spread out her quilt next to Kate's and took a seat, trying to mask her discomfort. "I didn't twist anybody's arm, but this baby is going to twist something of mine if I don't eat."

Retrieving her picnic basket, Kate knelt on the quilt and began laying out its contents. "You go right ahead and feed that baby. We can wait for Elijah."

Elizabeth stared at Kate, afraid to tell her perfect sister that her life had gone a bit haywire. Working to keep a nonchalant expression on her face, she waved her hand.

"He had to run in to the office to take care of some paperwork and doesn't know when he'll be able to join us. He wouldn't want you to wait."

Kate hesitated. "Are you sure?"

Avoiding her sister's penetrating gaze, Elizabeth nodded.

Kate wiped off her hands on a napkin and stood. "Well then let's gather up the troops, say grace, and dig in."

As soon as Kate announced it was time to eat, the hungry children came running and found a piece of quilt to sit on. Uncle Bill blessed the meal, then he and Adam took their plates to a nearby picnic table. Elizabeth and Kate helped the kids fill their plates and get settled before loading up their own.

Elizabeth skillfully spread out a small amount of food on her plate, hoping to create the illusion that she was satisfying a healthy appetite. Nothing could have been further from the truth. With so much on her mind, there didn't seem to be any room left in her stomach. She pushed the food around on her plate, taking a bite here and there.

Growing weary of the charade but not wanting to answer any difficult questions, she pushed to her feet, disregarding the need to wince at the spasm in her back. Swiping Madeline's soccer ball, she strolled to the open field and juggled the ball between her feet and knees.

"Elizabeth, what are you doing?" Kate's maternal side emerged. "I thought you needed to eat."

"We have all afternoon to eat. My doctor said exercise is good for both me and the baby, and I can do anything I did before getting pregnant including playing a game of backyard soccer with some kids." Elizabeth held the ball between her arm and her hip. "Who's in?"

"Are you kidding?" Kate popped to her feet and dashed ahead of Elizabeth calling over her shoulder, "I may be a bit rusty, but I'll take you on any day."

Elizabeth's lips curling in a satisfied grin, she pressed a hand against her back to fight off the dull constant ache and hurried to join them.

They split up the teams so that Kate had Dominick, Madeline, and Haley, the bigger twin, leaving Elizabeth with Zander, Chloe, and Bailey. They found trees to mark the goals and Adam and Uncle Bill strolled over to referee. As the teams took their places, Adam placed two fingers in his mouth and started the game with a loud whistle.

Kate's team got the ball first. Dominick dribbled it toward the designated trees and passed it to Madeline. Getting into position, Madeline booted it hard, only to have it blocked by

Zander. Elizabeth whooped and gave him a high five, her heart swelling at the pleased expression on his face.

Zander passed the ball to Chloe, who dribbled it down their makeshift field until Madeline swooped in and swiped it away. She kicked it hard, but too prematurely, and it rolled to a stop at Bailey's feet.

"Kick it, Bay!" Elizabeth shouted.

Concentrating, the seven-year-old balled up her fists and hauled her foot back. But just before she made contact, Dominick lunged forward, stealing the ball and making a break for the unguarded goal.

Elizabeth, closer to the goal, raced and beat him there, bracing to make the save. Dribbling the ball side to side, Dominick eyed her and sized up the goal.

"Shoot it!" Madeline called, forgetting he couldn't hear her.

Elizabeth crouched with her hands up, trying to predict where he'd aim.

"Elizabeth!" a voice called out from a distance.

"Elijah?" Straightening, she turned and spotted him at the edge of the parking lot. She lifted a hand to wave at the exact moment that Dominick fired the shot.

With no time to react, the ball hit her square in the stomach. Hugging her middle, she staggered back a step, and then sank to her knees. She glanced up as everyone rushed toward her, but she could only see the horrified expression on Dominick's face. Taking a few deep breaths, she resolved to protect her stepson.

Dominick slid to a stop next to her as if sliding into home plate, and his fingers started flying. "I'm so sorry. Are you OK? Is baby OK? I'm so, so sorry."

Elizabeth reached out and stilled his hands. Giving him a weak smile, she signed, "I'm OK."

With the happy sounds of the park adding a surreal effect to the moment, she scanned the worried faces surrounding her. It was up to her to ease the tension. She closed her eyes for a split second, summoning all her strength.

"Just for the record, I made that save."

Adam helped her up just as Elijah reached her out of breath. "Elizabeth! Are you all right?" Before she could respond, he turned to Dominick. "What were you thinking?"

Elizabeth touched his forearm. "It wasn't his fault."

Elijah shrugged her off, took a step toward Dominick, and pointed an accusing finger at him. "You know better than to throw or kick a ball at someone who's not looking."

Elizabeth's heart broke as she watched the look of guilt on Dominick's face morph into a fearful expression. Fighting off the sting of angry tears, she slipped an arm around her stepson's shoulders.

"Elijah, I was looking until you called my name."

Elijah planted his hands on his hips and stared at her, unbelieving. "Are you implying this is my fault? You shouldn't have been out here playing soccer in the first place."

Ever the peacemaker, Uncle Bill stepped between them and put his hand up, palm facing out. "Now, hang on, Elijah. I think Elizabeth is trying to say that this was an accident. No one's to blame." His gentle, unassuming voice smoothed some of the ruffled feathers between them.

Elijah's shoulders fell. His demeanor softened, but Elizabeth could tell that the sliver that'd been festering in his spirit for three long days didn't budge. "I'll be at home. We can talk more about this there." With that he turned on his heel and stalked off.

When he was out of earshot, Kate leaned closer. "What was that all about?"

Elizabeth sighed. The cat was out of the bag that she didn't have a perfect marriage. Now to cover up the reason why.

"He's been under quite a bit of stress at work—too many clients and not enough PTs." At least, she hoped that was the cause of his moodiness. "Between that, going to court for Dominick, and having a baby on the way, he's had a lot on his mind. Don't hold today against him."

Adam nodded. "I understand that. He'll be okay. Just give him time to blow off some steam."

"Thanks. I'm sure that's all he needs." Another lie. Shame colored her cheeks at the realization of how easily she could rip off a fib. "I don't mean to be a party pooper, but I'm going to head home and try to relax."

Alarm flashed in Kate's eyes. "Are you sure you're okay?"

"I'm fine. A little sore, but fine."

"Why don't you let the kids stay here with us for a while? You'll be able to rest better." Kate paused. "If nothing else, it'll give you and Elijah some time to talk."

Elizabeth knew her sister meant well, but at that moment her tone seemed condescending. Still, an hour or so of peace and quiet to curl up in her bed, enjoy a cup of her favorite tea, and get lost in a good book sounded like heaven.

"It's fine with me if it's okay with them."

The kids cheered, and Elizabeth translated to Dominick what was going on. "Have fun, behave, and I'll see you in a bit." She turned to leave but he reached out and snatched her hand.

With puppy dog eyes, he signed, "I'm really sorry."

Elizabeth pulled him to her and held him. After a long moment she stepped back and signed, "Stop beating yourself up. It was not your fault, okay? I love you very much. Now quit worrying about me."

"Not just you. Baby, too."

With her back screaming at her, Elizabeth bent over to look Dominick in the eyes. "Your brother or sister is fine."

His frown eased a bit. "How do you know?"

Her heart squeezed with hidden uncertainties that her smile masked well. "I'm a nurse. I know these things, but would it make you feel better if I went to the doctor first thing Monday morning?"

His lips curled upward and he nodded.

"You've got it." She rustled his hair. "Now go have fun."

As he ran off with Zander, Elizabeth waved good-bye to Kate, Adam, and Uncle Bill and walked with gingerly steps to her vehicle. Once inside, she started the engine and broke down.

"Oh, God, it hurts. My back is sore, and now my stomach is tender, but my heart is breaking."

A sob escaped her throat as she rested her head on the steering wheel and let the emotion flow. After the tears slowed, she gathered herself together and put the Mountaineer in gear.

"Please show me how to help my husband before it's too late."

After Saturday evening chores, Amy climbed up on a couple bales of hay stacked just outside the stable door, the perfect spot to watch the sunset over the hay field. Leaning against the wall, she tried to relax, but her thoughts drifted to her grandmother and this newly discovered information regarding her past.

"I could have an aunt out there somewhere." The thought almost made her mouth water. Her craving for a mother figure had eased up some since she'd grown closer to Anna. However, the longing still ate through her heart like a worm through an apple, remaining unnoticed until someone took a bite.

This news was a very big bite.

She flipped her phone over and over between her fingers. If her grandmother had kept this secret for so long, it was bound to be a touchy subject, and she certainly didn't want to hurt the woman who had done the best she could to be everything Amy, and later Dominick, needed.

"But she hurt me by not telling me." Jutting out her chin in defiance she punched a key on her cell phone twice and held it to her ear as it started to ring.

"Hello?"

Amy's heart hammered in her chest. Soon she'd receive some of the answers she'd been searching for.

"Hey, Grandma. I got the package you sent."

"Oh, that's good. Did you have a chance to look through it?"

"That's what I'm calling you about. You know the family tree inside the front cover?" Amy hesitated, unsure if she was more afraid of asking the question or of her grandmother's reaction. "Well, it says that you had a baby girl in December of 1955, but I don't recall you ever mentioning that you had a daughter."

Silence filled the radio waves between them.

Amy checked her phone to make sure the call hadn't been dropped. "Grandma?"

"I'm here. I knew this call would come. I thought I was ready to tell you, but . . . " A deep sigh filled Amy's ear. "What you read is true."

Not knowing whether to laugh or cry, Amy did a little of both. "Grandma, I can't believe this. Who is she? Where is she? What happened?"

"Whoa, Amy. One question at a time, please. Unfortunately, the only question I can answer is the last one."

Amy waited, making note that her grandmother had said "unfortunately" and wondering what exactly she was referring to.

"I had a crush on my older brother's best friend. He was getting ready to head off to the military. We were both scared—he of leaving our small town, me of never seeing him again. He made the suggestion, and I just went along with it. I discovered a month later I was pregnant."

Amy had a hard time imagining her grandmother so spontaneous, so rebellious . . . so much like herself. "What did he say?"

"He never knew about it. He'd already been gone for a few weeks by the time I found out, and he never came back to stay long enough for me to tell him. Several times I wrote him a letter, but I couldn't get up the courage to mail them. About ten years later he was killed in Vietnam. By then your grandpa and I were married, living here, and helping his parents' run the orchard. Your dad was toddling around the house, and I was very happy, but I still couldn't forget."

"I'm so sorry, Grandma."

Somehow after all these years, Amy felt a new bond form-ing with this woman who for the longest time she'd believed couldn't possibly understand anything she'd been through. But she'd been wrong.

As the sun sank lower, an invisible paintbrush streaked different pinks and oranges across the sky and Amy hoped it was as marvelous for her grandmother. "What did you do?" she asked finally.

"There wasn't much I could do. I was fifteen and this was the 1950s. After I told my parents, Dad sent me to live with my great aunt in the middle of nowhere until the baby came. I went into labor on Christmas Eve and delivered her on Christmas morning. The nurse was kind-hearted enough to tell me I'd had a girl and give me a glimpse of her perfect little face before they took her away to her awaiting parents."

Amy clutched her chest, feeling as though her heart exploded. "How awful! I can't imagine what that must have felt like." Even as she said it, she realized that her future might hold a similar experience. She swallowed the anxiety balling up in her throat. "Do you regret it?"

"Regret, no. I knew I'd done the right thing. I couldn't have given her the kind of life a child deserves. I was only a child myself. But to this day I miss her. I think about her all the time, especially on the twenty-fifth of each month. I pray for her night and day, that she's happy and healthy, that some-how she knows that I love her."

Tipping her head back against the barn, Amy felt silent tears slide into her ears. "So you don't know her name or where she is? Have you ever tried to find her?"

"I started to once, but I realized that I was searching out of my own selfishness. The second chapter in Philippians warns against doing anything through selfish ambition and instructs Christians to look out for the interests of others."

Amy's blood started simmering. "I can't believe that you of all people would use scripture to support your decision to not look for your own daughter. Did you ever consider the interests of your son? Don't you think Dad would've liked to know that he had a sister?"

"Amy—"

With her voice wavering, Amy plunged forward. "Or what about me? When Mom took off, you were the only woman in my life, and I'm thankful for that, but there were times, especially in my teen years, when I could have used another mother figure."

The radio waves carried soft sniffling to Amy's ear and guilt gripped her heart. "Grandma, I'm sorry. I didn't mean . . ."

"No, Amy. You're right to be upset. All these years I convinced myself I was protecting your dad, you, and even your grandpa, but I was really protecting myself. It hurt so badly to lose her once, I didn't know what I'd do if I found her and she rejected me. Forgive me?"

A fluttering just to the right of her bellybutton caused a powerful tidal wave of emotion to crash over Amy. "There's nothing to forgive, Grandma. I'm the one who should be asking for your forgiveness, but I just wish you would have told me about this sooner. You have no idea how it would have helped me."

"Well, I really wanted to tell you in person, but God's timing is perfect. When you said you needed a Bible, I knew in my heart that was the one."

Strokes of lavender and navy now colored the sky, concealing the waterfall that cascaded down Amy's cheeks and pooled in her lap.

"So, are you finding the answers you're looking for?"

"Not yet, but I think I'm getting closer." She wiped her face and took a shaky breath. "Speaking of which, I'd better get off of here. Sunday morning comes extra early when I have to get chores done before church."

"It's so good to hear you say that. I love you, Amy."

"Love you, too. Give Grandpa a hug."

They hung up, and Amy stared into the twilight. The mystery of Baby Girl Whitlowe had been solved, but her personal dilemma remained unanswered. New questions swirled in her mind, leaving her dizzy and even more confused.

Could she go through what her grandmother had experienced in order to give this baby to someone who truly wanted him? Or could she somehow learn to love this baby? And most important, could she live with her decision?

CHAPTER
Twenty-one

E ggshells were never meant to be walked on. Elizabeth
fully understood that after spending the rest of the
weekend pussyfooting around Elijah.

Monday morning, rocking gently in a pale yellow glider
in her obstetrician's cozy waiting room, she heaved a weary
sigh. *I guess I can't help him if he doesn't want to help himself.*

Frustration burned inside her. She'd bent over backwards
for him. Couldn't he at least lean a little in her direction?

One thing she knew for sure. Elijah's attitude didn't
change her new-found desire to become a foster parent. If
anything, his standoffish behavior fueled her fire. *I can't
change Elijah's past, but maybe I could change a child's future. I
could be the one to make a difference.*

A cheerful nurse in turquoise scrubs appeared in the
entrance to the hallway. "Elizabeth, you can come on back."

Elizabeth's mood lightened as she shifted her focus from
her distant husband to her little dream come true and followed the nurse to an examining room. After checking her
blood pressure and jotting down the information, the nurse
left Elizabeth to fantasize about filling her arms with the
swaddled, sweet-smelling, bundle of love. She imagined tying
bows in the baby's little tufts of hair and dressing her in frilly

outfits. Or maybe she'd have a little boy to dress in sporty shirts and overalls with pockets that he'd one day stuff frogs into.

She envisioned long walks in the park with the baby in a stroller. Maybe on days when they had Dominick, he would walk alongside her, helping to push. Or maybe he'd ride his bike in big long loops around them.

Contentment bloomed in her spirit when she pictured all the Thanksgivings, Christmases, Easters, and birthday parties in her future. Her home would be as full as her heart. Tears pooled in her eyes to think about her next Mother's Day. The holiday that had been physically painful would now contain more joy than she ever could have imagined.

A soft tap on the door returned her focus to her appointment. "Good morning, Elizabeth." Dr. Davis entered the room and flipped through her chart. "It says here you got hit with a soccer ball?"

"Yes. Saturday evening. It was just a fun game of backyard soccer with my stepson, nieces, and some of their friends. I wouldn't have even come in today except that I promised Dominick I would for his piece of mind."

"Well, that's as good a reason as any." Dr. Davis set the file folder aside. "Have you had any abdominal soreness or cramping since then?"

"I was a little tender right after it happened, but by Sunday morning I felt fine."

He patted the examining table. "Go ahead and lie back." Standing at the small sink, he washed his hands and dried them on a paper towel. "How have you been feeling otherwise?"

"Good. I had some lower back pain last week, but it's better now too."

"I see." Dr. Davis retrieved an electronic device and squirted some clear gel on what resembled a small microphone. "Did you lift something heavy or do something to strain your back?"

Hiking her shirt up past her bellybutton, Elizabeth shook her head. "I don't think so, but I've been pretty tense lately. I probably pulled a muscle without knowing it."

"This might be a little cold." Dr. Davis set the rounded, gooey end of the microphone on her skin and, right on cue, Elizabeth sucked in a sharp breath. "Now let's see if we can get a heartbeat."

Her own heart dancing at the thought of hearing her baby's, Elizabeth strained to catch a steady beating rhythm.

After a moment of picking up nothing but the whoosh of her insides, Dr. Davis moved the Doppler to another area of her abdomen and paused to listen. A few seconds later, he shifted it again, and then again.

Rising panic stifled the dancing inside her chest. "What's wrong?"

Dr. Davis slid the Doppler to another area and waited while the whooshing continued.

"Why isn't it picking up the baby's heartbeat? Is the machine broken?"

Dr. Davis picked up the handle of the Doppler and cleaned the rounded end. "No, it's not broken." He gave her a paper towel to wipe the goop off her belly. "Don't worry. Ten weeks is still a little early." He sat on the rolling stool and returned to her chart. "And with your history of irregular cycles, it's likely that your dates are off and you're not as far along as we think." He closed the file folder, tucked it under his arm, and stood. "I'm going to send you down to radiology for an ultrasound. They'll take measurements and give us an accurate indication of where you are in this pregnancy."

Elizabeth pushed herself to a sitting position. "Will they check to make sure nothing happened to the baby when I got hit with the ball?" She needed the reassurance for Dominick and now herself, too.

He strode to the door. "Absolutely. Let me give the techs a call to let them know that you'll be on your way. If there are no visible concerns on the ultrasound, I'll just see you back here for your next scheduled visit."

If? Elizabeth managed a wobbly smile and Dr. Davis disappeared into the hallway.

That little insignificant word haunted her as she left his office and waited for the elevator. *Of course there won't be any visible concerns. There can't be anything wrong. I've waited so long for this baby. I prayed and fasted and prayed some more. Surely God will keep this baby safe and healthy. He just has to.*

When the doors opened with a ding, she stepped inside and pushed the button for the first floor, hoping she wouldn't run into anyone she knew, most especially Nathan. She thought she might explode if she saw him and his condescending expression now while in such a frazzled state. Thankfully, the elevator didn't stop to let anyone else on, the doors opened on the first floor, and she made a beeline for radiology.

Elizabeth checked in with the receptionist, and then found a quiet corner in the waiting room to pass the minutes. The hard plastic chairs and drab walls added to her discomfort as she fought hard against mounting anxiety. Rubbing her forehead with her thumb and index finger, she considered her situation.

Okay. Let's think about this rationally. No, I didn't plan on having an ultrasound today, but by having it done, I'll know with one hundred percent certainty that everything's okay. And I'll actually get to see my baby. A little bubble of excitement started at her toes and floated up her body, lifting the corners of her mouth as it passed by. *I'll actually get to see her.*

The bubble reached her brain and popped, her small smile falling, as she thought about Elijah. Wishing she could share that moment with him, she felt a heavy cloud of loneliness settle on her. *I wish I could share a lot with him. Dear God, what happened to the closeness we once knew? And will we ever get it back?* Her eyes grew damp. *I miss him.*

"Elizabeth? Are you ready for your ultrasound?"

Elizabeth turned toward the friendly female voice, her gaze landing on Julie, a tech she knew from high school, and she almost cried with relief. Surely the young mother would put all her worries to rest.

Elizabeth rose and offered her friend a smile. "Now I am."

"Well then, come on back." Julie led Elizabeth down a short hallway to a room where a high-tech computer with several knobs and wires sat on a large stand next to the examining table. "Hop up here and we'll get started in just a minute."

Elizabeth climbed onto the table, leaned back, and lifted her shirt again. "Hey, Julie, how common is it for the doctor to not find a heartbeat at ten and a half weeks?"

Julie began typing information into the computer. "Well, at ten and a half weeks, it should be detectable, but it's pretty common for women who have irregular cycles to think they are farther along than they really are." Julie dimmed the lights, squirted clear gel on Elizabeth's belly, and pressed a little rectangular mouse to her skin. "But we're going to clear that up right now."

Elizabeth gasped as she watched a picture appear on the computer screen.

"This is your amniotic sac." Julie shifted the mouse. "And this is your baby."

"Oh," Elizabeth breathed. Tears sprang to her eyes. The image was so tiny and odd looking, but she could easily make out the baby's head, and stumpy little arms and legs. "She's beautiful."

"Just like her mommy." Julie winked at Elizabeth. "Now let's get some measurements. First, we'll record the heartbeat."

Elizabeth watched Julie move the cursor over the baby's midsection, preparing herself to hear the heavenly rhythm of her baby's heart. But after a long moment of silence, she glanced at Julie.

"Why can't I hear the heartbeat?"

Julie's chipper expression had changed. Creases of concern crossed her brow as she double checked the switches and wires, and then returned her focus to the screen.

"Let me try this angle."

Elizabeth waited, her tears of joy transforming into liquid fear, her heart squeezing tighter with each silent second that passed. *Please find it. It's there. It has to be.*

Finally Julie turned to her with deep sorrow in her eyes. "I'm so sorry, Elizabeth. There's no heartbeat."

Elizabeth's heart screeched to a stop. All of her breath escaped from her lungs. "A-are you sure?"

Julie nodded and grabbed Elizabeth's hand. "I'm so sorry."

Those three words blew a hole through Elizabeth's emotional dam, and she began to wail. "No, dear God! Not my baby, please!"

Julie sat beside her and held her hand until her weeping subsided. After a while, she handed Elizabeth a box of tissues and solemnly returned to the computer.

Elizabeth sniffed. "What are you doing?"

"I still have to take some measurements. This will tell Dr. Davis exactly when the miscarriage occurred."

Miscarriage. The word caused a fresh stream of tears to flow down the sides of Elizabeth's face and land in the pool of hair on the hospital pillow. *This can't be happening. I saw the baby right there on the screen. She was perfect. How can there be no heartbeat?*

Her thoughts shifted to Dominick and a sob escaped her throat. *He was so worried. How am I going to tell him?* She realized that her sensitive stepson would immediately blame himself. He'd kicked the soccer ball. *But it's not his fault. I should have known better than to play . . . And I wouldn't have gotten hit if Elijah hadn't called my name. If anyone is to blame it's . . .*

"According to these measurements, Elizabeth, the sac is ten weeks old, but the baby only measures eight weeks."

Elizabeth scrunched her forehead. Amidst the fog of grief that had settled in her brain, she could hardly remember her name, let alone make sense of medical jargon.

"What does that mean?"

"Well, it appears that your pregnancy ended two weeks ago."

"Two weeks ago?" In her mind, she combed through the events that had taken place in that time frame. "But

I didn't do anything that might have hurt the baby then."

Julie handed Elizabeth a damp washcloth to wipe the goo off her belly. When she spoke, her gentle voice held a matter of fact tone.

"Sometimes it just happens." She helped Elizabeth sit up. "There's no reason or explanation. No one's to blame. It doesn't make sense, but it happens just the same."

Elizabeth dropped her head into her hands as another heavy wave of grief crashed over her. "I want my baby."

Julie slipped an arm around Elizabeth's shoulders, allowing Elizabeth to lean into her. "I know."

After several minutes, Elizabeth straightened and wiped her face with a tissue. "So what happens now?"

"I sent all of the images I collected from the ultrasound to our radiologist, who will call a report in to Dr. Davis. Take as much time as you need here. Feel free to call your husband or anyone else. Whenever you're ready, I'll walk you back to Dr. Davis' office, and he'll discuss your options with you." Julie moved to the door and paused. "I truly am sorry, Elizabeth."

Unable to force words past the big wad of emotion lodged in her throat, Elizabeth only nodded. Julie slipped into the hallway and pulled the door shut, leaving Elizabeth alone to process the overwhelming news.

Her baby—her son or daughter—was gone. In an instant, her lifelong dream had evaporated. Elizabeth would never know what color hair and eyes this little angel had. She'd never hear her baby say "Mama," or watch with pride as her little one took those first shaky steps. She would never fill her arms with this precious child and sing bedtime lullabies. There'd be no walks in the park or birthdays to celebrate.

Elizabeth's bottom lip quivered at the thought of enduring another childless Mother's Day. Her answered prayer had bounced like a bad check, leaving her more desperate than before.

"Why would God give me my deepest desire only to snatch it right back?"

As she tried to wrap her brain around her revoked blessing, her cell phone rang from inside her purse on a counter near the door. She climbed down from the table and crossed the room on weak knees to answer it. Her phone blurred behind unshed tears when she read Elijah's name on the caller ID. Now this nightmare would become reality.

She swallowed hard against the rising lump in her throat and pushed the green button. "Hello?"

"Hey. I had a second in between clients and since I hadn't heard from you I thought I'd better call to see how the doctor appointment went."

Elizabeth opened her mouth but her voice drowned in the silent river of tears and her words floated away.

"Hello? Elizabeth?" He paused for half a second. "Look, I don't have time—"

"I lost the baby, okay?" She burst out and broke down. "Dr. Davis sent me to have an ultrasound. I saw the baby, Elijah. Her round little head and tiny arms and legs . . . she looked perfect, but there was no heartbeat."

He took his turn at being speechless. When he finally recovered, his words stumbled. "May-maybe they . . . maybe they made a mistake. Y-you can get a second opinion."

Elizabeth didn't think it was possible to be any more miserable, and yet somehow she sank even further in her pit of despair. "There was no mistake."

"It wouldn't hurt—"

"Stop. Please don't make this more difficult than it already is." She inhaled a long shaky breath. "Now I have to go talk to Dr. Davis about my next step, and I'd really like to have you here with me."

"Okay. I'll get there as soon as I can."

Too numb to care either way, Elizabeth pushed the red button to end the call and tossed her phone back into the purse. Her heart limped along like a wounded soldier. She'd lost her baby, her marriage seemed to be headed in that direction, and she simply had to find a way to survive. Operating on autopilot, she gathered her belongings, opened the door, and met Julie in the hallway.

"I was just coming to check on you. Did you have enough time?"

"Yes."

"All right, then. Dr. Davis' office is expecting you. Let's head up the back way." Julie walked with her through the hallways reserved for doctors, avoiding high traffic areas and waiting rooms.

When they reached Dr. Davis' office, his nurse took over and led Elizabeth to a room. "Will your husband be joining us?"

"I think so. He shouldn't be long. He's a physical therapist here at the hospital so he just has to rearrange his schedule."

"I'll watch for him and let Dr. Davis know when he arrives."

"Thanks."

The minutes dragged on. Elizabeth stood and paced for as long as her rubbery legs would hold her. The longer she waited in that examining room the angrier she became.

Why couldn't he drop everything? He should be here by now.

The door opened then and the nurse ushered Elijah in. "Dr. Davis will be in shortly."

After the nurse closed the door, Elijah sat on the rolling stool and scooted closer to Elizabeth. "How are you?"

She stared at him in disbelief. "How do you think I am?"

He held his hands up defensively. "I'm sorry. I don't know what to say. I don't know what to do."

"Then don't say anything at all." Tears tickled her nose. "Did it ever occur to you to just hold me?"

Before Elijah could move, Dr. Davis tapped on the door and entered the room. He shook Elijah's hand, and then turned to Elizabeth. "I'm sorry, Elizabeth."

She nodded.

"Take the time you need to grieve this loss, but understand that this doesn't mean you won't get pregnant again. Maybe you'll need another round of fertility medicine, maybe you won't. But statistically speaking, about one in five women have miscarried and go on to have normal, healthy pregnancies. So don't lose hope, okay?"

Elizabeth sucked in a sharp breath as Elijah leaned forward. "I'm sorry. What did you say?"

Confusion creased Dr. Davis's brow. "Not to lose hope?"

Elijah shot daggers from his eyes at Elizabeth. "You took medicine without me knowing? How could you? You knew how I felt about it."

Dr. Davis cleared his throat. "Uh, let's get back to the matter at hand. For right now you have two options. I can schedule you for a D and C, or you can wait for your body to expel the miscarriage naturally. There are pros and cons to both. Obviously, a D and C is a procedure so there are certain risks involved, but it is quick and thorough, with a minimal amount of pain. Some women feel more comfortable going with the natural route, but with as far along as you were, you'll likely experience a considerable amount of pain. Plus there's a chance that not all of the tissue from the pregnancy will get expelled naturally and I'll have to perform a D and C anyway."

Elizabeth opened her lips, but she didn't recognize her own voice. "Then I guess you can schedule me for a D and C."

As soon as the words were out, hanging heavily in the room around them, she wished she could take them back. But what other choice did she have?

"All right, then. Stay right here. I'll have one of the ladies up front schedule it and get you all the information you need." He moved to the door and grabbed the handle. "Again, I'm truly sorry."

Fifteen minutes later, Elizabeth and Elijah left the room with the procedure set for the next morning and several pamphlets describing in great detail exactly what the procedure entailed. Just holding it made Elizabeth nauseated.

It was the right decision. It was her only decision.

So then why does it feel so wrong? She sensed another ferocious wave of emotion coming, and she quickly reinforced the dam that maintained her composure. *Because mothers aren't supposed to lose their babies.* A tear slipped out of the corner of her eye, the only sign that her insides were being battered and bruised by a tempest of emotions.

But when she pushed through the door to the waiting room, the strong, secure dam proved to be no match for the awaiting tsunami.

CHAPTER

Twenty-two

*M*ovement at the door that led to the examining rooms caught Amy's eye. She glanced up from the magazine she'd been thumbing through and stifled a gasp as she watched her biggest fear unfold. Her blood turned to ice and her heart froze solid as she met Elizabeth's wounded stare. Elijah followed her into the room.

"Amy?" Elizabeth's voice wavered as two tears followed the identical trails of mascara down her cheeks. "W-what are you doing here?"

"Uh." Amy glanced down her front to the slight bulge of her belly. Try as she might she couldn't keep the sarcasm from her voice. "It's really not that hard to figure out."

Unbelievable. Of all the doctors in this hospital, Dr. Kimball had to refer me to Elizabeth's.

Obviously confused, Elijah rubbed his chin. "I thought you . . . "

Amy's eyes widened and, pressing her lips together, she gave a firm shake of her head.

Elizabeth didn't seem to notice. Releasing a shaky breath, she wiped her blotchy face off with a crumpled tissue and blew her red nose. "Look, I know that it's your night with Dominick, but can you please bring him by the house after school. I have something to tell him. It'll just take a minute."

Expecting Elizabeth to judge or criticize her, Amy was thrown for a loop, but she quickly recovered. "Yeah, sure. No problem."

A sob escaped from Elizabeth's throat then, and she dashed out of the office. Amy shifted her questioning expression to Elijah. He shoved his fingers through his hair and sank to a chair across from her.

"She lost the baby."

"Oh no." Amy groaned, her calloused heart breaking a little for the couple, but a lot for Dominick.

Tears sprang to her eyes as she imagined how crushed the poor boy would be. She wondered how she could help her son through this or be any kind of a support to Elizabeth when she was carrying a baby she didn't want. A sense of her own hypocrisy stabbed her hard in the gut.

I'm the one who should have miscarried, not Elizabeth.

Amy met Elijah's weary gaze, remembering Owen's advice to open her heart, and, on a whim, she decided to take a chance. "I'm so sorry. Is there anything I can do?"

"Just pray." Visibly disheartened, Elijah shook his head. "I can't even tell you what to pray for specifically, but just pray."

Amy cringed. Of course he'd request the one thing she couldn't do. Thankfully, she didn't have time to respond as a nurse pushed through the door and called her name.

Avoiding eye contact with him, she pushed to her feet. "I'll bring Dominick by this evening."

"Hey, Amy," Elijah called as she reached the door the nurse had appeared in.

Amy glanced over her shoulder.

He offered her a weak smile. "I'm glad you didn't 'take care of it.'"

Amy returned his hint of a grin and hurried off to follow the nurse through the hallway. After stopping to briefly check her blood pressure and weight, and the nurse showed her to an examination room.

"Dr. Davis will be in shortly."

In the silence of the pale blue, sterile room, she thought about Elijah's request. *Pray?* Grimacing at the bitter taste the word left on her tongue, she thought of the last time she'd prayed. She had been twelve, and she asked God to bring her dad back home safely. She dropped her gaze to her hands in her lap, surprised by how the disappointment still stung.

I can't pray. I just can't. But I can open my heart and try to love this baby. I don't know how that would help Elizabeth, but maybe it will help ease some of Dominick's disappointment.

She glanced down at the roundness under her shirt and pressed her hand against it. *Looks like I'm going to be keeping you.*

As if in response, she felt a flutter against her fingertips, which caused a wad of emotion to lodge in her throat. Was that a sign? Had she made the right choice? Would she be able to see past that terrible night when she looked at this baby?

A soft tap on the door caused her to snap her gaze up as Dr. Davis entered, smiling. "Hello again, Amy. How have you been feeling?"

"Pretty good, I guess."

Dr. Davis patted the head of the table, gesturing for her to lie back. He washed his hands at the small sink in the room, pulled out a small tape measure from his lab coat pocket, and measured the roundness of her belly. "Looks good." He slipped the tape measure back into his pocket and retrieved the Doppler and gel. "Are you feeling the baby move?"

"Yes."

Dr. Davis squirted some gel on the end of the Doppler. "This might be a little chilly." Almost as soon as he set the Doppler on Amy's belly a strong, steady heartbeat filled the room.

Amy's heart sped up to match it. That was the baby, a life that would depend on her for a very long time.

Dr. Davis studied his watch for a minute. "One hundred forty-two beats per minute. That's very good." He lifted the Doppler off her belly and handed her a paper towel to clean off the extra goo. "So have you decided what you're going to do about this baby?"

She nodded and swallowed the last of the balled up emotion. "I'm keeping him." Putting a voice to the decision seemed to set it in stone, and her anxiety levels skyrocketed. This meant she would have to tell Dominick. And what if her ten-year-old boy asked about the circumstances—the hows and the whys and the whos?

She would also have to tell Owen, and, sitting on the examination table at that moment, she thought that might break her heart more than telling her son. What if he rejected her? She reasoned it'd probably be the smartest move he ever made, but it'd take her a long time to get over losing his love.

Maybe even the rest of her life.

"Amy?"

Amy shook free from her gloomy thoughts. "I'm sorry. Did you say something?"

"I just asked if you were sure."

Amy remained silent, her lips unable to form the word *yes*.

"You have time. This isn't a decision to be rushed." He jotted down some notes in her folder and returned his compassionate eyes to her. "Let me know if you want to talk to someone about the adoption process."

She lifted her chin. "No need. I'm keeping him."

He stared at her for a moment, his friendly eyes seeming to bore a hole through to her shaky insides. Then he nodded. "Good. This baby will be blessed to have such a wonderful mother."

He smiled warmly, patted her knee with the file folder, and tucked it safely under his arm. "The ladies up front can check you out. I'll want to see you back in another four weeks. Call if you need anything in the meantime."

"Thank you."

She sat there for several minutes after he left the room, her lips curving upward at his words. *Wonderful mother. No one has ever called me that before.* She hopped down from the table. *I've been so worried about not turning out like my mother that I've lost sight of the fact that I'm not her.*

Smiling, she headed down the hallway to check out. *This baby is mine, and I'm keeping him.*

But even as the thought formed, Amy recognized the difference between determination and love.

Elizabeth sat for hours in the room they'd started preparing as a nursery, making the slightest movement in her grandmother's antique rocking chair, heavy grief washing over her in powerful waves.

Her cell phone rang, and Elizabeth checked the caller id hoping to see Elijah's number. *Kate.* Disappointment weighed on her heart like a bag of cement. *She's probably calling to see how my appointment went.* The thought brought on another surge of emotion and she wailed into her hands.

"My. Baby. Is. Dead." She lifted her tear-streaked face toward the ceiling. "Dear God, I don't understand. How could this happen? You made me to be a mother, I know You did. So after I tried for so long You gave me a baby, and then took her away before I could hold her or rock her or do any of the other things mothers do. Why, God? Why?"

Her body wracked with sobs, and she rubbed her belly, having a hard time fathoming that she still carried the tiny lifeless body. "Is it too much to hope that Jesus will bring this baby back to life like he did Lazarus? Please, dear God. I want my baby back." She doubled over her knees, covering her face with her hands, and wept hard.

A moment later, the doorbell rang. Elizabeth checked the time on her phone. *Two-thirty. A little early for Dominick to be here, but maybe Amy picked him up early.*

She'd been dreading this short visit and still hadn't come up with any kind of explanation suitable for a ten-year-old. Uttering a quick prayer for wisdom, she sucked in a deep breath, rose, and slowly started down the steps. The doorbell sounded again as she reached the bottom step.

"I'm coming!" She reached the door, swung it open, and the gentle face that met hers blurred behind fresh tears. "Uncle Bill! What are you doing here?"

He held out a foil covered pie pan. "Wilma baked this for you."

Elizabeth offered him a weak smile in return for his gift. Though she had no appetite and didn't expect to gain one anytime soon, the rich apple spice aroma that wafted out from under the loose foil smelled heavenly.

"And I wanted to check on you. Been thinking of you since Saturday."

Elizabeth's bottom lip quivered. "I'm fine." She moved into the living room, setting the pastry on a decorative table along the way, and sank to the sofa just as her composure crumbled. "But the baby's not."

Uncle Bill joined her in the living room and sat in a chair adjacent the couch. "I'm sorry, Elizabeth."

Beginning to grow weary of hearing those two words, she wiped her face with the back of her hand and sniffed. "Yeah, me, too. I've been sitting here trying to make sense of it all, but I can't. Why did this happen, Uncle Bill?"

He shook his head. "I don't know, Lizzie. I don't know."

At the sound of Grandpa Clayton's special nickname for her, she gave in to another round of torrential emotion. "With everything in me, I don't want to blame God. I don't. But I just can't understand why He'd give me my heart's deepest desire only to take it back. I mean, doesn't the Bible say, 'Delight yourself also in the Lord, and He shall give you the desires of your heart.' "

"Indeed it does, but it also says, 'Trust in the Lord with all your heart, and lean not on your own understanding.' "

Elizabeth nodded. Kate had told her the same thing. Still . . .

"Trust in the Lord. Sometimes that's a tough thing."

"It sure is, but it's going to be all right. You'll see." He reached out his long slender fingers and patted her knee.

"Remember the God of the mountain is still the God of the valley. It's just harder to feel, see, or hear Him right now because of all the shadows. Take this time to grieve. Just remember, weeping may last for a night, but believe me, kiddo, your joy is coming in the morning."

A sob escaped Elizabeth's throat. "It hurts, Uncle Bill. It hurts so much."

Uncle Bill scooted to the sofa, slipped an arm around Elizabeth's shoulders, and held her just like Grandpa Clayton always had—strong, yet tender. Sometimes Elizabeth found it hard to believe that he and her grandfather had only been friends and not brothers.

After several moments the tears subsided, and Uncle Bill pushed to his feet. "I better get back home, but let us know if there's anything we can do for you."

Elizabeth stood on wobbly knees to walk him to the door. "Thank you. And tell Wilma thanks for the pie."

"Will do."

Just as he stepped onto the front porch, Amy pulled into the driveway. Elizabeth's heart screeched to a stop. She wasn't ready to explain this to her stepson. She wasn't ready to make it real. *Dear God, give me the words.* She lifted up the simple prayer and pasted on a smile as Amy and Dominick climbed out of the car and headed up the sidewalk.

Reaching Elizabeth several steps ahead of Amy, Dominick wasted no time in moving his hands, his expression hopeful. "Did you have your doctor's appointment?"

Elizabeth bit her bottom lip to keep it from quivering. "Yes."

Amy joined them on the porch and the women locked grim gazes.

Unable to keep herself from glancing at the slight bulge under Amy's oversized T-shirt, Elizabeth felt her shoulders sag under the weight of inadequacy. She signed and spoke the words, "Why don't you come in and sit down?"

Dominick's smile faded as he plopped onto the sofa and watched Elizabeth perch herself next to him. His expression and hands spoke for him.

"What's wrong?"

"Well, sweetie," Elizabeth inhaled deeply, thankful to break the news with her hands since the lump in her throat was impassible, "when the doctor checked out the baby there was no heartbeat."

Dominick stared at Elizabeth in confusion.

"The baby died."

In a panic, he shook his head frantically and pointed at his chest.

Elizabeth held her hands up, a tear slipping out of the corner of her eye at his reaction. When he calmed down a bit, she tried to explain with her hands.

"It wasn't your fault. The doctor was able to tell that the baby died two weeks ago." Staving off a surge of emotion, she shrugged. "Sometimes things just happen."

Dominick lunged at her, wrapping his arms around her neck and heaving loud, pathetic sobs. Tears streamed down Elizabeth's face as she met Amy's damp gaze over Dominick's head.

After several long moments, Dominick pulled back, wiped his face, and spoke with his hands. "Is brother or sister in heaven?"

Elizabeth's breath caught in her throat. Still struggling with what she hadn't allowed to sink in, she realized that

Dominick needed reassurance. Yes, she'd lost the baby, but his brother or sister wasn't gone forever. Still, answering the question would mean she'd have to accept that she'd never see or hold or rock her baby in this lifetime.

Her fingers trembled with her response. "I believe that with all my heart."

He offered her a wobbly smile. "Me too."

At that moment, the front door swung open and Elijah stepped through. Shifting his gaze from Elizabeth to Dominick to Amy and back to Elizabeth, his face clouded over with a potent mixture of anger and hurt.

"You told him without me?" He threw his keys onto the table near the pie. "Darn it, Elizabeth. He's my son. Don't you think you should have included me?" He threw his hands into the air. "But why should I have expected anything else?"

Heat rose to Elizabeth's cheeks, and she thought flaming emotion would spew from her like a volcano. For the sake of Dominick's feelings, she bit her tongue so hard she tasted blood and only glared at her husband.

Elijah rubbed the back of his neck and slid his gaze to Amy. "Do you care if he and I go shoot some hoops? Maybe talk a little about this . . . " He waved his arm in the air searching for the right word. " . . . situation."

Picking at her thumbnail, Amy appeared to be considering Elijah's request. "You know, I don't want to make a habit of rearranging our schedule, but it just so happens I've had something come up unexpectedly, and I was kind of hoping you wouldn't mind if Dominick stayed here tonight. You can still have your regular Tuesday."

Glancing at Elizabeth, he nodded before she had a chance to respond. "Sure. No problem." He grabbed the front door handle and motioned for Dominick to join him. "Come on, sport. Let's go play some ball."

Dominick hugged Elizabeth one more time before racing off with Elijah. In the awkward silence that followed, Elizabeth shifted uncomfortably on the couch and stared at her still trembling hands.

"Well, I guess I should go." Amy started for the door.

"Thanks for bringing Dominick over on such short notice."

Amy nodded, reached for the door handle and froze. Hesitating for a long moment, she turned back to face Elizabeth. "Hey, are you okay?"

"Not really." Elizabeth's gaze fell to Amy's belly again. "Are you?"

"Oh." Amy glanced down the front of her. "Yeah, I'm fine. I mean, it certainly wasn't expected, but you learn to play the hand you're dealt, you know?"

Elizabeth pushed to her feet and trudged to the table where the pie sat. "Well, I'm having a hard time playing this hand." She carried the pie to the kitchen counter, uncovered, and, after grabbing a knife from the drawer, sliced it. "Would you like a piece?"

Amy stared at Elizabeth for a second with an uncertain expression. Moving to a chair at the kitchen table, she nodded. "Sure."

Elizabeth retrieved two plates from the cupboard, dished out two pieces, and carried them to the table. Her stomach turned. She had no desire to eat a piece of pie, but it was better than sitting in uncomfortable silence. She stabbed at the wedge of pastry with her fork.

"I have to tell you, I'm surprised Dominick hasn't told us that you're pregnant. He was so excited about . . . " She nearly choked on rising emotion.

"He doesn't know. No one does but you, Elijah, and one other person, and I'd prefer to keep it that way for a little while longer."

Elizabeth set her fork down. "Well, how far along are you? If you're past the first trimester, you should be safe."

Amy chewed and swallowed. "I'm at twenty-six weeks, but it has to do with the circumstances." She set her fork down and stared at Elizabeth. "Please, don't say anything to Dominick. I'll tell him when I'm ready."

"It's not my place. I won't say anything."

Amy took her last bite of pie, chewed and swallowed. "I don't mean to pry, but is everything okay with you and Elijah? I mean, he seemed a little edgy just a minute ago."

"I kept something from him that I shouldn't have." Elizabeth swallowed hard against the thick lump of emotions. "He's angry on top of being disappointed about the baby, and he's dealing with it all in his own way."

Amy stood and carried her plate and fork to the sink. "Thanks for the pie, but I really need to go. I do have some business to take care of."

Elizabeth walked her to the door. "Thanks for letting Dominick stay tonight."

Amy stepped out onto the porch and turned to face Elizabeth. "Let me know if I can do anything else."

Elizabeth offered Amy a weak smile. "Thanks. I'll keep that in mind." She watched Amy walk to her car, warmed and somehow strengthened by the caring gesture of this woman who not so long ago was her adversary.

Thank You, God, for answering that prayer and forming some sort of a relationship between Amy and me.

Closing the door, Elizabeth trudged to her bedroom and collapsed onto her bed with a deep sigh. Exhausted in every way possible, she crawled under the covers and tried to forget that after her procedure the next morning, her womb and her dream would be completely empty.

CHAPTER
Twenty-Three

Amy stood in the doorway of the kitchen, an unnoticed spectator as Anna busily baked pumpkin-shaped sugar cookies with a handful of her grandchildren. With the patience of a saint, Anna guided the kids through the recipe, helped them roll out the dough, and use the cookie cutters. She dried the tears of a pig-tailed little girl whose cookie fell apart before she could get it to the baking sheet. She laughed when an older boy turned the mixer on too high and became doused in a cloud of flour. She cheerfully helped a corkscrew-headed girl fish out a couple pieces of eggshell from the mixing bowl.

Amy reflected on the story Anna had told her that evening in Kennedy's old room and wondered how a broken young woman could become a confident and capable grandmother. Where did all that pain go?

"Oh, hey, Amy." Anna greeted her with a warm smile. "Want to come join us?"

Amy held a hand up, palm out. "Watching is enough entertainment."

Anna chuckled and returned her attention to a grandson who was working on rolling out his dough. "Baking with these kiddos is always an adventure."

Amy moved into the kitchen and sat at the table. "You're a brave woman."

"Lookit this punkin, Grammy," the pig-tailed little girl squealed with a big toothless grin.

"It's perfect. Good girl, Haley." Anna helped the little girl place the cookie on a baking sheet. Then she slipped the sheet in the oven, set the timer, and turned to Amy.

"Where's Dominick? He should join us."

"He's spending the night with his dad and stepmom." Amy picked at her thumbnail, her nerves kicking into overdrive. "And, uh . . . " She'd made an honest effort to open her heart, but it put her so far out of her comfort zone that she needed a map to find her way back.

"Amy? Is everything all right?"

"Yes. I . . . well, if you have a minute I need to talk with you."

"Oh, sure. Let me just get cleaned up in here."

Anna shooed the younger grandkids into the other room and enlisted the older children's help in tidying up the kitchen. When the timer dinged, she pulled the cookies out of the oven and one by one slid them off the baking sheet onto a cooling rack. Finally, wiping her hands on a towel and calling to Jacob that she was stepping out for a minute, she smiled at Amy.

"What do you say we go for a walk?"

Amy rose and followed Anna out the back door.

The late afternoon sun had begun its descent in the early October sky. The slight chill in the air carried the earthy scent of autumn as the two women strolled across the lawn in silence toward the path that led to the pebbly beach at the back of the Sullivans' property.

Anna reached down and plucked a dandelion. She held it out and twirled it between her fingers, watching the white fluff let go and drift away on the breeze. "You know, people are a lot like dandelions. They grow and change and eventually have the ability to plant seeds, but it often takes a supernatural force to get them to let go."

Amy quickly glanced at Anna, and then back at the ground. "What did it take for you to let go of your past?"

"Ah, see that's where people go wrong. I didn't let go of my past. I had a wonderful childhood, and the time I spent with my mom before she died was precious. I'll hold those memories close to me all my life." Anna wrapped the bare dandelion stem around her finger. "What I had to let go of was the pain."

It took a minute for Amy to find her voice and another minute for her to gather all her courage. "H-how did you do that?"

"For me it was a process, and the biggest part of that process was forgiveness."

Amy thought of Steph's testimony that she shared over three months earlier: *"When you finally reach a point of acceptance and complete forgiveness, your chains will be gone and you'll be free."*

Maybe there was something to what Steph had said, but . . . "I'm not sure I can do that."

"It's not easy, that's for sure."

Amy kicked at a dirt clod. "For me, it just might be impossible."

"It's funny you should say that. Owen said the exact same thing after he lost Julia and his son."

At the mention of Owen's tragedy, Amy missed her foot-
ing on the uneven ground and stumbled, but quickly recovered. "You know that he told me?"

Anna nodded. "I suggested it. Thought it just might do
you both some good."

A twitch near Amy's bellybutton fought for her attention,
and she wrapped her arms around her middle as if covering
the mouth of a noisy child. "But that was an accident. Who
did he have to forgive?"

Anna stopped and captured Amy's gaze. "Himself."

Amy wondered if Anna knew how close to home she hit.
"And . . . " She didn't mean to invade Owen's privacy, but she
had to know the answer. "Did he? Forgive himself, I mean?"

"Yes. It took time, but yes."

"How did it happen?"

"Well, if you want the specifics, you'll have to ask him,
but I think it came gradually as he began to recognize the
good God had worked through his loss."

Amy thought of Elizabeth and the pain so visible in her
violet eyes. "It doesn't seem like a fair tradeoff."

Anna slipped her arm across Amy's shoulders. "It's not for
us to determine what's fair and what's not."

Silently, Amy soaked in Anna's words as they began to
stroll along the path again. "Does good always come from the
bad?"

"If you let it." Anna paused thoughtfully. "And sometimes
it happens whether you want it to or not, and you just have to
open your eyes to see it."

"Is that what the rest of your story is about?"

Anna nodded. "You see, the nurse who took care of
me after I lost my baby, when I was battered and broken

physically, emotionally, and spiritually was Eva Sullivan, my future mother-in-law."

Stunned, Amy stared at Anna, her mouth falling open. "You're kidding."

"Nope. It's the truth. Eva nursed not just the bruises and broken bones, but also my suffering spirit."

While they walked and talked, Amy felt the bond between her and Anna tightening. But she remained cautious, knowing all too well that a bond of any strength can be broken.

"How did she do that?"

"Well, after I was released from the hospital, she invited me to go to church with her and her family. She even told me she'd pick me up. I had no desire to go to church, was sure with all I'd done God didn't want to have anything to do with me."

Heat rose up Amy's neck and settled in her ears. "I can relate."

"I thought maybe you could." Anna slipped her hands into the pockets of her lightweight jacket. "But I was missing my mom and craved that female attention so badly I think I would've gone just about anywhere to get it. So I accepted the invitation and I kept going. Soon I was staying in the afternoons to have lunch with them. Eva talked to me a lot about Jesus' redeeming love and how it didn't matter what my past looked like, but instead what my future could be."

Amy thought of Pastor Ben's sermon the Sunday before, but it didn't make sense. How could God overlook her shady past?

"It took many months, but with Eva's help and guidance, I accepted Jesus as my Savior. Shortly after that, I began dating Jacob. It made all the difference in our relationship to grow together in our relationship with the Lord."

Relationship with the Lord? Amy was curious as to exactly how someone developed a relationship with the Lord, but she didn't ask for fear of the answer. In her experience, relationships required sacrifice and, more often than not, ended with an irreparably broken heart.

They reached the clearing that kissed Lake Erie at that pebbly shoreline just as the sky began to turn several shades of fuchsia and lavender. Anna closed her eyes and inhaled deeply.

"I still miss my mom and daughter. I think about them every day, but I'm able to accept that I had to walk down that path to get to where I am today." Anna gazed out over the pink-tinted, diamond-studded water with an expression of joy and contentment. "And I have to say, it's a pretty incredible view."

The hard thud of hooves on the well-worn path caused Amy and Anna to turn simultaneously.

Amy's breath caught in her throat as when she saw Owen sitting atop Moses with the same easygoing demeanor that had drawn her in on her very first day in Harvest Bay. At times it felt as if ages had passed since that afternoon in the Bayside Café, but at this moment it seemed like a breath ago.

With one hand holding the reins, Owen guided Moses toward them, while leading Angel by her reins with the other hand. Lips curling upward, Amy marveled at how far that broken but beautiful animal had come in just a few short months. She watched in amusement as Angel fidgeted, and in response Moses patiently turned his big head toward the little paint and snorted.

It's kind of like Owen and me, she mused. *He's been my source of reason every single time I get worked up.* In that moment, she knew that not only did she love this man, but also that she didn't want to keep anymore secrets from him.

Owen pulled back on Moses' reins, bringing the horse to a halt, and swung out of the saddle. "It'll be dark soon and two ladies shouldn't be out here alone after dark."

Anna met Owen and took Moses' reins from him. "You're right, son. And I have a handful of grandkids that are probably running all over their poor grandpa."

Owen chuckled and assisted Anna into Moses' saddle.

"C'mon, big boy. Back to the barn." Anna clicked her tongue, and Moses took off at an easy trot.

Amy's nerves kicked into overdrive as she became very aware that she and Owen were alone in this intimate setting. A fluttering near her bellybutton matched the fluttering in her heart as she wondered if she had the guts to come clean with him once and for all, just lay it all on the line and prepare for the worst, while hoping for the best. From several paces away, she met his warm gaze and her chest tightened.

Owen closed the gap between them and handed her Angel's reins. "She's been waiting for you." He reached out for her free hand and intertwined their fingers. "And so have I."

Heat climbed her neck and settled in her cheeks. "Owen, I . . ." Revealing this secret could change everything between them, but how much longer could she keep it going? She sucked in a sharp breath, deciding it'd just be best to get it over with. "I have something to tell you."

His expression darkened. "I have something I need to tell you too."

Warning bells sounded in her brain. She yanked her hand free and crossed her arms. "What is it?"

Owen stuffed his hands in his pockets and stared at her intently for several seconds.

Trying her best to brace herself, she waited on pins and needles. "Well?"

He rubbed the back of his neck. "I didn't know for sure until it was confirmed yesterday at church, but I'm going to be leaving Harvest Bay for a while."

All the moisture from Amy's throat relocated to just behind her lashes. She blinked twice and swallowed hard. "What do you mean?"

"I volunteered to be on a mission team, but the trip had been put on hold because of political unrest in nearby areas. Sunday I found out we've been cleared to go. We leave next month and will be gone until January."

A bubble of panic started at her toes and worked its way to her brain. Her breath came out in short puffs. "A mission trip?"

Owen nodded. "I was hoping we wouldn't leave until after Christmas when you and Dominick will already be gone, but part of the purpose of the trip will be to take gifts from the church to the kids in the village orphanage."

Visions of tearful good-byes followed by the shock of tragedy flooded Amy's mind causing the pocket of anxiety to burst. "You can't go." The words were out before she could stop them. Although they were an order, they showed her weakness—the ultimate mistake—and she wished she could take them back.

He planted his hands on his hips and studied her critically. "Excuse me?"

Feeling her heart begin to take a nosedive, she backed up a few more steps to make plenty of room for the inevitable crash landing. "W-well your family needs you here. And what about the fire station? Two months is a long time."

"My family will be just fine without me, and I've put in for a leave of absence from work." With one step, he closed the gap between them and encircled her waist with his arms. "Now tell me the real reason why I can't go."

She made the crucial error of gazing into his sincere blue-gray eyes and melted a little into the comfort of his strong arms until the fear of never being like this again with the only man she ever really loved nearly suffocated her. She broke free of his embrace, gasping for air.

He held his hands out in desperation. "What do you want from me?"

An emotional storm brewed in her soul, churning faster with each breath. She knew he'd eventually grow weary of pursuing someone who kept pushing him away. It's what she intended all along. Unfortunately, now it was too late to save herself.

"Nothing. Nothing at all."

"The morning of the Fourth of July in Angel's stall, you said you'd consider staying if you had a reason. I took that to heart and have since given you dozens of reasons to stay."

Her vision blurred with unshed tears. "I never wanted you to. I never asked for any of this."

"What do you want now?" His peaceful, gentle eyes suddenly became as stormy as her soul. "Why should I stay, Amy? Give me a reason."

Of all the conflict she'd faced in the past ten years, this was by far the most painful. *Because I love you . . . Because if you go you won't come back . . . And because I don't want to live without you.* They were all valid reasons in her mind, but that's where they stayed trapped. She couldn't form the words on her tongue and spit them out.

Owen nodded and took several steps back. "That's what I thought." He snorted. "It's what I deserve, taking a chance on opening my heart to someone who doesn't want it." He shrugged. "It healed once, it will again." As he turned and started down the path, he called over his shoulder. "I'll see you when I see you."

As he disappeared around the bend, the dam burst and tears flowed down her cheeks. She opened her mouth to call out to him but the words were washed away. The grenade in her heart detonating, she stood there weeping until the weight of her world crashing down around her brought her to her knees.

Elizabeth stirred when Elijah slipped into bed late that night. She rubbed her eyes and squinted at the alarm clock. "One o'clock? Have I really been sleeping that long?"

"Yeah. Sorry. I didn't mean to wake you."

She propped her pillows up a little, with the hope that he might want to talk. "It doesn't matter. It wasn't a sound sleep anyway. I kept hoping this was all a nightmare."

Elijah didn't respond. Instead he pulled the covers up to his chin and rolled over.

She lay there for the rest of the night listening to Elijah's soft snoring and clutching her chest as she silently wept into her pillow. It was excruciating enough to lose her baby but to feel her marriage slipping away at the same time was almost more than her heart could take.

The silence lasted throughout the morning. In the kitchen, the first rays of dawn streamed through the window as Elijah sipped his coffee.

Elizabeth stood in the doorway marveling at how handsome he still was after their seven years together, though somehow the events of the past week had seemed to age him. "Dominick's almost ready for school."

He nodded.

"We'll be a little early, but we can head into the hospital after we drop him off."

"Okay." He drained his coffee cup and set it in the sink.

"You've been awful quiet." Taking a chance, she crossed the kitchen and reached out to him.

To her relief, he took her in his arms, but his embrace lacked any real emotion. "I don't know what to say anymore. I don't know how to feel. I just don't know."

Biting her bottom lip to keep it from quivering, Elizabeth never realized that four words could cause such loneliness.

They arrived at the hospital shortly after eight and Elizabeth checked into outpatient surgery. Finding a seat next to Elijah in the waiting area, she sat in the uncomfortable plastic chair feeling no closer to him than if she were sitingt all the way across the room. Sometimes, she guessed, tragedy brought people closer and other times tore people apart. She rested her hands on her belly, praying for not just one miracle but two.

At her request, they performed another ultrasound to confirm the findings of the first. After that, the procedure went as planned—quickly with no complications, except for those in her heart. Elizabeth had a hard time dealing with the

cold, hard, medical facts of the D and C. Following the procedure, she spent a brief time in recovery but she was sure she'd
never recover from this excruciating emptiness.

She fell asleep in the car on the way home and awoke several hours later on the sofa.

Uncle Bill rocked in an adjacent recliner, studying her
with concern.

Propping herself up on an elbow, she scanned the room.
"Where's Elijah?"

"He went in to the office for a while."

Elizabeth lay back on the couch pillows, covered her face
with her hands, and wept hard. "Why, dear God? Why? It's
hard enough to lose this baby, but my marriage too?"

Uncle Bill scooted to the end of the couch by her feet.
"Lizzie, why do you think you're losing your marriage?"

The tiniest bit of peace eased her heart at hearing
Grandpa Clayton's special nickname for her. "He's been so
distant and short with me. Trying to have this baby almost
came between us and now . . . " Her voice trailed off, replaced
by quiet sobs.

"Now, now. Elijah loves you. And every marriage has its
peaks and valleys. This is just a bump in the road, kiddo."
Uncle Bill patted her leg. "Elijah just needs some space to
deal with this in his own way. Give him some time. He'll
come around."

Elizabeth sniffed and wiped her eyes with the back of her
hand. "You think so?"

He gave her a wink and a smile. "I'd bet my bottom dollar."

Just then the doorbell rang. Elizabeth planted the couch
pillow on her face, stifling a moan.

"I don't want to see anybody. Can you please tell whoever it is that I'm resting?"

Uncle Bill rose and headed toward the door, but not before the bell chimed again. He opened it, and Kate stepped inside.

"I came as soon as school dismissed." She slipped out of her jacket and draped it over the back of a nearby chair. "How's Elizabeth doing?"

Uncle Bill gestured toward the couch where she lounged . Elizabeth met Kate's worried gaze and a wave of dread washed over her. She loved her sister, but had no desire to look at her perfection and listen to her sympathy.

Kate hurried to her sister's side and knelt on the floor. "How are you feeling?"

Elizabeth stared at her incredulously. "How do you think I'm feeling?"

"You're right. I'm sorry. I just don't know what else to say."

"You don't have to say anything. There's nothing anyone can do." Elizabeth closed her eyes. "What I need more than anything right now is rest. So don't feel like either one of you has to stay. I'll be fine until Elijah gets home."

Uncle Bill picked up his jacket. "I do need to get back home to Wilma, but I'll call later to check on you."

Elizabeth managed a weak smile. "Thanks."

He nodded and let himself out.

Moving from the floor to the end of the couch, Kate turned to Elizabeth. "How does this affect your ability to get pregnant again?"

Elizabeth shrugged. "It shouldn't at all, except that it was a miracle we got pregnant in the first place." She fingered the edge of the afghan, tears coming again. "That's not true. It wasn't a miracle at all. It was all medical. I'd been taking fertility drugs without Elijah knowing. I took God out of the equation and look what happened." A sob bubbled out of her throat. "It's my fault."

"No, Elizabeth. Every pregnancy is a miracle regardless of the means of conception. This is nobody's fault. Miscarriages happen. It's just life."

"And now my marriage is on shaky ground, but how can I expect anything else. Elijah may never trust me again."

Kate reached out and took Elizabeth's hand. "What can I do to help you?"

Elizabeth shook her head, feeling more distant from God than she ever had in her life. "Pray. Just pray."

Twenty-four

A my spent the next several weeks searching her soul as
never before. Owen avoided her, which she guessed was
for the best, but it hurt like crazy, especially when she worked
with Angel. She'd reached the point in her pregnancy where
the doctor advised against horseback riding so she reluctantly
asked for Kennedy's help. She hated seeing Kennedy on "her"
horse, but it was exactly what she needed to be one hundred
percent certain of what she wanted . . . and what she didn't.

She still hadn't told the Sullivans about the baby, though
she suspected they'd figured it out. It was getting harder and
harder to hide as her biggest T-shirts were becoming less and
less baggy. And it wasn't that she was trying to hide it anymore, but more due to the fact that she just didn't know what
to tell them.

Late Thursday afternoon, with Halloween just days away,
she sat under the shade tree writing in her journal while
Dominick played in the yard with Harley.

Well it's been four and a half months since we arrived in
Harvest Bay, and I've noticed improvements in every area of my
life except two—faith and love. Dominick will be away at Boy
Scout camp with Elijah this weekend, so maybe I'll have an oppor-
tunity to work on one or the other or both.

The crunch of tires on the gravel driveway made her turn, hoping she'd see Owen's truck. Instead, she groaned inwardly as she recognized Steph's car. Amy took a deep breath and closed her journal as Steph started across the lawn toward her.

"Hey, Amy." Steph called out as she drew near.

"Oh, hey."

Steph squatted down next to her. "We've missed seeing you at the meetings the past few weeks. Everything okay?"

Amy picked at the grass. "Sure. Everything's fine. I've just been preoccupied lately."

"I don't mean to pry, but is it about the baby?"

Turning her frigid gaze to Steph, Amy warmed up a bit when she took in Steph's genuine expression. "Partly." Amy returned her attention to the tuft of grass. "Mostly I've just been trying to figure out how God can make good things come from the bad in our lives. Sometimes it doesn't seem possible."

"With God all things are possible."

"You would know, wouldn't you?" Afraid her vulnerability might be revealed in her eyes, she quickly glanced at Steph. "The first night I met you, you gave your testimony and talked about forgiveness."

Steph nodded. "I remember."

"Well, this may sound like an odd question, but how do you forgive someone?"

"That's not an odd question at all." Steph settled in, sitting cross-legged next to Amy. "Forgiveness comes when you accept that things didn't turn out the way you expected and they'll never be the same again. Then you make a conscious effort to let it go."

"Just like that."

"No. I said you make a conscious effort. That means you pray about it daily, sometimes several times a day, and you keep turning it over to the Lord until peace fills the place where that burden used to be."

Amy's shoulders fell. "Well, there's another problem. I don't pray."

"Why not? You don't want to? Don't believe in it? Or don't know how?"

Amy snorted. "All of the above."

"It never hurts to try." Steph scooted a smidge closer. "I can help you if you want."

Help? I don't need help . . . Before she'd finished the thought she remembered Owen's advice to open her heart and let someone help her. Sucking in a deep, shaky breath, she nodded.

"Okay. What do I have to do?"

"Think of someone you have to forgive."

Immediately, her mother came to mind. "I've got her."

"Can you accept that things didn't turn out the way you expected?"

"I'm not sure. No one expects her own mother to run out on her. How do I just accept that?"

"You acknowledge that she's human. She made a mistake—"

"Made a mistake? She abandoned her husband and three-year-old little girl, just left me standing at the door crying as she drove away. And she never looked back."

"I can't imagine how that must have hurt."

Biting her bottom lip to keep it from quivering, Amy only nodded.

"What she did wasn't right, but she's not perfect, and neither are you or I. We are all sinners and yet God loves us just the same."

Amy picked at the grass contemplating what Steph had said.

"Forgiveness is for you, Amy. Not her. She's going to go on living her life regardless." Steph met Amy's gaze. "What do you say? Can you accept that she wasn't there for you and choose to forgive her?"

"Acceptance means I think that what she did was okay, but it's not."

"No. Acceptance is acknowledging that it happened and you're okay anyway."

Tears blurring the tuft of grass she picked at, Amy shrugged. "But I don't know if I'm all right."

A warm smile crossed Steph's face. "I think Dominick would say you're doing just fine."

Thoughts of her son filled Amy's mind. She mused how their bond had grown stronger as she grew stronger every day that they'd been in Harvest Bay.

"Yeah, I guess maybe I am."

A sudden sense of something wrong cinched her spirit. A strange smell reached her nose. She sniffed the air twice.

"Is someone burning leaves?"

Steph inhaled. "It smells like someone's burning something."

High-pitched yelping drifted to Amy, and she scanned the yard. Warning bells rang loud and clear when she didn't see any trace of Dominick. She sprang to her feet and searched for the source of the frantic barking.

Pure panic flooded her as she found Harley and took in the horrifying scene. Harley stood barking and yelping at the door of the big, red barn that housed the farm equipment, where the barn dance had been held. Smoke billowed out of every opening and flames shot through the roof.

"Dominick!" She raced toward the barn, shouting over her shoulder, "Call 911! Hurry!" She reached the big double doors, her eyes already watering from the smoke. "Dominick!" Even as she screamed her son's name she knew it was futile.

He couldn't hear her. She'd have to go in and find him.

"Dear God, help me now!" she cried out in her desperation.

As she took a step forward, a brawny figure dashed past her. It only took a split second to register that Owen had run into the burning building to save her son.

"Owen, stop!" But he'd already disappeared into the thick smoke, and fear like she'd never known gripped her heart.

Sirens filled the distant air as Jacob ran across the yard toward them shouting, "My barn! Good God, all my equipment!"

Anna followed close behind. "Amy! What happened? Is anyone in there?"

Amy nodded, her throat so constricted with emotion when her words finally came out they were drenched with tears. "Dominick and Owen."

"Oh dear God!" In slow motion, Anna sank to her knees, lifting her face heavenward.

Instantly, Steph flanked her. Clasping hands, each woman took turns praying for safety and protection.

Listening to their fervent prayers, Amy's anxiety grew with the volume of the sirens. It didn't take a trained medic to understand that each second in a smoke-filled, blazing building was critical.

Okay, God, You can come to the rescue any time now. A few more seconds passed. I wouldn't expect You to listen to me, God, but aren't You listening to them? Are You really even there?

Her breaths came in short panicky puffs. Stepping closer to the door, she felt a flutter in her abdomen. She knew taking in even a small amount of smoke could seriously hurt her baby. She didn't want to take that chance but she couldn't just stand there while her son and the love of her life were in very grave danger.

"What am I supposed to do?" She shoved her fingers through her hair, hot tears streaming down her face. Uncertain and so afraid, she whispered, "God, I need You."

"When you walk through the fire, you shall not be burned, nor shall the flame scorch you."

The familiar voice—Was it Justin? Maybe her dad? Or someone else?—spoke the scripture verse louder than the approaching sirens. Still, she wondered if she'd heard it correctly until it came again louder and firmer than before.

She couldn't mistake what she'd heard that time. Pressing her medallion against her skin, she filled her lungs with clean, fresh air, summoned all her courage, and dashed into the barn.

The darkest Iraqi night didn't compare to the blackness in the barn, and this enemy was every bit as intimidating. Willing to take the risk of allowing smoke into her lungs in order to find the two people who meant the most to her, she choked out, "Owen!"

Above her in the hay loft, the fire roared like a powerful waterfall, and Amy knew it was just a matter of time before the barn caved in on all three of them. Panic seized her, and for one fleeting moment she considered doing what she did best—running, saving herself and the baby. After all she'd been through in this pregnancy, how could she think about sacrificing this innocent child now?

"Because I could live with myself if it meant saving my son and Owen."

The revelation mixed with the think smoke caused fresh tears to blur what little vision she had. The intense pressure in her lungs brought on a case of lightheadedness, and she mused that no oxygen at all might be as harmful to the baby as breathing in the smoke. Blinking back the tears, she dropped to her hands and knees on the dirt floor, took a small breath of the cleanest air she could find, and crawled farther into danger.

"Owen!" The quick burst of air it took to call his name was more than she could afford, but in her desperation she couldn't think rationally.

In that moment, however, some things became perfectly clear.

Oh God, what have I done? I'm so lost. I don't know which way to go, and now I'm so turned around I don't even know how to get out. I'm trapped. She swallowed hard against rising emotion. She had to keep it together, keep a level head. *What else did I expect? This has been my life for so long—a burning barn so full of smoke I can't see anything but the trouble I'm in.*

A sob started in her chest and bubbled up her throat. Seeing that no amount of swallowing would keep it down, she lay flat on the ground for the cleanest air supply. "Dear God, I accept that this isn't the life I've bargained for. I forgive myself for the bad choices I made and for turning so far away from You that I couldn't even see wrong from right. I want the future I know You see for me, like the potter sees when he looks at a ball of clay."

Tears slid down her cheeks. Whether from her emotions or the smoke, she didn't know, but the salty moisture felt somewhat refreshing.

"I want more time to train Angel. She's already come so far. I have hopes and dreams that I shared with Dad a long time ago. Angel could be a part of that. So could Dominick and Owen." Her body wracked with sobs. "Oh, dear God, I missed out on so much of Dominick's life. I want to see him grow up now. But I don't want to live another day without Dominick or Owen. Please help me find them."

Her cheek pressed against the dirt ground, she sucked in a deep breath. Lifting her head, she summoned all her strength and screamed, "Owen!"

The rafters creaked above her. She glanced up as burning ash fell like snow from hell. Surprised that it hadn't already happened, she knew that the barn was about to cave in on top of her. Covering her head wouldn't provide her much protection in such a dire situation, but it was all she could think to do.

This is it. I'm going to die. She envisioned seeing her dad and Justin again. That is if I make it to heaven. The stark realization filled her with new resolve. There was a time not too long ago when I would have welcomed a one-way ticket out of here, far away from the pain and sorrow. But now I want to live.

She choked on her tears and the thick, putrid air. "Dear God, I want to live for You!"

Through the roar of the blazing fire, a dog barked.

"Harley?" Amy squinted in the blackness and made out that beautiful old farm dog. "Harley!" Her laugh came out as a deep cough, and she reached for the animal.

In the next instant, a strong arm wrapped around her waist and lifted her to her feet.

"Owen?"

"Home, Harley!" Owen's weak voice didn't diminish the urgency of his command, and the dog dashed off barking and yelping all the way. Gripping Amy's hand tightly and carrying Dominick over his shoulder, he rushed after the sound.

Holding her breath, Amy allowed this man to lead her to safety. It seemed only fitting. He'd already saved her from an empty, meaningless life. She focused her watery eyes on Dominick's frightened gaze, and for the briefest moment relief washed over her. She had her two loves.

Horror returned to her, however, when a large beam cracked and fell in a fiery heap a few feet in front of them, showering them with sparks. Owen glanced up at the groaning rafters.

Just beyond the burning beam, flashes of red cut through the smoke, and in the hayloft's second-story opening, Amy could see a firefighter at the top of a ladder holding a mammoth hose trained on the flames. But she could see that the structure had already been too heavily damaged to save.

Wasting no time, Owen stepped closer to the burning beam and, grunting with the effort, heaved Dominick to the fireman who raced toward them on the other side. Before Amy could protest, he pulled her close, brushing his lips softly against hers. Then with one last tender look, he shoved her into the waiting armsof a paramedic.

As the paramedic raced her out of the barn on the heels of the fireman carrying Dominick, Amy's heart seized. Justin had done the same thing right before . . .

With an eerie groan, the roof gave way and collapsed.

Continuing to put one foot in front of the other, Elizabeth graduated from living a moment at a time to day by day. Still, the death of her dream left a crater-sized whole in her heart that nothing else could fill. Somehow she figured out how to cope with it. It took more effort to shake off the comments of well-meaning friends.

"It's probably for the best. Maybe there was something wrong with the baby."

Each time she tried to ignore the stabbing pain in her heart and simply offered the gentle rebuttal that it wouldn't have mattered. She'd love her baby regardless of any health issues. Elizabeth still loved her little angel, and it surprised her how much she missed the baby.

It helped some that her relationship with Elijah seemed to be improving. He became affectionate again and they talked more, but every time she brought up the loss of their baby or the possibility of trying for another one, he shut down. She'd always enjoyed roller coasters, but this one made her sick.

Nothing else, though, compared to the stress of dealing with her shaken faith. Finding little comfort in the Word, she grew distant from God.

Where she'd once felt excitement about going to church, she now experienced deep dread. Her powerful prayer life had been reduced to a weak one sentence prayer whenever she hit a rough spot: "Just help me get through the day."

With Halloween drawing near, a spirit of discontent filled Elizabeth as she visualized all the cute little trick-or-treaters dressed up like princesses and superheroes. Standing in front of a display of overpriced bags of candy at the Pit Stop Gas and Grocery, she considered leaving her porch light off this year and skipping the holiday altogether.

Her cell phone rang and she answered it, dismally pushing her cart away from the display. "Elizabeth, this is Anna Sullivan."

Creases formed in Elizabeth's brow. *Anna? That's odd.* "Oh, hey, Mrs. Sullivan." A nervous knot formed in her stomach. "Is everything okay?"

"No. There's been a fire. Dominick and Amy are being transported to the hospital to be treated for minor burns and some smoke inhalation."

Intense fear gripped Elizabeth's heart. Suddenly, Dominick wasn't just her stepson. She loved him like her own, and for the moment it didn't matter if she never got another chance at motherhood. Dominick was all she needed.

"I'm on my way." She disconnected the call, grabbed her purse, and dashed out of the grocery store, leaving her cart in the soup aisle. Climbing into her Mountaineer, she punched the button for Elijah's number on her speed dial.

Elijah picked up on the second ring. "Hey, Elizabeth. I'm busy right now. Can I call you back?"

"No!" she barked at him blinking angry tears. *God, why does he have to be so insensitive?* She backed out of her parking spot, threw the gearshift into drive, and tore out of the lot. "Look, I don't know details, but there's been a fire and Dominick is being taken to the hospital. I'm heading that way now."

Silence filled the air waves, and Elizabeth wondered if he'd hung up before she got out the reason for her call. "Elijah, did you hear me?"

"Yes." His whispered response revealed deep emotion.

"Are you okay?"

"Yeah. I'll go see what I can find out and meet you in the ER waiting room."

"I'll be there in ten minutes." She disconnected the call, tossed her phone in the passenger seat, and stepped on the accelerator.

Making record time, she whipped her Mountaineer into a parking space and popped open the door before she even cut off the engine. She climbed out and sprinted to the sliding glass doors. Scanning the emergency room lobby, she quickly found Elijah standing off to the side, staring out a window. Fear tightened its hold on her heart and squeezed out a small bubble of panic. It was all she could do to get to his side without tripping over herself.

"Elijah, what did you find out? Is Dominick okay?"

Elijah nodded, his damp gaze meeting and holding hers. "The doctor is running some tests—a complete blood count and an arterial blood gas—but he seems to be optimistic that there's no permanent damage."

A small tear slipped out of the corner of his eye as he reached out and drew her to him in a fierce hug. "I'm so sorry, Elizabeth. I'm sorry for all you've been through, for all I put you through."

"Shhh." She held him close, hoping he felt safe and secure in her arms. "It's okay."

"No. No, it's not. What does Proverbs 3:5 say?"

Caught off guard, Elizabeth had to search her brain for a

moment. "Trust in the Lord with all your heart, and lean not on your own understanding."

"I didn't trust God's plan for my life. I was afraid of being a parent, afraid of making the mistakes my folks made with me, and it made me angry to know that's all you ever really wanted." He shook his head. "Today, though, I became more afraid of not being a parent. I don't know what I would have done if I'd lost that boy in there."

He pointed toward the hallway that led into the emergency room, then hooked his finger under her chin and tilted her face upwards until their lips were a mere breath apart. "And I don't know what I would do if I ever lost you."

A steady stream of tears flowed from the corners of her eyes and soaked into her hair. "Oh, Elijah, you weren't the only one who didn't trust God. I'm so sorry I lied to you. I just wanted a baby so bad, but now all I want is Dominick safe and healthy. Please forgive me."

He kissed the top of her head and smoothed her hair. "There's nothing to forgive. I'm sure I wasn't easy to talk to. I should have been more considerate of your needs."

She offered him a weak smile. "Thank you for that, but I see now that I should have been a little more sensitive too."

He wiped away her tears, kissed her sweetly on the lips, and cocked his head to the side. "Come on. Let's go see our kid."

They walked hand-in-hand through the emergency room to the room number Elijah had been given, tapped softly on the door, and waited.

"Come in." Amy's weary voice floated to them from the other side.

Elizabeth entered first and took in the scene with misty eyes. The curtain separating the two beds had been drawn back, revealing one empty bed. In the other bed, Amy cradled and comforted her son.

Dominick clung to his mother, his head resting on her chest, silent tears spilling down his cheeks. His fingers lay across Amy's neck, and Elizabeth's heart squeezed as she realized that feeling the vibrations was his way of hearing the lullaby Amy hummed.

Elijah moved in and sat at the foot of the bed. "Hey, Champ. How are you feeling?"

Dominick recapped the incident, while Elizabeth interpreted. The faster his fingers moved, the harder his tears flowed.

"My fault. I wanted to be ready for camp so I practiced making a fire with my flint and steel. Before I knew it, all around me the hay burned and smoked." The boy's hands trembled as he signed, "I was so scared until Owen came. He saved me but he's hurt now. And it's all because of me." Dominick tipped his head back and howled in deep grief.

Her heart breaking for this boy she'd grown to love so deeply, Elizabeth patted his back to get his attention and moved her hands as she voiced her words. "This was an accident and accidents just happen. No one blames you—I know that Owen certainly wouldn't—so don't blame yourself, okay?"

Whimpering, Dominick nodded and nuzzled closer to Amy.

Given the angle of the distraught boy, Elizabeth was sure he couldn't read her lips, but she still kept her voice low as she turned her worried gaze to Amy. "Are you okay?"

Amy nodded. "A little shook up but I think we'll be fine. We should be discharged soon."

Elizabeth hesitated. "And the baby?"

"The ultrasound showed the baby moving and the heart rate is good. But other than that, I guess we'll have to wait and see." Amy sniffled, her bottom lip quivering.

Wanting to comfort this woman, once an enemy and now an ally, but afraid of overstepping her bounds, Elizabeth simply rested her hand on Amy's shoulder. "Don't worry. I'm sure the baby will be just fine."

Amy heaved an exasperated breath. "I'm not worried about the baby." She covered her eyes with her hand, tears slipping out from under her fingertips. "It's Owen. The barn caved in on him just after he got Dominick and me to safety."

Elizabeth gasped.

"I tried to go back after him." She threw her hand into the air in frustration. "I mean, less than a year ago I went after casualties in a war zone, for God's sake. I could have helped, but the paramedic wouldn't let me."

Elijah shook his head. "The paramedic did the right thing keeping you safe and getting you and Dominick to the hospital to get checked out. It's what Owen would have wanted." He stood and moved toward the door. "I'll go see if I can get any information on Owen's condition."

Amy's lips curled in a weak smile. "Thanks." As soon as the door closed behind Elijah, she fell apart. "I've been told God can make good come from bad, but tell me, Elizabeth, if I lose Owen what good can come from that? I have to tell him . . . " She met Elizabeth's gaze, glanced away, and dropped her voice. " . . . thanks for saving me."

Tears pooled in Elizabeth's eyes. "Aw, Amy, you'll get that chance." Sitting on the edge of the bed, she rested her hand on Amy's arm that cradled her distraught son. "There's so much that I don't understand, especially lately. But Elijah reminded me that we are to trust in the Lord with all our heart and not lean on our own understanding."

Like someone standing at the edge of a high dive, debating whether or not they wanted to jump, Amy stared at Elizabeth. After a long moment, Amy took a deep breath and dove in.

"I'm scared. I'm so scared."

Elizabeth realized immediately how hard that must have been to admit for someone who'd been strong for so long. Now, in the midst of her weakness, she'd have to be the strong one.

"I know, but I'm here, and I'll help you through whatever is to come."

The promise was made and she intended to keep it. Somehow.

God, don't let me down this time. Amy needs You. We're both trusting you.

"My grace is sufficient for you, for My strength is made perfect in weakness." The response fluttered from the depths of her soul like a butterfly landing silently on her heart, bringing with it enough peace and hope for the moment.

CHAPTER
Twenty-five

"Well, the hospital staff wouldn't give me any information on Owen's condition since I'm not family," Elijah announced returning to Amy and Dominick's room.

Aware of the privacy laws, Amy wasn't surprised, but her heart sank just the same.

"But I found someone who would."

Anna appeared in the doorway, her eyes dark with anguish.

Had Dominick not been asleep on her chest, Amy would have jumped out of the bed at the sight of this woman who'd graciously given so much for her sake . . . quite possibly even her own son.

Elijah motioned for Elizabeth to join him. "Let go to the cafeteria for a cup of coffee."

Pulling up a chair, Anna reached for Amy's hand. "Are you and Dominick okay?"

Amy felt as though she would drown in her sorrow. "We're fine, but . . ." Her voice thickened with tears. "How's Owen?"

Anna dropped her gaze.

Amy's heart plunged to the pit of her stomach, a lump of panic rising in its place. "He's alive, isn't he? Please tell me he's alive."

"Yes, thank God, but he's been hurt pretty bad. Amy, he can't feel his legs."

Her short-lived relief morphed into heavy grief. "You mean he's paralyzed?"

"We don't know the extent of his injuries yet. The CT scan showed considerable swelling so for now the doctors are treating that until more tests can be done to determine if there is damage to the spinal cord and exactly where it's at." She squeezed Amy's fingers. "He's in good hands—the doctors' and our Father's—and I'm choosing to believe that with our love and prayers and extensive therapy he'll make a complete recovery."

A wild storm brewed in Amy's heart as she imagined her strong, brave Owen in such a dire condition . . . all because of her. No amount of mental toughness could prevent the emotional hurricane from battering her weathered spirit and wiping out every defense she'd ever put up. Remembering all Owen and Anna had done for her caused the creek of tears to quickly flood its banks as sobs rose from the depths of her soul.

"Oh, Anna. I'm so sorry. You and your family took us in when we had nowhere to go. You not only gave us a place to stay, but you gave me a new purpose. Somehow you and Owen have always been there right when I needed someone. And what have we done in return? Burn down your barn with all your equipment inside, seriously hurting your son in the process. If I never would have come to Harvest Bay . . . "

"Now stop right there. Don't think that even for a minute. God brought you to Harvest Bay for a reason. He brought you to us for a reason. The fire was an accident and insurance will cover it, but you, my dear, are no accident. We are all better for having known you and Dominick." Anna leaned in closer. "And I'm certain Owen would agree."

Amy moaned. "If you really knew me, you wouldn't think that." The flutter in her abdomen reinforced her words and made her glad Dominick was still asleep.

"I know all I need to know." Anna's firm tone, laced with understanding, not judgment, planted a tiny seed of acceptance in Amy's heart.

"Before the fire I was talking with Steph about forgiveness."

"Mmm." Anna nodded. "Important topic, but not always easy."

"She said forgiveness is accepting that things didn't turn out the way you expected, and you make a conscious effort to let it go." Amy swallowed. "Think Owen can ever forgive me?"

Anna's lips curved upwards. "There's only one way to find out."

A short time later, the nurse delivered Amy's discharge papers, and they were free to go. As much as Amy wanted to keep Dominick close to her, she recognized Elijah's need to be with him as well and suggested that he and Elizabeth take him home for the night.

"I have some business to take care of here, and I don't know how late I'll be." She spoke slowly and clearly so Dominick could read her lips. "Go get a good night's sleep at your dad's, and I'll be there to get you first thing in the morning."

Dominick moved his fingers while Elizabeth put a voice to his words. "Will I have to go to school?"

Amy chuckled and rustled his hair. "After what you've been through, I think you deserve to play hooky." She held her breath as he hugged her tightly just above her growing waistline, and heaved a silent sigh of relief that, after being active all day, the baby had seemed to settle down. She could put off discussing this situation with him a little longer.

They walked together through the emergency room and parted ways at the lobby—Elijah, Elizabeth, and Dominick exiting out the sliding glass doors, while Amy headed toward neurology. Weaving her way through the hallways and up the elevator, Amy wracked her brain for the words to say, but there were no words to describe the whirlwind in her heart. When she reached the room number Anna had given her, Amy took a deep breath and knocked.

The door cracked open, and a nurse slipped out pushing a small cart with a blood pressure monitor and a pulse oximeter. Wedged under her arm was Owen's chart.

Amy eyed her, formulating a quick plan on how to hijack the chart. She wanted to pore over it, learn the treatment plan, the prognosis, whatever was necessary for her to help Owen recover.

The nurse met Amy's gaze with an annoyed expression. "Can I help you?"

"Oh, no, thank you. I'm just visiting the patient."

"I'm sorry, ma'am, but it's a quarter after eight. Visiting hours on this wing ended fifteen minutes ago."

Amy's shoulders fell. "But you don't understand—"

The nurse put a hand up, cutting her off. "Hospital policy. You can come back tomorrow morning at ten."

The nurse started to step around her, but Amy blocked her, chin lifted defiantly and shoulders squared her. "Listen, that man in there saved my son and me today. I would have been up here sooner, but I just got discharged from the ER. Now, we can make this easy and you can look away while I slip in. Or we can do this the hard way, which will include a scene and possible bodily harm. But I promise you that one way or another I'm getting in that room. So what's it going to be?" Amy crossed her arms and hoped the nurse wouldn't call security right then.

The nurse's demeanor softened slightly. "You've got fifteen minutes," she mumbled.

Backing down, Amy offered an appreciative nod. "Thank you."

"Fifteen minutes," the nurse reminded her as she pushed the cart away.

Amy's heart began to hammer in her chest as she turned back toward the door and tried to prepare herself for the scene that lay just beyond. After everything she'd experienced in Iraq, including watching helplessly as Justin died in her arms, she bet her bottom dollar that this would be the one to break her heart. Sucking in a breath, she stepped into the room and pulled the door shut.

In the dim lighting, it resembled every other hospital room she'd ever been in—drab, boring walls, one window with a view of the parking lot, and the faint smell of disinfectant in the air. Tiptoeing farther inside, she peered around the curtain and froze. Her blood turned to ice, her breath caught in her throat. The standard, ordinary hospital bed held the most extraordinary man she'd ever known, her once in a lifetime chance at love, and her hope for a fulfilling future.

His eyes fluttered open. With a weak smile, he held up his heavy hand.

"Hey."

"Hey." Determined to hold herself together, she blinked back the tears that pooled beneath her lashes and moved to the side of the bed. "How are you feeling?"

"Well, from my waist down, not much of anything."

Amy could have kicked herself for her thoughtless choice of words until she spied the smirk on Owen's face, and found herself snickering. "Once a wise guy, always a wise guy."

Owen shrugged. "Some things never change."

Amy pulled up a chair and lowered herself into it. "How exactly did this happen?"

"When the roof caved in a rafter fell and hit me just below my shoulder blades." He rubbed his forehead. "At least I think that's how it happened."

"Owen, I don't know how to tell you how sorry I am."

"Then don't. This isn't your fault."

"Indirectly it is. If Dominick—"

"It isn't his fault either." Owen's gaze met hers with an intensity that pierced her to her soul. "Look, Amy, you've been running from ghosts, but I've been chasing them right into every burning building we get called to." He shook his head. "This time was different, though. When I ran into the barn I wasn't trying to redeem myself for the umpteenth time for not being there to rescue Julia and my son. This time I could only think of you and Dominick." He closed his eyes. "Somehow I survived losing them, but I don't think I'd make it a day without the two of you."

Amy sniffled and swiped at the tears streaming down her face. "It's amazing what the human brain thinks of in such a short amount of time when there's a chance you just might die."

He shifted his attention to her. "Care to share?"

"Well, basically I realized that while I've done a lot of things wrong in my life, I've done some things right too, and one of the best choices I ever made was coming to Harvest Bay."

His lips curved in a soft smile. "Does that mean you won't be leaving after Christmas?"

"I believe I said all the way back on the Fourth of July that we'd be leaving unless something happened to change my mind."

"I remember. So has something happened?"

In an instant, her heart catapulted to her throat, making it impossible for words to pass. Swallowing hard, she nodded.

"Well, good. Angel's done so well with you training her. I'd hate to have her regress."

"I thought of her while I was in the barn. She's come so far in just a few months—from a broken, angry horse to trusting enough to let someone get close again."

"It's been a remarkable transformation." Owen reached out his hand. "Kinda sounds like someone else I know."

Slipping her hand into his, she closed her eyes, knowing there was no other hand she ever wanted to hold. "And I knew I couldn't die without telling you . . . "

"Yes?"

There was so much she had to tell him, she wondered where to start. "I need to tell you why I didn't want you to go on that mission trip."

Owen snorted. "Well, I don't think that'll be an issue now."

"Maybe not, but I want you to know." She dragged a long shaky breath from her throat. "When I was twelve years old, my dad left on a mission trip and he never came home. On his return trip, his plane went down and I lost him. Forever." She gazed at him hoping he could see in her eyes everything she held for him in her heart. "I didn't want to lose you too."

His fingers tightened around her hand. "You can't get rid of me that easy."

Her heart squeezed even tighter. "I wouldn't be so sure. There's one more thing you need to know."

"Lay it on me."

Amy opened her mouth but fear paralyzed her vocal cords.

Owen glanced down the front of his blanket covered body. "Amy, look at me. I'm not going anywhere. Whatever it is, I can take it, and we'll get through it just like we'll get through all of this. Together."

Once again he came to her rescue. Even in his condition, he gave her the strength to go on.

"I-I'm pregnant." She braced herself for the response—the look of disappointment, the judging scowl—but finding only his tender gaze, she continued. "Not by choice or even by accident for that matter. I was raped by some guys from the Iraqi military during my last deployment. I didn't tell you or your mom because I was afraid after how easily you accepted me, you'd reject me without a second thought. But I can't hide it much longer, and . . . "

She gazed at him with more love than she knew she had in her. "I don't want to hide anything from you anymore. Ever."

He reached up and brushed his fingertips across her temple. "Good because I want to know everything about you." He paused. "What are you going to do about this baby?"

"I don't know. I thought I'd decided to keep it, but when I was in the fire, my only concern was you and Dominick." Fresh tears slid down her cheeks. "I just can't love this baby like a mother should."

"Come here." He held his arms out to her.

Amy stood, leaned over the bed and allowed herself to be enveloped in a warm, safe, loving embrace. She didn't pull away. She didn't try to run. Instead she rested her head on his chest and wept with an odd mixture of grief and joy.

"I wish I could take that whole situation and all the pain that comes with it away from you, but I promise you that whatever you decide, I will not leave you. Ever."

Another wave washed over her, but this time it was relief, and it refreshed her soul and strengthened her spirit. She lifted her head and gazed into the beautiful eyes she could lose herself in.

"I'm going to help you through this too. You will be walking again in no time, you hear me?"

Owen chuckled. "Yes, ma'am."

"Well, I better let you get some rest. Can I bring Dominick by in the morning? He'll want to see you."

"I'll be counting the minutes until you do."

Impulsively, Amy leaned forward and brushed her lips softly against his. "Have a good night."

Owen grinned. "I will now."

Smiling naturally for the first time in a long time, she straightened, turned, and headed toward the door.

"Hey, Amy."

She did an about face. "Yeah?"

"You never told me what happened to change your mind about staying."

"Oh, that's an easy one." Amy's smile brightened, and a warmth radiated through her that rivaled that of the afternoon sun. "I fell in love."

Standing in the doorway of Dominick's room, Elizabeth watched him sleep and tried to wrap her brain around the events of the day. From behind, Elijah's strong arms encircled her waist and she leaned heavily against him.

"You okay?" His tender murmur against her ear caused a small earthquake in her heart.

Her voice came out in a hoarse whisper. "He must have been so scared. Imagine not being able to hear in the midst of such danger and confusion."

Elijah rested his chin on her head. "I can't imagine."

Turning in his arms, she buried her face in his chest. "We almost lost him today."

"I know. It scares me to think about it too." Drawing her into their bedroom, he sat with her at the edge of their bed. "You know what else scares me?"

She sniffed. "No. What?"

"Standing in the way of God's plan for your life."

Creases of confusion forming on her brow, she gazed up at him with damp eyes. "But you are God's plan for my life."

He held up a finger. "I'm only one small part of it. I've been too selfish to understand that your desire to be a mother is your calling, not an obsession."

Elizabeth pulled back slightly. "Right now Dominick is enough for me." It was the truth. She could be content with being a stepmother for the rest of her life.

He held his hands up. "I guess I deserve that, but it does-n't seem fair to all those kids who crave a woman's nurturing love and compassion."

Elizabeth eyed him with cautious optimism. "Elijah, what are you saying?"

"I'm saying that we should try to have a baby again, whether we go to the fertility doctor or not. And in the meantime, I think we need to start the paperwork to become foster parents."

Her lips curved in a slow smile. "Really?"

Elijah nodded.

"But what about you? After all you've been through as a kid, I thought becoming a foster parent would be too hard."

"This isn't about me. It's about doing what's right and following God's will." He shrugged. "And, besides, what better example do I have to follow than our Father?"

Joy flooded Elizabeth's heart, the excess washing away her voice and pooling behind her lashes.

"What do you say?" Elijah squeezed her hands. "Will you pray with me that God's will is done in our home and our hearts?"

Following his lead, Elizabeth slid to her knees. Awestruck, she listened to Elijah's heart-felt plea to God. It had been months since they'd prayed together, and yet on the heels of this second miracle in one day, in the depths of her soul, she still felt hollow.

"In twenty counseling sessions, it seems I've changed the most after this week." Sitting on the sofa in Dr. Kimball's office, Amy flipped back in her memory almost five months to that first appointment and saw a different woman sitting in her place—a woman weighed down with years of baggage, a woman living in her shell. Now, however, she'd transformed into a butterfly, light with hope and love, ready to take a chance and spread her wings.

Appearing nearly perfect in her crisp navy suit, with her dark curls piled on her head, Dr. Kimball tapped a perfectly manicured fingernail on the arm of the chair. "And why do you suppose that is?"

"I think I've finally discovered who I really am. All the grenades life lobbed at me—from my mom leaving to losing my dad and Justin, from becoming a single parent of a special needs child to the attack that resulted in this pregnancy— might have helped shape me, but they don't define me. I made peace with myself for mistakes I've made, and I figured out what I want out of life."

Dr. Kimball nodded, a satisfied expression on her face. "Sounds like you've made quite a bit of progress in your journey to self-discovery. Was it as painful as you thought it would be?"

"At times."

Entwining her long slender fingers, Dr. Kimball brought them to her chin. "Making peace with yourself, owning up to your own shortcomings, is often the biggest and hardest step to take. Have you noticed a decrease in your nightmares and anxiety?"

"Yes, but I thought it was because I've worked so hard with Angel and now with Owen in his rehabilitation."

Dr. Kimball shook her head. "It might all be related, but true healing has to come from inside you first." Her lips curved in a smile that reached her twinkling crystal blue eyes. "Congratulations, Amy. I think your time here is done."

Amy stared at Dr. Kimball, a strange twinge penetrating her heart. She'd grown to depend on and even enjoy her weekly hour-long sessions with her therapist. Dr. Kimball had become more like a trusted friend, one of the few people she ever completely opened up to, and at that moment her relief and happiness over her healing was partly clouded by the fact that she wasn't sure she wanted to let that go.

"This is it?"

"Amy, you've come so far. Be proud of this accomplishment." Dr. Kimball reached out and patted Amy's knee. "I'll always be here if you ever need me, but you're ready. You're really ready."

Amy could only nod as a lumpy mixture of joy and sorrow lodged in her throat. Dr. Kimball's beautiful, delicate face reflected Amy's conflicting emotions. Rising, she crossed the room to her coffee pot.

"So what do you want for your future?"

Amy's thoughts drifted to Owen and all he'd done for her and Dominick, all he meant to her. Somehow he'd become her roots and her wings. He kept her grounded and yet gave her the courage and confidence to try things she'd never thought possible. It felt as if she'd loved him all her life instead of just a few short months, and she believed with all her heart that she'd never love anyone else so completely. A blissful smile crossed her face.

"True love. Real happiness. A family."

Filling a mug, Dr. Kimball stirred in some creamer and sweetener. "Sounds like things are going well for you and Owen. From what you've said, Dominick must be happy about that."

Amy wondered if this perceptive psychiatrist could see the stars in her eyes. "They are and he is."

Dr. Kimball quirked an eyebrow. "But does a family include this baby?"

Amy hesitated, and then blew out a breath that ruffled her bangs. "I still don't know. I thought it did, but the fire changed everything."

"What do you mean?"

"Well, when Dominick and Owen were somewhere in that burning barn, I realized that I could go on without this baby, but I couldn't live a day without my son or the man I love." Amy leaned forward, resting her forearms on her knees and folding her hands. "Is that terrible?"

"No. It's honest." Leaning against her desk, Dr. Kimball sipped the steaming liquid. "What's keeping you from making a decision?"

Amy shrugged. "I want to make the right one."

Cradling the mug in her hands, Dr. Kimball returned to her chair. "Just remember we all have issues. It's called life, and life isn't perfect no matter who you are. Pray about your choices, listen to your heart, and your baby will be just fine."

Pray. Amy's stomach turned as she thought of the one area in her life she still had to work on. She'd been putting it off, resorting to prayer only in moments of desperation, but maybe the time had come to try.

"Back at the end of July when I first told you about this baby, you said that I've been given the opportunity to be a hero. How do you know that? How do you know that I won't be looked at like a coward who ran away from her problems?"

"Amy, if you think you can't love this baby like you do Dominick, then giving him a chance at happiness with someone who will only get to experience motherhood through your sacrifice is the most heroic thing you could do. Trust me on this one."

The words held more than a therapist's wisdom, and Amy eyed Dr. Kimball, idly wondering exactly who she was. But after a moment, she sucked in a lungfull of air and stood up.

"Well, I guess this is it."

Dr. Kimball set her mug on the coffee table and once again got to her feet. "It's been a pleasure to watch you become a little stronger every week. It might have taken longer than you expected, but you made it."

Acting on impulse, not knowing or caring if it was the proper thing to do, Amy reached out and embraced her therapist. She closed her eyes soaking in the moment. A chapter in her life was ending, but oddly enough it seemed as if this story was just beginning.

Opening her eyes just before releasing Dr. Kimball, Amy glanced over her therapist's shoulder and spotted a black-and-white photo in a small gold frame propped up near the computer. She squinted to bring it into focus better. In twenty weeks, Amy thought she'd stared at every frame, book, and knick knack in this office, but she didn't remember seeing this photo. She stepped out of Dr. Kimball's arms and walked over to get closer look.

"This picture. I've never seen it before. Where'd you get it?"

"From the social worker I told you about." Dr. Kimball stepped next to Amy and gazed at the old photo. "That is a real-life hero, Amy. She's my birth mother."

A missing piece of her life fell into place as Amy shifted her attention from the picture to this woman who'd done so much for her. Her smile reached her tear-filled eyes.

"That is my grandmother."

With each passing week, the incredible discovery lost some of its wonder, replaced by more turmoil and confusion. Amy had made the decision to keep the baby, a decision she was prepared to live with. But after seeing with her own eyes how successful and well-adjusted Dr. Kimball had turned out, new uncertainties filled her.

You have been given the opportunity to be a hero not only to this baby, but to some woman out there who will get the chance to be a mother only through your sacrifice.

"Hey, you're awfully quiet," Owen said as they worked on his exercises before church. "What's going on in that pretty little head of yours?"

Amy shifted her focus from her daunting situation to Owen's progress and a smile easily returned to her face. "Just thinking about how much progress you've made."

She blinked twice to keep the moisture from building in her eyes. "I'm really proud of you."

By three and a half weeks after the fire, the swelling in his back had decreased enough to show little damage to his spinal cord, which restored hope and endless possibilities as far as his complete healing. The doctors released him from the hospital with a list of daily rehabilitation exercises and scheduled trips to physical therapy several times a week.

As fate would have it, Elijah was assigned to his case and pushed Owen just as hard as Amy did.

"Well I haven't had much of a choice. You can be a regular drill sergeant when you want to be. You know that?"

Amy chuckled. "I guess you can take the girl out of the military, but you can't take the military out of the girl." Her words struck a nerve and her grin faltered as the baby shifted in her round belly. "Now back to work. You've got five more reps."

He reached for her hand, placed a kiss on her palm, and wrapped her fingers around it. "Thank you."

The affection twinkling in his eyes caused her knees to wobble. "For what?"

"For changing your mind. For staying."

"Well, I haven't had much of a choice," she mimicked with a smirk. "I mean, really, you sat in a wild horse's stall and ran into a burning barn for me. After that, I'd say you're stuck with me." She stood and patted his knee. "But I've still got chores to do, so we're done for now. I'll let your mom know that she can help you get ready, and I'll see you in just a bit."

Owen reeled her back in by the hand as she turned to walk away. "I love you, Amy, and someday I'm going to walk again for you."

She kissed the top of his head. "And I love you, but you've done enough for me. You're going to walk for you."

The peaceful stable provided little comfort for her troubled mind, and by the time she settled into the pew next to Owen, it'd become a full fledged firestorm. She didn't just need answers. She needed the right ones, and her patience was growing as worn and raggedy as a child's treasured blankie.

With people streaming in, Owen adjusted his wheelchair as close to the pew as possible. "I thought you said you didn't want to hide anything from me anymore."

Feeling like a cornered animal, Amy put an extra inch between them. "I'm not hiding anything."

He eyed her dubiously. "You seem to forget how well I know you."

Amy narrowed her eyes at him. "If you know me so well, then you know I'm not going to talk about it." Her demeanor softened and she reached for his hand. "At least not yet."

Owen laced her fingers with his just as the pianist's fingers danced over the keys, filling the church with the first few measures of an old familiar hymn. He leaned in, his whisper tickling her ear. "This isn't over."

During the prelude, while everyone else prepared their hearts and minds for worship, Amy drifted back to the fire— her desperation for Dominick and Owen and her disregard for the baby. Her desire to live.

But I want to be able to live with myself. I've made so many bad choices that have affected my whole future.

Anna's words floated back to her. *"I'm able to accept that I had to walk down that path to get to where I am today."*

Glancing at Owen, Amy melted a little. *I'd have to say this is a pretty incredible view too.* The baby shifted and her spirits fell. *Almost.*

As the music faded, Pastor Ben made his way to the pulpit and, with the exception of a fussy baby, a hush fell over the congregation. "Grace and peace to you from God our Father. As most of you know, we recently had a team of men and women from this church leave on a mission trip."

Amy glanced at Owen, guilt pinching her heart. *He should be on that trip instead of stuck here in a wheelchair.* He gave her hand a reassuring squeeze, and her heart warmed at the realization that he knew her so well.

"With today being the Sunday before Thanksgiving, I'd been thinking about a message illustrating the importance of being thankful for what we have, while supporting those in need. I remember several years ago, when I served on a mission team, we went to a village in Cambodia where I met a young man just beginning his ministry. He'd graduated from Bible college in Cincinnati, and returned to his homeland to put his faith and education in action as headmaster of the Christian school our church supported. When I found out he is spending the holidays with his family in southern Ohio, I invited him to come and share his testimony with you. So, without wasting another second, please help me welcome Joshua Sovann Smith."

Applause echoed through the sanctuary, and Amy unenthusiastically joined in as a young Asian man made his way to the pulpit, clutching an old, worn Bible to his chest. She'd looked forward to the way Pastor Ben unerringly found a way to challenge her every Sunday. He made her think, and she had so much she needed to think about.

"Good morning. Thank you, Pastor Ben Andrews and all of you for having me here today. I also want to thank you for supporting the missionaries in your congregation. I am living proof of how important mission work is."

Amy tipped her head to the side, impressed by his clear English. She barely detected a foreign accent.

"I'm going to read a passage that I know you're all familiar with." Joshua flipped his Bible open to a marked page. "Romans 8:28 says, 'And we know that all things work together for good to those who love God, to those who are the called according to His purpose.' We are all called to serve God and help complete His will in whatever we are gifted in."

Leaning forward, Amy chewed on a thumbnail and listened intently.

"My story begins in Cambodia. My mother was sold to a brothel by her father at the age of thirteen. She was young and beautiful and, from what I'm told, earned a considerable amount of money for the brothel owner, averaging eight men a day. That is, until she became pregnant with me. The brothel owner insisted that she have an abortion, as is common with such prostitutes and, I've recently learned, is unfortunately an added expense that indebts these women to the owners longer."

As Amy listened, she slid her hand over her belly, connecting to this woman in a way she didn't understand. *No woman should become pregnant as a result of a crime. It's just not how it's supposed to be . . . and yet, I'm staring at the result.*

"But by the grace of God my mother escaped the one-room prison they kept her in and sought the help of a missionary. This man took her to an orphanage run by a young American couple. There they took care of her until I was born, and they would have allowed her to continue to stay, but she ran away."

She ran away. That sounds familiar. But it wasn't like she was planning on being a mother. She was probably so scared she didn't know what to do . . . kind of like I am now.

"The situation seems grim, but I'm here to tell you that sometimes when life's storms are the roughest, that's when God is the closest to you, working things out for your best and for His glory, without you even realizing it."

"*Open your heart to the possibility . . . Try seeing with your heart instead of your eyes . . .* She searched through her grandmother's Bible until she found Romans 8:28 and read the words silently. "*And we know that all things work together for good to those who love God, to those who are the called according to His purpose.*" When she was trapped in the barn fire, she'd said she wanted to live for God. She'd meant it with all her heart, but now thinking of her father, she wondered if she could.

"That couple adopted me and brought me up knowing and loving the Lord. Just before I started school, we moved here to Ohio, where I got an education and other opportunities I'd never have received in Cambodia. I understand that God has worked good through my mother's miserable situation and selfless decision. I wouldn't be who I am today if she hadn't been brave enough to give me the chance at a life abundant with the love of a mother and father, with educational and spiritual opportunities. I've never questioned my identity because I believe that God created me to grow in my birth mother's womb and my adopted parents' heart."

Amy's gaze shifted to the left side of the altar, where Elizabeth was signing Joshua's message for the hearing-impaired congregants. Compassion flooded Amy as it dawned on her that in kind of the same way Dominick had grown in Elizabeth's heart. Even after the loss of their baby, Elizabeth and Elijah had been preparing for foster children that would grow in their hearts. Amy wished she had the ability to love like that, but at this point her heart only had room for Dominick and Owen.

"But even more than that, I can see that because of one man's actions, my earthly life as well as my eternal life was saved. I don't know what happened to that missionary, but before he left he gave my mother his Bible and marked this verse, which he'd translated into her native Khmer language." Joshua flipped open the Bible and read. "'Have I not commanded you? Be strong and of good courage; do not be afraid, nor be dismayed, for the Lord your God is with you wherever you go.'"

Amy stifled a gasp, and her hand flew to her pendant.

"That verse is from the first chapter of the book of Joshua, my namesake and a source of strength and encouragement for any situation I might face. And it was all because a man by the name of David Beauregard cared about one lost soul."

"Dad?" The tearful whisper slipped from Amy's throat.

"I can't say whether my mother received Jesus as her Savior or not. I pray for her salvation daily, but I know that because of this brave missionary I have been saved."

Owen slipped his arm around her shoulders and hugged her as close to him as he could.

Like a train rolling out of the station, her pulse picked up speed, her breath coming in short puffs. "Dad?" The squeak of her voice was barely audible behind the waterfall of tears. "How can that be?"

Owen wiped away her stream of tears. "Your dad was a hero, Amy. Just like you."

"I lost him, but because of his sacrifice this man isn't lost." She sniffed and wiped her face with the sleeve of her sweater. "And I don't know if I'm okay with that."

"In closing, I just want to stress that God is constantly at work—in your lives, in this church, in the world around us, and He can use every situation for His glory. I want to thank you again for supporting your missionaries, and I daily thank God for this very special missionary." He held up the Bible that had belonged to Amy's father.

Amy's heart hammered in her chest. Anxiety rose with the thick lump in her throat. She tried to focus on her deep breathing techniques, but Joshua had unknowingly torn the eighteen-year-old gash wide open, and the searing pain carried each breath away before she could grab it. Black spots floated through her vision. The sanctuary started to tilt.

Her chest heaved as she battled a rebel sob trying to escape. "I've got to get out of here."

Before Owen could remind her that running wouldn't solve anything, that she'd promised not to hide from him, she slipped out of the pew, maneuvered around his wheelchair, and dashed through the back doors.

With a wrenching sob, she hit her knees in the church yard. "Angel," she choked. "I need Angel."

Pastor Ben approached the pulpit as Joshua made his way to the front pew. "Thank you for that message this morning, Joshua. I'm sure I'm not the only one who felt the Holy Spirit moving among us as you spoke."

Elizabeth worked hard to mask her disappointment as she stood in front of the congregation. Pastor Ben might not have been the only one who felt the Holy Spirit, but she for one hadn't.

She used to be able to close her eyes and sense the Spirit all around her. She could breathe Him in and be instantly rejuvenated, but she hadn't felt God's presence in months, and it was becoming more difficult to put on the charade for her friends every week. She'd managed to fool Elijah for a while, but now he could see through her act.

Lately he'd been more excited about furthering the process for becoming a foster parent, while she'd become weary of the paperwork and home inspection and all the other hoops they had to jump through. More than once she'd asked herself, "Is it worth it?" And she received the same answer every time.

"My grace is sufficient for you, for My strength is made perfect in weakness."

She believed the Lord's promise somewhere down deep in her soul, but the emptiness still prevailed. It'd been almost seven weeks since she lost her baby, and some days it still felt as if all she was doing was surviving, just putting one foot in front of the other. The very idea of trying again—the waiting and hoping and wishing—drained her past the point of desperation to near hopelessness.

"The altar is open at this time. Please come as you feel led." From the piano rose the beautiful melody of "Here I Am, Lord." "Let's remember our missionaries and all those who may be going through a time of uncertainty right now. And if you don't yet know Jesus Christ as your Savior, I encourage you to take that step. Let Joshua or me pray with you today so you can begin to see all the good He can make come from your life."

As congregants began to migrate toward the altar, Elizabeth stepped down and sat in her spot next to Elijah. She looked down at her Bible in her lap, and the gold lettering blurred behind unshed tears.

Where are You, God? Here I am. Have You forgotten me? All my life I've known I'm supposed to be a mother but now . . . I'm so lost. She flipped to the verse in Isaiah that served as the inspiration for the sweet hymn. *"Also I heard the voice of the Lord, saying: 'Whom shall I send, and who will go for us?' Then I said, 'Here am I! Send me."* Her heart begged the words as she read. *God, just fill me up again. Give my life purpose. Make something good come of this.*

"Elizabeth?"

She snapped her gaze toward the soft voice. Meeting Uncle Bill's gentle gaze, she pasted a smile over her desperation and loneliness.

"God gave me a verse for you. Isaiah 54:1. I'm still praying for you, kiddo." He squeezed her shoulder, shook Elijah's hand, and joined Wilma at the altar.

Craving a heaping helping of inspiration, Elizabeth flipped to the passage Bill had just given her, and as she read her pleading heart nearly stopped in her chest.

"Sing, oh barren, you who have not borne! Break forth into singing, and cry aloud, you who have not labored with child! For more are the children of the desolate than the children of the married woman,' says the Lord." She read it again and once more after that. She recognized the promise, but still hesitated to rest her hope in it.

What are you saying to me, Lord?

The question remained unanswered as Elijah led Elizabeth to the altar. Kneeling in prayer, she wondered if Godcould possibly give her an empty promise.

The service finally concluded, but the sanctuary remained full of mingling congregants and a few still lingered at the altar. Grabbing her coat and purse, Elizabeth spun on her heel, ready to high-tail it out of there.

"Elizabeth!"

The urgency in the voice stopped her in her tracks. Turning with worry in her eyes, she met Sarah's gaze. "What's wrong?"

Sarah closed the gap between them. "I just got a call from our case worker. They have an emergency situation and need an immediate placement for a six-year-old deaf girl. You and Elijah just finished your paperwork, right?"

For a moment Elizabeth stood in stunned silence. Could this be the child she'd prayed for? Was this what God was try-ing to tell her?

Basking in the light of God's promise, her heart blos-somed, tickling her insides and causing a new warmth to radi-ate through her. "What's the number?"

As Sarah scribbled it on a corner of her bulletin, Elijah walked up with Dominick by his side.

"We have to go," he said. "Something's going on with Amy. An anxiety attack, maybe. Owen said she left in a hurry and now she's not answering her cell."

Elizabeth took the scrap of paper and met Sarah's gaze with tears pooling behind her lashes. Then she, Elijah, and Dominick dashed down the aisle and out the door, the bright rays of her new-found hope clouded over by deep concern.

Twenty-Seven

Tears blinded Amy as she and Angel tore down the dirt path to the clearing by the lake. The pounding of Angel's hooves on the ground matched the rhythm of Amy's heart. She'd never pushed the horse—or herself—so hard. At thirty-six weeks into her pregnancy, she was well past the point of horseback riding, especially at such a breakneck speed, but there was nothing else that could soothe her. She'd have to deal with reality soon enough, but at that moment she couldn't face it. Nor could she fight the urge to be carried away.

The cold late autumn breeze bit at her face as she reached the clearing. Skidding Angel to a stop, she swung out of the saddle and stumbled to the pebbly shoreline. Tiny shells and stones crunched under her as she sank to her knees.

"Why, God?" A sob erupted from her and, finding a large rock, she catapulted it into the lake. "I was only twelve and he was all I had." She reached for a heavier stone and heaved it into the frigid water. "He. Was. All. I. Had." She dropped her face into her hands and wept.

Be strong and of good courage; do not be afraid, nor be dismayed, for the Lord your God is with you wherever you go.

She sniffed and wiped her face with the sleeve of her sweater. "I know, I know. But You couldn't tuck me into bed at night and sing to me. You couldn't push me on the tire swing or take me riding. I *needed* my dad."

"Someone else needed him more."

Amy started. Swiveling her gaze toward the voice, she found Anna approaching her, Dixie's reins in her hand.

"Losing him changed my whole life."

Anna tied the reins on a branch near Angel and squatted next to Amy. "I understand that, remember?" She situated herself on the damp pebbles. "So what are you going to do about it?"

Amy silently tossed another rock into the water with a small splash.

"The only guarantee that we have in life is that things change. It's up to you now to accept it and make the best out of where the Lord has brought you. Or you can continue in this rut, keeping everyone who cares about you at arm's length while you hang on to the grief and sorrow." Anna reached out as Amy prepared to launch another rock. "Amy, you have to let go."

"I can't remember his voice or the way my hand felt in his." Staring at the smooth pebble in her hand, tears flooded her eyes again. "I can't see his face in my mind anymore."

"Honey, that's just the effects of time, and it's going to happen whether you let go or not." Anna hugged her knees to her chest. "Tell me some of your favorite memories."

Amy sniffed. "He bought me a horse named Mercy. We had a dream of opening a therapeutic equine program for disabled kids."

"What else?"

As Amy rattled off several more of her favorite memories, she found her heart lightening with each one.

Anna slipped her arm across Amy's shoulders. "You see? You're dad is never going to be gone as long as you keep him close to you in your memories. He's a part of the amazing boy Dominick is, and he's very much alive in Joshua's testimony." Anna smoothed Amy's stylishly unkempt hair. "Your dad saved a life for all eternity. That's something to be proud of."

Relishing Anna's motherly care, but still clinging to her independence, Amy straightened. "I am, but he would be disappointed in the way I've acted."

Anna shook her head. "No. You accepted it in God's perfect timing."

"He would be disappointed that I turned away from God."

Anna took both of Amy's hands in hers. "It's never too late to return."

Amy hesitated. Living for God meant committing to a life of discipleship, and she didn't know if she could give herself to something she didn't know much about.

"I'm sorry. I can't." She shrugged. "I don't understand it."

"Oh, Amy, there are things about Jesus' teachings that I still don't get. You don't have to understand. You just have to believe."

Amy scooped up a handful of pebbles and let them run through her fingers, making a sound like rain as they cascaded to the ground. It reminded her of that miserable day at the women's clinic. If the Lord had delivered her from that situation and sent Steph just when she needed someone, why hadn't He provided her with another solution, one she could live with?

At the sound of snapping twigs, she looked over her shoulder. Her heart leapt as Owen emerged into the clearing, with Elijah pushing his wheelchair. She met Elizabeth's concerned gaze and the baby kicked inside her round belly.

Amy's shoulders fell at the reminder of her dilemma, and she scooped up another handful of pebbles. "It's not easy to believe."

"Of course it isn't. If it was, Peter would have met Jesus on the water. But when he started thinking, he started sinking." Anna shoveled up her own handful of shells and stones. "You have to make the choice to see with your heart instead of your eyes."

Amy reflected on Maggie's similar advice. She caught Owen's intense gaze from several yards away, and somehow it all started making sense. "And open your heart to the possibility."

To her amazement, the heavy fog surrounding her spiritual eyes began to dissipate. New understanding filled her as she began to see how God had guided her steps, putting people in her path, starting with Justin, who would lead her to this moment.

"I want to believe." Amy shifted her tearful gaze back to Anna. "Will you help me?"

Anna's smile shined from her caring eyes. "Every step of the way."

While Amy prayed to accept Jesus as her Savior and begin living each day for Him, eighteen years of heavy grief melted into hope, and true peace settled in her soul. The melody of her special lullaby floated across the lake to her, and she once again felt loved and safe.

She'd returned home.

"Amen." Renewed, Amy filled her lungs with the fresh, crisp air and pushed to her feet. Her joyous demeanor faltered, however, as a gush of wetness oozed down her leg, soaking through her dress pants. Fighting off rising panic, she reached out for Anna.

"I think my water just broke."

Excitement lit up Anna's face as she turned to the others and announced, "We're having a baby."

Amy clung to Anna. "But it's too soon. I haven't decided."

"Don't you worry about a thing, Amy. We're going to take care of you." Anna pulled out her cell phone and pushed a button. "Ken, it's mom. I need you to bring the truck back to the clearing and take care of putting Dixie and Angel up. Amy's gone into labor."

Like a deer caught in the headlights, fear knotted Amy's muscles and locked her joints. She swiveled her gaze from Anna to Elizabeth, her eyes screaming, "Help me!"

It was the choice she'd yet to make that petrified Amy. Should she keep this baby and hope to become the mother he deserved? Or should she give him to another woman who already loved him and hope he'd never hold it against her?

Within minutes, Kennedy arrived in a white extended-cab pickup. Leaving the engine running, she hopped out and hurried to the horses.

"Good luck, Amy. Have someone keep us up-to-date," she said as she rode off on Dixie, while leading Angel.

Anna shuffled Amy into the passenger seat, hurried around to the driver's side and slid behind the steering wheel.

Elizabeth reached through the window and patted Amy's shoulder. "We'll be right behind you." Tenderness gleamed in her violet eyes. "It'll be okay. I promise."

Anna put the truck in gear. kicking up dirt clods as she sped down the path onto the old country highway.

God, I need to know what You want me to do? That's all that is important now—Your will, not mine—and I'll be okay with whatever it is. Just, please, tell me.

A contraction tightened her abdomen, and she leaned forward to breathe through it. *It'll be okay . . . It'll be okay . . .*

With each breath, an answer came together like pieces of a jigsaw puzzle, fitting so perfectly Amy was certain it had been God's plan all along. She just couldn't believe that it had taken her so long to figure it out.

Elizabeth's pulse matched the speed of Elijah's car. She had no idea why her nerves were jitterbugging through her body, but glancing over her shoulder, she suspected she wasn't the only one experiencing a raised level of anxiety.

In the back seat, Owen sat staring intensely out the window and rubbing his palms vigorously on the tops of his legs.

She faced Elijah. "Can't you go any faster?"

"I'm already going ten over the speed limit." He placed a reassuring hand over hers. "We'll be there in a few minutes."

True to his word, Elijah pulled up to the main entrance of the hospital in record time. He helped Owen into his wheelchair, and then went to find a parking place while Elizabeth pushed Owen with quick steps in the direction of the obstetrics wing.

The elevator doors slid open on the fifth floor with a ping. Finding Anna in the small family waiting room, Elizabeth rushed to get a report on Amy.

"She's in a room. The nurse examined her and called the doctor. Labor seems to be progressing quickly." Anna glanced at Owen with an apologetic expression. "She wants Elizabeth in the room with her."

Confusion knit Elizabeth's brow. "Me?"

Anna nodded. "Go on. She's in room 547. We'll be here waiting for an update."

Owen reached out and squeezed Elizabeth's hand. "Take care of her."

"I will." Her comforting smile contrasted sharply with her apprehensive heart. True, she was a nurse, but she knew little about childbirth. Puzzled, she started down the hallway. When she reached the door, which was slightly ajar, she tapped lightly before slipping into the room.

Breathing through a contraction, Amy shifted her gaze to Elizabeth. After the contraction subsided, she leaned back heavily against the pillows.

"I'll bet you're wondering why I asked for you to be in here with me."

Elizabeth stepped up beside the bed. "It crossed my mind."

"I don't expect you to believe me—I can barely believe it myself—but God revealed something pretty amazing to me."

Elizabeth's soul stirred. "W-what did He tell you?"

A powerful contraction hit and Amy doubled over, trying to focus on taking slow, steady breaths. Feeling helpless, Elizabeth rubbed her back, encouraging her.

Bustling into the room, the nurse deciphered the output from the monitor and evaluated the situation. "Looks like your contractions are coming just a few minutes apart." She snapped a pair of latex gloves on. "After this one we'll check how far along you are."

When the pain eased some, Amy sank back against the pillows and the nurse performed a quick exam. Elizabeth took it all in, grateful that Amy was allowing her to witness this miracle. At the same time, a dull ache filled her empty womb at the realization that she might never experience such a moment firsthand.

"Amy, this baby is coming. I hope Dr. Davis makes it in time." The nurse slipped off the gloves and tossed them in the trash. "As for the pain, I can get you some medicine to knock the edge off of these contractions, but I'm afraid the anesthesiologist will say it's too late for an epidural. You're almost ready to push."

Amy leaned forward with another contraction and grunted between breaths, "Don't need meds . . . Been through worse than this."

"Well, it's available if you want it." The nurse went to the door. "Let me go report to Dr. Davis. Then I'll get the area prepped so we'll be ready to deliver this baby as soon as the doctor arrives."

The contraction faded and Amy worked to catch her breath.

Elizabeth's face lit up with excitement. "It won't be long, and your baby will be here."

Amy shook her head. "Not my baby. Yours."

Elizabeth's eyes flew open. "What? Amy, what are you saying?"

"It's been God's plan all along." Amy stared at Elizabeth, determination sparkling in her emerald eyes. "This baby might have grown in my womb, but he's been growing in your heart."

Tears spilled over Elizabeth's lashes and cascaded down her face, dropping unto their clasped hands. "I don't know what to say."

"Then don't say anything." Amy groaned as another contraction hit. "This . . . is how . . . it's supposed . . . to be."

Amy pressed Elizabeth's hand to her belly and right on cue the baby softly tapped against it.

A tearful giggle escaped Elizabeth's throat. "That's my baby?"

Quickly becoming weary, Amy could only nod.

Now Elizabeth encouraged Amy through each contraction as before, but with a new purpose. *This is my baby. Amy has held the answer to my prayer all this time . . . This is my baby!*

Dr. Davis arrived ten minutes later, donning green surgical scrubs, two nurses flanking him. "All right, Amy. We're going to wait for a contraction, and then you're going to push for me, okay?"

Amy didn't have to wait long. A contraction slammed her body, reading off the chart on the monitor, and she bore down.

Wincing with Amy's pain, Elizabeth squeezed her hand. "That's it, Amy. You can do it. Just a couple more minutes."

Twelve contractions later, the first wails of a healthy baby boy pierced the air.

Elizabeth wept. "That's the most beautiful sound I ever heard."

Dr. Davis cut the umbilical cord and handed the baby to the nurse, who swaddled him in a blue blanket and placed the ruddy-faced infant in Elizabeth's arms.

"Oh," she breathed. "He's so perfect." Elizabeth hugged him to her, rocking him gently, an empty, cold part of her suddenly overflowing with warmth. As she stared down at this precious gift, the connection between them was instant.

Uncle Bill had been right. Her joy had come after all, and it was worth every tear she'd shed. She soaked up the moment, letting it fill the depths of her soul, basking in it like the warm sun after spending so long in a dark, lonely valley.

From a corner in the back of her mind, part of Psalm 107 emerged, and Elizabeth once again rejoiced in its message. *"Then they cry out to the Lord in their trouble, and He brings them out of their distresses. He calms the storm, so that its waves are still. Then they are glad because they are quiet; So He guides them to their desired haven."*

"After the storms I've weathered, God is faithful to keep His promises. You, little one, are His promise. You are my Haven." She paused, gratefully meeting Amy's satisfied gaze, and turned back to her newborn. "Welcome to the world, Haven William."

From somewhere in the hallway, she heard a lullaby playing.

Epilogue

*A*my awoke with a start that late spring morning, her heart hammering out an erractic pattern that resembled a Morse code message. The sun already streamed through the window, lighting up the bedroom. Jerking her gaze to her alarm clock, she threw off the covers and sprinted across the hall to the bathroom.

"Nine o'clock! The bus is going to be here in half an hour."

She couldn't be late for one of the biggest days of her life. She only wished her dad could have been there to share it with her.

After a quick shower, she dressed in the same white capris and navy sweater that she'd worn to the Fourth of July party ten months earlier. Glancing in the mirror, she grinned at the realization that the only thing that remained the same was the outfit.

She applied some mascara and a thin layer of lip gloss while she whispered a quick heartfelt prayer. "Thank You, Father, for never giving up on me even after I gave up on You."

Tamping down a rising bubble of exuberance, she glanced at her reflection one last time and dashed out the door. Her easy stride broke as she rounded the corner of the garage. Taking in the sight that awaited her, she slowed to a stop.

"What's all this?"

A wide red ribbon stretched across the big double doors to the new arena Jacob and Anna had built with part of the insurance settlement from the fire. Above the doorway, a large rectangle was draped with a thick bed sheet. And clustered in front of the arena stood everybody who meant the most to Amy, who had touched her life in one way or another—Anna and Jacob; Steph, Maggie, and little Justin; her grandpa, grandma, and Dr. Kimball; Elijah, Elizabeth, their deaf foster daughter, Janessa, and baby Haven. And front and center, were the two loves of her life—Owen in his wheelchair and Dominick flanking his left side.

Even after her recovery, the instinct to immediately be on her guard still lingered. She crept toward Owen, keeping her eye on the others. "What's going on?"

"Amy, you've worked hard to make this dream a reality. Everyone here believes in you and what you're doing. We just felt you deserved a proper dedication." Owen nodded at Dominick who reached up and pulled the linen off the rectangle to reveal a brightly colored sign with a rough drawing of a horse with a music note sitting on top of it.

Amy's hand flew to her mouth but didn't make it in time to cover her sharp gasp. "The Lullaby Ranch," she breathed. "It's perfect."

"Something else is perfect."

Amy blinked back threatening tears and returned her attention to Owen.

"You are. For me." Owen locked his wheels and flipped

up his foot rests. With incredible effort, he pushed himself to his feet.

Amy's eyes widened, tears spilling down her cheeks. She reached out to help him, but he put his hand up.

Concentrating on every movement, he took a step toward her. "I've known it since your first day in Harvest Bay." He managed another step. "And every day that has gone by just confirmed what I already believed." Stepping forward again, he glanced over his shoulder at Dominick, who hurried to his side. "God brought you to Harvest Bay for many reasons, but one of those reasons was me. He knew I needed you and Dominick." He held his hand out to Dominick.

On cue, Dominick dug in his pocket, pulled out a little velvet box, and placed it in Owen's hand.

"And I don't want to spend another day of my life without you." He flipped open the box to reveal a beautiful antique princess-cut diamond ring that sparkled as it caught the morning sunlight. "In my heart I'm down on my knee as I ask you, Amy, will you please marry me?"

Every ounce of her being wanted to leap into Owen's arms, and all that kept her from doing it was that she knew he wasn't strong enough yet. Instead, she gently looped her arms around his neck and nodded.

"Yes, yes, a hundred times yes. Owen Sullivan, I will marry you."

He leaned in and softly brushed his lips against hers. Then he slipped the ring on her finger and kissed her hand as the small group of onlookers erupted in applause.

The sounds of gravel popping under tires caused them all to shift their attention to the driveway. Right on time, the school bus pulled up, the door opened, and out poured students with special needs. A lift on the back of the bus let down two wheelchair-bound children. There were thirteen children altogether.

Amy's heart soared as high as her ribcage would let it. *This is it, Dad. Our dream is coming true. She touched the medallion that hung around her neck. I wish you were here, but I know you're always with me.*

Jacob stepped forward and handed her a pair of scissors. "It's time to officially open the Lullaby Ranch therapeutic equine program for kids with special needs."

Amy took the shears and prepared to cut the ribbon, but stopped. "Wait. We're missing the most important part."

"Not anymore," Kennedy's voice echoed from inside the arena. Flipping on the light switch, she walked forward, Angel's reins in her hand.

Feeling as close to heaven as she ever could on earth, Amy cut the ribbon and made her dad's dream come true. Soothing classical music piped through speakers in the corners of the arena while Amy rode students around on Angel. Bella and Beau were in a stall for the students to groom and feed under Anna's supervision. Kennedy used Moses to teach some of the more advanced students the basics on leading a horse.

After forty-five minutes, the students boarded the bus, chattering about how much they loved the horses, and returned to school while Amy breathed a blissful sigh.

Elizabeth sidled up next to Amy. "What does success feel like?"

Her smile reaching her eyes, Amy turned to face Elizabeth. "I don't know if it's a success yet, but that felt pretty fantastic."

"Congratulations on your engagement. Owen said he had an important announcement to make, but he didn't say what it was. Let's see the ring."

Amy held up her hand, admiring it herself. "I don't think I've ever been so happy in all my life."

"That makes two of us." The joy in Elizabeth's heart gleamed in her eyes. "Elijah and I are having a baby. I'm due December first."

Amy pulled Elizabeth to her in a fierce hug, and then gingerly let her go. "How are you feeling? Is everything okay?"

"I'm already passed my first trimester and we are both doing great."

Elijah approached the women toting Haven in his carrier, with Dominick and Janessa trailing along behind.

Amy chuckled. "You guys are going to have a full house." She peered into the carrier at the sleeping baby. "And those kids are so lucky because you are an amazing mother."

Elizabeth touched her baby's feathery tufts of black hair and ran a finger down his light brown cheek. She shrugged. "I just love them. That's all I know to do."

Owen wheeled up next to Amy and captured her hand, and unknowingly her heart, in his. Like Elizabeth's, Amy's dream had come true in more ways than one, unfolding more beautifully than she could have ever imagined. The pain she'd been through only made this joy that much more satisfying.

The memory of the battles she'd fought inside herself for so long served as a guarantee that she'd never take this peace for granted. She realized that the love she thought she'd lost had never really left her. Yet new love had found her, and she vowed to never let it go.

Together, the foursome headed toward the farmhouse for an engagement brunch, but with each step, Amy relived the events of the morning. As soon as she got a chance she'd record it all in her journal. She never wanted to forget this day—the day she learned that promises were kept, dreams did come true, and there really was such a thing as true happiness.

The first day of the rest of her life.

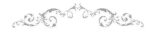

Reader Discussion Guide

Elizabeth Truman

1. In what ways can you identify with Elizabeth? Discuss her strengths and weaknesses.

2. Elizabeth's major conflict throughout this book is waiting on the Lord's timing and understanding that her plans for her life might not be the Lord's. Have you ever experienced such a conflict? Who or what helped you through that time?

3. Initially Elizabeth's struggle is intensified by the arrival of a stepson she never knew she had. But gradually the Lord softens her heart and turns her feelings of hurt and inadequacy into genuine love and acceptance. Have you ever experienced a time when the Lord turned a hardship into a blessing? Tell about that experience.

4. Read Philippians 4:11. How could this verse be used as a theme for Elizabeth's faith journey? How could you apply it to your own personal faith journey?

Amy Beauregard

1. In what ways can you identify with Amy? Discuss her strengths and weaknesses.

2. Amy's major conflict throughout this book is her lack of faith that God is real and cares at all after all the heartache and loss she experienced throughout her life. Have you ever struggled with this? How did you overcome it—or have you?

3. Amy eventually learned to trust Owen and his family because they never gave up on her. They saw the good in her when she couldn't even see it in herself. Think about someone in your life who never gave up on you. Tell about that individual and what he or she means to you.

4. Read Joshua 1:9. How could this verse be used as a theme for Amy's faith journey? How could you apply this verse to your own personal faith journey?

Elizabeth and Amy

1. Two broken women, initially at odds with one another, grow to become kindred spirits. And through this process, healing occurs for them both in amazing and miraculous ways. Have you ever experienced a relationship that began on rocky terms, but eventually, with prayer and patience, blossomed into something beautiful? Tell about that experience.

2. Read Romans 8:28. How could this verse be used as a theme for this friendship? How could you apply this verse to relationships and/or situations in your own life?